RICHARD RUSSO'S
MOHAWK

RICHARD RUSSO

MOHAWK

VINTAGE CONTEMPORARIES

VINTAGE BOOKS

A DIVISION OF RANDOM HOUSE, INC.

NEW YORK

VINTAGE CONTEMPORARIES EDITION, November 1989

Library of Congress Cataloging-in-Publication Data
Russo, Richard, 1949–
Mohawk.
(Vintage contemporaries)
A Vintage Original.
I. Title.
PS3568.U812M6   1986   813′.54   86-40133
0-679-72577-6 (pbk.)

The author gratefully acknowledges support from the Penn-
sylvania Council on the Arts and Southern Connecticut State
University. And special thanks for faith and assistance to Jean
Findlay, Mrs. Richard LeVarn, Jim Russo, Kevin McIlvoy,
Robert C. S. Downs, Kjell Meling, Kitty Florey, Ken Florey,
and Greg Gottung.

The town of Mohawk, like its residents, is located
in the author's imagination.

Manufactured in the United States of America
10   9   8   7   6   5   4   3

For Barbara, Emily, and Kate
And for Dick LeVarn
In Loving Memory

But Faith, like a jackal, feeds among the tombs, and even from these dead doubts she gathers her most vital hope.

Herman Melville, *Moby-Dick*

PART
ONE

1

The back door to the Mohawk Grill opens on an alley it shares with the junior high. When Harry throws back the bolt from inside and lets the heavy door swing outward, Wild Bill is waiting nervously in the dark gray half-light of dawn. There is no way of telling how long he has been pacing, listening for the thunk of the bolt, but he looks squitchier than usual today. Driving his hands deeper into his pockets, Wild Bill waits while Harry inspects him curiously and wonders if Bill's been in some kind of trouble during the night. Probably not, Harry finally decides. Bill looks disheveled, as always, his black pants creaseless, alive with light-colored alley dust, the tail of his threadbare, green-plaid, button-down shirt hanging out, but there's nothing unusually wrong with his appearance. Harry is glad, because he's late opening this morning and doesn't have time to clean Wild Bill up.

When Harry finally steps aside, Bill scoots by into the diner and climbs onto the first round stool at the end of the formica counter. Harry hooks the heavy door to the outside wall so the delivery men can come in the back way and the place can air out. A few flies will wander in off the street, but will end up stuck to the No Pest Strips dangling from the ceiling. Harry throws open the large windows in the front of the diner, creating a cool draft that stands Wild Bill's thinning hair on end. Bill is in his middle thirties, but his baby-fine hair is falling out in patches and he looks as old as Harry, who is almost fifty.

"Hungry?" Harry says.

Wild Bill nods and studies the grill, which is sputtering butter. Harry lifts a large bag of link sausages and tosses several dozen on the grill, covering its entire surface, then separates them with the edge of his spatula, arranging them in impressive phalanxes. "It's gonna be a while," he warns.

Wild Bill is beginning to look less anxious. The sputtering sausage calms him, and he watches hypnotized as the links spit and jump. The grease begins to puddle and inch toward the trough at the edge of the grill. Wild Bill would prevent its escape if he could because he likes the taste of sausage grease. Sometimes, when Harry remembers, he will scramble Wild Bill's eggs in it before cleaning the surface. But Bill only gets eggs when he has money, which is seldom. Bill himself rarely has more than a few nickels, but for the last ten years, at the first of the month, an envelope has arrived at the Mohawk Grill containing a crisp ten-dollar bill and a note that says simply, "For William Gaffney." Where it comes from is the only genuine mystery in Harry's life. At first he thought the money came from the boy's father, but that was before he met Rory Gaffney. Harry has met just about everyone who knows Wild Bill and determined by one means or another that it's none of them. The money just appears. When it's used up, Harry can be depended upon to stake Wild Bill to coffee and one of yesterday's sticky buns before his customers come in, but Harry's generosity has its limits, and he seldom gives away food that isn't headed for the dumpster. Once, on Christmas two years before, Harry had got to feeling pretty blue about things in general, so to get rid of the depression he had cooked Wild Bill a big breakfast—juice, eggs, ham, pancakes, home fries, toast, jelly, and maple syrup—which the younger man wolfed, wide-eyed and grateful, before going out into the alley to be sick. Since then, Harry has been careful not to make the same mistake.

"I want you to take out the trash this morning," Harry says, turning sausages with his spatula.

Wild Bill watches each flip like an expectant dog waiting for a mistake.

"Hear me?"

Wild Bill starts and looks at Harry.

"I said I want you to take out the trash. You can have some toast."

"Ow?"

"Yes, now."

Wild Bill is reluctant to leave—he likes to watch the sausage—but slides off the stool and goes to the back of the diner where Harry has stacked several bags of garbage. The flies have already discovered them and are attacking the plastic in a frenzy. Wild Bill deposits each of the bags in the dumpster and returns to his stool just as two pieces of toast pop up golden brown. Harry butters them sparingly and puts the toast on a saucer in front of Wild Bill. He almost asks if he'd got into a fight during the night, then decides not to. If Bill had, there would be the usual signs, because he isn't much of a fighter. Usually, whoever starts the fight will give Bill a fat lip and then get embarrassed when, instead of getting mad, Wild Bill would just stand there, his arms dangling at his sides, looking as if he might cry.

"You ain't found yourself a girlfriend, have you?"

Bill shakes his head, but he stops chewing his toast to look at Harry, who wonders if he might be lying, if he is capable of lying.

"I promised your uncle I'd tell him if you got into trouble," Harry warns.

But Wild Bill has gone back to his toast, which he chews with exaggerated concentration, as if he fears making a mistake. There is a thud against the front door of the diner and Harry goes to unlock. The rolled up *Mohawk Republican* is lying in the entryway, and Harry returns with it after checking to make sure he didn't hit the number the day before. The *Republican* knows its readership and prints the three-digit number in the upper left-hand corner of the front page above the headline, which today reads, in somewhat bolder type than usual, TANNERIES BLAMED FOR ABNORMAL AREA CANCER RATE. Harry skims the first short paragraph, in which a university study of Mohawk County concludes that people living in the county are three times more likely to contract cancer, leukemia, and several other serious diseases than elsewhere in the country. Persons who work in the tanneries and leather mills themselves or who reside near the Cayuga Creek, where the Morelock, Hunter and Cayuga tanneries are accused of dumping, are ten to twenty times more likely to contract one of the diseases listed on page B-6. Spokesmen for the tanneries deny that any dumping has occurred in nearly two decades and suggest that the recent findings are in all probability a statistical anomaly.

Harry leaves the paper on the counter for anybody who wants to check Friday's late racing results. The sausages done, he scoops them off the grill and into a metal tub. He will toss them back on to warm for a minute as the orders come in. What doesn't get eaten by breakfast customers he'll use in sandwiches later in the day. He knows within a link or two what is needed. There are few surprises in the diner, for which he is thankful. With the long spatula he moves the puddle of grease toward the trough before lining the glistening surface with rows of bacon strips.

"Hey," he says. Wild Bill's busy thumbing toast crumbs off his saucer. "You don't ever drink out of the crick, do you?"

Wild Bill shakes his head.

Harry shrugs. It was just an idea, but it would've explained a lot. Harry wasn't around Mohawk when Wild Bill was a boy, but some people said he'd been normal once, more or less. The bacon begins to sizzle. Harry belches significantly and wipes his hands on the stomach of his apron. He feels the way he always does on Saturday morning after a hard night's drinking. He has come directly to the diner without any sleep, and the sweet smell of frying meat has his stomach churning. It's not his stomach he's worrying about, though. He has proposed marriage to some woman during the course of the evening. When drinking, Harry is indiscriminate about women, to whom he invariably proposes. The women Harry ends up with on Friday nights usually say yes, and then he has to renege. On the plus side, they know he hasn't any intention of marrying, so their feelings are never hurt. They say yes because it's a long shot and their lives are full of long shots. They know Harry doesn't need a wife and could do better if he were serious about taking one. There was a time when they could've done better than Harry, but that was several presidents ago. The calendar above the grill is for 1966, a year out of date. Whoever gave Harry the calendar the year before didn't give him a new one this year. The months are the same and Harry doesn't mind being a few days off.

"Don't get hooked up with women," he mutters.

"Ow?"

"Any time."

Harry sees Bill eyeing yesterday's sticky buns beneath the glass dome. He hands Bill one and dumps the rest. The bakery man will be along in a few minutes. Harry flips the bacon.

On the other side of the wall is the sound of tramping feet on the staircase, which means the all-night poker game on the second floor is breaking up. This in turn means that Harry will have some early business. When the front door opens and several men enter, Wild Bill starts to leave, but Harry puts a hand on his shoulder and he settles back on his stool. Ordinarily, Harry doesn't want him around after his paying customers start coming in, but he knows these particular men are not squeamish. At the moment they are barely awake. After taking stools in the center of the counter, two of the red-eyed men order big breakfasts—ham steak, eggs, home fries, toast, coffee—and the other two just coffee. Harry doesn't have to ask who won. John, the lawyer, usually wins and hangs on to his winnings until he goes to Las Vegas, usually twice a year. Then Vegas usually wins. One of the noneaters pulls out the day's racing form. The other grabs Harry's *Mohawk Republican* and folds out the sports page. "What was yesterday's number?" somebody says.

"Four-two-one," Harry growls.

"I haven't had a number in three years."

"So what? I haven't been laid in pretty near that long."

"I can get you laid if you can get me a number," says John, who is reputed to be a ladies' man. He's the only one who looks relatively fresh after the long night's work.

"Anybody can get laid," another agrees.

"Some of us prefer girls."

A mock fight breaks out. Wild Bill watches the men, a little alarmed at the feigned hostilities. One of the men nods a hello in his direction.

"Oughta," Bill says.

"Yeah," the man says, rolling his eyes at Harry. "Oughta."

"Oughta," the rest chime in. "Oughta, Harry."

"Lay off." Harry wishes now that he'd let Bill, who is grinning happily at this camaraderie, clear out when he'd wanted to. He sometimes wishes Wild Bill would just go off some place and not come back. He's a burden at best. Still, Harry doesn't like people making fun of him.

"How long does it take to fry a couple eggs?" the lawyer wants to know. "They oughta be done by now."

"Oughta," the others say in unison.

The man with the sports page leans back on his stool so he can see the street outside. "Stay away from my car, you fat shit." Officer Gaffney is studying the three illegally parked cars at the curb. A recent ordinance prohibits parking on Main Street. "If I get a ticket, I'm going temporarily insane."

"I'll take your case," John tells him.

"Even you could win it," somebody says.

Harry doesn't even bother to look. He knows Officer Gaffney and also knows that no tickets will be written until he finds out who the cars belong to. Gaffney likes to drink coffee in the diner, and he leaves Harry's customers alone.

The door opens and he strides in, a large man, but soft-looking. Even the boys who race their bicycles down the Main Street sidewalks are unafraid. They do wheelies behind his back as he guards the traffic light at the Four Corners and are gone again before he can turn around. Only Officer Gaffney takes himself seriously. He wears his thirty-eight slung lower than regulation on his right hip. "Boys," he nods, taking a stool at the opposite end of the lunch counter from Wild Bill.

"Oughta," somebody says.

Wild Bill is clearly nervous again, fidgeting on his stool and never taking his eyes off the policeman. He is made uneasy by uniforms, even those worn by familiar people. Wild Bill hasn't had much luck with uniforms.

"Who owns the Merc," Officer Gaffney asks. He pours two level teaspoons of sugar into the steaming coffee Harry puts in front of him.

"Murphy," says the lawyer, jabbing his eggs until they run yellow. "He'll be down in a minute if he doesn't kill himself."

"You could've bought him breakfast, at least," says one of the coffee-drinkers.

"I offered. He said he wasn't hungry."

"I hope his kids aren't either. Not this week, anyhow."

"This month."

"He isn't the only one took a bath," says the other

coffee-drinker, anxious that the absent Murphy not hog all the sympathy.

"Yeah, but did you see the look on his face when he lost on that aces-over-boat?"

Devouring the bleeding eggs, John chortles at the recollection. "Shit," he says appreciatively.

When Wild Bill slides off his stool like a scolded dog and slinks out the back, Harry doesn't try to stop him. The men watch him go. The man reading the sports page has now folded the paper back to the front. "He must drink out of the Cayuga," he says. Everybody but Harry laughs.

"What the hell is 'oughta' supposed to mean?"

"It means Howdy," Harry says.

"How do you know," John asks. "You look it up in the *Morons' Dictionary?*"

"It means Howdy."

"You can settle this, Gaff," the lawyer says without looking up from his breakfast. "You're his uncle."

Officer Gaffney goes deep purple. Though he and Wild Bill look about the same age, he is indeed the other man's uncle. Not many people in Mohawk know Wild Bill's last name, so he seldom has to admit to being related. Now they all know.

"I do see a family resemblance, now that you mention it," somebody remarks.

"Say *oughta,* Gaff."

"Can it!" Harry thunders, so loud that everybody including the policeman jumps. Harry's normally red face is even redder, and he brandishes his long, thin spatula like a sword. To someone wandering in off the street, Harry would look more comic than menacing, but anyone wise and within striking distance of his spatula takes him seriously.

It's the lawyer who breaks the tension. "You must have got married again last night. Always makes you pissy. I can have it annulled by noon unless it's consummated."

"Consummated? Harry?"

Everybody laughs, and Harry lowers his weapon. He doesn't mind them kidding him, but he's still angry. "He's just a poor moron. Give him a break, can't you?"

"Sure, Harry. We really oughta."

When the men pay up and leave, Harry and Officer Gaffney have the place to themselves. It's early still. The policeman reads the front page of the *Republican* while Harry dumps a small tub of home fries onto the grill. He probably won't see Wild Bill again until Monday morning, and that's just as well. Harry wonders where he goes, what he does with his days and nights. By the time the policeman puts the paper down, Harry's fries are good and brown underneath, but they look cold and unappetizing. The cars that were out front are gone, except for the Mercury.

"This Murphy character a customer?"

Harry says he isn't.

Officer Gaffney pays for his coffee and goes back outside. Harry can see him bend over the Merc to write a citation on the hood. Harry turns the home fries and looks around his diner. He hasn't many regrets about his life, nor does he want a lot that he doesn't have. The diner is just about right. He wishes now that he had scrambled Wild Bill some eggs in the sausage grease, but that's the only regret he can think of.

2

"I think the house will be *just* fine," Mrs. Grouse said
when her daughter Anne turned the corner onto Oak.
The older woman was still in her Sunday outfit, a belted,
cream-color dress, the fabric of which she smoothed
over her knees with gloved fingers. Mrs. Grouse disliked riding in automobiles and refused to do so except
to attend church or visit her older sister Milly, which
was, in fact, where she and her daughter were now
headed.

Anne drew over to the curb. "Do you want to go
back and check the house again, Mother?"

"Whatever for, dear?"

"I have no idea. But if you have doubts, let's go
back . . . by all means. Otherwise you'll be wondering
out loud all afternoon."

"Nonsense."

"I agree," Anne said, pulling back onto the street.

When they had gone about a block, Mrs. Grouse
said, "I locked *all* the doors."

"Yes, Mother."

Mrs. Grouse didn't look at her daughter. "There isn't
a thing in the *world* for you to be upset about. But with
your father in the hospital, the house happens to be
my responsibility."

Anne knew it was pointless to continue the conversation. Most things, great and small, fell under the general heading of her mother's responsibility, and Mrs. Grouse shouldered them all bravely on her slender frame. The two women had been feuding since the attack that hospitalized Mather Grouse earlier in the week. Since then, they had alternated staying with him at the hospital, waging the same subtle war they'd been engaged in as long as Anne could remember. Not surprisingly, Mather Grouse seemed to prefer the company of his grandson Randall to either of them.

"Randy has the number . . . ," ventured Mrs. Grouse, who never in her life left a doubt unvoiced.

"Yes, Mother. Please, let's not worry everything to death."

"What are you talking about? I simply said—"

"I know what you said. But in a few minutes you'll be with your sister and then you'll forget about everything. You'll forget that the house exists. In the meantime, can't we have some peace?"

Milly was pushing eighty, nearly fifteen years older than Anne's mother, but the two women were spiritual twins. They hadn't been particularly close until the four sisters between them in age died. Since then, the two women began rewriting their pasts until both believed that they had spent every day of their girlhood in each other's exclusive company, when in reality the decade and a half that separated their births had made them relative strangers. But they unburdened themselves of this constraining reality for the sake of the vivid, shared recollections that lacked even the slightest basis in fact. Old Milly took spells when she confused Mrs. Grouse with their sister Grace, dead the best part of twenty years. Fortunately, Mrs. Grouse had little trouble shifting gears, and she cheerfully assumed the dead sister's identity lest she upset the living one. To Anne there was something a little spooky about her mother's easy metempsychosis on such occasions, but she never said anything.

Of course the sisters shared some recent memories more firmly grounded in historical fact. It was Milly's husband who had been responsible for Mather Grouse's coming to Mohawk shortly after his marriage to Anne's mother. The town had seemed alive and healthy then, though the leather business was already showing signs of decline that no one imagined would be permanent. All the tanneries and glove shops were hiring, at least seasonally, and Mather Grouse had gotten work in the same shop that employed Milly's husband. When things began to go bad, everyone blamed the Depression and said things would boom again once the economy recovered. When Pearl Harbor was bombed, Mather Grouse enlisted, confident that he would return to the same job he left.

But the war changed everything. In order to escape high import duties the more unscrupulous shopowners began to bring into the country as unfinished goods gloves that required only the fastening of a single button to become "finished," and in this way the demand for the skills of Mohawk's cutters was controlled. Never again would there be more work than men, and competition for the existing work drove wages lower. Very few of the men knew what was happening to them, and those who did were afraid to speak out.

Still, the years following the war were not bad ones, at least for the two sisters. They were veteran "visitors" and took turns entertaining each other to pass the long afternoons when their daughters were in school and their husbands at the shop. Serving fancy pastries on lace doilies, they gossiped harmlessly, sticky fingered, on many subjects. Who among the cutters was getting the best leather, who was likely to get laid off if the work did not last through the winter, and the like. Both women had delivered their children very late in the natural scheme of things, and mothering did not come easy to either of them. Anne and her mother cared for each other after their fashion. But they were very different, and neither mother nor daughter had spoken of loving one another since Anne was a very small girl.

Milly, since her husband's death over a decade ago, lived with her daughter and son-in-law on Kings Road, in one of the few remaining neighborhoods in Mohawk that had not seen better days, where there was some real money. Though it was in the same end of town as the Grouse home on Mountain Avenue, the latter neighborhood was beginning to exhibit, in chipped paint and rolling, cracked sidewalks, signs of the town's general decline. On tree-lined Kings Road the earth never shifted, and the smooth, wide sidewalks ran straight and true. The houses themselves were set far back off the street, each home with its own manicured lawn and tall, symmetrical hedges. Despite frequent visits, Anne could never remember seeing anyone in the act of mowing or clipping. The seventh, eighth, and ninth holes of the Mohawk Country Club doglegged lazily around these homes on Kings Road, a dead-end street whose residents' lives were punctuated by worries no more serious than the occasional slice or duck-hook. When Anne pulled into the driveway and stepped out, she heard the distant crack of a fairway wood and the mild curse of a man with a monied voice.

Diana Wood, Anne's cousin, met them at the door,

her mother limping up behind. Old Milly and Mrs. Grouse greeted one another as if they had endured a separation of many months instead of two weeks. That they did not see each other daily was the fault of "the young people." Di Wood looked ragged and tired, and after witnessing the too-fervent reunion of the sisters, she exchanged with Anne the look of a fellow sufferer. "How's Uncle Mather," she asked when they were out of earshot of the kitchen.

"They're talking about releasing him tomorrow."

"We've been meaning to visit, but things are never easy to coordinate around here. Any other time Mother would already be there."

"Dad doesn't expect it. He doesn't appreciate visitors there any more than he does at home. Besides, you look beat."

From the kitchen they were able to see into the living room where the sisters sat facing each other on the love seat, their knees actually touching. Di Wood shook her head. "We'll be dead long before they will," she said half seriously. "You ought to get out while you can. You're still young enough."

Anne smiled at the observation. "I'll be thirty-five in a few short months. Which means that unless you've gained ground you'll only be forty."

Her cousin took a glazed ham out of the refrigerator and set it on the cutting board. It was very beautiful, topped with cherries and pineapple slices. The Woods always entertained Anne and her mother lavishly on Sunday afternoons. There was always a ham or roast or leg of lamb, along with several fancy salads. Since there was no way to reciprocate in kind, Anne wished her cousin wouldn't go to the trouble. Milly was more or less housebound since fracturing her hip the previous winter. But Di claimed to derive pleasure from "doing."

"Look at me if you don't think I've gained ground," she said cheerfully.

This much was true. Diana had never been a pretty girl, though during her early twenties, shortly after her marriage to Dan, she had possessed a fragile, vulnerable loveliness that people often remarked on after regretting the plainness of her features. Now she could easily pass for fifty and her former fragility was supplanted by a kind of solidness. She looked like a woman who had spent her whole life waiting in line.

"What you and Dan need is to get out," Anne said, as much to change the subject as anything. "Your mother could certainly survive a weekend. Mother and I could look in."

Diana's electric knife curled thin, admirable slices off the ham, each falling obediently on top of the last. "We were supposed to go away last weekend. We even hired a nurse. But when mother got wind of it she threw such a tantrum we didn't dare go."

"You should've anyway."

"I know," Diana conceded. "But after a while you lack the necessary will. It would've been just a gesture anyway. We wouldn't have enjoyed ourselves."

In the living room Mrs. Grouse and Milly had not moved. Their knees still touching, they faced each other, their eyes widening at the exchange of trivial information. Neither heard very well, and together they were too intent on each other to suspect that they were the topic of conversation in the next room. "Look at them," Di smiled. "It's as if they didn't need another thing in the world."

Anne would have liked to share her cousin's sympathy and generosity, but it wasn't easy. She found little to pity in strength, and old Milly, though physically feeble, was capable by sheer force of will to have things pretty much her own way. Anne's mother shared the family trait of passive aggression and determination. When Anne studied her mother she felt certain that the American wilderness had not been subdued by courageous men, but by their indomitable, sturdy wives—tamed by an attitude, a certain slant of the jaw, expressed only in the female, a quality she herself sadly lacked.

Di arranged the sliced ham on a large platter garnished about the edges with generous sprigs of fresh parsley. "They're lucky when you think about it," she said. "Everybody should have at least one other person in the world who is all her own. Someone she doesn't have to share."

Now it seemed to Anne that the same old thing was between them again, the way it often seemed to be, though Anne was never quite sure it was real. Just when she began to feel an almost painful intimacy with her cousin, she would become aware of its presence, as if each was able to read the other's thoughts and unwilling to indulge intimacy too far. "I wish you'd let me do something. To help."

Di looked around the kitchen as if for a task and, though there must have been many, came up empty. "Why don't you go say hi to Dan. He heard the car pull up, and he'll think you're ignoring him."

"Do you really suppose men suffer such insecurities?"

Di smiled sadly, and Anne felt the same twinge of intimacy again. "They claim to."

"I thought maybe it was just us."

3

Dan Wood was on the far side of the pool skimming leaves when he heard the sliding patio door and looked up. It did not look to Anne like he was making much progress. The wind was up and the brittle autumn leaves seemed attracted to the placid surface of the water. Even with the long-handled skimmer, the middle of the pool was well beyond Dan's reach from the wheelchair, and the multicolored leaves lay there several layers thick, like a bright counterpane on a rippling waterbed. "Judging from the look on your face," Dan said, smiling, "you're about to tell me that I'm losing this particular battle with nature."

"Why do you bother?"

"The goddamn filter will croak," he said. It was a matter of intimacy between them that Dan swore. Diana did not appreciate profanity, and such language confirmed for old Milly the many doubts about her son-in-law that she had freely voiced during the last twenty-or-so years, the majority of them under his roof. Dan's oaths were always quiet and reverent, though, and he never swore when he was genuinely angry, at which times he became peculiarly restrained.

He offered no objection when Anne relieved him of the skimmer and began working on the carpet in the center of the pool, which she herself was barely able to reach by leaning. For a while he would be content to watch her work. "If I had my way, I'd just fill the bastard with cement and be done with it. Who needs the aggravation?"

"Di never uses the pool?"

"Occasionally," he said, as if this concession did not exactly invalidate his point. "I should've drained it in September. I must've been thinking about Indian summer." Wheeling over to do the deep end, he extracted a plastic lawn bag from a box sitting on the diving board. "The two of them going at it in there?"

"Nose to nose."

"They'll be good for the afternoon. How's Mather?"

"Anxious to be released."

"Legend has it you acted heroically."

Anne banged some clinging leaves off the skimmer and onto the deck. "Talk to my mother if you'd like a balancing view."

She had come home from work and found her father half dead. Though it was the second week in October, it was so hot the tar glistened on the roads the way it did in July and August. Mather Grouse had collapsed over his chair, the one he leaned forward onto when he needed to catch his breath, and then slumped to the floor where he lay precariously balanced against the wall, one leg beneath him, the other straight out as if in a cast. He was shirtless in the heat, the skin along his shoulders pale and translucent. When Anne came in, he was staring at nothing in particular, his eyes wide with fear, an expression his daughter had never seen in them before and that made him look like someone she didn't know. His inhaler lay a few inches from where his hand twitched, and he pulled at the air in short, quick gasps, the oxygen stopping far short of his straining lungs. He might as well have been under water.

Mrs. Grouse had been there in the living room, too, standing stiff with fright, several feet from where her husband lay. When Anne came in, she merely nodded toward Mather Grouse. The only thing that needed saying she said several times. "The ambulance is on its way. Everything's going to be *just* fine . . . *just* fine. The ambulance. . . ."

Kneeling beside her father, Anne tried to get his attention. Mather Grouse's eyes refused to focus behind their fluttering lids, and his chest leapt under the force of each convulsive breath. His mouth opened wide, then snapped shut again, like a child's toy, against his rising chest. When Anne picked up the inhaler and inserted it into her father's mouth, Mrs. Grouse recoiled in horror. "No!" she cried. "You'll burn his lungs. The men . . . they'll be *right* here—"

"He can't breathe, Mother. He's dying." Her father's chest heaved angrily, as if in response to the word.

"The men. . . ."

Ignoring her mother, Anne timed Mather Grouse's gasps, which were growing more and more feeble. She depressed the inhaler twice, just a few seconds apart. At first her father showed no sign, but then his eyes, which had begun to roll back, registered something. Pulling him away from the wall, she tried to get him on all fours, the position he once confessed was easiest for him to breathe in. She had caught him that way once, on his hands and knees, his head hung low, and he had been so embarrassed that he vowed never to assume that position again, preferring, as he put it, to strangle like a man than become an animal. But when Anne pulled up on his belt and the seat of his pants, he seemed to understand and even tried to help by pushing up with his forearms. He managed one decent breath before the strength went out of his limbs and he drove forward, chin first, into the carpet.

"Help me!" Anne ordered her mother, who was watching from across the room, having backed away until she finally came up flush against the wall. Mrs. Grouse balked, but then did as she was told. For a terrible moment, once they had succeeded in getting him to his knees again, Anne was afraid her mother had been right, for her father appeared to stop breathing altogether and there was a dreadful rattle in his chest. Then he began to choke, expelling yellow bile from his lungs. But he also caught his first real breath, one that went all the way down, and he hung onto it like a drowning man. By the time the ambulance arrived, some of the icy blue had begun to drain from his cheeks. In the interim he had not objected to remaining on all fours, apparently grateful, at least for the moment, simply to be. Even as an animal.

"So," Anne said, picking a particularly bright leaf off the skimmer, "I'm in the doghouse."

Dan Wood, who had listened to the story somewhat abstractedly, began stuffing the soggy leaves into the bag with a large scoop. "I'd like to sympathize, but you're old enough to know better than to disobey your mother. Just who did you think you were, saving your old man's life after you'd been expressly forbidden to?"

"But I didn't save his life, you see. The ambulance men get credit for that. What I get credit for is fracturing his jaw."

"Ah."

There were still plenty of leaves to skim, but Anne suddenly collapsed into a deck chair, letting the skimmer balance against one knee. "It's funny," she said. "When I was younger and things first started going wrong between my father and me, I had this daydream where I would rescue him from a burning house. I knew it was silly, but I indulged the fantasy all the time. He would be unconscious and I'd have to drag him out through the flames. Lord knows where Mother was when all this rescuing was going on."

"Dead, according to Freud."

"Oh, stop it."

Dan ducked the swatch of leaves she threw at him. "Anyhow, it turns out I got my wish. And do you know what I did when I saw him in the hospital the next morning? I apologized for fracturing his jaw."

"And so you're ticked off at your mother."

Anne studied him, surprised by his tone, but he did not meet her eye. "What's your point?"

"No point. I just wondered about Mather's opinion of the whole episode."

"He's got a fractured jaw, remember?"

"Mmmm," Dan said. "You should get one of those drawing boards they have for kids. The kind you write a message on and then pull up the plastic sheet and the whole thing disappears. T-H-A-N-K-S, then zip—clean slate."

Anne glared at him until he apologized, then added, "Don't go telling me things if you don't want my goddamn opinion."

She did regret telling him. She might've guessed what his reaction would be. "It's another of my idle dreams that you two will like each other one day."

They were talking directly to one another now, not looking away. "That's like me dreaming about walking again."

"What's wrong with that?"

"Only everything."

"I don't see why you and my father shouldn't like each other. You're a lot alike, when you think about it. For instance, you're the two most bullheaded men I know."

"Excepting Dallas."

"Naturally," she admitted. Her ex-husband. "Always excepting Dallas."

"Well," Dan smiled. "I don't much appreciate being called bullheaded. And I don't like your father. Never have liked him, never will like him. And there's nothing you can do to change my mind."

Anne couldn't help grinning back at him, as always. They would be on the brink of a serious falling out when suddenly the danger would pass as if it had never existed—"like a fart in a gale of wind," as Dan liked to say. He had a way of saying the most patently offensive things, plain or profane, without offending. A rare gift, she concluded. The other men in her life somehow always managed to offend even when they were tiptoeing.

"Anyway," Dan said, "I'm glad he's better."

"He isn't, really. The doctor says it's just a matter of time before he has another attack. An oxygen tank in the house would help."

"How's that a problem?"

"I'm not certain. I've been instructed to butt out, though. Mother insists he's too proud, but I suspect she's the one. You know how she is about the house— the first set of slipcovers is to protect the sofa, the second set is to protect the slipcovers. An oxygen tank in the living room would be like admitting the unspeakable."

"Milly's the same. We do nothing without permission. Di doesn't even buy for our bedroom without consulting."

Dan wheeled along the deck from pile to pile, scooping leaves into the lawn bag. She knew she should help but suddenly felt leaden and stayed where she was, watching. She had once thought he'd never grow to fit the chair, and for the longest time after the accident she kept expecting him to get up out of it and trot away. But now the chair was part of him. His once trim abdomen was showing signs of a paunch. She knew he was drinking heavily, and while she didn't blame him, thinking of him the way he had once been always brought her to the verge of tears. She felt them start to well up now and had to look away.

"I used to look for little things to burn her up," he said. "A couple years ago I ran across one of those little mechanical obscenities that works on a pulley. This little guy had a prick the size of a leg. Did lewd things with it when you pulled a string. Gave it to her on her birthday, all boxed up and wrapped nice."

The idea was very funny, and quickly Anne didn't feel like crying any more. He *was* the same Dan. "I wish I'd been there."

"No you don't. She went all gray and I thought 'Uh-oh.' Diana was fit to be tied, of course, and I've been a good boy since then, more or less. I guess there's no good reason to torment old women."

"Remind me again why they're supposed to torment us."

Before he had a chance there was a whistling sound, something cracked, first on the pool deck, then against the metal shed. Dan wheeled over quickly and picked up the golf ball. "Good one," he said, holding it up for Anne's inspection. "Titleist. Just missed you, too."

Opening the door to the shed, he deposited the ball in a bucket that must've contained a hundred others. "When I get out of this chair I'm going to take up golf again," he said. "It's a shame people don't lose clubs."

"You've decided to go ahead and try the operation?"

"What the hell. It's only money, and according to the quack-of-the-month there's a chance. You think I'm crazy?"

"No. I don't."

"Neither do I. My mother-in-law says I'm crazy. But since she plans to inherit all this when I'm gone, she dislikes my spending money."

"Hey!" called a voice that belonged to the head of somebody just tall enough to see over the top of Dan's redwood fence. "Golf ball come through here?"

"Nope," Dan smiled cheerfully.

"Sure." The man frowned, then muttered, "Brand new Titleist."

"What would I be likely to want with a golf ball?"

The man noticed the chair then and went pale. "Jesus, Mac, I'm sorry."

"Forget it," Dan said. "Drop in some day. We'll have lunch."

When the man disappeared, the patio door slid open and Di was out on the deck. "Stealing golf balls again?"

"You bet," her husband admitted. "What's more, I have an accomplice for once."

"God will get you."

"He already has."

"Lunch is on the table. Bring your accomplice." Diana surveyed the yard. "Nice job, by the way."

Since Anne had stopped skimming, the pool had filled again with blown leaves. When the door closed behind her cousin, Anne noticed that the air was suddenly chill. Nothing was more unrelenting than a Mohawk winter, and Anne wasn't sure she was equal to another one, not this year. "Shall I give you a push?" she suggested.

"Provided you turn me around first. You'll notice I'm headed for the water at the moment."

Anne lifted the heavy, leaf-filled bag and set it on his lap. Near the door were three large plastic trash cans, and Anne wondered if Di had to lug these all the way out to the curb herself. "Di looks exhausted," she said before they turned toward the house.

"She's dead tired all the time."

"I wish there was something I could do. But I wonder if it isn't hypocritical."

"I don't think so."

"If she knew, do you think she would have forgiven us by now?"

"Yes. Long ago."

"I'm not sure I could. If I knew for sure. All these years, she's never asked?"

"Not even a hint," he said. "I don't know what I'd tell her. She's too nice a girl to lie to."

"Or hurt."

"Yeah, or hurt."

Inside, Mrs. Grouse and old Milly had not budged. If anything had changed, it was their posture, for both were sitting straighter now, and they looked stronger, somehow, as if being joined at the knee had worked some sort of transfusion. Milly looked up smartly when Anne and her son-in-law came in. "Diana," she called.

"Are we all going to die of famine, or is there some food in this house?"

"It's on the table, Ma," Dan said from the doorway. "If I can see it without standing up, I guess you can too."

The old woman turned back to her sister. "I haven't eaten a thing all week," she said. "But right now I could eat a cow."

"You know what, dear?" said Mrs. Grouse. "I'm hungry too, for some reason."

"For some reason," Anne said under her breath. For some reason she herself had lost her appetite.

4

Dallas Younger grunted loudly and rolled over in bed. He had been dreaming vividly and wanted to go back to sleep so he could find out how the dream ended up. Not knowing would bother him the rest of the day. He'd waste a lot of time trying to remember the dream's details, examining them for clues, until consciousness finally banished the whole thing. Dallas never paid any attention to completed dreams, but fragments were worrisome.

The alarm clock on his nightstand was quivering and buzzing weakly, the way it always did when he allowed it to ring for a long time before shutting it off. Dallas opened one eye and peeked at the clock suspiciously, not wanting to believe, at least not yet, that he had overslept again. Then a horrible idea struck him and he ran his tongue along the roof of his palate, encountering there nothing but gum. Unwilling to accept the evidence of a mere tongue which, now that he thought about it, tasted suspiciously rancid, he stuck his index finger into his mouth and felt around. No doubt about it. His bridge was gone again.

When he heard something in the hall outside his apartment, he vaulted out of bed. This was the third bridge he had lost in as many months, and it occurred

30

to him now with startling clarity that someone had to be stealing them, actually sneaking into his room and removing them as he slept. Benny D., in all likelihood, as a practical joke. It wouldn't be difficult, for Dallas always slept with his mouth open, one of a dozen personal habits Anne had irrationally held against him, as if he had control over them. He ran to the door and flung it open in time to discover his neighbor, Mrs. Nicolella, after locking the door to her flat, deposit something into her purse. Whatever it was sounded to Dallas Younger a little like teeth, and he regarded the woman suspiciously.

What Mrs. Nicolella saw when she looked up was a thirty-six-year-old man, naked, who looked like he had just awakened with something on his mind. Something to do with her, a middle-aged widow woman, living alone, except when her daughter visited, which was practically never.

For his own part, Dallas became aware of two things simultaneously: first, that he had no clothes on; and second, that Mrs. Nicolella was no teeth thief. The expression on her face was ample testimony. "My teeth," Dallas tried to explain, having difficulty with the *th* sound.

"Your what?" said Mrs. Nicolella, confused, expecting from the naked man another sort of communication entirely.

"Teeth," Dallas repeated. This time the sound he made more closely approximated his meaning, and he succeeded in reducing at least one level of his neighbor's confusion.

"You aren't wearing any," she reported. Then, seeing that he still eyed her purse, his brain refusing to surrender completely the sound it had first recognized as that of falling teeth, she opened the purse wide so he could see. No teeth.

Back in his apartment, Dallas commenced a thorough search of the premises, though he knew in advance it would be futile. He was thinking more clearly now and the former certainty that his teeth had been stolen began to seem rash. His two-room flat was easy to search. Once he examined the sink and shower, stripped the sofa sleeper and plunged his hands down along the seams, he was more or less finished. His quest was not without its immediate rewards, however, for he found, among other things, his nail clippers, a dollar and a half in change, and a paperback Mickey Spillane, its spine broken and pages falling out. But nothing even vaguely porcelain. He gathered up the Spillane and put it in the trash, figuring that if the urge to finish the book ever became unbearable he could pick up another copy. This particular edition had disappeared months ago without his noticing, so that was unlikely. In the long run he would probably worry more about how his unfinished dream was supposed to come out. In the closet by the hall door he went through the pockets of all his clothes, clean and dirty, finding a number of interesting things but not what he was looking for. Giving up, he put on the only clean workshirt in the closet—this one happened to have *Cal* stitched in script over the pocket—and made a mental note that it was time to do his laundry. The last two days he had worn shirts with other people's names on them, and that was a sure sign he was running low on everything.

Actually, the loss of his teeth was not tragic this time, since he had displayed uncustomary foresight in ordering a spare set the last time he woke up toothless. The spares he found in their pink case in the medicine cabinet where he had stashed them behind the bottle of Old Spice someone had given him two Christmases ago and which he'd been meaning to use. He slipped the bridge in place and it fit perfectly, even better than the old one. Instead of angry and embarrassed, he began to feel pleased with himself for the way he had providently provided against mischance.

Since he was already late for work, he decided to stop and see his brother's widow, remembering, for some reason, that today was his niece's birthday. Mother and daughter lived in a small, square house on the outskirts of town near Mohawk Sand and Gravel. Dallas parked at the curb, since the driveway was strewn with children's toys. Although they had been married in their teens, Loraine and Dallas's younger brother David didn't have their child until they were in their late twenties, after they had just about given up. David was so excited about the baby that he spent every spare penny on his daughter, not that there were so many pennies to spare. When Dawn was one and he discovered he had cancer, David went a little crazy, taking out a substantial loan so he could buy the little girl twenty years' worth of presents. They filled up the walk-in closet of the spare bedroom, each package wrapped and dated: Merry Christmas 1985; Happy Birthday 1987. Loraine had shown Dallas the closet the day after David's funeral, and he remembered the way she had stared blankly at all the brightly wrapped gifts, still awed, perhaps, by her husband's great need to enter and enrich his daughter's life over the long years from the grave.

Dallas found Dawn swinging in the back yard, her white-sneakered feet straight out in front of her. She didn't quite have the hang of pumping but was doing the best she could. When she saw her uncle, the little girl scuffed to a stop and ran up to meet him. "Pow!" she said, poking him in the forehead with her index finger when he picked her up.

"How old are you?" he said.

"Two old."

"I'm the one that's too old, you knucklehead. Besides, you're three old today. Don't you know your own birthday?"

Loraine then appeared at the screen door and studied her brother-in-law wearily. She was still in her bathrobe. Actually, it looked like it might have been David's. "You again," she said, holding the door open for Dallas to come in without having to set his niece down.

"That's a nice hello after you don't see me for a month."

Loraine cocked her head and frowned at him suspiciously. "You were here last night in case you forgot. Three in the morning."

Dallas did not know whether to believe her or not. He had no recollection of visiting his sister-in-law last night, but then he had next to no recollection of last night. For some reason though, when he first saw her standing there on the other side of the screen, he had imagined—could it have been a memory?—that she had been wearing a nightgown, the shadowy outline of her breasts just visible behind the fabric. Dallas tried to think why he should have imagined such a sight. "What would I have been doing here," he asked, genuinely curious.

"You were drunk. I told you to get lost. You really don't remember?"

"Did I have my teeth?"

Loraine shot him a pained look that contained little sympathy. "Not again. . . ."

Dallas nodded, pulling a chair from the kitchen table, and sat, the little girl still on his lap. Dawn pulled up her dress to show him her panties, which featured an embroidered pig. She leaned back as far as she could, her knees high in the air, so he could have the full benefit of the pig. "Will you take me to Chickey Fried Chicken?"

"You mean the Kentucky Colonel? All the way to Schenectady?"

Dawn nodded eagerly and smoothed her dress back down.

"At times I still can't believe you and David were brothers," Loraine said.

"Uncle Dallas says it's my birfday."

"How would he know? He doesn't even know where his teeth are." Loraine squinted at him. "What are those in your mouth?"

"Spares. You mean it's not her birthday?"

"You insisted the same thing last night. It isn't till the middle of the month."

"And I had my teeth?"

"It was three in the morning, Dallas. I don't remember. Though I think I would have noticed if you didn't."

Since there now appeared to be a consensus that today was not her birthday, Dawn squirmed down from her uncle's lap and went to her mother, clutching her robe with one hand, inserting the other, nearly the whole fist, in her own mouth.

"Come back here."

"No," the little girl said, coyly refusing to look at him.

"What was that on your underwear?"

"Pig," said Dawn through her fist.

"I don't believe it," Dallas said, but his niece refused to take the bait.

"Go back outside if you're going to sulk," her mother said. "And take your hand out of your mouth."

When Dawn didn't obey, Loraine removed it. "Don't want to go outside," Dawn whined, her eyes filling with tears. "It's my birfday."

"Thanks a lot," Loraine said.

"Come here," Dallas clapped his hands. "Be my girl." But instead the child ran outside and let the screen door slam behind her. In a minute the swing squeaked into motion.

"I could make you some eggs," Loraine offered.

Dallas shook his head. "I'm late for work."

He didn't object to the cup of coffee, though, which Loraine poured without asking him. "Then I lost them someplace between here and home. Assuming I went home."

"You promised you would," Loraine said. "You were talking about stopping by the grave, but I made you promise not to."

Dallas frowned. "Grave. What grave?"

"Your brother's. Whose do you think?" She sat down opposite him and put the cream pitcher between them.

"Why would I go there?"

"You were in one of your maudlin moods. I really wish you'd stay away when you get like that. I feel the same way half the time myself, and I don't need any encouragement."

Dallas said he was sorry, and he was, too, though in much the same way he was sorry about a rainy day or something else he had no control over. When he drank too much, he nearly always blacked out and had to depend on people to tell him what he'd been up to, and because he was often told that he became sentimental at such times, he supposed it must be true, though he couldn't say for sure.

"My daughter doesn't need to be woke up in the middle of the night either," Loraine went on. "She's got enough on her mind. She's been scared as hell ever since David."

"Scared of what?"

"She doesn't know. Who ever needed a reason?"

Loraine looked a little scared herself right then, and Dallas felt ashamed of his behavior. He wished he could remember his behavior, so he could feel even worse about it. It wasn't fair that Loraine should feel frightened, and even more unfair that little Dawn should be. When he finished his coffee, Loraine quickly cleared the cups and saucers, and he watched her at the sink, trying to think if there was something he could do for her or the little girl. He had promised his brother he would do what he could for them, but even at the time he hadn't any idea what that might be.

Loraine rinsed the cups in the sink and dried them carefully with a thin dish towel before putting them back in the cupboard. When she and David had married, Loraine was a very pretty girl with soft skin and lovely brown hair. People had wondered out loud how such a shy, studious boy like David had done so well, especially since in addition to being pretty Loraine had a reputation for being a little wild. Those who made book on other people's chances gave them long odds. But David was kind and attentive, qualities that were more or less new to Loraine and that she discovered she liked. According to those who knew her best, she simply changed overnight, returning her husband's devotion as if, without a word of discussion, he had somehow convinced her to forget about wildness in favor of himself and the life he had to offer, which was pleasant and satisfying if not always terribly exciting.

Loraine also discovered early in their marriage that there was nothing she could do to alter his love for her, and when she first noticed that she'd put on a few pounds, that the curves of her body were straightening, she refused to be disappointed in herself. Since he didn't appear to notice the way she was thickening, she repaid the favor by telling herself that she did not mind her young husband's receding hairline, nor that the drain was always full of his dark hair after he showered. Only Dallas, who often visited them on Sundays, made her feel a little self-conscious about her appearance, because he was an unmerciful tease. After a while, though, he stopped ribbing her. She never knew why. At first she thought maybe David made him stop, but then a more plausible explanation occurred to her—that Dallas stopped the ribbing when what he was saying became too true to be good fun any more. She had got very big with Dawn and somehow never quite lost the shapelessness of postpregnancy. Now she thought it might be nice if Dallas would start teasing her again, but he never did. When he commented at all, it was to say that she looked well, and since she knew that wasn't true, the compliment had the opposite effect of what was intended.

Indeed, as he watched her at the sink, he did feel bad for Loraine. With her husband gone and more than half her life ahead of her, it seemed to him that she needed to be prettier than she was. "So," he said when she turned around and discovered him looking at her, "how are you making out?"

She dried her hands on the dish towel and looped it through the refrigerator door handle. "Fine. How can you look at these lavish surroundings and ask such a question?" Her sweeping gesture included not just the kitchen, but the rest of the house, the yard, the neighborhood, and probably all of Mohawk.

"I'm serious," Dallas said, feeling immediately the silliness of his remark, since Loraine was obviously serious too. Her attitude in this respect was inexplicable to him, partly because her surroundings *were* quite lavish compared to his. Admittedly, there was a threadbare quality to the house. Even when David was alive, they had been forced by necessity to make do with things until they were used up. Now what had once been simply thin was close to transparent, like the dish towel Loraine had used to dry her hands. But that was one of the things Dallas had always liked about his brother's house. Dallas himself never wore anything out. He lost it before wear-and-tear became an issue. His clothing was never ragged, because when he went to the laundromat he always managed to leave at least one load in one of the machines. Loss was perhaps the central feature of his existence, and he had learned to accept it the way one does a scraped knuckle or skinned knee. In the long run things equaled out anyway. For every load of clothing he forgot in the washing machine, he gained another in the dryer. Tumbling towels and shirts inside one dryer often bore a striking resemblance to those in the next, and more than once Dallas had discovered, after shoving the spun-dry contents into his duffle bag and going home, that it was some other man's wardrobe he had inherited. Provided the clothes fit, or near enough, Dallas was content and his life various.

Only when he visited his brother's house and saw the sameness of things, the continuity of familiar objects, did he feel keenly dissatisfied with the lack of control he exercised over his daily affairs. He had always liked Loraine's house and was more comfortable there than just about any place he knew, except maybe the track or Greenie's Tavern after work. He was so comfortable in his brother's house that he disliked even the smallest changes or additions, and on those rare occasions when Loraine bought something small and bright and new for the house, he couldn't help but wonder what she wanted with it. Fortunately, she wasn't one of those women who liked to move furniture around. She was far too sensible to suppose that rearranging resulted in improvement.

"You never see anything," she told him, "but the whole place needs work. The cold seeps in everywhere during the winter. The lower cabinets are rotting where the plumbing leaks. None of the doors hang right anymore. I can't even close the one in the bathroom. Not that it matters."

"I could—" Dallas began.

"Don't go making offers. I'm just fed up, that's all."

"I—"

"Don't," she insisted. "You'll promise and then half an hour from now you'll forget, and then I'll dislike you for a while until I forget. Then in a few weeks you'll remember and be mad at yourself until you forget again. So spare us both."

Dallas could tell that she was already angry with him, and he knew, of course, that what she said was true.

He doubted she was miffed about this, though. And he knew enough about women to guess that she wasn't mad about anything as obvious as his having awakened her in the middle of the night. No, she was mad at him for something else, and she wasn't going to tell. That much was for sure. In the three years he was married to Anne she was always miffed and never once willing to say what about. Maybe Loraine just needed to hurt somebody's feelings, and he was handy. He hoped it was just that and nothing more. He liked Loraine. She was one of the few people who seemed to know that he had feelings to hurt. They weren't, he had to admit, regular and predictable like other people's feelings; they came and went in ways that Dallas himself didn't begin to comprehend. After he left Loraine's house, he'd probably get sidetracked and not think of her again for a long time. The little girl's birthday would come and go. Maybe that was why he had convinced himself it was today, knowing that when it really did come he'd be someplace else. "I guess you married the right brother," he admitted.

"A lot of good it did me." She had her back to him and was staring out the tiny kitchen window above the sink as if something outside had caught her attention. "Why don't you run along to work," she suggested. "I've got a lot to do and for some reason I didn't get much sleep last night."

Dallas started to leave, then noticed that Loraine was crying. When he touched her, she broke down completely. "Christ, I miss him."

"I know," Dallas said weakly, guessing that maybe something was required of him but having no idea what it might be.

"Of all the people in the world that God could have

taken, and it wouldn't have amounted to anything. No loss. . . ."

What she said was true. Dallas knew practically everyone in Mohawk, and there weren't many that God, if there was one, wouldn't have been smarter to take. "Like me," he admitted, since it was something he'd thought many times since his brother's death.

Loraine spun around to face him, her face desperate with rage and pain. "Yes, damn it!"

He figured there wasn't anything to do but leave, so after muttering something like an apology, he did. But Loraine caught up to him before he could drive away. He would've been gone already if he hadn't stopped to check the floor of the car and under the seat for his teeth. "I'm sorry, Dallas," she cried through the rolled-down passenger-side window. "God, I don't know what made me say that."

"Forget it," he told her. "Besides, it was true."

"No," she insisted. "I was just mad. If I were you, I'd go see Anne and make her marry me again. You're a nice man. You just need somebody to look after you."

"Or five somebodies."

She smiled and snuffed her nose. "David worshiped you, you know. You were the only one in the family he cared anything for, really."

"And vice versa."

She looked off down the street and neither said anything for a while. "I guess I've got to forget him," Loraine said finally. Then she studied Dallas through the open window. "So do you."

"I have."

She smiled. "Then why do you come around here still expecting to see him?"

The remark took Dallas so off guard that he didn't know what to say. At times when he visited Loraine and Dawn, his brother's presence was so tangible he half expected to see David materialize in the kitchen doorway wanting to know who stole the sports page.

"How would you like to do a favor for somebody who just treated you pretty rotten?"

"Sure, if I can. . . ."

Loraine ran her hands through her hair. Once a lovely, shining brown, it had lost most of its luster. "I'm going to have to go back to work pretty soon. The insurance money's about gone. For some reason David had it in his head that twenty grand would set us up for life."

"It does sound like a lot."

"Not when you're paying off medical bills the insurance didn't cover."

Dallas said he would keep an eye out.

"Thanks," she said. "And I'm real sorry about your teeth."

"I'll find all five sets someday. They're probably in a pile someplace."

They both laughed, and Loraine looked a little better. Dallas knew she never stayed down long. "How come your shirt says Cal?"

"That's what Cal always wants to know. You really think I should bother Anne again?"

A doubt registered in Loraine's eyes, but passed. "Sure. If not her, bother somebody else. What would your son think about it?"

"Hard to say. I don't think he likes to talk to me. I don't even know him any more."

"He's the same kid."

"I didn't know him before either."

Suddenly Dawn was there with them, climbing up her mother until she could see in. Dallas leaned across and gave her a kiss.

"When're we going on Paris wheel?" she wanted to know.

"The Ferris wheel?"

"Yeah, Paris."

"You'd get scared."

"My daddy takes me all the time," she said, glancing up at her mother—waiting, apparently, to be contradicted. "He's taking me tomorrow."

"I know a little girl," said Loraine, "who wants a spanking."

5

The old Nathan Littler Hospital stands atop a steep hill at the base of Myrtle Park, overlooking the rooftops of the junior high, the Mohawk Grill and the rest of downtown Mohawk. Only one wing of the old hospital is currently in use. The rest is dark. The new hospital on the outskirts of town near the new highway has opened, but the transition from one facility to the other is incomplete. Mohawk Medical Services Center is a political hot potato, years behind schedule and many hundreds of thousands over budget. The grand opening and ribbon cutting have been delayed yet again, this time because inspectors discovered that the wiring in the emergency and intensive care units is not up to code. This is also true of the wiring in the rest of the hospital, but the other units have already moved in, and to make them move out again is unthinkable. So, despite the complications it causes, the emergency and intensive care units are still operating out of the old hospital, a hulking, four-story brick affair replete with climbing vines. The rest of the building, now vacant, looks as if it had been gutted by fire. The windows have been exploded by rock-throwing boys who climb the hill from the junior high during their lunch hour. At first there was a public outcry against the vandals, and Willis Anders ran an editorial in the *Mohawk Republican* urging that where the old hospital was concerned, youth might better be restrained than served. But since the old hospital is to be torn down as soon as the transfer is complete, the boys continue to knock out with impugnity the windows of the various vacated wards, giving the impression that those left inside are being pursued from room to room. Now no windows are left to break, except a few in the emergency wing, but the boys still climb the steep hill on their lunch hour, pockets heavy with rocks, and perch in the trees that border the back lot, impatient. Broken glass crackles beneath the wheels of Mohawk's two ambulances when they snake their way around the back of the building to the hospital's emergency entrance.

Tonight both ambulances are on duty. Saturday nights are always busy in the emergency room of the old Nathan Littler Hospital, especially around two in the morning when the bars are closing and people are forced to consider the prospect of returning home with so many of the night's dreams unfulfilled. What follows are the usual brawls and the battered wives and husbands and girlfriends who limp up Hospital Hill—some afoot, some in wobbly old cars—to be sewn up and sent home. Some are bleeding, the majority terribly drunk, and all but the most tragic cases must wait in line for attention from the sparse, overworked staff. Among the throng awaiting attention is a couple in their late twenties. Both are huge, but the woman is slightly larger. Still, it is the man who grabs one's immediate attention. Shoeless, he is wearing a bright orange beach towel about his middle in lieu of trousers. The towel sticks out in front comically, and the large woman stares down at the protuberance maliciously.

"*Look* at you, you dumb fuck," she says. Her voice, though not loud, is brittle and carries marvelously even in the crowded room.

"Look at yerself, if you can stand it."

"You don't even have enough sense to feel like the dumb fuck you are," the woman says. "Everybody's looking at you, you dumb fuck."

This happens to be true, but the man wearing the beach towel is undaunted. He uses a simple four-letter word to describe his companion and it is a part of her own anatomy. Despite the name-calling, neither is truly angry. Their language alone is inflationary. They've been calling each other such names for so long that it's now beyond the power of mere words to stimulate passion. At this moment they are closer to humor than anger.

"You'd see what a dumb fuck you was if you wasn't so proud of yerself. You just never had no hard-on get so big and last so long."

"I just wisht I had a woman worth it."

She ignores this. "I don't see why yer so proud, anyways. It ain't every man has a weeny the size of a wedding ring."

"Least I got a weddin' ring, which is more than you'll ever have."

This is clearly the best shot in the volley, and the woman reacts as if he has punched her good. "How'd you like me to slap that worthless little weeny, dumb fuck."

The man turns away from her. "You're just mad 'cause I won the bet."

"I shoulda knowed, that little thing. . . ."

Someone in the room wails loudly, and the man and woman are no longer the center of attention. People crane their necks to see who howled, but no one looks particularly guilty. When one of the emergency room doors slams open, an ambulance siren is heard—at approximately the same pitch as its human counterpart—and everyone concludes it must've been the ambulance siren all along.

The ambulance driver winds the vehicle around the back of the hospital, over the trail of broken glass toward the yellow crease of light at the end of the long drive. In the rear is a fifteen-year-old who probably will not live to see the morning—after a wreck that took the rescue workers half an hour to get her out, she's in very bad shape. Inside they will do what they can, then take her by helicopter to Albany Medical, but the driver knows the girl is too badly broken to live no matter what they do. He's a young man himself and he doesn't like to think of her young life ending, but there is nothing he can do about it. For all he knows, she's already dead. Sometimes they tell him when a patient dies; other times they let him drive like hell with the corpse. As he nears the leaking yellow lights, he hits the brake hard to avoid hitting something in the road, which disappears immediately. There is a chorus of "Heys!" from the rear. When the driver docks beneath the red EMERGENCY sign, the back doors fly open and the young girl is hurried inside, which means that this time, anyway, he has been transporting a living person.

Rather than get out, the driver sits by himself in the ambulance, staring out the window at nothing in particular, listening to the thick static on the CB and the low twang of a country singer on the conventional radio. After a few minutes he remembers and grabs a flashlight. Fifteen minutes later, one of the ambulance attendants finds him far down the drive at the base of the hospital's gutted south wing, shining the flashlight into the cavelike windows.

"What was it—some kinda animal?"

"I guess."

"Next time, hit it."

"How's the girl?"

"Just died. Come on. There's busted glass all over the place."

They walk back toward the red EMERGENCY sign, but every now and then the driver looks back over his shoulder at the dark windows along the third and fourth floors. He's not certain that what darted in front of him was an animal, but it must've been.

6

Randall Younger stared out the second-floor classroom window at the dark, weatherbeaten statue of Nathan Littler, the town father, on the sloping lawn in front of Nathan Littler Junior High. Already several members of the gang of boys who called themselves the Cobras were beginning to congregate at Nathan's feet, even though last period had over fifteen minutes to go. For Randall, last period was math, and he was bored. The material his teacher was trying to cover should've been clear to anybody who'd read the book, but most of Randall's classmates didn't read books of any description and would never have allowed themselves to be pressured into reading a math text. The private school that Randall had attended in the city had been much more demanding, and in the two years since he and his mother had moved back to Mohawk, Randall had occupied his time waiting for his classmates to catch up. It was exhausting work. The Mohawk kids had pretty high opinions of themselves, but most of them lacked natural ability and desire, at least when it came to schoolwork. As a result, Randall was fast coming to the conclusion that the only way he'd ever be accepted was if he regressed. To that end he had recently adopted a few simple measures. By purposely flubbing questions on exams, he was able to avoid the chorus of groans that had for more than a year greeted his announced test scores. Perfection rankled just about everyone, including the teachers, whereas mediocrity made people feel comfortable. The Jewish kids could get away with excellence because it was just the way they were brought up, but Randall was not Jewish. His father was just a mechanic at the Pontiac dealership, so better things were expected of him. Therefore, instead of scoring a perfect hundred on a recent science test, Randall had allowed himself a mere eighty-eight, and the prettiest girl in the class had smiled at him approvingly. Indeed, if she hadn't been going with the best wrestler in school, Randall might've asked her out to a movie some Saturday afternoon. He wasn't exactly afraid of the wrestler, just aware that he had a way to go before his own credentials were rock solid.

When the bell rang, Randall tossed his things in his locker and drifted along with the crowd toward the double doors, ducking into the gym at the last moment so he could slip out the door that opened on the alley behind the Mohawk Grill. Randall didn't believe in tempting fate. The day before, he was waylaid by Cobras who insisted he join. For a dollar a week, they'd make sure nobody bothered him. That wouldn't have been such a bad deal except that the Cobras themselves were the only ones who ever bothered him. Only the biggest and most athletic boys escaped paying dues. Randall himself had avoided the issue for over a year because no one knew exactly who he was and because he had a way of blending in. But now Boyer Burnhoffer, the Cobra leader, who had already spent two years in reform school, had him figured, and Randall knew he'd have to join pretty soon if he expected to escape a thrashing. The Cobras bragged that they had once killed a boy who refused to join. Randall didn't believe it, but it was vaguely unsettling to know that it was murder they aspired to. They had stopped Randall at the foot of Nathan Littler's statue, and Boyer Burnhoffer—his shirt unbuttoned to the waist in the late October chill, his breath reeking of onions—had wondered out loud, his nose only an inch or two from Randall's, what the boy could have against becoming an honorary Cobra. Randall had known they wouldn't dare to beat him up there on Main Street in front of the school, so he stalled and made an excuse about his grandfather waiting in the hospital. That wasn't true, of course. Mather Grouse had been released earlier in the week, but the ploy for sympathy worked and Randall got away after promising he'd join by the end of the week.

The situation was far from critical. All he had to do was make sure he always had a dollar in his pocket and exercise normal vigilance to avoid parting with it until he had to. It wasn't forking over the dollar that bothered him, but giving people money not to beat him up seemed a bad precedent. By leaving through the gym, he was able to flank the Cobras, who were quite attached to Nathan Littler, in whose august presence they swore and smoked and said mildly obscene things to passing girls. It would probably take them a month or two to figure out how it was they missed him every day, which left only the men's room to steer clear of. And when they finally discovered his flanking maneuver, he could still join the chess club, which met after school in the library.

When Randall emerged into the alley behind the Mohawk Grill, he came face to face with Wild Bill, who appeared headed in the wrong direction. The alley ran along the junior high until it dead-ended at a tall chainlink fence at the base of Hospital Hill. The man had apparently been absorbed in his own thoughts, because when the gym door opened, he started visibly. His longish black hair covered his ears completely, though patches of leprous white scalp showed through where hair inexplicably refused to grow. Randall had seen Wild Bill on the street many times but had never before come face to face with him. But if he was rattled, Wild Bill was more so. He stared at Randall as if he recognized in him someone who had once played a dirty trick on him. Then Wild Bill's expression changed and, as usual, he looked just goofy. "Oughta," he said cheerfully.

"How are you?" said Randall, trying not to appear nervous. His grandfather had told him that the best way to deal with dogs was to show no fear. According to Mather Grouse, dogs could smell fear in people, and Wild Bill, who had a distinctly canine appearance, might have the same ability, it seemed to Randall. There were many legends concerning Wild Bill, stories that Randall had never credited when he saw the other man slouching harmlessly along Main Street, but that, now alone with him in the alley, Randall remembered. According to some eighth graders, Wild Bill was an ax-murderer escaped from Utica. Others said he had once been a perfectly normal teenager until he encountered Myrtle Littler's ghost one night in Myrtle Park, at which point he'd gone crazy. One girl claimed to have watched Wild Bill urinate on the street and, whenever she had listeners, she described the event horrifically. Randall would've almost preferred that his path be blocked by eight or ten angry Cobras than one benevolently beaming Wild Bill, who seemed unable to do anything but nod and grin. When the awkward face-off became unbearable, Randall croaked "I have to go now," whereupon Wild Bill, as if he had been waiting for precisely this intelligence, danced nimbly out of the boy's way like some some shaggy doorman who'd nodded off waiting for instructions.

Before Randall could complete his escape, Wild Bill had stuck one hand into his own dusty black trousers and drawn out a small package, which he then thrust into Randall's hand. Much to Randall's relief, the back door to the Mohawk Grill opened and Harry Saunders, its cook and proprietor, appeared with a bagful of trash for the dumpster. When he saw Randall and Wild Bill, he stopped and surveyed them critically. "You get on home, Bill," he advised.

That must have seemed like good advice to Wild Bill, who resumed his course up the blind alley the wrong way. Once he was out of earshot, Harry turned to Randall angrily, "Just what's wrong with you boys, would you tell me that? None of you got nothing better to do than torment that poor man. Cheating him out of what little money he's got, getting him to trade dimes for nickels, then giving him a bloody nose when you're tired of his company. And all because you can't figure how else to amuse yourself—"

"I never—" Randall began, but Harry wasn't in a mood to listen.

"What ever become of decency? That's what I'd like to know." He still held the sackful of garbage but seemed to have forgotten it. "What ever become of decency?"

"I don't know," Randall admitted.

Harry then remembered the bag and tossed it into

the dumpster, wiping his hands on his grimy apron. "Garbage!"

On Main Street Randall turned right to head home, then stopped to see if Wild Bill would retrace his steps when he discovered there was no outlet to the alley. When he did not, Randall went all the way back to the gym door, from which point he could see the entire alley in both directions. Wild Bill had vanished. On the other side of the chainlink fence was the sheer hillface, heavily wooded all the way up the slope to the old hospital. The only place Wild Bill might conceivably have gone was in through the rear door of one of the other shops that fronted on Main, something Randall was certain he had not done. Then he remembered the small package still in his pocket, and when he took it out, Randall did not immediately know what it was. "Ribbed and lubricated for maximum pleasure," the little package promised. He quickly shoved it back in his pocket, just as he heard someone call his name. Randall half expected to see Boyer Burnhoffer, but when he turned, he recognized his father coming out of the Mohawk Grill. His shirt said *Steve* above the pocket.

"What's up?" Dallas said, falling in step beside his son.

"Nothing."

"Something must be up."

Randall insisted there wasn't anything up that he knew of, the end of the line for that conversation. He saw his father very seldom, and when chance threw them together, it was always a struggle to discover something to talk about. Most subjects just naturally fizzled after two or three exchanges.

When they passed the sloping lawn of the junior high, Randall heard his name again. The Cobras were still congregated at Nathan Littler's feet, and they all waved. "See you tomorrow," Boyer Burnhoffer called.

"Those boys friends of yours," Dallas asked.

"Sort of."

Dallas nodded thoughtfully, and they walked a ways in silence. "Anybody ever teach you to defend yourself?"

Randall frowned. "You mean fight?"

"You should know how."

Randall shrugged, seeing no advantage to it. If you knew how, you'd only be tempted. "Gramp says fighting is for people who can't think."

"Sounds like your grandfather. I can't recall him ever fighting over anything."

To Randall, the very idea of his grandfather raising his fists in anger was preposterous. Not that he thought Mather Grouse a coward. Rather, his grandfather simply would have nothing to do with people he considered unreasonable.

"Somebody said he was in the hospital," Dallas remarked.

"He's home now," Randall said, though he offered no free information. While his grandfather had never spoken ill of Dallas, the boy knew they didn't get along. Perhaps Mather Grouse considered Dallas unreasonable. Dallas once had borrowed a substantial sum and never paid it back, and Randall knew that his grandfather wouldn't want his private business, even his health, discussed with anyone so untrustworthy. This was the problem, of course. There were very few subjects his father ever introduced that Randall ever felt comfortable discussing.

"Your mother doing okay," Dallas asked.

Randall said she was fine.

"She ever see anybody?"

"See?" Randall played dumb.

"Go out—date?"

"I don't know—" he started, then felt his father's eyes. "I don't think so."

This seemed to cheer Dallas considerably, and the fact that the question had been asked cheered the boy, for it meant that their visit was nearly over. Randall's talks with his father always followed the same basic pattern. You just had to be patient, let things run their natural course and eventually Dallas would go away.

When they reached the firehouse intersection, they had traveled about five blocks together and Randall guessed they'd part company, Dallas heading back to the garage, Randall up Seventh toward home. If the traffic light had cooperated, their goodbyes would've been smooth enough, but as luck had it the WALK light flickered out just as they arrived at the crosswalk, forcing them to share a few more awkward moments in each other's company, each aware that their normal conversation had run its limited course and that anything further would represent a wilderness adventure. Had either been alone, he simply would've crossed against the light, for there was no traffic coming, but that wasn't possible now. Both felt duty-bound by the other's presence to wait for the signal.

Just as the WALK sign flashed again, Dallas thought of something to say. "You got any money?"

Randall hesitated, misunderstanding for a moment. Dallas must've guessed, because he looked hurt. "If you ever need any, you can just drop by the garage. I'm not always flush, but. . . ."

When his father didn't appear to know how to finish, Randall said he would remember, though it was difficult to imagine asking his father for money. He never doubted Dallas would give it to him, but there were just some people you didn't ask, even if they happened to be your father.

"Maybe I'll stop by the house sometime," Dallas concluded, a familiar promise that nothing would come of. Randall wished more than anything that his father wouldn't make it, and there were times when he thought that things might be all right between them if Dallas could somehow refrain from saying he'd stop by the house.

In the nearly two years since Randall and his mother had moved back to Mohawk, Dallas had "stopped by" only twice. He'd intended to many other times, probably even shaved and showered, but then would stop downstreet for a paper or something and would run into a guy who'd just heard something about a poker game, and he'd stop in for a hand or two since he was early anyway, and next thing he knew the sky was gray in the east and his recently clean-shaven face was rough, his eyes bloodshot, his hands unsteady. And what he would feel more than disappointment in himself was a sense of relief—that he'd very nearly done something foolish.

As Randall and Dallas parted, the WALK sign flicked off again, and when Randall looked back, he saw his father in the middle of Main Street, cars whizzing by him on both sides. He remembered, then, something he'd overheard his grandfather observe to his mother— that for Dallas life was a series of near misses. To Randall, his father now looked kind of sad, standing out there in the traffic, waiting for an opening so he could scoot the rest of the way. And it occurred to him that it might have been a kindness to his father if he had lied, told him his mother was serious about somebody, instead of getting his hopes up. When he was little, there had been a time when Randall had prayed his father and mother would get back together. Now he looked at things differently. To pick out all the things that were wrong with his father wasn't hard. His shirts never even said the right name and, though he hated to admit it, Randall was ashamed of him. Dallas needlessly complicated their lives, and his son couldn't help thinking how much simpler everything would be if his father weren't around.

Behind him tires screeched, seemingly in answer to the boy's innermost thought, but when he whirled around his father was disappearing into the *Mohawk News,* where he would get a number down before returning to work.

7

Mather Grouse was home from the hospital only a week before being readmitted on the advice of Dr. Walters, the family physician. Had it been up to Mather Grouse himself, he would've cheerfully ignored his old friend in this matter, just as he had in all the others over the past thirty years. But it was not up to Mather Grouse. His wife had insisted. Mrs. Grouse had great faith in physicians in general—Dr. Walters in particular—and she often argued their omniscience with blasphemers like her daughter Anne, who refused to accord them the reverence they deserved. Mrs. Grouse believed that physicians spoke concentrated wisdom, like Jesus in the parables, and one's duty was to be alive to possible levels of meaning. So, when Dr. Walters intimated that a series of tests might be beneficial, Mrs. Grouse saw to it.

She was convinced, for one thing, that Dr. Walters was concealing the real reason for the tests. He claimed that Mather's blood pressure had been high during his recent stay in the hospital, explaining that people with pulmonary disorders were especially susceptible to heart attacks. The effort they expended in breathing was greater than the human heart was designed to accommodate. Mrs. Grouse nodded politely when all this was explained to her, though, of course, she knew better. What Dr. Walters was really concerned about, she knew, was the damage to her husband's lungs resulting from her daughter's negligent use of the inhaler. It said, right there on the label, that frequent use damaged the inner lung. Dr. Walters was too kind to make an issue of Anne's carelessness. Mrs. Grouse had suggested a mild dressing down, but the doctor had just smiled like an old imbecile and said he didn't think the damage was permanent. But Mrs. Grouse took as a vindication of her own view his decision to admit Mather Grouse for further tests.

Over the years, Mrs. Grouse's only complaint with the family physician, who attended their church and was middle-aisle usher, was that he lacked sufficient sternness. Another doctor might have frightened her husband into quitting smoking sooner, whereas Dr. Walters, she suspected, secretly sympathized with her husband's backsliding. As a result, the entire burden had fallen on her. He never smoked in the house, but she suspected Mather Grouse of lighting up whenever he went outside to work in the garden or walk around the block "for exercise." Mrs. Grouse faithfully reported her husband's cheating, hoping that Dr. Walters could be induced to deliver a stiff lecture, but the more she detailed the lengths her husband would go to to sneak a cigarette, the more the old fool would smile and nod at her. And so Mrs. Grouse gradually took to sharing her husband's previously solitary walks through Choir Park and to poking her head outside every few minutes when he was gardening, to make sure he was all right. Insuring that he was never alone was no easy task, because Mather Grouse was slippery where smoking was concerned, and Mrs. Grouse estimated that despite her vigilance, he probably managed at least four cigarettes a day.

All along it was Mrs. Grouse who had looked after her husband's health, and for that reason she had no intention of allowing her daughter to claim credit for saving his life. They'd exchanged no words on the subject, but clearly Anne felt not even a twinge of remorse. And while her daughter would never dare say so, it was equally clear to Mrs. Grouse that Anne was critical of Mrs. Grouse's calm, responsible posture in waiting patiently for the ambulance, just as she had been instructed to do. Actually, Mrs. Grouse was a little foggy about what she was told on the telephone when she had called the emergency number. But she was pretty certain that she had not been instructed to do anything and, as anyone could see, that was practically the same as being instructed to do nothing. She was assured that the ambulance would be right there and imagined the vehicle rounding the corner onto their street even as she hung up the phone. And while it took longer than she had anticipated, the white-jacketed medics who threw the oxygen mask over Mather Grouse's mouth were responsible for her husband's salvation. Or, if not the ambulance people, then she herself, who had calmly dialed the number and explained the situation and given the address without the slightest hysteria. Had she not practiced that drill every night for nearly three years, and responded with skill and courage? All her daughter had succeeded in doing was fracturing Mather Grouse's jaw.

Now, with Mather in the hospital again, things were bitterly civil between Mrs. Grouse and Anne, who stayed strictly in the upstairs flat where she and Randall lived.

They took turns visiting him and could not agree on his condition when they compared notes.

"I think he's going to be *just* fine," said Mrs. Grouse when her daughter stopped downstairs on her way to work.

"Not fine, Mother. Just out of immediate danger. Have you made arrangements for the oxygen yet?"

"That's for your father to decide, dear," Mrs. Grouse said, her lips thinning perceptibly, as they did whenever Anne stepped across the invisible line. "But I can tell you right now he won't have one of those big tanks sitting in the middle of the room for everyone to see. He's a proud man."

"As long as he's alive."

Mrs. Grouse set her jaw firmly. "Don't start worrying him as soon as he gets home. You know what upsets do to him."

"I know what not being able to breathe does to him. I don't understand what you have against the idea."

"Me?" Mrs. Grouse pretended surprise, though she hated the prospect of an oxygen tank in the house. They were not only huge and ugly, but dangerous, too, or so Mrs. Grouse suspected. She knew the tanks were filled under enormous pressure, and she was unable to dispel from her imagination the possibility that the cap might come off one day and the tank fly around the room like a leaking balloon, bouncing off the walls, killing them all in the process before crashing through the front window and coming to rest in the middle of the street. "It hasn't a thing in the world to do with me," Mrs. Grouse said. "I just won't have your father killed with all these upsets."

Anne stopped at the door and turned to face her.

"We both know what he's going to die of, Mother."

Confronted with this obvious truth, Mrs. Grouse did what worked best in such situations. She changed the subject. "I think I'll have a pot roast for his first supper home. And banana cream pie for dessert."

"Whatever," Anne said. "Do you want me to pick anything up on the way home?"

"Like what?"

"Like a pot roast? Or bananas?"

"Don't be silly. I'll go right down to Howard's."

"I didn't think I was being silly, Mother. I was offering to save you a trip."

"What trip? Two itty-bitty blocks."

"Fine."

"I don't like things from those big supermarkets anyway."

Anne knew the best thing was to let her mother have her own way, since she'd end up doing as she pleased regardless. "Don't plan on me," she told Mrs. Grouse. "I've missed a lot of work and tomorrow's Friday. I'll probably have to stay late."

"I think that's terrible," said Mrs. Grouse, who never missed an opportunity to suggest that Anne was ill-treated at work.

"I'll tell my boss. He always looks forward to hearing your opinion."

"Well, I mean really. . . ." Mrs. Grouse elaborated, "I never heard of such a thing."

Anne resisted the impulse to tell her mother that there was a good deal she'd never heard of. Married to Mather Grouse at seventeen, she had never held a job outside the home she ruled as absolute mistress, whereas Anne, since her divorce, had been a professional woman and took pride in it, something Mrs. Grouse had no experience of. During the years Anne and Randall spent in New York, she and her mother remained at cross-purposes, Mrs. Grouse doling out advice in long letters to a daughter whose life was already broader and deeper by half.

"When Randall gets home, I want him to pick up his room. No heading off to the hospital until it's done either. I'll stop by the ward on the way home." When Mrs. Grouse didn't answer, Anne said, "Did you hear me, Mother?"

"Of course I heard you. I'm not deaf."

"Goodbye, Mother."

On her way Anne took the garbage pails to the curb and set them on the terrace. Mrs. Grouse called to her from the front window, "Did you put the handles up? The dogs—"

"Yes, Mother. I'm not a child."

Her mother was still talking when Anne got in the car and closed the door on her voice. Instead of driving away, she sat where she was and massaged her throbbing temples with her fingertips. Then she checked her appearance in the rearview mirror, suspecting for some reason that she must look terrible. She didn't, though. There were the lines beneath her eyes that had begun to appear shortly after her return to Mohawk two years before, but they had not deepened significantly. And besides, it wasn't really age she feared.

Two doors down the block, staring at her curiously, stood a mangy-looking dog of indeterminate breed. Anne returned his gaze until the mutt became self-conscious and, panting, walked a tight circle. For some reason, staring the animal down cheered her up a little.

When Anne backed out of the driveway, the dog's ears perked and his wet tongue lolled out of his mouth. When she disappeared around the corner, the dog loped forward toward the garbage cans.

8

Dallas Younger's life was place oriented, at least as far as it was oriented at all. At certain times of the day or week, only certain places would do, and if he happened to be anyplace else he was vaguely unhappy. He had started spending his Sunday mornings in his brother's wife's kitchen shortly after Loraine and David were married. He and Anne had recently split up, which made his Sundays seem pretty purposeless—the only day of the week when he felt any serious dissatisfaction with his life. On the Sabbath Dallas's two-room apartment, small and cramped and none too clean, always seemed to him small and cramped and none too clean. Only rarely did it seem that way on other days of the week, and when it did, he simply left. But on Sunday mornings Dallas's haunts were all closed, and the men he drank and shot pool with felt obliged to stay home with their families, at least until the ballgame came on and the bars opened at noon.

Loraine's kitchen, thick with the smell of fresh cinnamon rolls, *was* Sunday morning to Dallas Younger. Before his brother's death, Dallas, who had a key, would be waiting in the kitchen when they returned from church. He would cheerfully accept Loraine's chiding about being a heathen and David's pretended anger over his treatment of the Sunday paper, which got rearranged, its pages mixed up and folded the wrong way before David even had a chance to look at it. To make matters worse, Dallas would read aloud from the sports page. Both men were avid fans, but David always saved the sports for last, dutifully reading the other sections thoroughly before allowing himself the pure pleasure of box scores. He'd done things that way all his life. As a boy he separated Oreo cookies, first eating the dry cracker shell, saving for last the sweet white filling. No one had ever succeeded in breaking him of that habit, not even his brother, who always swiped the hoarded filling, stuffed it in his mouth and grinned, his mouth open far enough to reveal the depth of his child-ish depravity. Dallas, of course, had eaten his cookies in reverse order, as he had begun every endeavor with the part he enjoyed most. The landscape of his life was littered with classified sections and dry cookie shells.

But since David's death, Dallas had not been regular in his Sunday visits. Sometimes he didn't wake up until noon, which meant that Sunday morning had taken care of itself. Other times he didn't go over due to the vague feeling that Loraine wouldn't really want him there. And he hadn't been back since the morning he'd been confused about his niece's birthday and only now, as he pulled up in front of his brother's house, did he remember his promise to Loraine to keep an eye out for a job. He couldn't remember having heard of any-thing, though, and he was grateful for that.

Loraine answered the door in her bathrobe again, looking surprised to see him or, maybe, anyone. "What's the story," Dallas asked. "It's ten o'clock. How about getting dressed?"

"Thanks for the advice. For your information, I've

been up all night with a sick child. Hundred and two fever."

"How about me cheering her up?"

"Like hell. I just got her to sleep."

"Oh," Dallas said. He had wondered if he would end up sorry he came over, and sure enough he was. Loraine looked tired and grumpy, and there was no cinnamon-roll smell in the kitchen.

"Come on in, though. There's coffee, and I could use a little cheering up myself."

Dallas took his usual seat and immediately began to feel more comfortable. In the unlikely event that he ever owned a house, he would want it to be one like David and Loraine's. It wasn't that much of a house, really, but somehow it felt right. When coffee brewed, you could smell it everywhere in the house, and on holidays with a turkey in the oven you could feast on the aroma. Though today there were dishes stacked in the sink, several days' worth, and it occurred to Dallas that his sister-in-law's explanation for still being in her bathrobe might be a convenient excuse. She poured them each a cup of coffee. "The paper's in the living room if you want it."

"Maybe later."

Loraine stirred some cream into her coffee. "I figured you must be mad at me for treating you so rotten."

Dallas made a face. "You know better. I've been busy, is all."

"I know how busy *you* get," Loraine said. "That the same set of choppers you had before or different ones?"

"Don't get smart. What's wrong with Little One?"

"Flu, prob'ly."

"Want me to take her to the doctor?"

"Where? It's Sunday."

"There's the hospital."

Loraine shook her head. "I'm not that scared yet. Besides, I can take care of her. What I need is someone to take care of me."

"If it's money. . . ."

She smiled. "No. What I need is a good hot beach someplace. Where I can lie in the sand and have somebody whose only job it is to bring me those tall native fruit drinks with miniature palm trees in 'em. He could also rub suntan oil on my back if he felt like it."

Dallas was surprised by his sister-in-law's mood and, for some reason, a little embarrassed by it.

"You don't have to look at me like that," Loraine said. "There was a time when the boys would have fought for the privilege of greasing me up."

"What did I say?"

"Nothing. You're too kind to say it."

They drank their coffee, Dallas stirring his in order to appear occupied. Again it was clear to him that he shouldn't have come, and he wondered if there was any way he could leave without offending. He hated not knowing what people were thinking. It happened mostly with women. When he married, he had never known what to make of Anne, whose moods were unpredictable and far too subtle for him to read accurately. He always laughed at the wrong times, thinking he was supposed to, and then got serious when she was trying to joke with him. It made him grateful that women didn't play poker, because then he'd always be folding and raising at the wrong times, a problem he had anyway.

"Don't you ever wish someone would take care of you?" Loraine said. "Cook you a meal? Iron you a shirt? Someone who'd always know where your teeth were?"

"Keep it up."

She frowned. "That's no answer."

"No, then. I don't want anyone to take care of me. I live the way I want."

"That's crazy. Nobody lives the way they want."

"If you want to meet somebody new, get out of the house. Who's going to come over here looking for you?"

"That's just it. I'm not even sure I want to meet anybody. I hated dating, even as a teenager. All that being nice when you don't feel like it. All the time wishing you were cleverer and better looking than you are. I haven't got the stomach for it any more. I can't even get up the nerve to look for a job."

"I've talked to a couple people," Dallas lied. "Something will turn up." He made a mental note to really look around. He hated telling lies to people he liked, but maybe he would be able to find Loraine work. That would make up for it.

"Don't use up any favors," Loraine told him. "When push comes to shove, maybe I won't have the guts."

"What else can you do?"

"Sell the house, live off that for a while. After Dawn is grown up, I don't care that much."

As if on cue, the little girl cried out upstairs and Loraine started from the table.

"Want me to go up," Dallas asked.

"Not really. All you know how to do is tickle."

Alone, Dallas went into the living room and found the paper. He started with the sports section, which quickly absorbed his thoughts. It would've been nice to read out loud if there'd been somebody to read to. He would've liked to get his brother all red-faced just one more time. Subconsciously he lifted his bridge free of the roof of his mouth with his tongue, then let it slip back in again. He'd been without his own front teeth since he was nineteen, when he got into a fight and refused to give in, even after taking a terrible beating. The loss of his teeth didn't bother him much, even at the time, but his brother David had unraveled. Coming to see Dallas in the hospital, David didn't even recognize him at first. Dallas's face was swollen and gray and, when he grinned at his younger brother, the boy had broken down. Years later, after his marriage to Loraine, Dallas could still unhinge his brother by removing his partial and grinning at him. Once David was so angry he made Dallas promise never to do it again. "They're gone," Dallas had told him. "I don't see why that should bother you if it doesn't bother me." But after that he rarely removed his teeth in his brother's company.

When Loraine came back downstairs, Dallas was completely absorbed by the college football line scores, and she studied him with interest from the foot of the stairs. Her late husband had been slight of build, his dark brown hair thinning badly after his twentieth birthday. Later, after the treatments, he was completely bald. Dallas's hair was still thick and black, and he was sturdy at just under six feet. Anyone who didn't know him might have mistaken Dallas's thoughtful expression as he read the paper for profound intellect, and Loraine, who knew him well, couldn't help wondering if her brother-in-law's lunatic behavior might not mask a better mind than people gave him credit for. Everyone said his son Randall was very smart in school, and the boy must've inherited it from someone. Anne, perhaps, but maybe even Dallas. When people jokingly asked Dallas how he wound up with such a smart kid,

Dallas explained by saying he'd had a smart milkman. In truth, Dallas himself was not convinced of his son's intelligence.

He finally became aware of her. "Fever's finally broken," she told him. "She'd like to see you."

He quickly rose and went to the foot of the narrow staircase. "Where's my girl?"

From above there came a delighted peal of laughter.

9

Much to the delight of Mather Grouse, the autumn days stayed mild well into November. He felt like himself for the first time since early summer, and even the thought of the approaching winter and the bitter winds that would keep him housebound failed to dampen his spirits. Autumn had always been his favorite season, and in the afternoons he was able to take short walks without the cloth mask given him by Dr. Walters. The neighbors raked leaves and burned them in large drums, the sweet smell lingering in the neighborhood long after the leaves themselves had been reduced to white cinders. Mather Grouse enjoyed the scent of autumn because it reminded him of Keats's ode, which in turn made him feel better about life than was his custom. After summer, which exhaled suntan oil on sweaty limbs, the scent of nature incinerated was reassuring.

About the only part of summer that Mather Grouse missed was his little garden in back of the house—dead now for another year, the vines of his tomato plants brown and brittle. Today he got down on one knee to feel the earth. Inside the house he heard Mrs. Grouse humming tunelessly. In the kitchen, by the sound of it. When the humming moved to a more remote corner of the house, he pulled out a loose board above the cellar window and removed the plastic bag he'd hidden there. Inside the airtight plastic pouch were some Camels. He took one out, slipped it into his shirt pocket and quickly zipped his windbreaker to the neck before returning the bag to its hiding place. Fortunately, Mrs. Grouse was cleaning and wouldn't interrupt her sacred duty to take a walk with him, even though she would be suspicious and irritated when he returned.

Getting away with something sent a dark sensation through him, as when he was a boy. As far back as Mather Grouse could remember, he had always known the difference between right and wrong, though his mother had always pleaded Mather's defense with his father when the boy misbehaved, arguing that he was too young to grasp the significance of his misdeeds. But his father was a wise man who never suffered recriminations or self-doubts once he'd taken off his belt. Young Mather had always endured his punishments stoically, tracing the progress of the pain to its climax, then to its gradual decline until that time after the strapping when he could cheerfully pronounce it gone. He saw no good reason to resent punishment, at least at the time, for he knew in his heart that he was more often bad than punished, which was what kept life from seeming a shabby, piddling thing.

After his father's early death, the result of having whistled into too many empty gin bottles and having no one to strap him for it, Mather Grouse took upon himself the task of reining in his passions. His mother was far too weak and compassionate to help her son, so he donned the hair shirt pretty frequently—whenever it seemed like a good idea. He didn't overburden himself with commandments, but merely pledged to steer clear of women and mind his own business, which covered just about everything that was likely to cause him serious grief. By the time he reached his middle teens, he had made of himself a sober and industrious youth, and when he left his mother's house to take his first job, he was able to compliment himself that he had successfully held in check his innate depravity, though now and then he still enjoyed getting away with things. But at sixty-four his wife's vigilance took up where his own left off.

This afternoon he decided to walk through Choir Park—a good deal farther than he usually ventured, for he tired easily, but today he felt strong and it had been a long time since he'd truly tested himself. He enjoyed the symmetrical paths that wound among the hedges and pines. If he tired, he could always stop at the bandshell and rest on one of the benches. There weren't any flowers this late in the year, but with luck he'd catch the smell of burning leaves.

It was a gray afternoon, and when he arrived at the park, Mather Grouse was thankful for his windbreaker. He had the park to himself. There was no hurry, since Mrs. Grouse would be equally suspicious and irked regardless of the length of his absence. In the end he would still have to face her arched brow, the offended tilt of her slender jaw, the pursed lips, but in the meantime there was the autumn afternoon and the threat of an endless winter during which to remember it. When he arrived at the bandshell, he wasn't breathing heavily and the smell of the leaves made him feel young and strong. He sat down on a park bench, content.

He sat until he felt he had denied himself the final pleasure long enough. Then he took out the Camel, lit it and inhaled deeply. It seemed odd to Mather Grouse that nothing went all the way down any more except cigarette smoke, which somehow knifed through the phlegm and arrived at the very center of his body. At times he thought it would be the most exquisite pleasure in the world to smoke an entire pack of Camels, one right after the other, for it was only when he smoked that he had the sensation of truly breathing. Intellectually he knew it was cruel deception—that each Camel reduced the number of breaths allotted him—but there was no denying the experience. Even the pure oxygen he received at the hospital didn't penetrate the way Camels did, and he often smiled at the notion that what he needed was not to be hooked up to an oxygen tank but to an endless Camel.

Mather Grouse became aware that he was not alone precisely when he inhaled his last drag on the cigarette. A dark-complexioned man roughly his own age stood idly by the bandshell. Mather became aware of him just as it occurred to him that the afternoon had become bitter cold and that the park bench was acting as a conduit for the cold earth at his feet. There was no way to tell how long the man had been standing there, but he had the impression it wasn't a short while, because he'd caught no movement in his peripheral vision. Mather Grouse knew who the man would be even before he recognized him.

Rory Gaffney nodded at him and limped over—like his brother a large, soft man, but the way he moved, almost in slow motion, made him seem more menacing. No child ever taunted him the way kids on their bikes had their favorite police officer. Rory Gaffney's hair was tousled and his chin and cheeks perpetually gray, no matter how recently the straight razor had glided over them, his generally scruffy appearance in contrast to the lush, milk-white, leather coat he wore. Mather Grouse, who had worked with leather all his life, had never seen a more beautiful skin. It was the kind you paid your employer for the privilege to cut. Rory Gaffney stopped at the row of benches where Mather Grouse sat and sidled down the row.

"Mr. Grouse," said Rory Gaffney, reaching into his coat pocket for a pack of cigarettes. "How are you, sir?" The last word sounded anything but congenial.

"As well as I deserve," Mather Grouse said without turning. They might have been the only two men in a church, the low gray sky its ceiling, the bandshell its altar.

"Deserve!" said Rory Gaffney enthusiastically. "Deserve, yes. Well, thank the good God above we're none of us worse off than we deserve!" He jerked the pack of cigarettes, so the ones near the opening popped up part way. He lifted one clear of the pack before offering it to Mather Grouse. When he was refused, Rory Gaffney rather pointedly allowed the offer to stand by not withdrawing the pack, as if there should be no mistake.

"You don't see skins like this any more," Gaffney observed, extending one arm so that Mather Grouse could inspect the leather close up. To a passerby it would've looked like he was offering the back of his hand to be kissed. But there was no passerby. The park was still.

Mather Grouse admired the leather but declined to touch, even when it remained before him, as with the cigarettes. "The good stuff is a thing of the past," he said, wishing the arm away.

It went, finally. "Mostly," Rory Gaffney agreed

pleasantly. He lit a match on his thumbnail and the tip of his cigarette glowed red, the burning tobacco inching toward the man's parted lips. "You never come by the shop any more."

"Never," Mather Grouse admitted.

"A clean break from the past."

"Yes."

"I understand," Rory Gaffney said. He smoked cross-kneed, exhaling through his weedy nostrils. "It isn't like the old days. Things change."

"Not most things."

"No. But some things. You and I, we're old men, and that's change."

Mather Grouse smiled. He still had not looked at his companion. "The world will do fine without us."

"Ah, but how will we do?"

"As we deserve, I suppose."

Suddenly Gaffney snorted and coughed, the cigarette bobbing between his lips. But he left it where it was, though he gripped the park bench with both hands. "Deserve," he said. "It's always deserve with you, Mather. You always come back to it. You're going to tell me you're not afraid to die?"

"No."

"Good. Because you have a reputation for telling the truth."

Mather Grouse looked out into the leaves.

"Me? I hate the thought of dying," the other man observed. "There's no place better than where we are right now. I have some good years left, and I don't see why anything should spoil them."

This sounded to Mather Grouse like a question. "You've always been lucky."

"Right!" the other man agreed. "Luckier than I deserve, you may think, but that's life. I'd bet my luck will hold."

"Yes," Mather Grouse said, though without pleasure.

The other man seemed satisfied. "You should visit the shop. I still work a little, teach the young ones."

Mather Grouse shifted on the park bench. For many minutes he had become aware of a tightening in his chest that had now become a fist, and he was suddenly short of breath. It did not surprise him, though he had felt so well and strong a half hour before. The spells came and went without warning.

"Not that they want to learn the important things, these young ones," Rory Gaffney said. "For them there's nothing in life except today. Me, I live for the future."

That remark seemed so incomprehensible to Mather Grouse that for the first time he looked squarely at the other man, forgetting for a moment the problem of whether or not he could draw another breath. "And what do you see in your future?" he said.

"Everything," Gaffney answered.

"Everything?"

"Yes, everything. Do you understand?"

"No."

"Then let me explain. The other afternoon I picked up a hitchhiker. She was maybe fifteen. She pulled her shirt right up to show me." Rory Gaffney pulled an imaginary shirt up to his neck to demonstrate, holding his elbows straight out, and he left them there when Mather Grouse looked away. "Cutest little things you ever saw. You don't believe me?"

Mather Grouse bent forward to breathe.

"God's own truth."

They sat a while in silence. Gaffney showed no apparent interest in finishing his story, but presently said, "Most men our age live in the past. I say forget the past. Make like it never happened. Regret in the ground."

Mather Grouse said nothing.

"My wife left me, you remember. I regretted for a while. Then I said the hell with it. Regret in the ground."

Rory Gaffney ran his hands through his hair, then stretched. "You're smart to stay away from the shops," he said, apparently forgetting his previous advice on the subject. "You aren't a man to dwell on what's done and can't be undone."

"No."

"And I'll bet the good Mrs. Grouse is the same."

"She knows nothing of the past."

A gust of wind came up, standing Gaffney's thinning hair on end and revealing a larger extent of baldness than perhaps he would have wished. He smoothed the hair back into place, not bothering to transfer the cigarette to the other hand. A glowing red spark detached itself and settled onto the man's scalp, but if Gaffney felt it, he showed no sign. Instead, he rose and buttoned the milk-white coat. "You should wear something heavier, Mather. The long winter's coming. You should comfort yourself. A fine coat like this one would look well on you. You deserve one."

He turned up his collar and looked around the empty park. Mather Grouse did not get up. He wasn't sure he could; the fist in his chest hard and unrelenting.

Gaffney lit another cigarette. "Your daughter and grandson live with you?"

"Yes . . . upstairs."

"I have a granddaughter. Did I ever tell you?"

". . . no. . . ."

Rory Gaffney nodded. "Yes. Twelve years old. Take care of yourself, Mather. You don't look well."

Then he was gone, and Mather Grouse was left alone on the park bench in the gray afternoon. Someone had raked brown, brittle leaves from the flowerbeds into a pile near a large drum, but most of the leaves had scattered and drifted. Mather Grouse watched some leaves dance in a funnel that swirled vigorously, then abruptly died. Home was a very long way away, and he could not imagine where he would find the strength. He thought of his father and wondered for the first time if the man had drunk himself to death on purpose.

On the ground at his feet lay the butt of Rory Gaffney's first cigarette, flat and broken and covered with dry earth. He bent to pick it up and felt himself slump and the gray sky came into view. He watched the swiftly moving clouds until his grandson Randall appeared, his face ringed with the faraway branches of dead trees. When the boy handed him the inhaler he had left behind, Mather Grouse took it reluctantly, for his body had begun to relax. His first good breath hurt. The air had the sting of winter.

10

One weekday in early November Diana Wood and Anne Grouse met for lunch at the new Holiday Inn on the highway. Anne arrived first and took a table by the window overlooking the Cayuga Creek, which wound off into the woods some thirty yards away. Her father said there were trout in the stream when he came to Mohawk as a young man. But the fish began to come out looking bulbous, and the Fish-and-Game quit stocking it. Recently there was talk of restocking, and to show that the past was past the tanneries were in favor.

Anne smiled at the notion. The window reflected her face and she studied herself suspiciously. Her faint smile expressed little joy, but many would've found it lovely just the same, though she didn't know what to make of it herself. Though no longer vain, as she once had been, she nevertheless found it pleasant to think she was still attractive. Her hair was long and blue-black. Lately she had considered cutting it short. She never wore it down any more, the way men invariably said they liked it best. Earlier in the week she overheard a man at work, one to whom she had made excuses, refer to her as "a shame," and she took that as a compliment. In high school the boys had made the same comment about a pretty young girl who left school to join a convent, tragically just after her breasts had started to develop.

Di was late and Anne had nearly finished her Bloody Mary by the time her cousin slid into the booth. "Now *that's* a fine idea," she said, ordering the same for herself, along with another for Anne. "Are we on a schedule, I hope not?"

Anne said she didn't need to get back before mid-afternoon.

"Good," Di said. "Let's get roaring."

"Have you ever *been* roaring?"

"No," her cousin admitted. "And it's high time, don't you think?"

"I hope you won't be disappointed. It's more messy than anything else."

"I don't care. At least it's *my* mess. Not my mother's. Not my husband's."

"All right." Anne wondered what had brought on her cousin's uncharacteristic mood. Diana, after all, had majored in circumspection and graduated at the head of the class.

"I'm sorry I'm late, but Mother threw a fit when I told her I was going to the Holiday Inn. You know how she likes to eat out. Good food *for a change* is how she puts it. I had to take her over to your mother's to save her from a stroke."

"Mother's delighted, I'm sure."

"Poor Uncle Mather wasn't. You know that look of horror he gets when company comes?"

"He's terribly antisocial."

"And no good at concealing it."

"He isn't about to put a welcome mat on the front porch. He says people are literal-minded."

"I like him anyway."

"Me, too."

"I want shrimp," Di said with sudden conviction, without even looking at the menu. "Ice cold with cocktail sauce. These things make you hungry." She slurped the dregs of her drink through her straw.

They both ordered shrimp from a young waiter whom Di Wood, already a little tipsy, felt compelled to tease. "I only want them if they're large shrimp. Are they really large?"

"Yes, Ma'am."

"How many?"

"Four to an order."

"And how big?"

The waiter showed her with his thumb and index finger.

"Curled up or stretched out?"

"Curled up."

"Excellent."

The waiter went away and the cocktail waitress brought two more Bloody Marys. "Let's meet here every day and get ripped," Di suggested.

"I'm a working woman, remember?"

"What am I?"

"You know what I mean."

Di was having far too good a time to feel miffed. She had never been able to drink, and three was two past her limit. "I'm *enjoying* this," she said.

"You ought to have a cocktail at home now and then. Dan would enjoy the company."

"I'd end up pushing the two of them into the pool." Diana laughed out loud at the idea, then looked around guiltily, surprised by the volume of her voice and ashamed of her behavior. "If he doesn't hurry up and have that damned operation, I'm going to go batty. Battier."

"I thought it was tomorrow."

"Not soon enough to suit me. If he starts one more project I have to finish, I'll strangle him. I draw the line when it comes to the car. I know how he loves to tinker, but he can't reach—which means he has me in and out of the house. Do this, do that, right there under the manifold, as if I know what a *manifold* is. Then he gets tired or discouraged and guess who gets to clean up. All the while Mother's bellowing from the other end of the house that she's ready to get out of the tub and have I finally gone away and left her to drown."

When the shrimp arrived, both women ate eagerly. Di crunched hers all the way down to the tails. "God, they were good," she said once nothing was left but ice and cocktail sauce. "It's odd, too. I never enjoy food. Let's get some more."

"Let's split an order." Anne really didn't want any more, but neither did she want to disappoint her cousin. When the shrimp came, she insisted Di eat three out of four.

Everything was fine until Di, who was chattering happily, stopped and began to sweat. When she excused herself, Anne allowed her a few minutes before following into the rest room. Diana was on her knees, her head half in the commode. When she finished, Anne helped her to her feet and over to the mirror where Diana examined her streaked face and touched up her makeup as best she could. "You were right. It's mostly just messy," she said. "Leave me alone for a few minutes, okay?"

Anne went back to the dining room and paid the

check, then walked her cousin out to the parking lot. "Let me drive you home," she said.

"No. I left the alcohol inside, along with that beautiful shrimp. It's unthinkable to pay that price for shrimp and then leave it behind."

"These things happen."

"Not to me. Promise you won't tell Dan."

"Why? Lord knows, he's been there."

"It isn't that," she said. "I just don't want him to suspect how badly I needed to . . . to act like this. He'd feel bad if he knew."

"He's a big boy."

Her cousin smiled. "Not really."

"Drive extra carefully. I can't afford to lose my best friend."

Diana looked both surprised and pleased. "We *are* good friends, aren't we?"

"Of course."

Diana rooted around in her bag until she found the keys to her Volkswagen. She refused to learn how to drive Dan's customized Lincoln, afraid that in a moment of crisis she'd become confused and lose it. She turned the key in the VW's ignition, but only idled the engine. "Do you remember that night the four of us were coming back from the lake?"

"Yes, I do."

"I wanted to go in that night. God, how I wanted to. But I just couldn't. Isn't that sad?"

"I don't know. Maybe not."

"I think it is. I envied you so much, the way you always did whatever you wanted. I guess I still do."

"I'm not so wild any more."

"You can get mad, at least. Sometimes, I think if I

could just get good and mad. . . . I don't know. . . . I
envy you, anyway."

"Please don't, Diana. I mean it."

"How can I help it. Look at you."

Anne said nothing. Telling Diana that she was married to the man Anne herself had been in love with all
her adult life wouldn't be much of a comfort.

"I've always felt, somehow, that that night was a
crossroads for all of us. You and Dallas. Dan and me.
If I hadn't been so . . . who knows? Everything might
have turned out differently."

"I doubt it," Anne said truthfully. "There are times
when I suspect it's all mapped out before we're born."

"No," Diana said. "It has to be us. Otherwise there's
no sense. Otherwise. . . ."

Anne reached in and patted her cousin's hand on
the steering wheel. "Give Dan my best."

"I will," Diana promised. "Poor Dan."

11

Growing up in Mohawk, Anne Grouse had little opportunity to mix with any but the sons of shopkeepers and leather cutters and gas station owners. Of these, Dallas Younger had been the most dashing. By local standards he was an athlete of considerable skill, with just the hint of a bad reputation, which made him doubly attractive to Anne, a year his junior. After a quarrel with his family, Dallas had simply moved out of their home and into a room above the Scallese Drugstore, living the kind of independent life that made him the envy of every boy in Mohawk High. When a graduating senior got pregnant, suspicion had immediately fallen on Dallas Younger, because he and the girl had once dated and because a seventeen-year-old boy with a place of his own might be expected to put it to good use.

When Anne started going out with him, it was with the expectation that he would educate her. She, too, had a reputation for being wild, which she had done little to discourage and nothing to merit. More than anything, she feared that if she did not do something to authenticate her reputation soon, she'd risk losing it. To contemplate the depth and breadth of her innocence was far more frightening than any fear of pregnancy. Mrs. Grouse had shared no wisdom with her and her father was not the sort of man a young girl with questions felt comfortable approaching. Anne knew little more than that with boys came the danger of conception, and that with boys like Dallas Younger the danger was multiplied.

There was also the danger of destroying her father's dream—that she would win a scholarship to the state university. No one in his own or his wife's family had ever been to college. A man with eight grades' worth of education himself, Mather Grouse had spent the better part of his adult life doing what he called "improving his mind." His readings were eclectic, if wholly undisciplined, and by the time he was thirty, he knew a great deal without even beginning to satisfy his curiosity or discover its source. And he knew too that while he had read more than a great many educated men, the fact remained that they were educated and he was not.

From the beginning, Anne had shared her father's reverence for books, and he treated her to Saturday afternoons at the Mohawk Free Library the way other Mohawk fathers treated their offspring to movie matinees. By her sophomore year in high school, Anne was reading restless books that he himself would not have selected for her, and he had to comfort himself with the firm conviction that most of what he objected to in Mohawk and the world at large was not the result of people reading the wrong books, but rather of not reading any at all.

On the subject of boys, however, Mather Grouse was a stern lawgiver, reminding his daughter repeatedly that her future hinged on her ability to keep from falling in love with some local boy long on promises and short on ambition. "There is no disparity," he was fond of quoting from *David Copperfield,* "in marriage like unsuitability of mind and purpose." He didn't tell her that she was better than her classmates—just that it was unlikely she would meet anyone in Mohawk who wanted out of life what she wanted, or rather what her father wanted for her and trusted that in the end she would want for herself.

In the matter of boys in general and Dallas Younger in particular, it was odd that Anne for the first time in her life discovered an ally in her mother. Mrs. Grouse, who would not have said so openly, did not share her husband's ambitions for their daughter, partly because she feared a destiny far worse for the strong-willed Anne than the possibility of settling down to a responsible, dutiful existence like her own. And duty, that virtue she had tried to inculcate in her daughter above all others, would surely be driven home by necessity—the demands of a husband and children and a home. To Mrs. Grouse, her husband's efforts to raise his daughter's level of expectation had succeeded only in making her more vain and proud than she was by nature. The girl became more difficult by the hour, to the point of questioning the way her mother did things and demanding to know the reasons, openly expressing doubts that there were any.

Under normal conditions, even with his wife and daughter in cahoots, Mather Grouse would never have permitted Anne to date a boy like Dallas Younger. But as it happened, Mr. Grouse had recently averted what he considered a far greater threat to his daughter's well-being. Anne never understood her father's horror at seeing her on the street in the company of Billy Gaffney, a quiet boy who'd had a crush on her for several semesters. One afternoon the boy had finally summoned the courage to approach her, only to discover himself dumbstruck. Unable to ask for the privilege of carrying her books, he had finally, in utter desperation, yanked them away and refused to look at her as they walked, responding subverbally to her small talk.

That her father should explicitly forbid her to associate with the Gaffney boy, surely the most harmless of classmates, made little sense to Anne, but she had never seen Mather Grouse more adamant. Normally she wouldn't have given in, but giving up Billy Gaffney was a little like giving up liver for Lent. She felt sorry for him. Even once it was widely known that she and Dallas Younger were "going together," Billy Gaffney followed her home from school and stood across the street from the Grouse home as if awaiting a summons to dinner. Then something had happened to him—an automobile accident, people said—and he never recovered.

Having put his foot down about Billy Gaffney, Mather Grouse was reluctant to register another serious objection, though he never disguised his opinion that Anne wouldn't take long to discover on her own Dallas Younger's limitations. Ironically, the limitation she spotted almost immediately was Dallas's lack of worldly experience, for he turned out to be nearly as shy and inept as Billy Gaffney.

Dallas had some limited experience of girls, but none of "nice" girls, and no idea of how to treat a girl too pretty and well mannered to be comfortable with. They'd had several dates before Dallas brushed her lips with his. That quick, terrifying touch, the smell of her scented breath, convinced Dallas that life was deep down good. It convinced Anne that it must've been someone else who knocked up Mary Sue Bergen. The realization was stunning. After all, Dallas was known to hang around the pool hall, and he freely admitted to losing significant sums of money in poker games.

Innocence aside, there was much to admire. Dallas was independent, had a place and a car of his own, and wouldn't even have returned for his senior year if it hadn't been for baseball. He held down an afternoon job at a local garage and never seemed to want for ready cash. There was even something romantic about Dallas in his work clothes, which made him look more like a man than a boy. Anne sometimes would wet a tissue with her tongue and remove a smudge from his cheek, an act that seemed to both of them entirely wanton and exciting.

To say that Dallas "had a car" was somewhat misleading, because most of the time it was spread out all over the garage floor. No matter how you looked at a car, any car, it was impressive, but for Dallas perhaps the best way of looking was to lay all of its parts flat out there where you could see the full extent of your investment. On those occasions when he assembled the pieces, his car always ran, and on weekends he never had to ask his father for the keys to the family car. To Anne, Dallas was a sort of person she hadn't ever known, as well as an exciting contrast to her father. Each day Mather Grouse faithfully went to the shop, just as he had since Anne was a little girl, having acquired in all those years nothing except emphysema. In the autumn her mother would stock the pantry with canned goods in case his work did not last the winter. They had nothing but a small savings account, not even a family car.

There was a time when things looked as if they might improve, but it was brief. Mr. Grouse had been promoted to foreman at the shop, which meant not only more money but also a guaranteed winter. After a month, however, he went back to being a simple cutter. He had stepped down by choice; he told Mrs. Grouse that there was too much politics in the job and that he disliked wielding authority over men he had worked side by side with for so long. But for the first time in her life, Anne suspected her father of not telling the complete truth. A man he disliked was promoted to take his place, and the Grouses' new-found prosperity and security was over.

So, when Mather Grouse insinuated that Dallas lacked ambition, Anne had smiled bitterly to herself. It was true that Dallas had little interest in any of the things her father valued, but at eighteen the boy already had a place of his own and a car to boot. She didn't question her father's reverence for learning, his moral uprightness or his desire for more out of life than enough money to play the daily number and get drunk on weekends. But even measured by his own yardstick, Mather Grouse hardly seemed a success. And Dallas, feckless though he was, had more to show for his efforts—and a lot more fun than her father, for whom, it seemed to Anne, life was little more than a succession of sacrifices without even a slender promise of reward.

Anne Grouse, then seventeen, also feared that the world outside Mohawk County—the better life that for Mather Grouse was the promise of education and hard work—was naturally reluctant to embrace those who were not born into it. Her suspicions on this score derived from her reading and from a day at Saratoga with Dallas. She could tell when he picked her up that morning that life was pretty much the way he thought it should be. His car was waxed and shiny, and the sky was robin's-egg blue. The night before he had won nearly two hundred dollars at craps, and on the way to the track he gave Anne a complete rundown. She only half listened to his enthusiastic rendering, but she, too, was excited. Today was opening day at the flats, which meant that the horse people from up and down the east coast would be present. She'd heard reports of the pageantry, and was proud that Dallas wanted to show it to her at firsthand.

They arrived over an hour before the gates opened and, though Dallas was all for going directly to the track, when they drove past a grand old hotel with lush flowers all the way up the sloping terrace and people dressed all in white, breakfasting on the long, canopied porch, Anne made him stop. She immediately wished she hadn't. The parking lot was full of large new automobiles calculated to diminish Dallas's pride in his reconstructed Chevy. On the hotel porch the whiteness of the tablecloths and the new paint and the expensive summer clothing threw off a glare, and Anne could see that Dallas was none too comfortable even before the neatly jacketed waiter received them cooly.

Dallas, whose social graces did not include reticence, remarked audibly that in his opinion there were nicer spots right in Mohawk, and lots of them. The thin film of automobile grease that no amount of washing ever completely removed was suddenly very apparent to Anne, who wondered if all the summer people had noted this as well. In conversation over the linen, he waved his silver fork like a baton to music only he could hear.

At the track Dallas insisted on the clubhouse where the people around them were interchangeable with the ones on the hotel porch. The women wore jewels and their escorts seldom spoke above a whisper. Dallas, full of his expertise as a handicapper, freely offered tips to men who returned his friendly overtures with bored smiles and unfeigned indifference to his advice, which, had anyone taken it, would have proved disastrous. He lost everything he had won the previous night and then some. After which he announced that it was clear the jockeys had fixed all the races for the day, and the rest of the suckers could stick around to get fleeced if they wanted to, but he'd had enough.

On the drive home Dallas was morose, his recent exuberance and self-confidence dashed. He did throw his arm around Anne's shoulder when it was offered, but she could tell that the day's events weighed heavily on him. The car wasn't running as well as it should, it seemed to him, not even as well as it had that morning. He'd have to tear it apart tomorrow. When they drove past a sign that announced Mohawk County, Dallas was unable to suppress a sigh of relief. Even Anne, to whom Main Street now looked for the first time unrelentingly shabby, was happy, for both their sakes, to be home.

12

Sunday mornings, when his wife goes to church, Mather Grouse often sleeps sitting up in his favorite armchair. The house is quiet then, and he has faith that he will not die on a Sunday. Sometimes he will turn on a television evangelist. It doesn't matter greatly which one because Mather Grouse never turns up the volume far enough to hear distinctly what is being said. What he likes is the rhythm and, if it's the right sort of sermon, he will not only sleep but actually breathe with the cadence. Often his "religious slumbers," as he terms them, are the most peaceful time of his week.

Mather Grouse does not sleep much at night any more. Breathing is difficult when he lies down, and he often has nightmares in which his lungs don't take in sufficient oxygen. Each night he spends many hours perched on the edge of the bed, thinking about smoking cigarettes and how nice it would be to be able to recline and breathe at the same time.

But come Sunday morning his old chair is perfect. Its arms have been worn threadbare by his elbows, but he will not let Mrs. Grouse put a slipcover over it unless company is coming, which—when he has anything to say about it—is seldom. He believes that sick old men should be left alone, except when they don't want to be, and he has managed over the years to be left alone. This morning Mrs. Grouse and Anne and Randall will visit the Woods after church. He has been left a plate of something in the refrigerator for when he is hungry, but he cannot imagine being hungry today. The medicine leaves a brassy taste in his mouth, and any more he eats out of duty, to avoid weakness. He nods sleepily, his chin coming to rest upon his breastbone, his bald spot staring at the smiling black-and-white evangelist.

Mather Grouse is asleep only a few minutes when the doorbell rings. He ignores it, not even bothering to open his eyes. Odd people sometimes come by on Sundays, wanting to discuss Scripture. They are far more likely to go away if you don't answer the door than if you do and tell them to. Mather Grouse cannot remember if the blinds are drawn, but this doesn't matter. If they look in, see an old man slumped forward in an armchair and fail to raise him with the bell, they will depart. Basically they just follow Scripture, and Scripture doesn't have any advice about what to do in these situations. Soon he will hear the sound of their retreating footsteps.

When the bell rings again, Mather Grouse slyly opens one eye, just enough to see. A lone man is standing on the porch, but the blinds are half drawn and Mather Grouse cannot make out who it is. He can think of no one who has any business standing on his porch on a Sunday morning, but when the bell rings a third time, he pulls himself out of the chair and goes to the door where his old friend Dr. Walters is waiting patiently. "Are you going to invite me in, Mather?"

Mather Grouse decides not to, but he does pull open

the door and step out of the way. "You're not in church," he remarks.

"I don't go as regularly as I used to," the old doctor admits. "In fact I've been feeling particularly irreligious lately. I don't suppose it's good form for men our age to indulge in crises of faith, though."

Mather Grouse has already returned to his armchair. "Men our age shouldn't indulge in anything."

Dr. Walters takes off his outer coat and folds it neatly over the arm of the sofa. If Mrs. Grouse were there, she would hang it up and offer him a cup of tea, but Mather Grouse's inhospitality is legendary, even among his friends. "Any more I find myself a prey to young men's doubts. I've come to suspect there's something dark at the center. Don't you find that silly?"

"No."

"Neither do I, just now, but the feeling may pass. Still, I doubt you and I have ever been men of real faith. I much more enjoyed our friendly competitions than enything else about Sunday churchgoing."

Mather Grouse smiles. As ushers, they always made tiny wagers on who would take in more in the collection basket. "You could always afford to make up the difference. My side was always dimes and quarters, the occasional dollar bill. A crisp new ten-spot always turned up in yours. If it hadn't been for that, you'd never have won."

"You were better at making people feel guilty. They saw you coming and dug into their pockets. They saw me and said, let *him* pay. Perhaps if you came back to church I'd get my religion back."

Mather Grouse knows all this is leading somewhere. His friend is a master of indirection, but he will not be able to conceal the purpose of his visit much longer. "It was you who insisted I give it up to begin with."

"Yes," the other man admits, but his voice is tentative.

"Besides," Mather Grouse says, "I get all the religion I need right here." The two friends smile and watch the evangelist, whose face is aglow with love and makeup.

"I have another patient with emphysema," Dr. Walters ventures. "About your age, though according to the X-rays the damage to his lungs is far greater."

Mather Grouse says nothing. The two men are not looking at each other. It is very close now, and Mather Grouse begins to suspect the direction they are heading.

"The man is a mover. He carries people's furniture up and down flights of stairs. I told him this would have to stop. He has two big, strong sons. I said he'd have to let them do the heavy work."

"Very good advice."

"But you see what I'm driving at?"

"No," Mather Grouse lied.

"Here, then. You are suffering from emphysema, a disease we're only now learning about. We know it will gradually grow worse, because that's the only thing it can do. Eventually, unless you get hit by a car in the meantime, it will take your life. This much we know. But for a long time I've suspected—and now I'm certain of it—that you are sicker than you should be. Your lungs have suffered some deterioration, and there's the phlegm. But you should be able to breathe."

"That's very good to know. I promise to turn over a new leaf."

Dr. Walters frowns. Mather Grouse has always been difficult. He is resisting, and the doctor won't easily discover what he wants to know. If at all, perhaps. "Tell me about the bad days. When do they come?"

"Whenever," Mather Grouse says. "Sometimes I'm feeling good, then all of a sudden the tightness. If I happen to be awake, I have time to prepare. If I'm asleep, sometimes there isn't time."

"Do you dream?"

"Not often. Sometimes I have the sensation of dreaming, but when I wake up I can never remember what about."

"Tell me about the last attack."

Mather Grouse is growing annoyed. "I was in the park, sitting on a bench. I shouldn't have walked all that way."

"Why did you?"

"I don't know."

"Was Mrs. Grouse with you?"

"No."

"What were you doing?"

Mather Grouse decides to tell the truth, which might throw his friend off the track. "I was smoking. It felt wonderful."

"I see."

"I doubt it," Mather Grouse says. "I'll never be able to convince you, but it's not the cigarettes."

Mather Grouse steals a look and is surprised to see the other man looking so alert. So intense that he's nearly cross-eyed, the doctor is studying Mather Grouse as if he were something under a microscope. "I believe you," he says. "I have another patient. A little girl with asthma. Her parents are going through a divorce. A very ugly one. Her attacks coincide with her father's visits."

"My father is dead," Mather Grouse says. "You are the only one who visits here."

"Yes." Dr. Walters leans back against the sofa and crosses one knee. "But what I want to know is what you think about. What you think about and dream about when the tightness comes. That's what I want you to tell me, my friend."

13

Anne Grouse never set eyes on Dan Wood until he came home from Korea. By then she and Dallas had been dating for nearly a year. Dan lacked Dallas's good looks, but her first conscious thought, the afternoon they met at her cousin's, was regret that she had so openly committed herself to Dallas, whose light suddenly seemed dim. Not that Dan was a show-off. On the contrary, he was Dallas in geometric reverse. Where Dallas was garrulous, Dan was reserved. All the girls thought Dallas the handsomest man they knew, and Anne felt certain they would find Dan Wood plain by comparison, yet he was the most attractive man she'd ever met. She doubted that any girl, including her cousin, would ever value him at anything near his worth. What she admired most was his self-assurance. He wasn't always trying to say witty things, and when he did say them, he felt no need to repeat them for changing company.

Though she fought the feeling, Anne was jealous of her cousin's good fortune, for Diana and Dan were a match from the beginning. They had known each other before he went overseas and, though they'd never dated, he began writing letters. Those letters amounted to a courtship, and by the time he returned it was to a woman he'd never really known, except as she emerged through her responses on paper. If Dan was disappointed in Diana in the flesh, he showed no sign. For her part, Di was like the fairy-tale princess who waited, confident that every promise of future happiness would be redeemed in full, confident too that she would recognize the man she had waited for and that he would transform her. She had few physical charms, but when Dan came home from Korea, she simply opened her arms to him and in doing so became lovely in her own eyes and his.

For a long time Anne Grouse refused to admit that she was in love with her cousin's fiancé. No one suspected. The two couples double-dated frequently, often at Anne's suggestion, but despite their age difference, that seemed natural enough. There were times when Dallas would've preferred to have his girl all to himself, but when they were alone together, she was not as affectionate as he could've wished. She was far more agreeable, more willing to reciprocate affection, when they shared a cozy booth with Dan and Diana. Dan treated Dallas like a favored younger brother, humoring him, never showing him up, teaching him things without ever seeming to, providing Dallas with a social education as painless as osmosis. In turn, especially after drinking too much, Dallas was subject to flights of wild admiration for his new best friend. *"Helluva* guy," he would say once he and Anne were alone.

"Yes."

"One helluva guy," he insisted, bleary-eyed, as if he had detected some implied reservation. "I want us all to be best friends. We should all four of us get married right away. Til' death do us part."

Many an evening would have ended in a fight over

an imagined insult had Dan not been present. Dallas was ambivalent about the fact that no matter where they went, Anne was likely to be the prettiest girl. He took great pleasure from the fact when the night was young and he was still relatively sober, but later the knowledge weighed heavily, especially when other young men intruded on their happy foursome, wanting Anne to dance. Dan often defused the situation by taking Anne onto the dance floor himself, the quarrel fizzling for lack of a prize. Though he drank as heavily as Dallas, Dan was older and accustomed to it; Dallas went out with the idea of getting tight, and succeeded by forced marches.

At the end of these evenings, back in her bedroom in her father's house, the walls turning visible in the early morning light, Anne would try to hold onto the evening. But soon there was little but gray hopelessness. If things seemed fine when they were all together, when she was alone the fact that Dan belonged to her cousin, that they could not simply change partners, could not be ignored. To make matters worse, she had always been fond of Diana and genuinely pleased that the family prediction of spinsterdom would be foiled. If she was annoyed with her cousin at all, it was the result of a realization that came to Anne during the course of the summer—that Diana and Dan were actually lovers. At first she rejected the possibility as absurd. Diana had always been comically modest, not wanting to change into her swimsuit in front of other girls, failing to see the humor in dirty jokes. Moreover, she and Dan seldom showed the slightest public affection. Dallas always made sure he and Anne held hands, and often kissed her if he thought it was likely to be noticed. Though Dan and Diana were far more circumspect, the more Anne observed them, the more subtle signs of intimacy she began to detect. For the longest time she was unable to think what Diana and Dan reminded her of, then it came to her: a married couple.

Ironically, Anne's realization was compounded by a second intuition oddly out of synch with the first—that Dan Wood might have feelings for her. There never was anything overt between them, of course, and Dan never paid her any special attention, except when Dallas got too drunk to function, at which time Dan's attentions would take on the air of dutiful friendship by holding a chair or offering an arm.

Dancing had always been one of Anne's passions, and Diana, who danced indifferently, was always cheerful about lending Dan. Dallas danced like he did everything else, with wild enthusiasm and little staying power. The energy he put into a jitterbug often seemed comic, his arms and legs flailing about; with him for a partner, you danced at your own risk. In his rampant fits of dancing, his feet seldom firmly planted on the floor, fueled in part by drink but not quite drunk, he was always a threat to hurl Anne into tables of unsuspecting drinkers. Dan, on the other hand, moved effortlessly, always within himself, and he seemed as aware as Anne of the song's nuances. Their signals to each other were neither false nor obvious.

14

As usual, Wild Bill Gaffney stopped at the Mohawk Grill at three in the afternoon. He never used the front door like the real customers, but came through the door that opened onto the alley. As always, he waited until the midafternoon dead time when Harry was alone. If there were customers, he waited patiently outside until they left. Then Harry would be glad to see him, at least after a fashion, and maybe even treat him to coffee without being asked. Today nobody was in the diner to make him uncomfortable, but Wild Bill discovered after climbing onto his stool at the end of the counter that it was impossible to appreciate his new winter coat indoors. Harry's grill gave off enough heat to warm the whole place, and Wild Bill's stool was right next to it.

To make matters worse, Harry was acting suspicious, and when he asked where the new coat came from, Wild Bill didn't know what to tell him. The man who had given it to him had told him to forget it, so he had. Forgetting was something he was good at. Sometimes he just went ahead and did it without having to be told. The only trouble was that some things just wouldn't stay forgotten. Once he figured he had them erased real good, his memory would jog and there he'd be—remembering again before he could do anything about it.

He didn't want to remember who had given him the coat because he knew he wasn't supposed to, but the coat was so nice and warm that he couldn't help thinking about it. If he ever *needed* to remember, by concentrating hard and reconstructing the series of events that led up to having it, he'd be able to. First, he would recall where he had been and how he'd felt without the coat, and then how it felt not to be cold anymore, until the person who handed it to him and made him try it on to see if it fit became a clear image in his mind's eye. Just thinking about the process of remembering almost made him do it, but when he saw the image focusing he forced everything to go blank before any harm was done.

The coat was waist length, dark blue with white stripes along the sleeves. It seemed full of air and squeaked when he swung his arms. The coat made Wild Bill feel a little like a balloon. It was very warm, especially in the pockets where he stuffed his hands. Maybe he didn't remember exactly where it came from, but even Harry's needling could not shake Wild Bill's conviction that he hadn't stolen it.

Wild Bill drank his coffee quickly, his face sweaty. He was unaccustomed to such warmth and so many questions from his only friend. He had some coins and put them on the counter. Harry took one or two and shoved the rest back for Bill to put in his pocket. Outside, the November air was raw and the wind that howled down Main Street made Wild Bill feel comfortable all over again inside the coat. He neither sweated nor shivered. He hoped no one would take the coat away.

When he emerged from the alley, the junior high was getting out and some of the boys and girls along the other side of Main Street called to him. He waved and shouted back, which increased the general merriment. One of the boys began to walk with an exaggerated limp, his arms hanging down at his sides like a gorilla's. Wild Bill thought several of the young girls were pretty, though not nearly as pretty as the girl he had forgotten. At times, if he thought real hard, he could remember her, how she had looked with her long black hair and slender white arms, but because he was afraid his father or his uncle the policeman would catch him at it, he didn't think of her often. Sometimes, though, he would see somebody that reminded him of her, and there she was. She was beautiful to think about. Occasionally he waited for her in front of the high school, but she never came out, and he was always told to move along.

When the boys and girls were gone, Wild Bill zipped his coat and headed back up the alley between the Mohawk Grill and the junior high, still thinking about, and nearly remembering, the girl. He failed to notice that he wasn't alone until he had practically walked into the circle of boys. He recognized them immediately, though he knew none of their names. One of them had once punched him hard, and the blood from his nose had trickled down into his mouth and tasted like salt. When Wild Bill got closer, he saw that this boy had another pinned to the ground, one arm twisted up under his shoulder blade. The others were hooting encouragement. The smaller boy squirmed and, every time he tried to wriggle free, the boy on top grabbed him by the hair with his free hand and pushed his nose in the gravel. The victim didn't cry, though he was bleeding from the nose and mouth. Wild Bill thought he knew this boy, too, though it was hard to tell with his face so scraped and bloody.

Wild Bill drew closer and watched, at once concerned and skeptical, since these particular boys had once tricked him by pretending to fight among themselves. When he had tried to stop them, they hooted, made faces and told him to go do a bad thing with his mother. Then they ran away. Wild Bill was not at all certain that this wasn't a similar trick, despite the blood from the one boy's nose and the fear in his eyes.

Everyone seemed to notice Wild Bill at the same instant, even the boy on the ground. "Get out of here," said the larger boy, refusing to surrender his victim's twisted arm or let him off the pavement. Somewhat reluctantly, one of the boys stepped forward to prance around in front of Wild Bill, dancing left, then right, throwing up a small fist in the general direction of his frowning face. Bill neither dodged nor ducked, and the third jab landed and he felt his lower lip swell. When the boy swung again, Wild Bill pushed him to the pavement.

"Get him!" somebody yelled, but nobody moved after seeing their comrade dispatched with so little effort and respect. Finally the large boy got up to do the job himself. His opponent, now free, held his twisted arm like a broken wing, but didn't run away. This was definitely the boy he knew, Wild Bill decided, the one who made him think of the girl. As he was thinking about this he was doubled-over, punched hard in the stomach. But when the boy uppercut, his fist encountered Wild Bill's stony forehead and his knuckles cracked audibly. Bill sat down, then stood up immediately, determined not to be hit again and embarrassed to have been sat down. His belly hurt. When one of the other boys, finally shamed into action and heartened by seeing their adversary felled, offered to knock Wild Bill down a second time, Wild Bill caught him by the waist and flung him through the air against Harry's metal dumpster, where the boy's head rang against the steel. The sound took all the fight out of the rest, even the large one. They clustered around the dumpster. Each had seen his share of fights with bloody noses and chipped teeth, but they'd never seen anyone lie motionless like the boy on the ground, and the gravity of the situation struck them dumb. They forgot completely about Wild Bill, who had also forgotten completely about them and was grinning benevolently down at the boy he'd rescued. "Jesus Christ," muttered the large boy. "Jesus H. Christ."

When a delivery truck turned into the alley, the gang scattered, leaving only Wild Bill and the bloodied boy and the one motionless on the ground. The driver pulled up and got out, kneeled by the inert figure, quickly glanced up, then hurried into the diner. By the time he returned with Harry, the alley was empty save for the unconscious boy. It soon filled up, though, and the ambulance that screamed the short block and a half down Hospital Hill had to wait for the crowd of spectators to clear a path.

Wild Bill followed the boy at a discreet distance, first up Main Street as far as the fire station, then up the hill as far as Mountain. As the boy limped homeward, the man who followed—certainly sinister-looking, his hair long and scraggly, his face unshaven—felt his anxiety grow, for the boy appeared to be leading him to the one place in Mohawk he was most forbidden to go, and the further they went, the more he feared their destination. The tightening in Wild Bill's stomach had nothing to do with the fact that he'd just been slugged there. He'd forgotten all about the fight. Nobody had told him to, he'd just done it.

In horror he watched the boy cross the street and climb the steps of the house. Did the boy not know that this house was forbidden, that something terrible would happen if he didn't stay away? Wild Bill feared for the boy, because something terrible had once happened to him, though he had forgotten what it was and had been told that it would happen again if he ever remembered. Then the door to the house opened and she appeared from somewhere inside, the one he had forgotten and yet sometimes remembered, the one he'd been told was gone. She drew the boy quickly inside and the door closed again. Wild Bill waited across the street for a long time, but the door did not open again.

It was after dark by the time he got back downtown. The Mohawk Grill was crowded as he slipped unnoticed into the back, waiting to tell Harry the news. He never got the chance, though, because as soon as Harry heard the back door creak shut, he shoved Bill into the storeroom with the big cans of tomatoes and pumpkin pie filling. One man was too excited to speak, and the other sputtered. "You've done it this time," Harry said, his face bright red with fear and anger. "Nobody can fix this! Sweet Jesus, Billy, what came over you?"

Seeing his friend so worked up only increased Wild Bill's own sense of excitement, and he mistakenly concluded that they were excited over the same thing. He grabbed Harry's shoulders with such force that when the larger man tried to step back he discovered he couldn't. "Ive!" Wild Bill insisted, clutching Harry, who suddenly wished he had his spatula with him. "Ive!"

Pulling free, Harry pushed Wild Bill onto an empty crate and grabbed his chin with one paw so he could neither speak nor move. Actually, Bill didn't want to move, but having his cheeks pinched brought tears to his eyes, and he had not finished talking. The skin along his throat was feverish. "Yes," Harry said. "He's alive, but just barely. You're in big trouble and there isn't a goddamn thing I can do to help you. Can't you get that through your big numb skull? Can't you understand? I can't help you!"

Wild Bill stared dumbly at his friend, no longer struggling, but as soon as Harry's grip relaxed, he slipped free and shook his head vigorously. "Oh . . . oh. . . ."

Harry slapped him in the face then, hard enough to make his eyes water again. Their expression seemed to say that just about all the truly astonishing things that could happen in the world were happening within the space of a few hours, and he hadn't any idea where it would stop. "Don't tell me no!" Harry said savagely, grabbing his cheeks again. "Don't tell me no, goddamn you. You just sit there until I can figure out what to do. You hear?"

Wild Bill fought to get free, but this time Harry was ready for him and tightened his grip until his thumb and forefinger met, only the skin and stubble on Bill's cheeks between them. Not until he nodded that he'd stay quiet did Harry let go to return to his restless customers. He studied Bill sadly for a moment before leaving him alone in the storeroom among the high shelves stacked all the way to the ceiling with canned applesauce and kidney beans and cling peaches, burlap bags of sprouting potatoes on the floor, the darkness too complete with the door closed to read the labels.

15

One late August night they all headed for the lake. Everyone was on edge, partly because it had been hot and humid for a week, and because summer was nearly over. Even Dan seemed quietly out of sorts. Dallas was the worst. His car wasn't running, and that afternoon Anne had told him she was going to do as her father wished and attend classes at Albany State in the fall. It would be a shame to waste the scholarship she had earned, she said, but Dallas refused to be comforted by the fact that she would be only an hour away. He was clever enough to guess that her leaving was indicative of something, just as he knew that things had never been less intimate between them. He was far behind his own leisurely schedule, too. A whole summer had slipped away and he still hadn't discovered the courage to slip his hand beneath her brassiere. And here they were, practically engaged. He was cruelly ashamed of himself, and lately life had begun to seem shallow and worthless.

At the prospect of going away, Anne herself felt an odd mixture of hopelessness and resignation. In a way she welcomed September, which would give her the opportunity to break gradually with Dallas, whose feelings she had no desire to hurt. And seeing less of Dan might be for the best too. There was always the chance that her feelings might change, though she had no confidence they would.

"I guess it's up to me to cheer everybody up tonight," Di remarked when they were halfway to the lake and no one had said anything. They all seemed to know she would not be equal to the task.

The dance was not one of the regulars at the hotel. This one was being held in the rickety old pavilion on the other side of the lake, accessible only by a network of narrow dirt roads that wound among the campsites. In the still night the accents borne on the summer air were mostly from New York City. In August the whole metropolitan area seemed to empty into the Adirondacks.

"This is going to be full of city bitches and woodchucks," Dallas complained. He particularly disliked the latter, unworldly and unsophisticated, who found their way down the mountain on Saturday nights.

"At least there's a breeze," Di said.

Inside the pavilion, which was festooned with orange lanterns, they discovered they could only get drinks by going next door. After seating the girls, Dallas and Dan left for the bar, and by the time they got back, two good-natured hillbillies in black cowboy hats had invited themselves to the table and were entertaining Di and Anne with loud stories and enticing them to drink out of a large tin flask. Dallas tried his best to start a fight, but the two interlopers were far too amiable to be provoked and went away peacefully. It was a long shot, anyway.

Dallas drank purposefully and his mood did not improve. Before long, it was obvious to him that Anne didn't care for him as much as he could've wished.

"Admit it," he said suddenly, his reddening eyes full of anger.

"Admit what?" Anne said.

"You don't love me."

"I don't even like you when you get like this."

"Then admit it," he insisted.

Anne appealed to the others, but Di was looking carefully away and Dan somehow managed to give the impression that he really was someplace else. "Of course I love you," Anne said.

Dallas pondered his gin, as if it contained some melancholy truth. After a minute he said, "I can take it."

"Take *what*, Dallas. What can you take?"

"That you don't love me."

"I said I love you," Anne insisted. Di said she thought it was true.

"I know you love me," Dallas admitted. "Except not really."

"You're talking nonsense."

"No I'm not," Dallas snapped, his smile full of self-pity and gin. "I bet you love Dan as much as me."

Anne knew Dallas had no real suspicion on that score. He was just throwing it out to be contradicted. Yet she felt herself flush, and she didn't dare look at anyone for fear they would know.

"It's true," Dallas said, throwing his arm around Dan's shoulders. "I bet she loves you as much as me."

"There's no accounting for personal taste," Dan said.

The remark did not make immediate sense to Dallas, and he stared at his friend for a moment before breaking into wild laughter. "I love this guy," he roared. "You gotta love this guy. You gotta."

They all laughed, then, and even Dallas was relieved, though he would've been hard pressed to recall that he was responsible for most of the tension in the first place. At the moment he could think only that he was a lucky fellow. His personal landscape was filled with friends and he had the prettiest girl in the place. "Come on," he grabbed Anne by the elbow. "Let's teach these woodchucks how to dance."

She followed him onto the crowded dance floor where the hillbilly band was trying hard to master the subtleties of jitterbug rhythm. "Gangway," Dallas roared, taking his girl in his arms. And then his feet began to go, wildly, as if they possessed his very life.

When they left the pavilion that night, Dan at the wheel, Dallas drunk and melancholy in the back seat with Anne, Diana staring out the passenger-side window at nothing in particular, they had all reached the same unspoken regret that summer was indeed over. It seemed to Dallas that his heart was about to explode with love for his girl and his friends and just about everyone he could think of. Everything was perfect, and he did not want things to change. The black lake was shimmering like ink, small waves lapping gently against the shore.

"I love you all," Dallas said. "I mean it."

"Of course you do," Anne said.

"I do," he insisted. "You guys are . . . the best."

"True," Di said. She had nursed her two drinks all night long. They had made her tipsy, but she was sober now. Dan drove slowly, competently, given the amount of alcohol he had consumed. Anne watched him from the back seat, trying to read his thoughts, wondering if he minded her going away. He had said little all night and hadn't danced with her once, not the sort of conclusion to their reckless summer she had hoped for.

Something should've happened, she felt. Had there been some unmistakable sign between them, then going away would have been supportable. Instead, Dan seemed miles away.

"You're beautiful," Dallas told Di with such work-manlike sincerity that it sounded like false generosity. "I mean it. Good-looking, too. Damn good-looking. But you know what?"

Everyone wanted to know.

"I gotta stick with my girl," he said, pulling Anne to him, ignoring her resistance to his drunken embrace. "She's really beautiful. Really beautiful. You're good-lookin', Di. Don't get me wrong. But I gotta stick with my girl."

Anne nudged him, hard. Dallas never suspected when he was embarrassing people. Diana knew that she was far from pretty, and compliments from a melancholy drunk were sure to have the wrong effect. "You're bombed, Dallas. Even more than usual."

"I gotta stick with my girl," he repeated, planting a sloppy kiss on her lips.

Anne wished Dan would say something. If someone didn't distract Dallas, chances were that he'd continue in the present vein all the way back to Mohawk, and Anne was not sure she could endure much more of his foolish blubbering. He was too sweet to hurt, but she found herself dangerously close to telling him she thought he was a fool and that she couldn't wait to go away. She knew that would make the both of them feel terrible, and when they came to a stretch of road that was only a few yards from the lake, she said, "Let's go for a swim."

Dallas perked right up. "Skinny-skipping!" he said. "Dipping, I mean."

"I think we should go home," Di said.

"Stop the car!" Dallas roared, grabbing Dan by the shoulders and shaking him.

"It'll be fun," Anne said. "Some people might even sober up."

"Not me," Dallas threatened. He was already trying to get his shirt over his head, confused by the fact that it was a button-front.

By the time Dan eased slowly off the road, they had overshot the small inlet by nearly a hundred yards. Dallas, still struggling with his shirt, plunged blindly into the trees on what he was convinced was a shortcut. When Dan cut the engine, they heard Dallas crashing through the brush. He grunted once and they heard a thud, followed by a splash. "I found it!" he called.

"Don't look at me like that," Dan told Diana, the first time Anne could remember him raising his voice to her.

"This is crazy—"

"So what? Maybe we could all stand a little crazy. Maybe you could."

"I'm sorry," Anne began. "This is all my fault—"

Dan interrupted her. "You better catch up to Hawk-eye before he drowns himself."

Anne got out and began to feel her way toward the thrashing, splashing sounds, but when she looked back she could see that Di was still seated stubbornly in the front seat.

The moon was down and it was very dark, but by following the sounds Anne was able to locate Dallas at the water's edge where he was struggling to get his pants off, swearing angrily as he hopped about on one leg. Anne quickly stripped down to her underclothes and slipped into the water before he was even aware of her presence. When Diana and Dan emerged from the trees, he stood before them in nothing but his shorts and socks. "C'mon," he said excitedly. "You're way behind."

When Dallas took off his shorts, Di turned away and said she was going back to the car. This struck Dallas as an insult and instead of diving in, he stood his ground in his argyles. "Wassamatter?" he said. "We're all friends."

"Are you coming?" Diana said to Dan.

"Wassamatter?"

"Leave her alone, Dallas," Anne told him. "For once don't be a jerk."

"See?" Dallas said, surprised by her voice so close. Her presence seemed to him at that moment more significant than what she had to say. The fact that she was in the water made her an ally. "Anne's not ashamed, and she's better looking, too."

"Di can do what she wants," Dan said.

Had Dallas been a degree more sober he would've heard the warning in his friend's tone, but he wasn't. "Who cares?" he said. "She doesn't have to pretend she's a saint is all. Everybody knows she's putting out."

For an instant Anne was certain Dan was going to punch him. Dallas must've thought so, too, because he began to step back. The two men were only two yards apart, but the slope was steep. In the knee-deep water Dallas lost his balance and started over backward, then righted himself too much and lunged forward. Dan palmed the top of Dallas's head like a basketball, held him still for a second, then shoved him gently into the lake. By the time Dallas came sputtering to the surface, Dan had disappeared into the trees in pursuit of his fiancée.

Dallas now realized that he was alone in the lake

with his beloved and that the departure of their friends, once he thought about it, suited him fine. He spied the mound of Anne's clothes on a log nearby, but it was too dark to ascertain which garments were there. Here was an opportunity to make something of the summer after all. Turning around, he made out her dark silhouette a few yards away. His heart thumping wildly, he dived beneath the surface, hoping to surprise her from below, a manuever that struck him as a pleasing combination of foreplay and football. The problem was, it was even darker below the surface than above, and after several scissors kicks Dallas began to suspect he had miscalculated the distance between them. His strategy was determined, however, and he refused to surface until he felt naked flesh. For her part, Anne knew precisely what he was up to and was able to trace his progress easily since only his head remained thoroughly submerged. When he finally arrived, half oxygen starved, fully expecting to embrace the loins of his beloved, he was greeted instead by the small of her foot planted firmly in the center of his forehead. The surprise of finding himself propelled backward drove the remaining air from his straining lungs, and he sucked in brackish water before managing to surface.

The first thing he saw was Anne stroking shoreward toward the log and her clothes. Coughing and sputtering, he started in pursuit, not entirely certain he had been rebuffed. Clearly, unless someone else was with them in the lake, he had been, but he still couldn't believe it. Dallas also couldn't tell whether the figure retreating before him was naked, but it certainly looked naked, and he tried desperately to catch up. But where Anne seemed to knife effortlessly through the water, he pitched forward again and again as the sand gave way beneath his socks. His lungs began to fill with water, and he discovered, when he tried to call out, that he was capable only of gurgling noises. When he finally stumbled out of the lake, he was too exhausted and nauseated to mount much of an attack. Dropping to his knees in the sand, he sputtered "I . . . I . . . I. . . ." The tops of Anne's breasts glistened in the moonlight, and he felt his hopes plunge, so terrible was her beauty.

"You should be ashamed, Dallas," she said.

He struggled to his feet. "I—"

"Look at you."

Dallas did as he was told and was surprised to discover an erection in the very process of deflating. Mistaking her meaning, he said, "It'll come back. Just let me touch you."

But her permission wouldn't have made any difference, because the gin and lake water, churning more violently than ever, began to rise even as his penis descended. Burning with despair, he formulated a more modest plan. At the very least, if he lunged forward in a crude, last-ditch assault, he might bring her to ground and bury his sorrow in her breasts before she could summon the strength to cast him aside. Surely he deserved that much.

He was cheated, though, just the same. At first his legs refused to function, then they carried him in the direction opposite from the one he intended, off into the trees where he dropped to his knees again and began to retch.

Anne did not follow and, instead, found her clothes and shook herself dry as best she could after wringing out her long hair. Rather than put on her dry clothes over them, she removed her wet bra and panties and, after wringing them out, used them like a sponge to blot herself semidry. The night air was lovely and cool on her skin, and she felt the exhilaration of her nakedness, such an utterly abandoned and delicious and hopeless feeling that she wanted to cry, by herself, for a very long time. She had not heard Dan return; he stood watching her from the exact spot where Dallas had knelt a few minutes before. Somewhere out on the lake a night bird called. That was the only sound.

16

For several days after his beating, Randall Younger looked fairly impressive—one eye swollen shut, his cheek a purple fruit above the fracture, his lips and nose lacerated. His mother was terrified when she saw him, and he made matters worse by refusing to explain what had happened other than confirming the obvious—that he'd been in a fight. She was so frightened and angry that she threatened to transfer him to Sacred Heart, the Catholic junior high. There was no reason to fly off the deep end, he said, and that made her madder still.

Actually, as far as Randall was concerned, things hadn't worked out badly. Stories about what had transpired had widely circulated by the time he returned to school on the Tuesday before Thanksgiving, and when the other kids saw the way he looked, he recognized their admiration. Even better, the teachers made no objection to his wearing sunglasses indoors, a privilege never before extended. But strangest of all was the immediate camaraderie extended him by the very boys who had thrashed him so mercilessly. He met several of them in the halls that first day in school, and they all grinned knowingly, as if to suggest that in their book he was all right. They had shared something and were from that day forward blood brothers. They would do to anyone who bothered him precisely what they had done to him.

No doubt a significant portion of their newfound respect was due to the fact that Randall had stubbornly refused to implicate anyone. When the principal called him in, he denied having been in a fight at all, explaining he was playing basketball and had inadvertently run into the bleachers. Though the principal didn't believe this explanation, he was greatly relieved by it. He hated trouble, and it seemed that every time he took disciplinary action against a student, someone took disciplinary action against him. His tires were flattened, or an obscene suggestion was written on the hood of his car with shaving cream. Besides, at the moment the principal had real problems. Apparently a genuine maniac was on the loose. He had assaulted one of the boys on school property, injuring him badly, and the boy's parents, two huge, pear-shaped people who smelled of perspiration and, unaccountably, lemon juice, were threatening a suit. So he accepted Randall's improbable account.

Randall saw no reason not to be cheerful. Miraculously, he still had all his teeth, and his injuries had begun healing already. And it was difficult to hold much of a grudge against Boyer Burnhoffer, his tormentor, because he'd warned Randall for months that he was going to do it, and Randall himself had been prideful to assume that he could escape forever. Besides, the beating squared things all around, because he was no longer considered in arrears, the beating representing a kind of receipt for payment in full. Indeed Burnhoffer personally approved of this arrangement. Of late he'd been in more trouble than usual and knew that one more episode would land him back in reform school. He was resigned to returning one day but wasn't looking forward to it or to the necessity of killing the person responsible for sending him there when he got out.

Randall wasn't worried about being murdered by Boyer Burnhoffer, but the current misunderstanding about his rescuer did prey on the boy's mind. Fortunately, the now notorious Wild Bill Gaffney had somehow vanished. No one in Mohawk had seen him for days and wild rumors had begun circulating. Among the adolescents of Nathan Littler Junior High, he had long been legendary, largely due to his mutant appearance and vocal peculiarities. But special notice was now taken by their parents, who had self-consciously looked the other way whenever they encountered Wild Bill on the street. Since the assault their daughters had told them about Wild Bill's huge member, alternately compared to a rope and a garden hose, which someone had seen him use to water the side of the dumpster in the alley outside the Mohawk Grill. How many times the good people of Mohawk had passed him without suspecting how dangerous he was, never considering that he might be more than a simple retard. It was frightening. Several junior-high boys to whom Bill had made gifts of condoms now remembered and confessed, pulling them and their disintegrating plastic wrappers out of the secret compartments in their wallets where they had long awaited the right circumstances. The citizens of Mohawk could not have hunted more enthusiastically if they'd been on the trail of Jack the Ripper.

Very few people knew what really happened the day Wild Bill Gaffney came to Randall Younger's rescue.

Anyway, it was far more pleasantly chilling to think of Wild Bill Gaffney as a maniac and consequently the stories that began to circulate about him were increasingly colorful and imaginative. Soon the switchboard at city hall began to light up, everyone wanting to know what was being done to make the streets of Mohawk safe again. Some callers were Wild Bill's classmates many years ago, and they remembered him, now that they stopped to think, as never having been exactly right. For years he had been drinking the contaminated water of the Cayuga Creek, which had given him brain cancer. The whole town was on the lookout, conventional wisdom being that a man with a brain half-eaten away with contamination couldn't outsmart the constabulary and citizenry of Mohawk County for more than a few days. He'd turn up, all right.

When he didn't, the topic of conversation turned to what would happen to him when he did. At the junior high there was considerable speculation. Boyer Burnhoffer advanced a theory that wires would be hooked up to Wild Bill's head and then, *Zzzzzt!* Boyer demonstrated graphically, his knees and arms quivering, his jaw slack. "I don't see what good that would do," someone said. Boyer didn't know either, only that it was done. "It sure makes your pecker stand up," he observed. He'd been given a shock treatment once in reform school, and this unexpected effect had lingered in his memory.

The more Randall listened, the more uneasy he became. When school let out on the Wednesday before Thanksgiving, he had a knot in his stomach the size of a fist. Though he tried everything he could think of to ignore his gnawing conscience, nothing worked. He told himself that Wild Bill hadn't really rescued him.

Burnhoffer was nearly finished rubbing his face in the gravel when Wild Bill showed up. Everyone said he was crazy, and there were reasons to think so. Hadn't he forced the gift of a condom on Randall, a perfect stranger? Hadn't he done the same with half the young boys in Mohawk, as it now turned out? It was one thing to go out on a limb for a friend, but Randall couldn't see the advantage of doing so for the likes of Wild Bill. And in the long run the poor man would probably be happier where there were no kids to make fun of him. That night after dinner he decided he would sidle up to the subject with his grandfather, who always had pretty good advice when it came to thorny problems.

He found Mather Grouse seated in his favorite armchair in the living room, his face behind a book. Mrs. Grouse hummed quietly over the remains of the dishes. Once she finished this chore, she would take off and rinse out her stockings, hanging them to dry over the edge of the tub. When the bathroom door closed behind her, Randall opened the proceedings. He thought it best to keep things relatively abstract, at least at first. When his grandfather was reading, it was sometimes possible to carry on an entire conversation without his looking up from the page. He hoped this would be the case, for Mather Grouse had a penetrating gaze that Randall feared would pierce his heart, especially in its present swollen condition. "Is there any good way to know what's the right thing to do," he asked.

Mather Grouse immediately lowered his book a few inches and peered over the top at his grandson. Randall wasn't sure from this immediate reaction whether his question was very good or extremely silly. He anticipated a long involved answer full of qualifications, but again Mather Grouse surprised him. "No," his grandfather said with such conviction that Randall suspected that the single word might represent the end of the conversation. "Of ourse, you could always ask yourself what you want to do and then do the opposite, but even that isn't one hundred percent reliable because every now and then people actually want to do the right thing. I don't know why."

"How do you decide?"

"I forget. It's been so long since I've had a decision to make about anything important. Mostly I just try not to upset your grandmother."

"Were you ever scared to do what you thought was right?"

Mather Grouse frowned and found his bookmark. It looked like he might find it necessary to put the book down. "Yes," he said. "Many times."

"But you did the right thing anyway?"

"Sometimes. Not always."

"Can you tell me about one of the times you didn't?"

"No. I will not."

Randall nodded. He always understood his grandfather and wondered if that was why he loved him especially. The boy took a deep breath. "Have you ever seen the man who is always wandering around downtown? They call him Wild Bill?"

Mather Grouse started imperceptibly at the name and stared at his grandson as if he suspected the boy of clairvoyance. "His name is William Gaffney."

Randall nodded. "If you thought something bad might happen to somebody like that, on account of something that wasn't his fault, would you do something, even if it maybe meant trouble for yourself?"

Mather Grouse did not answer right away. His slender fingers tapped the scrolled, worn arms of his reading chair as if they were hitting notes on an imaginary keyboard. "It would be good," he said finally, "if you could help a William Gaffney. But there are many William Gaffneys and there is little that can be done for them. They can be given food or warm clothing or medicine, but the time is past for the William Gaffneys. Once somebody might've done something, and nobody did. But that should *not* be a burden upon you. I don't think you could do anything for a William Gaffney now. I doubt anyone could."

"Then it wouldn't be too bad if you didn't try?"

"It would probably be no good either way."

Randall went to bed early that night, but he remained awake long after his mother locked up the house and turned off all the lights. The house and street were silent, and there was no way the boy could've known that his grandfather lay awake a floor below and that Wild Bill Gaffney was also the subject of Mather Grouse's thoughts. Any more than he could've known that Mather Grouse would have to get out of bed and down on all fours, the cold seeping up through his palms and pajama knees until he was as icy as the hardwood floor he knelt upon, his ragged breathing tugging at him like some insistent beast.

17

Thanksgiving dawns gray and cold in Mohawk. Even Kings Road looks bleak, its tall skeleton oaks black as stumps after a forest fire, its groomed hedges stripped, looking like piles of balanced sticks. The golf course is deserted, the flag on the eighth green beside the Wood home flapping briefly before falling limp again. Diana Wood has prepared a turkey to place in the oven for the midafternoon meal, a huge bird that will take a very long time to cook. Diana cannot imagine how she and her mother and husband—none of them big eaters—will be able to make much of a dent in the animal. Already she knows that today will be one of her mother's bad days.

At eight-thirty, Milly cannot decide whether she will get up or not. She is cross with her sister's husband because Mather Grouse has vetoed Milly's suggestion that the two families celebrate the holiday together at the Wood home. It infuriates her that there should be so few means at her disposal to implement her will. Instead of getting people to do what she wants them to, she often has to satisfy herself with making them wish they had, and this constitutes a cruel diminution of power. Of course Mather Grouse has always been a tough nut to crack, always so insular and self-sufficient. No doubt her sister torments him for being so obstinate, but he will allow himself to be badgered only so far before calling a halt to it. The only way Milly can think of to get back at him is to have her daughter Diana rush her to the hospital. Her feet are swollen and she knows that if she complains of pain, her daughter will take her in at once. The flaw in this plan is that, once there, Diana will prove considerate and refuse to inform the Grouses until certain they've completed their holiday meal. She might not call at all, unless the situation is an obvious emergency, and Milly herself is doubtful she can parlay her swollen feet into a true crisis. The alternative to the hospital is to remain in bed and watch the parade on her portable set. Later she can always refuse to eat when Diana brings in the tray. That wouldn't be getting back at Mather Grouse exactly, but it would make her opinion known. A species of retribution, even if imprecisely focused. Milly wishes she weren't hungry.

"How about handing me my coat?" Dan says when his wife glides in from the kitchen.

Diana frowns. "It's cold out. Why don't you relax and watch the parade?"

"I'm feeling blue. The Rockettes can only make it worse."

Diana ignores him, listening. "Is that Mother again?" Theirs is a large house and her mother's room is at the other end. The old woman is capable of making herself heard, but she prefers to call feebly so that she can relate to her daughter how many pleas she made before anyone bothered to heed them.

"Take a pillow and smother her, will you?"

"That's not funny, even in joking."

"You're absolutely right. I'd never joke about such a thing."

Diana stops to think. Despite long years under the same roof, she has never sufficiently understood her husband's humor to feel confident about responding to it. What angers her is that he uses it to distance himself from her. She pulls his windbreaker from the closet and tosses it at him. "I'm sorry I'm no Rockette."

Dan realizes he has somehow contrived to hurt her feelings, that maybe he intended to. "What's the matter, sweet?"

Diana shrugs. "I'm sorry. I thought that was your point."

"Come here," he says, reaching for her hand. But Milly calls again, this time more audibly, and Diana turns away. On impulse he grabs a blue-green decorator pillow and flings it the length of the hall in pursuit of his wife; it lands at her feet. "You forgot something."

Dan Wood struggles into his windbreaker and wheels outside. The pool, now drained, is a gaping concrete maw in the center of his backyard, a few brittle leaves stirring near the drain. He watches them energetically dance and swirl up the turquoise sides of the pool before sliding back down to await another gust. It occurs to him that he had allowed himself to get more keyed up over the operation than he should've. The resulting disappointment was as slow and subtle in coming as the realization that, yes, once again he'd somehow gotten his hopes up. His grip on reality had always been a point of pride with him, and he felt a little like a backsliding AA member for losing that grip. Hope was a luxury he could not afford—a cruelty, really.

He didn't need anyone to tell him what the problem

was. He hadn't even seriously considered further operations until Anne's return to Mohawk. But seeing her again had recalled him from the comforting numbness that had made life bearable. Naturally, she didn't realize this. She was too kind to steal the anesthetic knowingly, and he couldn't think of a way to explain to her, even if he wanted to. And he didn't want to, not really. Even pain was preferable to numbness, at least for a while, and hope, once indulged, was only as delicious as it was short-lived.

He should've realized that it would be dangerous. From the beginning, everything about Anne had been risk. She had always seemed to him to be deep-down wild, the wilder because she harnessed that wildness most of the time. Never wantonly playing the part of temptress, she, nevertheless, remained his personal temptation. "I will never say I don't love you," she once told him. "I'll be as circumspect as you need me to be. We won't talk about what you want to avoid. But I will love you and go on loving you, and you'll have to live with that much, whether it embarrasses you or not."

In the beginning he had not believed she could be so circumspect. Neither Diana nor anyone else could have inferred anything between them from her behavior. Ironically, there were times when Diana probably suspected that her husband was partly in love with Anne, but only because Anne was so lovely that any sensible man would be in love with her, at least a little.

There was no way to know if Diana resented her cousin, no way to read what Diana wanted to remain a closed text. It was perhaps the oddest thing about his wife that she could be so open about her delights yet so secretive about her wounds, always retreating into some dark inner place to nurse herself back to health rather than admit to having been injured or reveal the scar. At her center was a code, something formulated when she was so young that the reason for it was long forgotten, a code that governed her most intimate thoughts and behavior and made her so fundamentally decent that she could never be otherwise. If Dan both admired and regretted any single quality in his wife, it was this profound spiritual stability.

And perhaps it was its lack in Anne Grouse that qualified her as his personal temptress. At her center was not law but profound lawlessness. Its initial revelation had left him stunned, excited, afraid—because it corresponded to something he had long suspected in himself. Her physical beauty seemed to him an expression of this inner wildness and was perhaps the reason Anne had changed so little since the night he had returned through the black woods to the lakeshore, moving quietly, holding his breath, until he stumbled over Dallas, passed out in his own mess, and finally found Anne, drying herself in the sliver of moon. She alone had remained unchanged throughout the years, when he himself had been reduced and Diana had been worn away by the friction of nearly constant giving. Even Dallas seemed diminished, as the already narrow circle of his experience and desire had tightened around him. But neither time nor childbirth nor disappointment seemed to have touched Anne, whose daily existence, the undeniable reality of it, seemed unconnected to that inner life, which remained as feral and hopeful as ever.

He had stayed away as long as he could, as if the length of time she required to seduce him might prove important later on, proof that he had not been utterly reckless. Since that night at the lake when they had kissed and each had felt the flush of excited confession—yes, I do love you, I've loved you from the start, as you know, as you must've known—he had not seen her for days nor called nor written. Then, on Friday, Diana had come down with a severe cold, and when Dan went to see Dallas, he found him at the garage with the thousand or so parts of his Chevrolet laid out before him on the floor, glistening, promissory.

Dallas himself hadn't seen Anne in the week following his disgrace. For two days he didn't see anyone, didn't stir from the sofa where Dan had deposited him, didn't go to work or even to the telephone. Now he was better physically, though still sick at heart. "To hell with her. She doesn't love me."

No, Dan thought. She loves me. But he felt no personal triumph. "Sure she does," he said. "She'll come back."

"She'll have to. I'm not going near Mountain Avenue, you can bet your ass."

"Give her time."

"She thinks she's going to fall in love with some millionaire at college. Mohawk isn't good enough."

"You're wrong."

"She listens to her old man all the time, and that's what he says. To hell with him." He made a sweeping gesture that encompassed his scattered Chevrolet, the garage, the county. "I love this place."

Dan left him and drove over to the *Mohawk Republican* where Anne was working part-time until school started. He parked at the curb, three doors down, and sat there thinking about fate. Finally he made a deal. It was five o'clock and there was a good chance that Anne, who worked irregular hours, had already gone home. There was an equally good chance that if she hadn't already gone home, she wouldn't notice him sitting there when she came out into the bright afternoon sun. She would head home in the other direction, or perhaps she'd be with someone. More likely still, she'd be angry with him for the long days, nearly a week, during which he hadn't even telephoned. There was also the remote possibility that during the week she had concluded that no decent people could afford to indulge the feelings she and he had confessed.

He waited until five-fifteen, slumped back against the door, smoking, watching the smoke crawl along the ceiling. Then the door on the passenger side opened and she got in. She didn't look at him right away, didn't move at all until he sat up straight and stubbed out his cigarette. Then she turned and smiled.

"Diana—" he began.

"Has the flu," she finished. "And Dallas is making love to his car tonight."

"Are you expected home?"

"Eventually. Not soon. If you don't kiss me in about two seconds, I'm going to slap you."

He did as he was told.

"And I want you to tell me you love me."

"I already have."

"I don't want there to be any mistake. We were drinking."

"All right: I love you. How's that?"

"Wonderful. I might make you tell me every now and then. My only demand."

"Fine," he said. "I just hope you won't make too much of it."

She laughed. "It only means everything. It means that we aren't bad people."

For her it was that simple, perhaps because she didn't love Dallas. Perhaps, Dan thought, because her love for him was all the credo she needed. If so, he was both frightened and grateful.

They drove to Albany and took a room in a small, out-of-the-way motel, and skipped dinner. He remembered thinking, as they made love, *I'm gone . . . too far gone to ever return.* He pictured himself breaking into the homes of all the respectable people he knew, and loading all their most valued possessions into a large canvas sack. He wouldn't get caught, either.

As he drove back to Mohawk, with Anne cradled against him, a twinge took his breath away.

"What's wrong?" Anne said.

"Nothing."

"You just shivered."

"The night air," he explained, rolling up his window. "There's autumn in it."

"I've never felt warmer," she said.

Dan Wood smiles at the recollection. Wheeling over to the shed, he unlocks it and pulls out onto the pool deck the large bucket of golf balls he has collected. He picks one out at random, fingering its dimples. He knows something about golf balls, how tightly wound they are, a mass of rubber bands wrapped under great pressure beneath deceptive white skin. He wonders, as he has since he was a kid, what magic is used to keep them from exploding. He gives the ball a heave in the general direction of the eighth green, watching its arc. But he can barely see the flag waving beyond the fence and cannot tell whether the ball has landed on the green. He flings another. It takes him twenty minutes to empty the bucket. Just as he unloads the last ball, the face of a teenage boy appears above the back fence. Undaunted by the frigid weather, he has undoubtedly sneaked on the course at number seven to get in some practice. He doesn't look particularly bright. "Hey! What are you doing?"

"Golfing," Dan tells him. "What does it look like?"

The boy stares stupidly, first at Dan, then at the green, now littered with over a hundred golf balls. "Which one is mine?"

"They're all yours."

"Really? You don't want them?"

"What good are they?"

"Jeez, I'll take them," the boy says, and disappears.

"You do that."

After a while the patio door slides open and Diana comes out. Watching from the kitchen window, she has waited until she thinks her husband will accept her company. In fact he's glad to have it. From behind his chair she rubs his shoulder blades, and he smells the reassuring perfume she has worn since she was a girl. "I love you, you know," she tells him.

"Of course you do." He smiles. "Who wouldn't? A big, virile hunk of guy like me?"

18

"Look at *you*," said Harry when the front door to the Mohawk Grill swung open and Dallas Younger sauntered in out of the gray afternoon. One of Harry's regulars, Dallas usually came dressed in work clothes, but today he wore a fresh shirt, neatly pressed pants and a Madras sportcoat that represented a momentary lapse in judgment. The lapse in judgment had not been in buying the coat, but rather in accepting it, because somebody, Dallas couldn't remember who, had given it to him, and this was the first time he had worn it. It had hung in the closet for over a year and for the last several months he had puzzled over its origin. The coat wasn't the sort of thing he lost sleep over, though. Things came and went in Dallas's life, and provided they came in at roughly the same rate as they went out, that suited him fine.

He was prepared for some razzing. As Harry opened his mouth to speak, Dallas held up one hand. "I always like to look my best when I'm in a classy place, Harry." He chose a stool near the center of the counter.

Harry had been of two minds about opening. He knew there would be no business to speak of. Christmas and Thanksgiving were two holidays when lonely people felt self-conscious about eating in places like his. Most would skip the meal entirely before they'd admit they've no place better to go. Like them, Harry had no better place, so he opened. "You must be on your way to see your ex," Harry said slyly. He was nobody's fool. Not that you had to be genius to read Dallas Younger.

"My kid," Dallas corrected him.

"Uh-huh."

"I'll take a cup of coffee if you aren't too busy."

Harry poured it and slipped a nondairy creamer on the side of the saucer. Dallas took the creamer and threw it playfully back at him. "Fifteen years I've been drinking coffee in here and you never got it right yet."

Harry tossed the creamer back in the bin with the others, happy to have saved it. Coffee cost the same one way or the other, and he liked the sensation of having made more money when his customers drank it black. "I never see her on the street," he observed.

Dallas shrugged. "You know how it is when you're too good."

Harry had seen Dallas's wife only once or twice before they split up but not once since her return to Mohawk. Still, she was not easily forgotten, and it made him feel sorry for Dallas to have lost someone so good-looking. Harry himself had lost his share of girls, but none of them were the sort you spent your life mooning about when they were gone. "I got some turkey and dressing," he offered. "Green beans, too. The whole shot for two and a quarter."

Dallas shook his head. "I'm supposed to be there for dinner."

Harry wasn't surprised. "I haven't served one dinner today," he admitted.

"I couldn't believe you were open. Too bad your

illegitimate nephew isn't around. He's pretty good at scarfing up food."

Harry involuntarily looked over at the vacant stool at the end of the counter. It was a matter of jest between Dallas and Harry that he and Wild Bill were related. Harry always pretended to blow up at the suggestion. Today, though, the joke was flat. "I ain't even seen him since he got in trouble."

The boy Wild Bill had flung against the dumpster was still in the hospital with a skull fracture and concussion.

"Serve those boys right if they all got their heads split, the way they torment him. Which is what I told the cops. His uncle was in here right away, all hot to arrest him."

"Naturally," Dallas said. Oddly enough, the subject of fighting was on his mind since Anne had told him over the phone that Randall had been in a fight and that it might be a good idea for him to have a man-to-man with his son. From what Anne said he couldn't tell if he was supposed to teach the boy to run away or play to win. Not that it mattered. If this conversation ran true to form, he doubted he and Randall would get anywhere. Everybody said his son was supposed to be smart as hell, but Dallas privately abstained. The boy just seemed odd. Of course most of the smart people he'd ever run across were odd, too, so it was possible.

"I told that fat fuck I didn't want him in here no more. He can write a hundred tickets out front if he wants, but he'll never get another cup of coffee off Harry Saunders."

"Gaff's all right," Dallas observed noncommittally.

"Sure," Harry admitted, "except he's an asshole, like his brother. The Gaffneys are all peckerheads, every one of them. . . . You sure you don't want some turkey?"

Dallas was tempted. The food smelled good and he wasn't looking forward to dinner at the Grouses. He'd been talked into it by Loraine, who said that if he called wanting to take his son out for Thanksgiving dinner, Anne was bound to invite him to eat with them. "And if that doesn't work out, you'll eat with us," she added. Unfortunately, the first plan had worked out. Dallas would have much preferred dinner at his brother's. Or rather his brother's wife's.

For a long time after they split up, Dallas had assumed that he and Anne would get back together. But then ten or twelve years slipped by, and one day it occurred to him that he might be wrong. Even more surprising was the fact that he didn't miss Anne very much, and couldn't remember having missed her, though he might've for a while and then forgotten about it. He was pretty content with his life, and Anne was more trouble than any other five women he knew. Even if by some stroke he should win her back—something he wouldn't make book on after all the intervening years—there would be the daily struggle to keep her and figure out why she wasn't happy. All of which he could live without.

There was a time when he hadn't minded fighting over women. He lost his front teeth over Anne when he was nineteen, in a fight people in Mohawk County still talked about, at least the ones old enough to remember it. The whole thing had started when he got off work one afternoon and ran into a buddy of his who told him he'd seen Anne parked outside the newspaper with Dan Wood, that the two were kissing. Dallas was too fair-minded not to give the boy a chance to take it back, but he stood grimly by his story, even after Dallas knocked him flat on the pavement. "It's the freakin' truth," the boy had insisted. "I can't take back the freakin' truth. . . ."

When Benny D. got to his feet, Dallas hit him again, but this time he managed to stay perpendicular and, seeing no alternative, took the liberty of breaking Dallas's nose. Despite being naturally athletic, Dallas wasn't much of a fighter. He was game to a fault, though, and took a terrible beating at the hands of his more talented adversary, who jabbed and ducked and weaved in workmanlike fashion. Time after time Dallas was surprised to discover himself on the ground, and he no sooner got up than he was promptly seated again. Soon Benny D. was covered with blood, which gave Dallas the unfortunate and entirely mistaken impression that he was unaccountably winning, despite being beaten to the punch on every exchange. He had no idea that his own broken nose was responsible for the ghastly appearance of his opponent. He actually expected Benny D. to concede at any moment, until the boy hit Dallas in the mouth so hard that several teeth gave and the pain was so bad Dallas couldn't hold back the tears.

The fact that he was crying made him mad. Giving up on his fists and lowering his head like a battering ram, Dallas drove forward into his opponent's midsection. Benny D., much surprised by this eleventh-hour tactic and suspension of the rules heretofore in effect, was lifted high in the air and brought back down to the pavement on his tailbone with a loud crack, whereupon all the blood went out of his face and with it the fight out of his heart. Dallas then sat on his chest and thumped his head into the pavement like a melon until Benny D.'s eyes rolled up in his head. Not one to press

an unfair advantage, Dallas then proclaimed the fight
finished, which of course it was.

In Mohawk news of fights traveled fast, and before
long Dallas's victory passed from fact to fable. Both
combatants were admitted to the hospital, Dallas with
a broken nose and smile, Benny D. with wounds less
noticeable but more severe. Both winner and loser
were tremendously admired, because it had been a real
fight, not just profane taunts and a little shoving. The
fact that the two were friends added a bittersweet quality and made the whole thing seem even more noble.
The fact that so much damage had been traded over a
girl elevated the contest into the realm of heroism.

After two days in the hospital, Dallas was allowed
to go home. Anne picked him up in his own car and
helped him up the stairs to his flat above the drugstore.
Her face was ashen and he was proud of having de-
fended her honor to the point of maiming and of the
effect his doing so apparently had upon her. For months
he had feared that she didn't love him as she once had
and was now delighted to discover how wrong he'd
been. On the way up the narrow stairs she let him lean
on her, and it occurred to him that there might be no
better time to press his advantage, even if he did look
like a B-movie zombie.

"Dan came by the hospital last night," he ventured.

"Did he," she said as if she hadn't really heard.

"He said he and Di are getting hitched next month."

"Yes."

"I guess I was the first one he told."

"Yes. Di told me this morning."

"I wish I didn't look so beat up. Otherwise, I'd ask
you."

She studied him, then—a little sadly, it seemed, and

not at all surprised, but with more affection than he had seen for some time. She took out a tissue, wet the corner with her tongue and touched it on one of his swollen eyes. "I wouldn't make you happy," she said. "Besides, I promised my father I'd give him one semester at school."

He shrugged happily, having anticipated a much more forceful objection. "How about January? I can wait."

She smiled. "People don't get married in January."

"They do in Austria."

"You mean Australia?"

Well, he had meant Australia. "I mean I love you."

His room overlooked Main Street, and from where they sat it was possible to see all the way up past the hospital into Myrtle Park, which overlooked the entire county. Only when Dallas finally noticed that she was crying did he realize how much she must love him, and he vowed from that moment to be worthy of her.

But it hadn't worked out. He did not blame her for ending the marriage when she did. She deserved better, and he couldn't see how there was much advantage to starting up again. He'd make all sorts of vows and end up breaking every one. He knew himself now, and he knew he could live without her.

"All right, Harry," he said. "Give me some of that turkey before you start crying. And don't be a cheapskate with the gravy, either."

19

Dallas Younger was Harry's last real customer at the Mohawk Grill, which meant there would be a special on turkey-and-dressing over the holiday weekend. Dallas lingered until late in the afternoon when he heard feet tromping up the stairs on the other side of the wall. Then he borrowed fifty from Harry and joined the game upstairs. The other players were family men who'd seen enough of their families and grown depressed by the sight of the turkey carcass.

Harry was cleaning the grill and preparing to close when Officer Gaffney came in. He was looking a little sheepish since Harry had read him the riot act. For two days he had obeyed the injunction not to show his face in the Mohawk Grill. But lacking a convenient place to drink coffee was beginning to wear on him, and he looked haggard.

"No," Harry said when the policeman straddled his favorite stool.

Officer Gaffney did not dare sit, though his rump hovered mere inches from the round stooltop, his legs bowed like a cowboy's. "Hell, Harry," he complained. "You can't refuse to serve me—"

"I can do anything I want. This is my place, paid for by me, run by me, according to my rules."

"Hell, Harry."

"Anyhow, I wasn't refusing to serve you. I was answering the question you'll get around to asking when you're through pissing and moaning. No, I didn't see Billy. No, I don't have no idea where he is. No, he's not downstairs hiding in the basement or the storeroom. And no, you can't just look around to make sure. No."

Gaffney squirmed, still astraddle the stool and unsure if he had permission to sit. "It ain't like we don't trust you, Harry. Everybody admires the hell out of Harry Saunders, and nobody's been better to that boy than you. We just need to talk to that boy for his own good."

"No," Harry said.

The officer lowered himself subtle fractions until he felt the stool. "Hell, Harry, I understand. Why wouldn't I understand? We're friends for God's sake. It's just I can't help being what I am. I got to enforce the law. A policeman's just got to."

Harry stopped working on the grill and turned. "We aren't friends, Gaff. Don't say so, because it ain't true. And don't talk about the law, because that's not it. If you're all worked up about the law, there's a game upstairs right now. Gambling's still against the law, so you can start right here where it's convenient. And when you're finished, there's some other things. I can tell you about who's stealing leather over to the Tucker Tannery, and who's cutting and selling it, too. Unless maybe you already know. And then you can go after Old Man Tucker himself and jail his ass for all that shit in the crick that's making the whole county sick. You could clean up the whole town, Gaff. Be a *regular* goddamn hero instead of chasing around the goddamn county after unfortunate retards like Billy that nobody cares nothing about until there's trouble."

Officer Gaffney blanched under Harry's onslaught and would have retreated a step or two if he hadn't settled onto the seat. The gleaming spatula Harry was using for emphasis was fluttering in front of his nose like a demented metal bird. It didn't seem right that anybody would talk to a peace officer in that tone, but Gaffney couldn't decide what to do about it in this particular case. Here he had come in to patch things up with Harry, and was worse off than ever. He was misunderstood, and that's all there was to it.

"The law . . . bullshit, the law," Harry fumed, though calmer now, having said his piece. He set the spatula down and returned to the brick. "Bill's nothing but a goddamn monthly check for your shit-heel brother. When was the last time he ate a bowl of soup under his old man's roof? When was the last time Rory gave him a pair of socks? It'd be a hell of an idea if somebody called them state people and asked them if they knew what happened to the money they sent every month." Harry was slowly working himself back into a fit. Chunks of the lava brick were crumbling onto the grill, whose surface shone angrily through the black ash. "The law—"

"I never meant for you to get all worked up on Thanksgiving," the policeman said. "I just come in for a cup of coffee and company."

"I hope you enjoyed the company, cause you ain't getting no coffee," Harry said without turning around.

Defeated, Officer Gaffney slid off the stool and left.

When Harry finished with the grill and refrigerated the perishables, he locked the front door and stuck the CLOSED sign on the window before turning off the lights. Then he peered outside between the blinds. On the other side of Main Street a cigarette briefly glowed red in the doorway of the drugstore. Two men stood in the shadows. One would be Officer Gaffney, and Harry had a pretty good guess who the second, larger man would be. They were positioned to see both the front entrance to the grill and the rear door on the alley. Harry smiled and watched as the cigarette glowed bright, then faded, then dropped to the pavement where it was extinguished. Finally, the larger man came out of the doorway and headed up Main in the direction of the firehouse.

The wind, which had been whistling all day, now howled up the corridor between the buildings that formed it. In the doorway of the Scallese Drugstore, Officer Gaffney turned up his coat collar. Inside the Mohawk Grill, Harry Saunders was warm.

20

"This is the *last* time you're going to be expected to climb these stairs," Mrs. Grouse said when she and her husband reached the landing. Not quite out of earshot, she and Mather Grouse had just finished Thanksgiving dinner upstairs in their daughter's flat. Anne had insisted on cooking the holiday meal, and of course the whole thing was a botch. Dallas had somehow gotten himself invited and then not shown up, which was typical, though they had waited for him until everything was ruined. Holding meals for people who were not punctual was something Mrs. Grouse herself did not approve of. Even when her husband was working, he knew what time dinner was served and knew better than to be late. He got off work at five, and dinner was on the table at five-fifteen, not five-twenty, because the walk home took fifteen minutes, not twenty. Occasionally Mrs. Grouse would stretch a point for the boy, but Dallas was a grown man, and there was no excuse for him. She would've said so, too, except that it wasn't her place and, besides, her daughter was really to blame for inviting him in the first place, knowing full well what was likely to happen.

"I'm fine," said Mather Grouse. He, too, was irritable, though for a different reason. "Take your hand off my elbow, for pity's sake."

"The idea of expecting you to climb these stairs and then wait around hours for your dinner. You must've been starved."

"I ate almonds. I ate walnuts. I ate deviled eggs. I ate grapes."

"That's not dinner."

"She went to a lot of trouble."

"I never said—"

They were at the bottom of the stairs now and entering their own kitchen, Mather Grouse holding the door for his wife. "Then stop being snippy. You're just bent out of shape because somebody cooked a dinner besides you."

"Who ever heard of leg of lamb for Thanksgiving?"

"I like it. I like lamb. I never get any."

"You can have leg of lamb any time you want. All you have to do is say."

"I've been wanting one for twenty years. How many have you cooked?"

"A greasy mess."

"Mmmm."

"The house smells for days," Mrs. Grouse said throwing wide open one of the windows, despite the bitter cold outside. "You can smell it all the way down here."

"Good," Mather Grouse said, inhaling deeply. "I like the smell. Until the leftovers are gone, I'm going to eat upstairs. Go help your daughter with the dishes. I'll be fine."

"Dirty lamb dishes. They'll never be clean."

Worn out by the discussion and the long afternoon

in somebody else's home, Mather Grouse retreated to the living room and his favorite armchair, stopping only to turn on the football game. He was still angry with Dallas Younger, angrier than he could ever remember being with his ex-son-in-law, and that was saying something. Mather Grouse had no use for physical violence, but for some reason he always felt like thrashing Dallas—a strange urge, because he liked a good many men less than Dallas and had little desire to thrash them. Dallas wasn't a bad fellow, actually. In fact, Mather Grouse could think of no one more genuinely harmless than Dallas Younger. And now that he thought about it, that was probably why he wanted to thrash him. With truly bad people even a horsewhipping did no good, but one might be just what Dallas needed, if only to make him pay attention.

If he turned up now, there was a good chance he *would* get one, and not by Mather Grouse. Anne was furious, he knew, and he couldn't blame her. It would've been nice to tell her so, but he couldn't. Since the afternoon she had recalled him from the dead, he'd wanted many times to tell her how much he missed the closeness they had shared when she was a girl. He knew he was to blame, but knowing and knowing what to do about it were two different things. He also knew she had concluded that the cause of their separation was his disapproval, and he had never corrected her misunderstanding. There was no way that he could make her see that starting from the time she began to change from a girl into a woman, she had simply frightened him. This wasn't just the matter of her womanhood. More than anything, it was the fact that she had inherited every significant feature of her personality from himself, except restraint, and not one thing from her mother. He began to suspect that only circumstance could keep her in check, her very virtues bordering on vice. She was too proud, too loyal, too ambitious, perhaps too beautiful. And she was too vulnerable, though Mather Grouse alone saw that side of her.

Mrs. Grouse joined him in the living room and looked at the television disapprovingly. "Are you going to sit there and watch, knowing how it upsets you?"

"Football does not upset me. I don't particularly enjoy it. Baseball upsets me. And it doesn't upset me; it excites me."

"You aren't supposed to get excited."

"I seldom do, thank you very much."

One of the more disagreeable features of Mather Grouse's existence was the never-ending debate over what upset him. Of late, Mrs. Grouse had come to see virtually everything he enjoyed as a potential source of upset. She seemed intent on making his remaining years one long Lenten season. When he objected, she reminded him that objections were upsetting. "Send the boy down, if he wants," Mather Grouse called after his wife.

Mrs. Grouse was at the kitchen door when the bell rang. She frowned at the clock on the wall. "Who could that be?" she said before she could think. Then it occurred to her that the doorbell at such a late hour on Thanksgiving might portend something about her sister, and she scurried back into the living room. "Who is it," she asked her husband, who had not budged from his chair.

"We won't know until you open the door. Whoever

it is, tell them to go away." Actually, he was curious. The porch steps usually groaned under a visitor's weight, and he hadn't heard them groan.

Mrs. Grouse tugged the front door open and peered into the dark. She was about to conclude that it was all a prank, when a large man stepped forward out of the shadows. Mather Grouse couldn't see who it was from where he sat, but he recognized immediately the deep, soothing voice.

"Mrs. Mather, I presume," said Rory Gaffney.

Mrs. Grouse instinctively stepped back and looked questioningly at her husband, whose expression had darkened. Her single backward step was enough for the man to insinuate himself into the doorway, which he pretty well filled. What Mrs. Grouse noticed most was the man's huge hands, which predisposed her against him. Her husband's hands were small, almost like a woman's, and they were one of the things she had always liked best about him. The world was full of men with swollen fingers and knuckles. The other hateful thing about their visitor was his eyebrows, black and unruly, and he used one of his paws to smooth them.

Rory Gaffney smiled and nodded as he carefully surveyed the living room and, like an auctioneer brought in for an appraisal, every object it contained. "It is exactly as I expected," he said. "Mather Grouse would provide just such a home for his family. Your husband was always a family man, Mrs. Mather. Never once got into the baseball pool or played a daily double. Never once in all those years. Some of the fellows at the shop didn't like it, but they weren't family men, Mrs. Mather, that's the thing. They had families, all right, some larger than they knew, but for the likes of these men there's always fifty cents for the number, a dollar for the pool.

There was always a little fun at the shop, you see. But not for Mather Grouse. Not for a family man."

Though flustered by the man's presence, Mrs. Grouse was too polite to interrupt, so he kept talking. What she found most odd about the situation was that the man was talking to her and somehow not really talking to her at all. He was looking right at her and certainly seemed to be speaking to her. But though he had his back to her husband, Mrs. Grouse felt it was Mather Grouse he was talking to, and that if she were to disappear from the face of the earth, the man might not even notice.

"No, some of the men didn't like it, Mrs. Mather. Some said Mather Grouse thought he was too good, but I always said it was because he *was* better than those fellows, and he had a right to think so if he wanted. That's what I always said, and that's God's own truth."

Mather Grouse had not stood up, and when their visitor finally turned to face him and offer one of his paws, Mather Grouse shook it reluctantly.

"A good handshake," Rory Gaffney said, not letting go when the other man tried to break it off. "One of the few pleasures left to old men like us." Having turned his back on Mrs. Grouse, he appeared to have forgotten her completely, and she then felt self-conscious about being in her own living room, much of which was blocked out by the broad expanse of the man's leather-coated back. When she announced that if no one minded she would go upstairs and help with the dishes, neither man seemed to hear.

She didn't go directly upstairs, though. Without knowing why, she went into the bathroom and lingered there. She washed her hands in cold water and dried them carefully, trying to understand her reluctance to leave her husband alone with this man who, now that she thought about it, hadn't even introduced himself. Despite the beautiful leather coat and his otherwise respectable appearance, the man was somehow unclean. When she finished at the sink, she turned out the bathroom light and stood quietly beneath the darkened door frame, hoping to overhear something of the conversation taking place two rooms away. With both the kitchen and the bathroom lights off, she decided it would be safe to sneak a peek into the living room. When she did, however, she received a jolt. The angle was wrong to see her husband, but the other man, who had seated himself on the sofa where Mrs. Grouse herself usually sat, was staring across the dark expanse of dining room at the doorway so that when Mrs. Grouse's head appeared, their eyes met in the split second before Mrs. Grouse withdrew as if from a flame. Getting caught flustered her. She was by no means an inexperienced spy, though sneaking up on Mather Grouse required no extraordinary talent. Their visitor, however, was apparently a different sort of man. He had met her only five minutes before, yet had predicted her behavior, something Mather Grouse seldom did after forty-some years of marriage.

The more she thought about it, the more Mrs. Grouse doubted the evidence of her own senses. In all probability the man had not seen her at all. With the lights out in the dining room, kitchen and bathroom, he couldn't have seen her; he just happened to be gazing in her general direction.

Mrs. Grouse was tempted to verify this second theory by peeking in again, but she did not dare. What if she were caught a second time? Instead of risking it, she turned and flushed the toilet to account for her presence in the bathroom and hurried out into the dark kitchen without even glancing into the living room. On the way upstairs she thought of, for some reason, the afternoon when she had been immobilized while her daughter had worked purposefully over Mather Grouse. Why she should have suddenly remembered that vexing scene was beyond her. Still, it might not be a bad idea to have her daughter go downstairs just to make sure. Though Mrs. Grouse was sure that everything was fine.

It was the boy who came down, though, all too happy to surrender the dish towel to his grandmother and curious as well about his grandfather's guest. Randall immediately recognized the man he had seen a month earlier in the park. He had waited then, because the two men appeared so confidential, returning to the bandshell only when he saw the large man shuffling away and his grandfather slumping on the bench. This man was again leaning forward confidentially, speaking quietly. "He has no money," the man was saying, "unless someone gave him some."

"I have not seen him in fifteen years," Mather Grouse said. He was not looking at the other man but seemingly at a random spot on the wall above the television.

"I thought he might've started up in the old way again—"

"I have not seen him in fifteen years," Mather Grouse repeated.

At this point the large man noticed Randall standing in the doorway and straightened, at the same time waving him in, as if he, not Mather Grouse, were the master of the house. "Grandma says not to tire yourself out," Randall said, which was neither true nor untrue. She hadn't said it just then, but she said it all the time and he felt sure she'd *meant* to say it.

Rory Gaffney rose, towering over Randall. "The grandson!" he said enthusiastically and extended his big hand. Randall shook briefly, withdrawing his hand before the man could get a grip. "I know your father, a good man, but you look more like your grandfather. A small Mather Grouse, if ever there was one. A fine, principled young man, I'll wager."

Mather Grouse had stiffened perceptibly at their handshake. "He's a good boy."

"Of course. A young Mather Grouse. I have a grand-daughter. Do you like girls?"

"Not much," Randall said, certain he would not like the girl in question.

"No," the man agreed. "But the day will come. And when it does, I hope you'll pay us a visit. It would be fine to know that my little one had young Mather for a friend."

"His name is Randall," Mather Grouse said.

"I will remember," Rory Gaffney said. "And you, Mather. I know you will remember. You will let me know—"

"Yes," said Mather Grouse, not an accomplished liar. His grandfather's real intention was so clear to Randall that he couldn't understand why the other man, now buttoning his coat to leave, was apparently satisfied with their arrangement. When Randall pushed the door shut behind him, Mather Grouse started to get up, then thought better of it. The inhaler was on the end table, and he used it, his grandson looking on. "You all right, Gramp?"

Mather Grouse nodded, closing his eyes.

"Want me to get Mom?"

"No!" his grandfather said emphatically. "Just look out the window and tell me where he is."

The boy did as he was told. "Gone."

"Look down both sides of the street."

"He's gone."

Mather Grouse shook his head. "Go to the back bedroom. Leave the light off."

"Okay. Sure," Randall agreed, excited by the adventure of it. When he returned a few minutes later, his eyes were wide. His grandfather nodded knowingly when the boy told him that the man had not gone away. Instead, he was on his hands and knees along the side of the house, trying to peer through the small, smoky window into the pitch darkness of Mather Grouse's cellar.

21

The policeman wasn't visible when Harry locked the front door of the grill and backed into the street, the pie tin full of turkey and dressing warm and snug under his coat. His car was parked half a block up the street. He took his usual route home, checking the rearview until he was sure no one was following, then circled back and parked on Hospital Hill on the opposite side of the street from the old Nathan Littler. Except for the emergency unit, the whole building was black and the broken glass crunched beneath his feet as he puffed up the incline and around the rear of the building, all the while trying to think of some plausible explanation if he were caught sneaking into an abandoned wing of a soon-to-be-demolished building at ten o'clock on Thanksgiving night. By the time he had climbed to the third floor, he was completely winded.

Wild Bill Gaffney, comfortable in his coat, was seated against one of the inner walls beneath a sign warning pregnant women about the potential dangers of x-rays. In profile Harry looked like this might apply to him, at least until he gave birth to the pie tin and handed it to Wild Bill, who'd been eyeing his friend's middle since the man came to a wheezing halt at the top of the stairs. Harry caught his breath while Wild Bill wolfed the food noisily. "Slow down," Harry said. "You'll be sick."

Wild Bill tried to slow down, but found he couldn't. He had been waiting for the food too long and was too happy to see it. In fact, he was obviously happy in general.

Harry studied him critically, wishing there was something he could do to make him less happy. Wild Bill had nothing to be pleased about, at least nothing Harry could see.

Wild Bill noticed he was being studied, and grinned gravy. "Ive," he said.

"Yeah, he's alive. But that's about all."

Wild Bill shook his head emphatically. "Ahn," he said before refocusing his attention on the pie tin.

"And what?"

Wild Bill nodded enthusiastically.

Harry shook his head. "You're looney, you know that? All week you've been saying 'and', but you never finish the goddamn sentence. And *what?*"

Wild Bill stared stupidly until Harry, exasperated, gave up. "We got to figure a better place. They'll level this pretty soon. And besides, it's getting too fucking cold."

Wild Bill thumbed gravy around the tin and did not appear overly concerned. Harry watched him, understanding, perhaps for the first time, why some people liked to abuse him. Just then, to slap him would've been nice. "Ahn," Bill said.

Harry massaged his temples, trying hard not to lose his temper. "I know. *Ahn.* Always *ahn.* But just listen a minute, will you? Fuck *ahn,* and listen to me."

Wild Bill suddenly looked so hurt that Harry broke off. In the dark Harry couldn't see the patches of baldness or the gauntness, and to him Wild Bill, all huddled up against the wall, looked a little like a teenager. And that, finally, was Harry's clue. He had never considered the possibility before, and it was staggering. He sat down next to his friend, putting a hand on a bony knee. "Ahn," Harry repeated softly this time. "Tell me, Billy, are you in love?"

22

Dallas lost Harry's fifty right away. But his timing was good because Benny D'Angelo, who owned the Pontiac dealership where Dallas worked, wandered in immediately afterward. So instead of having to drop out, Dallas borrowed another fifty from the boss and settled back comfortably, convinced that his luck had changed, at least in some respects. Sober, Benny D. was a hardheaded businessman with fish hooks in his pockets; but tanked he became one of the boys. As often as not, he was one of the boys. He and Dallas had been friends since high school, and before Benny D.'s old man kicked off he had worked construction with Dallas in Albany as well as points as far flung as Poughkeepsie and Binghamton. The old man didn't have a good thing to say about his wayward son, and everybody was surprised when he left Benny D. the dealership after swearing for years that he'd torch it first. No one was more surprised than Benny D., and his father's gesture made a fatalist of him. "Look at us," he was fond of observing to Dallas. "Three years ago I had shit. Now I got all I can do to piss it away. Three years ago you had shit and you still got shit. Who can figure it?"

Dallas had to admit he couldn't. Nor could he get a real good grip on the poker game either. He continued to lose, but whenever he got up to leave, Benny D. shoved money at him across the green felt. For a while Dallas kept a strict accounting of what he owed, but after the first two hundred he figured what the fuck. Benny D. was winning anyway, almost as fast as Dallas was losing, so nobody was getting hurt. Benny had brought along two bottles of good scotch that had circled the table, stopping meaningfully only before Benny D. and Dallas. As the evening wore on, the alcohol had a melancholy effect on Dallas, who began to talk about his brother.

"Who cares?" one of the other players finally said. "He's dead and buried. Play poker."

"Not fair," Dallas said.

"Right," Bennie D. agreed. He'd been at the scotch since midafternoon and saw the whole enchilada with startling clarity. "Not fair," he said. "Fate." Then he passed out, his chin on his chest, still gripping fiercely what turned out to be the winning hand.

"Three o'clock," said one of the other men, thoroughly disgusted. "Seven hours we been at this and I'm dead even."

Thereupon there was a general accounting, which revealed that everyone at the table was more or less even except for Benny D., whose considerable winnings had merely subsidized Dallas. To continue seemed pointless, and the game broke up. Benny D. was left where he sat, his broad forehead now resting comfortably on the table.

At three in the morning Main Street was so quiet that Dallas could hear the traffic light change from red to green a block away. There was nothing sadder and lonelier in the world, he decided, especially when you were all alone when it happened. What had he done to deserve such an experience? He remembered Anne and the fact that he hadn't even called to say he wasn't coming. Maybe that was it. He should've called, but it was too late now and besides, the traffic light had already paid him back. He never had been welcome at the Grouse home, not really. You could tell when you were really welcome, and the only place he'd ever felt it was at his brother's. His innocent brother, who never got drunk, never played poker, never catted around, never in his life caught a dose. Dead. And now Dallas had no place in the world where he was ever really welcome.

At the Four Corners Dallas headed north toward the cemetery, feeling sorry for the brother buried there and even sorrier for himself. By rights he should be the one in the ground, if only because nobody would miss him. Certainly not his ex-wife and probably not his son, who never said anything at all. Even the fast friendships of his youth had slipped away. If he ever saw Dan Wood, it was by accident. After he and Diana were married, he made all that money and moved into the house up on Kings Road. And they were friends with Anne, so to hell with them, Dallas figured. Yes, Dan had it rough, a lot of people did. Maybe not as rough as himself, but pretty damn rough just the same. Even as he arrived at this conclusion, Dallas was aware that he was posturing for his own benefit, something he did only when he was drinking. In the morning he'd be at a loss to discover much wrong with his life, assuming he still had his teeth. But for some reason, these periods of melancholy were important to him, and he rode them out the way some people did migraines.

The cemetery was closed, the grounds surrounded by a high iron fence studded with spikes along the top.

Dallas scrambled over with the nimbleness of a reckless drunk. Though when he felt one of the cold iron spikes graze his groin, he came to an important decision. He would end his meaningless existence and join his brother in the grave. If there was no justice, no God to insure that the innocent and the good were not spirited away while the guilty lingered, then he'd show them justice himself. That very night, before he had a chance to sober up and remember he didn't want to die.

David's grave was in the new section, but Dallas had climbed the fence at the other end, which meant he'd have to travel from past to present. The path in the old part wound through tall oaks that thrust upward, obscuring the stars, out of the hummocks. The night was clear now and the wind had finally died down. The gravestones angled crazily, two-centuries old, the result of deep restlessness below. Dallas had no desire to read what they said. That was the sort of thing Anne would do. They might have been interesting if the people beneath had done the writing, but the living had nothing worthwhile to say about the dead. As Dallas approached the present, the stones sat straighter and the stars began to peek through the bare branches of the smaller trees. Finally the stones disappeared altogether, victims of changing custom. Lying flat, they were invisible from the path.

Dallas knew where his brother's was, though, and walked right up to it, the emotion thickening in his throat. There was a fresh bouquet of flowers, which meant that Loraine had visited, probably that afternoon. They had a dusky smell, a little like Loraine herself. *I'd still be welcome in my brother's house,* Dallas thought. *Even at this time of night, I wouldn't get turned away*. This thought was quickly followed by two others—that it was wrong for any man to kill himself when there was a chance he might be welcome somewhere and that a man had obligations toward his brother's wife, obligations that might just improve his mood. Dallas had promised his brother to look after her and the child. How could he even think of killing himself when David's house needed so much work, and his sister-in-law a job? He hadn't really planned to do himself in, but to realize that he wasn't morally obligated to came as a relief.

The first thing was to go and tell Loraine to rest easy. He'd fix the plumbing, rewire the house, insulate the upstairs, give the whole place a fresh coat of paint. Dallas accomplished all of this in his mind as he hurried back along the path and scrambled over the fence. Since it was at least a mile to his brother's place, he began to jog. Then he thought of an even better plan and reversed his direction. Fifteen minutes later he arrived at the Grouse home, winded and perspiring, despite the cold. His breath billowed before him as he jogged in place, figuring. Some crushed rock was scattered along the perimeter of the porch, and Dallas grabbed a handful that rattled very loudly against his ex-wife's upstairs window. In a moment, a light went on and Anne appeared. At the sight of her, Dallas quailed a little. Despite his inner assurance that he was at this very moment turning his life around and that in time she'd come to understand the moment's significance, her beauty was still terrifying, and he felt afraid, the way he had when they were married, and even after. When she threw up the window, part of the pane of glass he had cracked with the barrage of gravel fell the two stories and shattered in the drive. "I'm sorry—" he began, startled by the strange sound of his own voice.

"Dinner was yesterday, Dallas. Go away."

The best thing was to ignore her. "I've got everything worked out," he said excitedly. "I'll start acting right. Starting today. Right now."

"Have you been reading Dickens?"

Definitely better to ignore her. Her remarks never made any sense. "Could you give Loraine a job?"

"Loraine who?"

"Sister-in-law, who'd you think?"

"Are you drunk?"

"Exactly. But would you?"

"Dallas—"

"Please. I won't bother you again. Ever."

"That's ridiculous. Of course you will. You bother everyone."

"If she came to the store, could you find something?"

"I don't know. Maybe."

"Great," Dallas turned to go. "Go'night."

His ex-wife's voice followed him. "You disappointed your son today."

Dallas shook his head. "No. He doesn't care 'bout me. Wish he did."

"Maybe he'd like the new you better."

Dallas hadn't considered this, and was cheered even more.

"In the meantime, you owe my father a new window. Should he put it on your tab?"

"Yes. I mean, I owe one. You'll never get another husband, you know."

"Thanks for the advice." The window slammed shut,

the rest of the broken glass falling around him before the light went out.

The remainder of the broken glass fell around him. Dallas was still excited, but the euphoria of alcohol was beginning to wear off so he alternated jogging and walking all the way to Loraine's. Despite the time, now nearly four in the morning, a light was on in the living room. Actually, it was just the television, all snow. Loraine answered the door right away and didn't seem at all surprised. "Come in," she said. "I guess Thanksgiving lasted a little longer than I planned."

For a moment Dallas took her literally. Her hair was fixed and she was dressed in a ruffled blouse, skirt and heels. She was a little wobbly. But there was no one else there and just the one glass beside the bottle on the old, ringed coffee table. All this he ignored. "I've got everything figured," he said.

"Then keep it to yourself," Loraine said. "I'm still figuring. Stuck at the beginning. Don't take all the fun out of it."

Did it always have to be this way with women, Dallas wondered. Didn't they ever want to listen? Did they always have to say things nobody could make any sense out of? "Just let me—" he began.

But he didn't get any farther. Loraine did the strangest thing any strange woman had ever done to him. Instead of letting him help her, instead of letting him tell her about it, she slapped him in the face. Hard, too, so hard it cleared his head.

"I feel like hell, Dallas. Can't you see I feel like hell?"

"I wanted to give you some good news," Dallas said weakly, now unsure that *any* news of his was likely to

be good. Anne had been right. It was his destiny to
bother people. If he'd learned anything in all the years,
he should have learned to pay attention to Anne when
she said things like that.

"I don't want any part of good news," she said. "I
want to feel like hell. Can't you understand?"

"Yes."

"You're just saying that. You aren't smart enough
to feel like hell yourself, or even understand when
somebody else does."

This struck Dallas as unfair, especially in view of the
fact that he himself had been feeling like hell so recently. Apropos of feeling miserable, he said "I saw
the flowers—" but then, for a moment, thought Loraine
was going to hit him again.

"Just shut up," she said quietly. "For once in your
stupid life, don't be stupid. David adored you, but he
was right. About most things you're dumb as hell."

Which sounded like the sort of thing Anne would
say, and Dallas guessed Loraine was probably right. But
he was confused, just the same. Not by what she said,
but the way she said it, her voice soft and sad. He
didn't understand until she came close. "Don't be dumb
for once," she said, her breath musky like the flowers
on her husband's grave. "Just be kind."

He was too surprised and scared to kiss back when
she kissed him. But he knew that he wasn't supposed
to step away. He might not be smart, but he was certain
of that much. As usual, he thought, just when I've got
everything figured, it turns out I had it all wrong. Like
cards, there was always something you didn't count on.
Usually something bad. Good things you didn't count
on were something new. If this *was* a good thing. The
more she kissed him, the more he wondered if it might

just be. Anyway, it didn't mean he couldn't paint the house and fix the plumbing if he wanted to. He would tell her about his plans later. "Scrooge!" he thought to himself suddenly, as the drift of his ex-wife's earlier remark became clear. Catching on, even belatedly, was pleasant.

23

Sunday morning after Thanksgiving, Anne Grouse informed her mother that she would not be going to church. "Why not?" Mrs. Grouse said. When her daughter made a point of not answering, Mrs. Grouse retreated, rhetorically, half a step. "I mean, if you're ill—"

"I know what you meant, Mother. I'm not ill. I'll drive you and Randall."

"No you won't. You'll go right back to your warm bed if you—"

"It's forty degrees out."

"Pooh. A few short blocks."

As they waltzed around the subject a little longer, Mrs. Grouse refused to surrender the notion that her daughter was ill, at least for the sake of public discussion. Privately, she knew better. Her daughter had been an infidel always. She went to services only for the benefit of the boy, who was beginning, Mrs. Grouse feared, to show many of the disturbing traits her daughter had manifested at the same age. More than once he had observed that the sermon made no sense. Mrs. Grouse was enormously fond of her grandson, but she was of the opinion that he was getting too big for his britches, and his mother remained living testimony to what could happen when such impulses were not nipped.

The more she thought about her daughter's sudden refusal to attend services, the more certain she was that Anne intended to corner her father and broach some proscribed subject. Mrs. Grouse had redoubled her vigilance of late, always guarding against upset. She took special care to insure that Anne was never left alone with Mather Grouse, lest she harp on the subject of the oxygen tank or introduce another one conducive to excessive enthusiasm on her husband's part. This latest tactic on Anne's part was unfair, for it invited Mrs. Grouse to shunt her Christian duty in order to protect her home.

In the car she smoothed her white gloves savagely and tilted her jaw in a fashion that suggested life's unfairness and a good deal more. "Your father had another bad night," she said when Anne slowed down. The traffic always bottled up in front of the church while elderly parishioners were extracted from cars and bundled across the street. "Neither of us had a wink of sleep."

Anne put the car in neutral to wait for an old woman who, suddenly disoriented, darted off in the wrong direction, was retrieved, then pointed in the right.

"The fourth night in a row," her mother continued. "Maybe he'll be able to doze while we're away."

Anne murmured in agreement, but Mrs. Grouse knew nothing was promissory in it.

"It's his time alone . . ." she ventured. By now they were at the crosswalk. Randall got out and held the door for her, but Mrs. Grouse lingered. Far back in the line of cars, someone honked.

"I'll pick you up in an hour," Anne said.

"Maybe we'll just walk."

"I'll pick you up."

"Why not come in. You're right here and all—"

"No thank you, Mother."

There was nothing to do but get out, so Mrs. Grouse did. "We'll say a prayer for her," she said to her grandson. "Won't we?"

"Sure," Randall agreed. "Why not."

Mather Grouse was indeed dozing when Anne returned, but he started awake guiltily. The television evangelist was gesticulating at him, but the sound was inaudible. To Anne her father had aged a great deal during the last year, even since October. His chest had become concave, and inactivity had added slack flesh to his middle. He looked more like a man deep in his seventies than one in his midsixties. The skin along his throat was pale and translucent.

"Go back to sleep," she urged softly, her mother's version of things suddenly too real and accurate to be ignored. Her father was a sick man, and she ought not to bother him.

"No," he said flatly. "Sleep is overrated. Have you ever noticed how it's always recommended to people anybody with half a brain can see need to wake up?"

Anne smiled, and remembered him always saying things like that when she was a girl. Long before she was able to figure them out, she had admired the way they sounded and her father's ability to say them when nobody else she knew could.

Mather Grouse apparently appreciated this one himself. "I wonder if I read that someplace or if I thought it up myself. I should write it down, just in case it was me."

"It sounds like you."

"I don't know. I'm suspicious."

Now that he was awake, she could see he was in a good mood, so she sat down. "It's nice to talk, just the two of us. Why don't we, ever?"

"It isn't permitted."

Anne frowned. True, she often blamed her mother in much the same manner, but her father's explicit criticism seemed unfair. He allowed himself to be badgered by his wife a good deal, but he always let her know when he'd had enough. And once the signal was given, she stopped. "It's not fair to blame Mother. We could if we wanted to."

"I guess we stopped somewhere along the line and just never started again."

"Let's. Now. If we didn't need a reason to stop, we don't need one to resume."

Her father looked dubious but did not object.

"Can we turn our friend off," she asked, getting up from the sofa and pushing the button. The reverend's face grew terribly thin for an instant, then disappeared, leaving father and daughter so alone that both wished him back immediately. "We're opening a new store," she said, trying for a simple, conversational tone.

Mather Grouse nodded, way ahead of her. "New York again?"

"The suburbs. Connecticut, actually. They're going to do a lot of hiring."

"You'd be better off."

"There's a lot more money. They want me to open the store at least. Then I can stay on if I choose. I'm wasted here."

"I seem to recall telling you that when you were fourteen."

"I guess I still have reservations. Different ones. But I'm afraid not to go. They've been patient, but I know how the company works. In the long run they'd rather ax you than not be able to tell you what to do."

"Perhaps they have your best interests at heart."

Suddenly Anne felt like crying. As usual, her father had refused to meet her eye. She couldn't recall the last time he really looked at her. For all she knew, he might still see a seventeen-year-old in his mind's eye when he listened to the sound of her voice. How startled he would be if ever he decided to look. "I guess I hoped you'd try to talk me out of it."

"No," he said, still staring nostalgically at the blank television screen. "I never thought your coming back was wise."

Anne struggled with the sudden tightness in her chest. "It was for you—"

"No," he interrupted. "I know your feelings for me, and I'm . . . grateful. But that's not why you came back."

"Then why?" She waited until it was clear that her father had no intention of speaking to that particular issue. And suddenly the silence rendered the whole conversation insupportable. In strength of will she had always been her father's equal, but they worked their wills in different ways, Anne through action, Mather Grouse through quiet patience. In the latter she was no match. He was far more comfortable with things unsaid than she could ever be.

"Anyway, there's this business with Randall. I think I'm beginning to lose him. We used to be so close, but I don't know what he's thinking any more. I know he hates school, and I doubt he's learning much of anything. The Connecticut schools would almost have to be an improvement."

"I wouldn't worry about him too much. Nothing can ruin a good boy except growing up, and he's going to do that no matter where you live."

"I hate to take him away."

"I'll miss him."

"And me?"

Mather Grouse paused. "Yes, I will. But I'll feel better about you in Connecticut. People sometimes get in the habit of being loyal to a mistake. They can devote their whole lives to it."

This time it was Anne who looked away, afraid that her father would choose this particular moment to meet her eye. They hadn't spoken of Dan Wood since the night fifteen years ago when she told him that she had agreed to marry a man she neither loved nor respected and that she was in love with her cousin's fiancée. "Then you know how much I still love him."

"Yes. I know you."

"Not even you could ever convince me that loving somebody is a mistake."

"It is though, just the same. Because as long as you continue, you'll be waiting for your cousin to die."

The harshness of this didn't surprise her; Mather Grouse had always been capable of cruelty. She shook her head. "It's even worse. Sometimes I wonder if I'm not waiting for *him* to die."

"Wouldn't it be kinder to leave him alone?"

"Yes . . . yes. It's just that for a long time now I've forced myself to be content with less than just about anyone I know. I see him rarely and almost never talk to him, really talk to him, except in my head. I've never once since their marriage encouraged the slightest infidelity. All I've asked is to see him now and then, listen to his conversation, and know that he's near. And

I'd like someone to explain to me why I should have to give up so little."

"It's like the penny on the sidewalk. It doesn't belong to you, no matter how much you need it."

Anne felt less like crying now. She had needed to explain herself to someone, even badly, for a long time. Now she had bottomed out in a different realm, where tears did not apply. "Did you read that somewhere, or was it you again?"

"Me, this time. I'm almost positive."

Anne took a deep breath, knowing that she was going to say it and that once said it would have to be done. "I'll go then. I just wish I got some satisfaction out of doing the right thing. Or strength. Something."

"You've always been strong enough," her father said. "I never know where you come by it."

"From you, of course."

Their eyes very nearly met. "No," he said so emphatically that Anne was startled. Her father had always been a hard man to compliment: He hated lies and was embarrassed by the truth. "Your mother will be waiting," he said before she could ask for the explanation he had no intention of giving.

24

The boys inside Nathan Littler Junior High hear the heavy machinery straining up Hospital Hill during third period, and despair—certain that the demolition will be completed before lunch break. Some of the braver boys decide to cut fourth period, duck under the chain-link fence at the end of the alley and climb the slope to the rear of the hospital. They perch there in trees on the far side of the ambulance service road. The rest of the boys will join them during the midday recess, praying in the meantime that something will be left of the building, for they harbor a terrible longing for the long-anticipated destruction. They want to see the steel ball crash through brick and mortar. The razing had been scheduled for Friday, but when the boys hear the groan of the heavy machinery and see the men in the yellow hard hats, they know that today's the day.

Their fears of missing out are ill-founded, as it turns out. The men in yellow hats have to put the machinery in place and wave blueprints at one another, pointing at the building. Sawhorse barricades are gradually erected to keep spectators at a safe distance. The town's curious, and there are many of these, have begun to congregate. The majority of those milling around were born in the doomed building, and have been back since.

The boys just released for lunch, too late to find seats in the trees out back, jostle for position along the barricades in front. All along Hospital Lane people line the upstairs and downstairs porches of the two-family dwellings fronting the old, ivy-crawling institution—at first just the owners and family, then friends, then friends of friends. When the crowded porches swell past capacity, the overflow spills out onto the porch roofs. People hang out of windows. Anticipation becomes electric, and the atmosphere up and down the lane becomes nervously festive, though the ballwrecker crouches idle between two bulldozers.

"What's holding things up?" everyone wants to know, and several theories, all authoritatively advanced, none correct, snake among the impatient. Most anxious are the boys from the junior high whose lunch hour is slipping away. Having so recently prayed the clock forward, they now curse their folly and weigh the considerable attractions of not returning to school against the inevitable retribution that failing to do so will entail. They band together, swearing solemn oaths that they won't go back until the hospital is rubble, arguing that so large a number of miscreants cannot possibly be effectively punished. Not if they stick together. But as the dreaded hour of one o'clock approaches, some of the boys, their hearts heavy with disappointment and a deep sense of injustice, slink back down Hospital Hill until only those who have bragged the loudest remain, prisoners of their own bravado. Even those who cut fourth period begin to drop like overripe fruit to the ground below, and with reluctant glances over their shoulders retrace the path down to the chainlink fence at the end of the alley. Only a few realize when they hear the heavy machinery awaken precisely at the stroke of one that they have been victims of anything more sinister than cruel mischance or bad timing.

With the majority of the schoolboys out of the way, the demolition crew begins with the most remote wing of the hospital, a section whose windows had been knocked out nearly a year before when the first ward had been evacuated to the new hospital. Unfortunately, the first swing of the ball is poorly aimed, plunging harmlessly through one of the vacant window frames on the second floor, eliciting a hoot from the crowd as the huge ball punches only a tiny hole in the red brick on its backswing. The next attempt, though, is on the mark, the black ball tearing through the brick and ivy with explosive force, blowing dust and smoke out the adjacent windows with a whoosh. An excited cheer goes up from the crowd, coinciding with a groan from the building itself, one corner of which shudders.

In the Mohawk Grill, Harry is perplexed by what's happened to his lunchtime crowd. The first explosion of the wrecker's ball is still reverberating when the bakery delivery man pulls open the alley door and backs in with a handtruck full of Sunbeam bread and hamburger rolls.

"What the hell was that?"

"The hospital," the delivery man says. "Wisht I could take the time. You oughta see the rubberneckers. Three deep."

The blood drains from Harry's face. The other man is too busy stacking buns to notice.

"Friday!" Harry shouts. "It's supposed to be on Friday!"

The man is startled by Harry's frantic expression. "Gonna snow by then. Maybe—"

"Jesus God," Harry says. "Jesus God."

He is a large man, and while his movements are efficient in the narrow space behind the familiar lunch counter, he's lost and sluggish in open spaces. He runs the first fifty yards to the base of Hospital Hill, but when he starts up the grade he slows like a swamp-bound dinosaur. Halfway up, he feels a tremor beneath his feet as a large section of wall collapses. All at once the air is full of dust. Harry imagines that he's still running, but only his crazy arm jerks suggest rapid motion. Otherwise he looks like a fat comedian doing an impression of an Olympic walker, all hips and elbows. He thinks of all those childhood dreams where he was pursued by something nameless and fearsome, his legs heavy and rooted like tree trunks. Near the top of the hill he has to stop and lean against the stone wall. The air is thick with the collective groans of men, machines and foundations. Even the people on the porches and rooftops are indistinct in the dust-fouled air. Their excitement is now fueled by sound more than sight. From where Harry slumps, panting, he can see that a large portion of the old hospital is already gone. The sight pushes him upward again.

On the other side of what remains of the building, a small knot of boys holds its ground despite the noise and dust and flying debris. Their original intention was to watch from high up in the trees, but the ground shudders each time the ball makes contact and instead they cluster at the top of the hill, prepared to retreat, if need be, down the slope. From their angle, the outline of the building looks a little jagged but not radically altered, for it is the front and side walls that are collapsing under the relentless attack of the ball. With each blast, though, dust and debris are exhaled from the windows. For a second at the moment of impact everything blurs before focusing again. The boys inexplicably find themselves rooting for the old hospital, seeing something admirable in its apparent defiance of the ball. When a section of roof collapses and the ground shakes, the air is so thick and dark they cannot see if the back wall is still standing. Gradually its form becomes visible again, though sagging badly. In a lull the air begins to clear, and what the boys see then they do not at first believe.

On the third floor, behind one of the broken windows, stands a stock-still figure. The boys see him clearly for an instant before the building suddenly vibrates and coughs forth another whoosh of dust. Not all of the boys saw the figure and when those who did point out the spot, it's gone.

Those who saw the man at the window are staggered. Each boy arrives simultaneously at the same conclusion. He has seen a man die. Nothing in their lives has prepared them for this, though they have seen men die every imaginable death in the movies and on television. They stare dumbly at the window, unable to break away, unable even to look at one another. The window becomes their focus and contains them. It is one of the boys who hadn't seen him, and therefore didn't know where to look, who spots the man when he reappears five windows down the wing. "Hey!" the boy cries, pointing. "Hey!" they cry together, their voices absorbed by the heavy air and the now constant tremors of the hospital. When another section of roof sags, the figure is gone again, only to reappear further down the wing. Whoever it is clearly is keeping a few rooms ahead of the searching ball. From where they stand, the boys can see he is nearing the end of the wing.

When Harry breaks through the line of wooden horses

on the other side of the hospital, he is collared by Officer Gaffney, who studies him with frank astonishment, partly because he has never seen Harry any place except behind the counter of the Mohawk Grill. To the policeman his mere presence is as confusing as his wild demeanor and apparent intention of running up the walk and into the collapsing building. Grabbing Harry firmly by the shoulders, the policeman asks the question that most troubles his imagination at the moment. "Who's watching the diner?"

"Billy—" Harry gasps.

Officer Gaffney nods knowingly. "We figured you had him, somehow. We figured—"

"No!" Harry's voice is full of exasperation. He tries to bull his way past the policeman but has left his considerable strength at the foot of Hospital Hill. Gaffney handles him easily. "In there!" Harry points.

Officer Gaffney looks at him blankly.

"Billy . . . in there—"

The policeman looks over his shoulder at what remains of the hospital for verification and, not finding any, simply says "No."

"Yes!" Harry insists.

Officer Gaffney studies the building. When what Harry has said finally sinks in, he still stands stock-still. "Well, then he's dead. And that's all there is to it."

"Stop the wrecker!" Harry calls, nearly crying now, but his frail shout is lost in the hubbub. He begins to cry in earnest, angry with his own weakness, his inability to break free of Gaffney's grasp. He would batter him silly if he could, but the policeman is right. If Wild Bill was inside, he's dead. He must be. Still, none of this slakes Harry's impotent rage. "You're a moron,

Gaff!" he says, clinging to the front of his uniform, *"A God damned moron!"*

Several onlookers have been following this sideshow with interest, but suddenly they're distracted by the shouts of people clustered on a single roof and gesticulating wildly. Everyone now cranes his neck to see what it's all about, but the air is too thick. People all along the rooftops take up the chant, though, pointing and calling to those below; and when Officer Gaffney loosens his hold, Harry shoves past. Immediately a section of wall collapses, sucking most of what remained of the roof into the building's open maw. As he makes his way through the rubble, other men are running, too, and one is climbing up the wrecker toward the cab. The machine's roar is so deafening that it isn't shut down until the operator is grabbed by the shoulder through the open window.

Gaffney catches up to Harry about twenty yards from what once had been the hospital's main entrance. Several others are already there, dashing toward the doorway. A few men have actually jumped down from the porch roofs across the street, and without hard hats they run skittishly among the mounds, arms above their heads as if to protect themselves from falling debris until they gain the metal canopy at the entrance, though this offers little more than symbolic protection, given the gaping rents in its sheet-metal fabric. Harry arrives near the back of the pack, but succeeds in pushing his way through to the threshhold, where he stops with the rest. All of them appear to be awaiting permission to enter. At Harry's elbow is Officer Gaffney, a picture of frowning puzzlement.

"That's not Billy!" Harry says after studying the

vaguely familiar boy who stands before them in the once blue-carpeted reception area, looking a little embarrassed amid a pile of mortar, brick and broken glass, utterly uninjured. "That's not Billy. That's some goddamn kid!"

25

On the corner of Sixth and Broad in Mohawk stood
Greenie's Tavern, which had the sole distinction of
being the gin mill closest to the largest of the Mohawk
tanneries. A low-ceilinged building, long ago a hand-
laundry, it now reeked of stale beer and provided a
bathroom whose door could never be induced to close
properly. The obligatory bowling machine stood against
one wall, its lights dancing seductively even when the
machine wasn't in use. Once a quarter was slipped into
its slot, the plastic pins clattered down from above and
quivered nervously in anticipation of the sliding puck,
which only appeared to strike them.

The man who owned Greenie's was not Greenie.
Neither were any of the several most recent owners,
though there was probably a Greenie somewhere in
the establishment's eccentric past. No doubt he had
drawn five hundred or a thousand kegs of draft, then
died or escaped to spend the money he'd made, fading
completely from the collective memory, leaving behind
only the neon script that subsequent owners never felt
sufficiently motivated to replace.

Greenie's seldom did any real business, except for
roughly one hour a day. During that hour it did the
best business in town. At a few minutes before five,

men from the tannery and surrounding glove shops began to drop in for a quick schooner on the way home to dinner. Between five and six, the bartender didn't bother to turn off the tap, and just ran his tapered glasses beneath the wide open spigot.

The second busiest man in Greenie's was Untemeyer, the bookie, who went through three tablets of paper slips, one hundred sheets each, looking up from his task only long enough to see whose name to write down next. Not that the slips were necessary. Untemeyer was acknowledged to have one of the finest memories in the county, and those who owed him money either steered clear or paid up, slips or no slips. He hadn't forgotten a wager in forty years, and sooner or later he got his money, because Mohawk was a small place and within its confines he was well traveled. Untemeyer was a workingman's bookie who took no heavy action, but no wager was too small and for this reason he was a favorite among men who often lacked the traditional two-dollar bet. Yet, these small wagers added up and had been doing so for a long time. A mugger, had there been one in Mohawk, could have done far worse than to find Untemeyer when he left Greenie's at six-thirty. Of course only a stranger could've robbed him, because he knew everyone else. But a stranger wouldn't have known enough to, for only a mind reader could've guessed Untemeyer had anything worth taking. He always wore the same shabby black alpaca suit, liberally dusted with cigar ash. Despite his being a public figure, only a very few men knew where he lived. Several women had known, once upon a time, but they were all married now, or dead or both. With a bookie, all you had to know was where to find him, and Untemeyer's movements were precise. If ever he happened not to be at the end of Greenie's bar at five, you could find him at the morgue.

The only visible sign of wealth Untemeyer allowed himself was a large diamond ring set in gold. It hadn't been off his thumblike ring finger in thirty years. Dallas Younger, one of Untemeyer's better customers, liked to tease him about it. "Don't you worry about that ring, Bill," Dallas would whisper. "When you die, I'll be right there with a hacksaw." Then he'd hold up his own ring finger to illustrate. "Right here at the joint." The otherwise unflappable Untemeyer—no doubt visualizing Dallas, saw in hand, grinning down at his corpse—always came unglued at this comic threat. "If I could get it off, I'd give it to you right now, you son-of-a-bitch. Get away from me," he'd growl. "I'll piss on your grave, anyway. See if I don't."

He straddled his corner stool and wrote out his slips, tearing them off one after the other until he had accumulated an impressive pile of coins and bills. In the bulging jacket pockets of his black alpaca suit, he carried coin wrappers.

Two weeks before Christmas there was a warm spell, and perhaps it was the unseasonable weather that produced at Greenie's an unusual customer. At five forty-five most of the men in the bar were finishing their third quick one and fishing around in their trouser pockets to see if they had money to pay for another. With this important business to occupy their minds, most didn't notice when a quietly well-dressed man in his sixties entered, squinting in the dark, smoke-filled interior, and took a recently vacated seat at the opposite end of the bar from Untemeyer. Apparently unwilling to shout his order, he sat for some minutes unattended. Most of Greenie's clientele were too young to know who he was, or how unusual the fact of his being there. They were of another generation and couldn't know that for over thirty years this man had gotten off work with all the others and walked past Greenie's open door, the raucous laughter of his fellow workers spilling out into the street along with the clacking of the bowling machine and the smell of stale beer and urinal cakes. This man had never once entered. Tonight only a handful of this older man's generation was present, and none immediately recognized Mather Grouse, their old coworker who, once he was finally served, drained half the beer before setting the glass back on the counter.

Mather Grouse very much liked the taste of beer, though he almost never drank it. Occasionally, when he was a younger man and still working in the shops, he would pick up a six-pack of ale at the market on his way home from work, and then after dinner—there was never a spare moment before—he would drink a bottle very slowly while he watched the news. He had stopped the practice one winter when there wasn't money for beer and never started up again, having found another use for the extra money about that time. Mrs. Grouse didn't object to her husband drinking a beer with the news, but she disliked having to rearrange their small refrigerator to accomodate the bottles, and Mather Grouse was never permitted to put in the whole sixpack at once. The best he could hope for was two bottles in the door rack, where Mrs. Grouse would lay them flat among the condiments, convinced they would tumble out onto the floor if they were set upright, though anyone could see by examining the racks that this was a geometric impossibility. In the door the beers never got as cold as Mather Grouse liked them. Greenie's beer was very cold, and Mather Grouse drained the remainder of his glass with satisfaction, then ordered another. On the way home he would stop and buy beer, and when he got there he'd make Mrs. Grouse stand all six bottles upright in the back of the refrigerator. Never before had he realized that this issue was worth a fight, but there were going to be other changes as well.

Almost contentedly Mather Grouse surveyed Greenie's. In his present mood, the dark, dingy bar seemed exactly the sort of place it ought to be, and for some reason the odor of stale urinal cakes was not nearly as nauseating as he had often thought when passing by on the sidewalk. It was simply the smell of humankind, and after all, it was pointless to disapprove. Greenie's served very cold beer, that was the main point. Mather Grouse decided that from now on he would drink cold beer whenever he felt like it. At the moment he was in a rare period of ascendency as regards his wife. Normally he would've considered suicidal a contest of wills with that good woman. Granted, she gave ground once the battle lines were drawn, but she always had a way of gaining that ground back again, and a little more, in the long haul of days, months, years. However long it took. You could win a skirmish here or there, but then you paid.

This evening Mather Grouse had simply informed her that he was going out for a beer, and Mrs. Grouse, who had not lived forty-odd years with him without being a shrewd judge of his moods, especially those rare ones when he would not be trifled with, registered no formal objection. But her lips drew together until they were a thin white scar. Nevertheless, Mather Grouse felt confident that on this occasion he would successfully prevent her from exacting slow retribution. If he had never been able to prevent it before, never mind. She was a woman, and mortal. All his life he had known men who beat their wives just to get their attention. Maybe it was a little late to start beating Mrs. Grouse, but he thought there might be some middle ground between physical abuse and unmanly acquiesence. Though he wasn't sure, there just ought to be. The first step in searching it out was to start thinking independently again. Casting about for something wild and independent to do, he noticed Untemeyer at the other end of the bar. Mather Grouse knew him, of course. When he was younger, the bookie had made the rounds of all the shops. Now the mountain came to Mohammed, as Untemeyer was fond of saying.

The majority of his business concluded, Untemeyer was making neat stacks of his dollar bills and paper slips, after which he would thumb quarters into the paper coin rolls. Everyone knew that he didn't appreciate taking further action after six, after he began tubing paper with rubber bands. "Yeah!" he barked whenever he sensed a laggard customer at his elbow. He never bothered to look up.

"I wish to play a number," Mather Grouse said.

The voice, together with the formal phrasing, jolted him, and he peered up over the rims of his owl-eyed glasses. "Well, I'll be damned."

"Perhaps not," said Mather Grouse.

"Mather Grouse."

"What is a good number?"

"602," Untemeyer told him honestly. He himself had never played a number, but had he been a betting man he'd often thought he'd play 602. Actually, this was the first time in forty years that anyone had asked his advice. The men and women of Mohawk were fiercely loyal to the numbers they selected. They played the last three digits of their license plates, the birthdates of their children and lovers, the death dates of local suicides. They didn't need Untemeyer to tell them what to play, and Untemeyer would not have presumed. "How much?"

Mather Grouse put a crisp ten-dollar bill on the bar. Untemeyer blinked. "Are you all right?"

"Perfectly," Mather Grouse said. In fact, doing something this abjectly foolish made him feel wonderful. It wouldn't do to make a habit of it, but the novelty was delightful. "Thanks so much for asking."

Greenie's was now beginning to thin out, and on the way back to his stool Mather Grouse spied Rory Gaffney at the bowling machine, surrounded by a small group of men. The sight of him caused Mather Grouse a fleeting moment of panic, although his coming to Greenie's in the first place had much to do with Rory Gaffney. Hadn't he lain awake half the night planning and rehearsing the meeting? Why the old panic, then? Now of all times, after he'd convinced himself that such feelings belonged to the past. Why the paralysis, the sudden impulse to slink out before he was noticed? Mather Grouse gathered all his self-control to keep from throwing the remainder of his money on the bar and bolting for the street.

Instead, he ordered another beer and again quickly drained half. The beer had a warming effect, and Mather Grouse felt something of his former determination restored. He was happy to feel it, too. The moment of panic had been senseless but real. He had felt it before, many times, and not always occasioned by Rory Gaffney. And perhaps it was foolish to force a confrontation.

The boy was responsible. Facing annihilation, he had entered the collapsing building even as the very roof and walls were giving way, and in so doing had saved the life of the very man who had not been out of Mather Grouse's thoughts for a single day for over fifteen years, and who had made him a virtual prisoner in his own home. In a single stroke the boy had redeemed his grandfather, saved his life more surely than Anne had done the afternoon he had collapsed after seeing the ragged bum urinating on the lawn and recognized in the man's decrepit state and shameless behavior another man entirely.

Had it not been for his daughter, Mather Grouse would have died that afternoon. But she hadn't been able to bring him all the way back to life, not the way the boy did. *Think of it!* Mather Grouse had said to himself over and over. *Just think of it.* No man could have done it. Only a boy. But just the same. The boy calmly stepping through the chaos, hearing behind him the shouts of the other boys who had spied the figure at the window. Think of him leaving the others behind, gauging it all correctly, intuitively, knowing there wasn't time to go back down the slope, around the school and back up Hospital Hill. Gauging correctly that even if there had been time, he wouldn't have been able to make anyone believe him. Think of it: calmly climbing through the rubble, in through one of the broken windows on the ground floor, bricks and wiring and wood falling all around, the walls shuddering under the impact of the ball, the air too thick to breathe, at least not deeply enough to do any good. And then, once inside, even worse: the mayhem, the groaning intensified, and think of it, going on, never guessing that it was two lives he was saving, the second his own grandfather's, as if Mather Grouse had been there in the building beside William Gaffney, the two of them fleeing room to room, just ahead of the massive ball.

Surely if the boy could do that, Mather Grouse could follow through and say what he should've said over fifteen years ago. Rory Gaffney, when you and I are finished with this conversation, you will never speak to me again. If we meet on the street, you will pretend you do not know me. You will never again address a member of my family. You will neither come to my home, nor drive past my house in your car. If you should ever do any of these things, if you should ever acknowledge that we are acquainted by so much as a nod of the head, then by God I will do what I should have done so long ago, and then you will get what you deserve. Yes, deserve.

Mather Grouse had entered Greenie's confident that he would deliver just such an ultimatum, and that once this was done he would again be a fully vested member of the human race. But somehow the sight of the man— encircled by his cronies, all of them in turn leaning forward over the bowling machine, nudging it, caressing it, cajoling it—had disheartened him. Between himself and the others there had always been a gulf, and he was never sure that he wanted to bridge it. Was this not an unholy brotherhood founded on ignorance, self-satisfaction, fear and promiscuity. You cover mine, I'll cover yours. If he stood against Rory Gaffney, he would have to stand against all of them, for Rory Gaffney *was* all of them, magnified, or so he seemed to Mather Grouse. Nor was that the whole story. The effect Rory Gaffney had on Mather Grouse, the very real panic Mather always felt when near him, could not have resulted from anything so abstract. Mather Grouse's loathing was instinctive, a combination of fear and re-vulsion that like nausea came over him in waves. Gaff-ney always seemed obscene, and he often reminded Mather Grouse of an incident early in his childhood when a fat ten-year-old had called him into an alley between houses and exposed himself. What the young Mather Grouse had felt—he still remembered vividly the complex emotion—was anger and revulsion at the sight of the boy's angry red member, as well as sinking sympathy, for the boy was obese and vile. For this reason, he remembered thinking, God invented hell, not to punish but to separate the clean from the un-clean.

Mather Grouse was snapped from this reverie by the sound of his own name, spoken close-by, and he started visibly. The man who had spoken was not the one he feared, but another, roughly Mather Grouse's age, dressed shabbily except for a cheap new lemon-yellow windbreaker. The man was no more than five feet tall, and everything he wore appeared at least one size too large. He was very drunk. "It *is* you, Mather Grouse," the little man said with boozy enthusiasm. "I knew it. Don't you remember me?"

Once he studied the man, Mather Grouse was sur-prised to discover he did. "Why, yes, Mr. Anadio. I do."

The little man was greatly pleased. "We was just talking about you," he said. "Wasn't that your daugh-ter's boy out there at the old hospital?"

"Yes," Mather Grouse said. "My grandson."

The mere mention of the boy instantly restored Mather Grouse. It made the boy real. Both the grand-son and the act of heroism had seemed to pale in the dank light of Greenie's, as if here they might not apply. Rory Gaffney, still hunched over the bowling machine, twirling the puck with doughy fingers, seemed far more tangible. Mather Grouse watched him, forgetful of the man at his elbow. It was the tenth frame and Rory Gaffney calmly rolled a strike to win the game. Money exchanged hands. Even from across the room it was plain that Rory Gaffney had faulted by releasing the puck well over the red line. But no one objected, probably because they all routinely faulted. A strange way to play, it seemed, and Mather Grouse's heart sank.

"Of course you heard *my* news." Mr. Anadio was saying.

Mather Grouse admitted he hadn't.

"Oh," he said. "I'm dying, Mather." He said it almost cheerfully, as if delighted to find someone at this late date who hadn't already heard from somebody else. "Cancer," Mr. Anadio explained. "Like all the rest. Cancer and leukemia, that's us, Mather."

He had been paying so little attention that it took a minute for Mr. Anadio's words to register. And when they finally did, Mather Grouse didn't know what to say.

"They killed us, Mather. All them years. They just plain killed us, and I told 'em so, too. Young Ralph Tucker and Mike Littler both, right to their face. Ten times the national average. It was right in the *Republican.* Ten times the average, but the bastards still won't admit they done it. Killed us, but they won't admit it." Tears were welling up in his eyes. "They wouldn't admit it if it was a thousand times the average. A million. Not them bastards."

Suddenly Rory Gaffney was standing with them.

Mather Grouse didn't have to look over his shoulder to know it. When Gaffney's soothing voice interrupted, he was prepared.

"You made your living in those shops, Mr. Anadio," he said mildly. "Who else would've paid a man like you? Men like all of us."

"But they made us *sick,* Rory Gaffney," Mr. Anadio pleaded. "They didn't have no right to make us sick."

Gaffney put a hand on his shoulder. "I'm not sick, Mr. Anadio. I worked in the shops all my life. And look at our friend Mather Grouse here. He's a different kind of sick, but you don't hear him running down the shops that gave him a living. Mather Grouse is a man who keeps his peace. If I *was* sick, I'd thank the shops anyway. Where would men like us have been without work? We're all of us the same, men like us."

Mr. Anadio had lost interest in the dispute. He was too intent on fighting back the tears. He wished he could stop crying, but he couldn't. "No kee-mo," he said to Mather Grouse, his voice suddenly full of defiance. As far as he was concerned Rory Gaffney was no longer there. "I told 'em, too. Not me, I said."

"I'm very sorry, Mr. Anadio," Mather Grouse said.

"Not me," the little man insisted. "I told 'em, too."

"You should let the doctors cure you," Gaffney said.

Mr. Anadio spit. "Cure! Not me, Mather. Maybe I'm sick, but no kee-mo. I even told young Tucker that."

Then Mr. Anadio turned and walked out into the early evening. He left Mather Grouse weak and sick to his stomach, as if he had just given blood. "I had better go home," he muttered. Mr. Anadio's troubles had somehow made clear to him that he wouldn't say what he had come to say. It was the boy's courage he had felt, not his own. Men in their sixties did not make new beginnings.

"Yes, Mather, home," Rory Gaffney said. "That's the place."

Untemeyer watched Rory Gaffney and Mather Grouse thoughtfully from the other end of the bar. His work for the day was finished and with money and slips safely tucked away in his deep pockets, he indulged himself with a boilermaker, as he did every day when Greenie's emptied out. Once the two men were safely out the door, he and Woody the bartender would have the place to themselves. A strange pair, Untemeyer thought, as Rory Gaffney took Mather Grouse's arm and steadied him toward the door. Then he remembered a strange story Dallas Younger had told him on the QT. If he remembered right, Mather Grouse had appeared one afternoon at the garage where Dallas worked and thrust twenty-five dollars into Dallas's jacket along with instructions to buy a heavy winter jacket for, of all people, Wild Bill Gaffney. Give it to him yourself, Dallas had suggested. No, you, Mather Grouse had insisted, and to sweeten the pot he said that if Dallas did this one favor and never let on to anyone, he would consider Dallas's debt squared. A strange story, Untemeyer thought. Maybe even true, and stranger still.

The door swung shut behind the two men, and Mr. Untemeyer grunted, downing his whiskey. Strange indeed. Somehow he had the impression that Mather Grouse and Rory Gaffney might even be blood enemies. But then life was strange, it occurred to him, as it did every afternoon at Greenie's as he drank his boilermaker and looked to the silent Woody for companionship.

26

That men who don't make friends easily seldom have any trouble making enemies is perhaps ironic, at least in the sense that intimacy is at the core of both relationships. In the leather shops where Mather Grouse worked, he had no friends, though with the majority of his fellow workers he was on congenial terms. Even so, they had cause to be suspicious of him—the way he went directly home after work each day, never playing a number or double when Untemeyer came around in the afternoon, never getting into the baseball pool, which cost only fifty cents, no matter how much money had accumulated when no one had won it for weeks on end. He never spoke up at shop meetings, though everyone else griped. And there was plenty to gripe about. Low wages, the poor quality of the leather, the seasonal layoffs, widespread rumors that some of the shops were going to close. Many speculated that before long the cutters would not be needed at all. In these meetings nothing was ever resolved, but everyone had the opportunity to blow off steam and went home happier for having voiced their opinions in a free country. Mr. Maroni, a wizened Italian who had worked leather for fifty years, always had the last word, and it was always the same. "Mr. Chair!" he would cry, his small voice all but lost in the shouting, until the noise finally subsided and he was recognized. "Mr. Chair! I wanna say wonna thing about the peep. You no can satisfax ever one. Ever one make a mistake. I am too."

Since Mather Grouse sat almost apart from these proceedings, he was not to be trusted. Some whispered that he might be an informer, working for the owners, a thesis that would have gained more currency had it not been for the fact that Mather Grouse prospered less than any man present, routinely getting the worst leather to cut, expert and diligent as he was at working around the flaws, carefully, methodically, unwilling to give in to them. The men were paid according to the number of skins they cut, and while Mather Grouse was universally considered one of the finest cutters in Mohawk, come Friday afternoon his pay in no way reflected his talents.

Mather Grouse and Rory Gaffney had little enough to do with each other until the former, much to the surprise of everyone in the shop, was suddenly promoted to foreman when the man he replaced was discovered stealing leather and fled town before he could be arrested. Mather Grouse had hardly assumed his new duties when Rory Gaffney followed him into the washroom one afternoon. Nothing would be required of him. He would simply look the other way. Skins were always disappearing, and had been disappearing for so long that if they stopped disappearing it would be noticed and then a lot of people would be in trouble. Besides, the owners were the biggest crooks of all, only for them it was all legit. That's the way it was in America. The owners saw to it that the workers remained poor and desperate. Why did Mather Grouse suppose they allowed and even encouraged Untemeyer to come around during working hours? Why did they promote Mohawk as the leather capital of the world and encourage new workers to settle there when everyone knew there wasn't enough work to go around as it was? They paved the swimming pools in their back yards with the sweat and dedication of men like Mather Grouse. This was his chance to get even, at least a little.

"What about the others?" he had objected. "What about Mr. Maroni?"

Rory Gaffney shrugged. "Like the old guy says, 'You can't satisfax all the peep.' "

And so Mather Grouse had contrived an excuse to return to his old job and, when the bad season came, was laid off like Mr. Maroni and the rest. He never told anyone, not even Mrs. Grouse, partly because the situation was ethically complex. Though he considered himself an honest man, Mather Grouse knew that in the last analysis he had been no less appalled by the dishonesty of Rory Gaffney's proposal than by the notion of throwing in with a man whose fingernails, though always cut obscenely close to the quick, were black. Gaffney was the sort of man he had always held in utter contempt—crude and vulgar and unapologetic. A man who smelled of his own fermented sweat and sperm and wanted no more out of life than what he already possessed. Only more of the same and more regularly.

Two men could not be more different. Mather Grouse never thought of himself in terms of his profession. Not that he harbored dreams of grandeur, though there was a time when he had dreamed. But necessity had made a realist of him, and he learned quickly that to be anything more than a simple leather cutter he needed either luck or daring. But he was conservative by nature, and luck was seldom a factor for those who didn't choose to roll the dice. Actually, he had nothing against being a leather cutter. He had mastered his craft and derived considerable satisfaction from it. Nevertheless, he realized that even if he lived to be a hundred, he would be essentially the same person doing the same tasks, neither better nor worse. He wasn't jealous of those who had more money than he did, though to have more money would've been nice. But it was change he longed for, and he often thought that in an ideal world people would change their personalities every decade or so, possibly learning something to boot. Each metamorphosis would necessarily be a change for the better. No butterfly, no matter how faded or imperfect, was ever uglier than the larva it emerged from.

Mather Grouse was not naive, of course. He knew that most people who had enough money to embrace sweet change were sidetracked before they got around to changing much of anything. They changed their wardrobes, or rotated their tires. But no beautiful butterfly was ever formed. Still, young Mather Grouse concluded that this was their own fault. The opportunity existed, even if most chose to ignore it.

For men like himself, though, destiny was rigid. The cards had been dealt and the only choice was to play them well or badly. He himself chose to play them well but was never able to stifle the regret of the deal, of not being able to play all the hands around the table. He didn't despise men who held winning hands, but he did object to men who held cards not all that different from his own yet were too stupid or crude to feel regret. They saw nothing wrong with the lives they led. They did not notice the film beneath their fingernails or, if they did, found it charming. Good manly grime. They noticed only its absence in other men, and were suspicious. They discussed their members proudly, explaining where they'd been and where they planned to go next. Gave them nicknames.

The low sameness of life gnawed at Mather Grouse like a sharp-toothed rodent, and dictated, even when he was young, that his only pride in life would derive from taking the less traveled path. And so he went home after work when he would've preferred a cold glass of beer. He stayed clear of gambling, though he would've loved to take part. He held his tongue and kept to himself, because to do things any other way was not so much wrong as self-defeating and common.

Long after he had quietly surrendered his personal dream, Mather Grouse continued to dream for his daughter. At the risk of turning her into a snob, he began to suggest to Anne that there was more to life than Mohawk had to offer. This message was not easily conveyed, however, especially with Mrs. Grouse undercutting her husband's efforts with her own brand of stoic resignation. But Anne was bright and very beautiful, even as a child, her skin radiant and slightly darker than either parent's, her eyes darker still, her hair so black it threw off an almost blue sheen. To her father she was so lovely, so true, that he convinced himself that she existed on a plane that transcended ordinary destiny. She was one of the lucky ones exempted from fate, a child with unearthly defenses all her own. One such defense was a stubbornness of will equal, if not superior, to her mother's. Anne also possessed uncompromising honesty and a hatred of injustice that made her eyes leap with fire. Mather Grouse loved her so deeply that he was almost beside himself with pride and hope.

But his cherished faith that Anne would somehow

prove exempt from common fate was tested during her junior year, when it occurred to Mather Grouse that what he had viewed as her natural defenses against the crudeness of Mohawk County might under different circumstances become tragic flaws. And he suspected that she might be more cruelly vulnerable than he himself had ever been. Her recklessness, which would have terrified many a father, gave him little cause for alarm. Mather Grouse understood that such spirit would frighten the sons of Mohawk who, while as ready and willing as their fathers to plant their seed in any convenient place, would blanch at the notion of approaching Mather Grouse's daughter. Whatever stoked the fire in her eyes made them timid, as her beauty made them unsure of themselves. They would slink up the back stairs of dark three-family houses to relieve themselves in the loins of some lonely, middle-aged woman of reputation, but like their fathers they lacked courage and will, not to mention intelligence.

No, Mather Grouse's fears were of an entirely different cast. Anne was far too intelligent to be lastingly intrigued by these Mohawk boys. Her mind was not the problem—but what of the heart? Beneath her almost cruel beauty, she had little of the innate haughtiness that might've served as a shield, leaving her heart all too approachable. Instead of revulsion, she often felt sympathy, and unfairness always melted her. Her father's fear on this score came to be personified in young Billy Gaffney.

The other men in the shop knew nothing of what had taken place between Rory Gaffney and Mather Grouse. The latter sometimes wondered what side they would've taken had they known, or even if they would've believed. Only the shrewdest saw what finally was plain—that Rory Gaffney prospered out of all proportion to his co-workers. Somehow he always got the best leather to cut, while the other men spent more time concealing the flaws in theirs. They might've resented Rory Gaffney had he ever given any indication he considered himself superior in any way, for democratic assurances counted a good deal among men with very little. For a man with money to put on airs was all right, but not a workingman. Gaffney wasn't that way. He'd tell a joke and shake a hand and, if it so happened that he prospered, he'd buy a round at Greenie's. It was Mather Grouse, who prospered as little as anyone, who suffered on this charge.

If they'd given the matter some thought, these men would've been surprised at the animosity they had collectively harbored against a man who had never wronged a single one of them. But when the opportunity arose for them to retaliate—as they saw it—not a single man abstained. It happened one warm spring afternoon, and the huge, ceiling-high windows had been pushed out to allow air to circulate in the stifling, smoke-filled shop. As they worked, the men closest to the open windows peered out wistfully into the bright sunshine. When the high school let out, pretty girls with armloads of books began to pass by below. Occasionally someone in the shop would whistle, but for the most part the men were circumspect, since they were, after all, their own daughters passing below. With older women, of course, it was a different story, and the men hooted enthusiastically, especially if they recognized the woman as the wife of a fellow worker.

They all knew Mather Grouse's daughter on sight— the prettiest of all the girls, with the most womanly figure. When they saw her coming, they always nudged one another and exchanged knowing glances. Mather Grouse, though he worked at a window table, never indulged this afternoon pastime, never encouraged his daughter to stop in to see him. Perhaps this, too, was held against him, because he made the men feel unclean in their desire.

Though it was rare for any boy to find the courage to walk with Anne Grouse, some followed her progress in cars, circling the blocks, slowing down along the curb, talking to Anne and her girlfriends, hanging out the windows. Usually, she walked with a girlfriend, or alone. No one had ever seen her in the company of a boy whose father cut leather with Mather Grouse, until the afternoon she was spied in the company of young Billy Gaffney, who shuffled along beside her stoically, trying in vain to think of something to say. They walked in awkward silence, Billy scowling at himself yet very happy.

The men in the shop were also happy. At first there were only a few random hoots, but before long these were accompanied by explicit suggestions, and soon the men were hanging out the third floor window, each offering lewd encouragement to Rory Gaffney's son, who showed signs of lapsing into neurotic lunacy as the advice rained down upon him. Embarrassed and confused, he didn't realize that many of the anatomical suggestions were facetious. The more he was jeered and encouraged, the more confused he became, for the advice was varied and he seemed expected to carry it all out at once, despite the fact that none of these suggestions were on his agenda and some required more expertise than he possessed. He had never been in the company of a girl before, and the only advice his father had given him was never to be around one without a

Trojan, advice Billy had neglected—and with disastrous consequences, just as his father had predicted, if he had followed the instructions of the men hanging from the windows.

Anne herself added to his confusion. If she had shown signs of being offended, he would've known how to react. Instead, she ignored the men as if they didn't exist, never so much as glancing upward in their direction. This left the boy utterly confounded. Did she as well expect him to behave in such a way? The horror proved too much. So he ran. With her books, until she called after him, and then without, having dropped them unceremoniously in the grass. Later, when his father taught him to forget, he was grateful.

In the shop the festive atmosphere was slow to dissipate, but when it finally did the men were conscious of having misbehaved, though no one was prepared to admit it. One man asked when Mather Grouse expected to announce the banns, and everyone laughed nervously. During the entire episode, Mather Grouse, after looking out the window only once, had returned to his work. The skin along the back of his neck glowed bright red, but he had not uttered a word.

Nor did he say anything at dinner that night, still too full of powerful emotion to react wisely. Strangely equidistant between grief and rage, he trusted neither. To put this humiliation behind him was not impossible, nor even that difficult in the long run. What he was unable to shake off was the new sense of his daughter, seated across the table from him, suddenly a vulnerable young woman. She had changed so quickly he had somehow failed to notice. Her girlishness had been so self-sufficient that he hadn't worried, as if girlishness itself were a potent charm. Now the angular, little girl had become softer, lovelier, weaker. She no longer seemed the equal of anything she was likely to encounter, and seeing her today, in the company of the son of the man who most embodied everything he wished his daughter to escape, had cut him adrift. What if, despite her great gifts, she also ended up trapped? Would she pity some poor boy and marry him, set up house in some rundown second floor flat to wait patiently for him to come home from Greenie's, their meager meal sitting idly on the back burner? In another year would she be pregnant beneath her flowing graduation robes? In ten years would he, Mather Grouse, himself older, too old, climb the stairs to this rancid flat only to discover her finally gone, perhaps with the children, perhaps not?

This particular evening, such a scenario did not seem melodramatic. For such was the basic plot of the Mohawk tragicomedy, staged again and again. Rory Gaffney's own wife had tolerated him as long as she could, then one cold winter afternoon, with no luggage, had walked downtown to the Four Corners and climbed aboard the Greyhound to Syracuse and points unknown. Mather Grouse had never met the woman, but felt sure that he knew her. And as he studied his now mature daughter across the table, the other woman's story became hers.

To make matters worse, that night Mather Grouse dreamt about his daughter in a way that left him so angry and ashamed that he got up from bed and went into the bathroom where he cried quietly in the dark until he regained his composure. So it is me, too, he thought. In spirit I was among them today. Hanging out the window, shouting lewd, indecent things. I *am* no different. Neither beauty nor innocence nor the best of intentions can alter that which has always been.

So Mather Grouse thought in the dark. And then he thought, Maybe it isn't true. She still is the same. Still innocent. And if I were to go into her room, I would find the same girl that I have tucked in every night since she was an infant. And if I were to do it now, I could banish for good the ugliness of my thoughts. Mather Grouse went to the door of his daughter's bedroom, but did not enter. What if she were awake? he thought. What if she suspected his dream? It was as if father and daughter had grown up at the same moment.

27

At two in the morning Mohawk is chilled and asleep. In the whole town not one person is abroad in the brittle night air. If anyone were awake indoors, he might detect the first snow of the winter gently dusting the town. By morning it will have disappeared, or remain only as frozen ice crystals on the sidewalks, and the small boys hoping to make a dollar before Christmas will be disappointed.

The traffic light at the Four Corners clicks green, then yellow, then red. No car has passed beneath it in half an hour, and no one would be inconvenienced if the light didn't change until five-thirty when the milk trucks begin their rounds. On weekdays no policemen are on duty once the bars close, though one sleeps at the switchboard in the station in case there's a call. In Mohawk there is no all-night diner or all-night anything. Harry tried to keep the Grill open for a while, but it was more trouble than it was worth. The night-man treated the business as if it were his own—which is to say, he kept the profits. In midweek there isn't even a poker game upstairs.

In front of the Grouse home on Mountain sits a large moving van. The driver had pulled in late that afternoon and left it parked there so they could get an early start in the morning. To load the furniture and boxes from the upstairs flat won't take long. The truck is already three-quarters full with the belongings of a Rochester family moving into a four-bedroom in the Stamford area. Anne Grouse can see the top of the truck from where she sits, surrounded by boxes, on the sofa. Her bed and frame are disassembled, and if she sleeps tonight, it will be right where she's sitting. Her intention was to work through the night, but Mrs. Grouse and Randall have pitched in and everything's ahead of schedule, leaving her with nothing to do but battle the vague presentiment that going away amounts to running away. Still, she is as committed as a person can be, having signed agreements, made promises, paid money.

The house is so still that when the refrigerator clicks on, she's startled. She decides to look in on Randall, not because he needs looking in on but because she needs to look in. The move will be good for him, at least, especially now that he has been formally elevated to hero status with his picture in the *Mohawk Republican* and three civic groups fighting over dates to honor him in official ceremonies. He has dealt with all of this better than she herself has. But then Randall has always been contemptuous of the opinions of others, even when that opinion happened to be flattering. He is a strange boy. Just when she's convinced that he's going to pass through life aloof, a wry critic, he risks his life for a perfect stranger. And Billy Gaffney, of all people. The symmetry is so perfect as to suggest there might be a Supreme Architect after all, or something.

Billy Gaffney—she hadn't thought of him in years. For the longest time after her father had put his foot down about him, Billy had followed her home from school, pretending he had some legitimate reason for standing on the corner, watching the house. Perhaps he was awaiting another surge of courage, or for the sense of humiliation to diminish, or to explain or apologize for the men in the shop. He continued to haunt the neighborhood even after she and Dallas started dating. Then, suddenly, he wasn't around any more. She had known that he was in love with her, but she was discovering some things about love herself at the time—like the fact that it was just as easy to fall out of it as into it, and with as little reason. Dallas didn't require much time to teach her that. She assumed that Billy Gaffney had made a parallel discovery.

According to the newspaper, he'd been living in the abandoned hospital. Well, he wouldn't have to any more. After Randall told his story about what had really happened in the alley the day the boy was injured, charges against Wild Bill were dropped. Unfortunately public sentiment still ran against him, and he was packed off to Utica for observation until his fate, which had already been decided, could be formally ratified. The fact that a good boy had very nearly been injured on Wild Bill's behalf proved, if further proof was needed, that Wild Bill was at the very least a public nuisance. When she heard, Anne was furious. If unfortunates like Billy Gaffney were summarily institutionalized, she told her father, then half of Mohawk County could well end up behind bars. Mather Grouse agreed, having always believed that half of Mohawk County belonged behind bars.

Randall rolls over in bed but does not wake up. Asleep he is beginning to look more like a man than a boy, and it occurs to Anne that youth must have something to do with movement. Perhaps this explains why it's so difficult to judge someone's age from a photograph. She has a recent snapshot of Dan Wood, asleep by the pool in his back yard, one arm draped over his head, that makes him look twenty. He had dozed that way, briefly, some fifteen years ago in a motel room in Albany. She had watched him sleep, wanting to run her fingers through his damp hair, but not wanting to wake him. Since then, he has always been there to touch. Now, as then, she has refrained.

Outside, the lazy snow forms a halo around the street lamp. There is a stirring sound below, and Anne wonders if her father is awake. He has begged off helping with the packing, probably because it meant something like goodbye. Anne turns out the light and, after undressing, pulls a quilt over her on the sofa. Two-thirty. Mid-December. Very nearly the longest night of the year.

Downstairs, Mrs. Grouse rolls over in bed and opens her eyes. The bedside clock says two-thirty. She sees that Mather Grouse's bed is empty, the covers thrown back. No doubt he has gone to the bathroom. Mrs. Grouse resolves to remain awake until the toilet flushes, a comforting sound. She doesn't get up to check on her husband, because it angers him to be checked on, especially at night, on the toilet, where he claims any man ought have a little peace. Sometimes he just sits there in the dark, behavior which frightens Mrs. Grouse, though she doesn't know precisely why. "What do I need a light for?" he complains when questioned. "I know what I'm doing. It's not a complicated process." He can be a thoroughly hateful man.

But Mather Grouse is not in the bathroom. He is

in the living room in his favorite chair, his head slumped forward. When a car goes by, its headlights send patterns around the room, waving over his face and torso, though he doesn't react. Mather Grouse is not thinking about what has troubled him so deeply of late. Nor is he thinking about the afternoon over fifteen years ago when something inside him snapped. Sitting in that very chair, from which he could see the street outside. Young Billy Gaffney was there, just as he had been there for nearly a month, watching patiently, just as Mather Grouse watched him, though the boy had no idea. And as he sat there, Mather Grouse heard afresh the hooting and jeering, and saw again the men dangling out of windows. The boy was not to blame, of course. No longer even an issue, really, since his daughter was seeing another boy now. No reason, but the Gaffney boy weighed on Mather Grouse. That way he had of just standing there, utterly relentless, as if he knew that time was on his side, as if his private oracle had counseled patience. It was not a moonstruck boy that Mather Grouse saw standing there, but rather the personification of his own straight-jacketed existence. Mohawk was waiting there for her, confident that sooner or later she would come out and offer her embrace. And sometimes Mather Grouse imagined that it wasn't Bill Gaffney at all, but his father, a goatlike presence, come to claim her. And so something inside Mather Grouse snapped and he went crazy, if only for the time it took to make a phone call. Almost before he set the receiver down, Rory Gaffney pulled up in his ramshackle old car and shoved the boy roughly inside. Twice more the boy appeared, and twice more Mather Grouse had used the telephone, each time making the threat more explicit. Then the boy missed the last week of school before summer vacation, and for a month no one saw any of the family. Gaffney's wife had disappeared, and some said he'd gone after her. Then he walked back into the shop, and everyone began to say he was the most unfortunate man who'd ever lived. Not only had his wife managed to stay missing, but his son had been in an accident and, well, damaged. There was a brief flap, because some people wanted to know more. Rory Gaffney himself appeared shaken for a while, but before long he was his old self again. One day he had the opportunity to say a word to Mather Grouse, privately. "You don't have to worry," he whispered. "Not about my poor boy." There was complicity and friendship in his manner as well as a distilled hatred that took Mather Grouse's breath away.

But Mather Grouse is not thinking of these things, as he has been, increasingly, since his afternoon at Greenie's. Rory Gaffney's whispered confidences and innuendos do not turn like a knife in his heart as they have for the last fifteen years. Nor is he thinking any more about the possibility of redemption, of getting one good, long, cleansing breath, deep into his lungs, burning away with its icy purity the yellow bile that has collected there. He is having no trouble breathing. His chest neither rises nor falls.

The car going by awakens Mrs. Grouse again, and seeing that her husband has not returned to bed, she sits up and works her feet into the slippers at the foot of the bed. When she finds Mather Grouse in his chair, she isn't surprised, for he often sits there at night when he cannot sleep.

"Dear?" she inquires.

Mather Grouse does not respond.

"Dear?"

When she touches his hand, it is cold, and Mrs. Grouse steps back quickly, fear registering in her expression. Luckily, she has encountered fear before and quickly banishes it. For a moment she is immobile, but then she takes the heavy quilt from the sofa and covers him, careful this time not to touch his cold flesh. "There," she says, her voice rather louder than she intended. "Warm."

Mrs. Grouse returns to the bedroom, but not to sleep. She is a patient woman. Morning will come.

28

There were problems from the start, especially finding pallbearers. Mather Grouse had no relatives outside the immediate family, and Anne didn't realize how small the circle of his acquaintance was until she began to call the few names she and her mother were able to recall from his working days. Randall would be a bearer, of course, and Dr. Walters had called immediately to offer. But from there it wasn't easy. Dallas called and asked if there was anything he could do, but she put him on hold. He often forgot important engagements, and besides, more than once he had borrowed money from her father and not repaid it. After several phone calls to people she didn't know and who didn't know her, she became so depressed that she called the Woods. Blessedly, Dan answered. He and her father never had much good to say about each other, but under the circumstances Anne knew that she could count on him to be kind. Yet, it annoyed her when she confessed her predicament that Dan professed no surprise. What he did offer, as usual, was help, suggesting a nephew, a few years older than Randall, who owed him a favor. "Did he know my father?" Anne said.

"I haven't any idea. Is that the issue?"

"No . . . you're right."

"He'll be on time, and he'll wear a suit. Wish I could do the deed myself, kid."

Cheered by this qualified success, she went back to her list and succeeded in enlisting two more. One was an old Italian by the name of Maroni, who was clearly delighted. "I wanna say wonna thing about you poppa," he told her over the phone. "He was gooda man. Everybody make a mistake. I am too."

That left them one bearer short and when Dallas called back a second time, Anne relented. He not only offered himself but a couple of his cronies. "I know a couple of guys—" he began.

"We're going to be all right, I think," Anne said. Mr. Maroni had sounded positively ancient, but she had to assume he wouldn't die until the funeral was over.

"I just thought you might be short—"

The whole world seemed to know what had occurred to her within the last twenty-four hours—that her father had died essentially friendless.

At the viewing, the day before the funeral, Anne admitted to herself that she was in bad shape. All the arrangements, it turned out, were her responsibility. Each time something came up, she asked Mrs. Grouse if she'd rather, and each time her mother had looked unsure and said, "Maybe you'd better." Only once everything was taken care did she understand that Mrs. Grouse had done her a favor. Now she felt herself slipping into a black numbness from which she was able to extract herself just enough to get annoyed at people who didn't deserve it. The Woods arrived at the funeral home early, and to everyone's surprise they brought old Milly, who hadn't been out of the house on Kings Road since October, except for emergency trips to the hospital. The old woman immediately hobbled over to Mrs. Grouse and proclaimed in her loudest voice, "You poor dear, I never *heard* of such a thing." Just a figure of speech, Anne knew. All her life the women of Mrs. Grouse's family had "never heard of" life's less pleasant aspects. Still, Anne had to fight back the urge to attack—"Never heard of death, Aunt Milly? Eighty years old, a husband in the grave, and you've never heard of such a thing?"

She was not the only irritant. Diana joined the receiving line as a bereaved survivor, which made that line longer than the line of potential mourners it was meant to receive. Dallas arrived fresh from work, his hands and work clothes greasy. He was full of apologies for his appearance, and reiterated that he knew a couple of guys. Benny D. said he would, and Benny was all right. Even Dan annoyed her by stopping to chat with one of the mortuary employees before coming over to her. The only person Anne felt sorry for was Randall, who had said next to nothing in two days, and whose eyes had remained full the whole time. He refused to inspect the casket and stood so that it wasn't even in his peripheral vision. Anne suspected that he might be in worse shape than she was, but feared that if she tried to console him she might come unraveled herself.

Things remained askew throughout the evening. Dan remained on the edges. He didn't want to make things awkward with the chair, and so Anne was unable to draw strength from his proximity. In fact he scarcely looked at her. To her relief, Dallas finally left, but then turned up again half an hour later, this time scrubbed and jacketed. As ex-son-in-law, bearer-to-be, he made the receiving line even longer. Then he tried talking to his son, but this was rough sledding and he finally gave up and returned to where Dan sat, the two of them looking extremely dejected, as if by the absence of a wet bar.

Including the receiving line and the employees of the home, there were never more than twenty people in the room at once, and of those that came, Anne knew only a handful. Neighbors and a few old acquaintances. A few others introduced themselves in ways that clarified neither who they were nor how they had known her father. Two men claimed to be high-school classmates, but she couldn't place them and suspected they were confused. In any case, life had not been kind to them, and the slack-jawed admiration with which they regarded her made Anne wonder what their wives must be like. An ugly little man wearing a black suit and smoking a particularly foul cigar came in and stood for a moment, stared at the casket, and then abruptly left. Anne did not speculate until far into the evening that some of the shabby people who paid their respects were present simply to be out of the cold, because it was the bitterest evening of the winter and there was a nice fire in the foyer.

Actually, Anne paid scant attention to any of it. She could feel herself sinking lower and lower, and she raised herself to half-consciousness only when a hand was offered or someone wanting to explain who he was appeared before her. A few people wanted to talk about and pay her father compliments, but she could think of nothing to say in return. Her mother told everyone that he had died "peacefully, as he lived." Which seemed plainly untrue, as least the last part. His existence had been full of hard work and dust and noise and shameful worry over money. Anne was glad that it was his heart that finally gave up, that he had not choked to death, gasping for oxygen, because he'd already had a lifetime of choking want and restriction. A peaceful death didn't begin to balance the scales. Mather Grouse was owed a great deal, and now he couldn't collect.

Mrs. Grouse, on the other hand, was a wonder. She had been no help in making the arrangements, because doing things was outside her traditional purview. But Mrs. Grouse had no equal when it came to passive, stoic suffering, unless it was her sister Milly. During all the lean years when Mather Grouse came home after Thanksgiving with his pink slip—Christmas and the long winter ahead of them and little prospect of work—Anne could never remember her mother complaining. It simply meant that they would have to make do until spring when things would probably get better again. After all, hadn't she been storing canned goods and hoarding small sums in anticipation of this very event? Hadn't she even bought an early Christmas present or two? As for the rest, she would simply stretch what needed stretching—clothing and food—as need be. She would've shrunk in horror if anyone had suggested that she herself find a part-time job, not that anyone would have. But at skipping meals herself and finding ways to make a quarter pound of fatty bacon feed three people, she was a marvel.

Anne herself was no stranger to adversity, but she had always hated any situation that could only be endured. She was able to summon the necessary courage for a bold, confident stroke, but simply getting by left her dispirited, and it seemed that the older she got, the more frequent these situations became. The next day, as she stood with the small company beside the open grave, waiting for the clergyman to begin, the ugly truth of this situation came home to her. She was going to be thirty-five, and she hadn't anyone of her own. No one, as Diana once remarked, she "didn't have to share." There was Randall, but sons grew up and married, and Anne wouldn't have wanted to hold onto him even if she could have. Once upon a time, she was confident, Dan had thought her the most important person in the world. Once he had even said so. But that was a long time ago, and such sentiments needed periodic validation. She didn't doubt that he still thought of her, maybe even thought of her often. But she doubted he thought in terms of her. She doubted he asked himself a hundred times a day, when he read something in a magazine or saw something on the news, or met someone—what would Anne make of this?

The Woods were a few feet away, across the semicircle that enclosed her father's grave. She watched Dan until he felt her and their eyes met. His expression was tender, as always, and genuine. But it was an act of kindness, arising out of what he felt was her need, not his own. Dallas was there, too, and if smiling had been a possibility, she would've smiled then. Dallas, as she might have predicted, was wearing a blazer that neither fit him nor matched anything else he was wearing. Despite the subfreezing temperature, he wasn't wearing an overcoat, and Anne still knew him well enough to guess why. No doubt he owned several warm jackets but none of them would be long enough to cover the blazer, which he wore so seldom that he had no reason to invest in an outer garment to cover it. A simpler and far less expensive solution was to pretend he wasn't cold, which now he was valiantly doing. She wondered from time to time what her life would've been like if she had tried to tough out the marriage. Though it was conceivable she might have developed a sense of humor, she doubted it.

One night a month earlier he had awakened her at three A.M. to ask her to give his sister-in-law Loraine a job, which she had done. Then, yesterday at the funeral home, when the poor girl was kind enough to pay her respects to the family of a man she'd never met, he had cut her as if she had the plague. Dallas, always careening about town, out of control, always landing on his feet, always vaguely wondering about the sound of screeching tires and crashing metal wherever he went, never suspecting a causal connection.

And, of course, there was her mother. It would have been comforting to think that Mather Grouse's death would draw them closer together. After all, in a sense they'd been fighting over him all these years. And certainly there ought to be some way that two grown women could keep from agitating each other. But so far there was no indication that things would change. They hadn't talked much since that morning when Mrs. Grouse climbed the stairs, a very few minutes before the moving crew arrived, to tell her daughter what had happened in the night. "Your father has died," she said firmly, as if Anne might not trust her diagnosis and rush downstairs to administer mouth-to-mouth. "We had better call the people."

Mother and daughter had shared no moment of grief together in the days that followed, though from her mother's swollen eyes Anne could tell that she'd wept privately. But Mrs. Grouse had little need of strength. If she needed to lean at all, she could lean on Milly, who rose up like a mountain of granite for the occasion. Usually a bundle of infirmities that prevented her doing for herself what she had grown accustomed to her daughter doing for her, Milly put age and infirmity on hold, and the two old women clasped hands and teetered against each other in a way that would've made anyone who didn't know them fear for their collective safety.

With the service at the grave concluded, people began to file back to the procession of cars, eager to warm up again. Randall walked part way with his mother, but within sight of the black limo he said he'd rather walk home. She couldn't think of any reason why he shouldn't. There were times when she couldn't understand him, and others when she understood perfectly. On this day, so bitter and cruel, he wanted no part of warmth and comfort.

Diana offered to return to the house with them, but that would've meant old Milly coming too, and Anne doubted she could suffer even one of the old woman's remarks. Dallas, in a moment of uncharacteristic humility, thanked her for letting him be a pallbearer, even reminding her that he had owed "Pa" money. She resisted the temptation to tell him that she herself had repaid her father, and that if compelled he could always pay her instead. The postponed move was going to cost more than she could afford, and the money would've been a godsend. But Dallas wouldn't have it, anyway. He looked pitifully cold, and there was no future in being mean to men like Dallas. After all, she had married him out of pity, and that was mean enough.

At the cemetery gates, the small procession of cars broke ranks, their unity of purpose having dissolved. So, Anne thought, it's over. She and her mother, alone in the huge back seat of the limo that would drop them off in front of Mather Grouse's home on Mountain

Avenue before returning to the funeral home to wait for another death and short drive. When they arrived, the driver got out and helped Mrs. Grouse to the curb before getting back in and driving off. Mrs. Grouse, showing her first signs of distraction in the entire ordeal, stopped at the foot of the porch steps and rummaged through her purse. To Anne, she suddenly looked old. "I have the keys right here," Mrs. Grouse said, and indeed they could both hear the keys jingling. Neither noticed the man in the black suit standing near the corner at a respectable distance. Only when he was at her elbow did Anne start, and look at him so maliciously that he removed the big cigar from his face and mumbled something about their time of grief. Then the hand not holding the cigar disappeared into a pocket and emerged with a fistful of money, which he thrust at Mrs. Grouse, who backed away as if from a knife.

"Your husband . . . ," Mr. Untemeyer said. "The number."

But he was no good at talking to women, having had little practice in decades, and quickly gave up. "It's yours, damn it," he said gruffly.

But Mrs. Grouse continued to retreat up the porch steps. "No," she said. "Oh, no."

Untemeyer was clearly nonplussed, having absolutely no experience of people refusing money. This struck him as unnatural, even perverse. He turned to Anne, who was only slightly less confused than her mother. Was there some grotesque Mohawk lottery that her father had won by dying on a certain day? "My father was just buried," she told the man. "Won't you please go away?"

In fact, Untemeyer looked as if there was nothing

in the world he would've liked better, but he stood his ground, fanning the thick wad of bills like playing cards. "It's *yours,*" he insisted. "Your old man hit the goddamn number. It ain't my fault."

To Anne's surprise, her mother stopped backing up and confronted her husband's accuser. "There is some mistake," she said. "My husband was no common gambler."

The bookie was prepared for this defense. He never went anywhere without his slips, and Mather Grouse's, which he had been carrying around for a week, was right on top, handy. "See?" he said, showing Mrs. Grouse her husband's clearly printed name. "See?"

But the good woman was firm. "I'm *very* sorry," she said.

"Jesus Christ, lady," said Untemeyer. But realizing he wasn't getting anywhere, and after one more futile thrust of the money, he returned it to his own pocket and stumped off, still shaking his head.

Once they were safely inside, Anne noticed that her mother, who was peering between the blinds as if she expected him to return, was crying quietly. "Why are there such horrible people in the world," she asked, as if she really wanted to know and thought perhaps her worldly daughter might be able to explain. Still gazing fearfully out the window, Mrs. Grouse then said something even more surprising. "You won't go now, of course. You won't go anywhere. You'll stay right here."

Anne understood her mother perfectly. By "now" she was not referring to Mather Grouse's death, but rather to what had just happened. It was the man who had so rudely pushed money at her that had forced

Mrs. Grouse to look squarely at an uncertain future. She was afraid, perhaps for the first time since her wedding day.

"Of course not, Mother," Anne heard herself say. "We'll stay as long as you want."

PART TWO

29

Harry Saunders looks around the Mohawk Grill and considers that life is change, an idea that occurred to him only recently and has given him little comfort. Indeed he had always embraced the opposite philosophy, or rather it had embraced him. Until recently, his days were arranged like dominoes spaced far enough apart to fall independently, victims of repetition, not necessity, the end result an unbroken black line, definitely headed somewhere or other.

Today would be the last of life as he knew it. Tomorrow, the men from Blackstone Construction would knock out the wall between the grill and what briefly had been a bookstore. Before that it was a beauty salon, and before that a men's clothing store. In the twenty-five years since Harry bought the grill, eight or ten businesses had come and gone next door, each more ill-fated than its predecessor. They all opened with a flurry, the traditional quarter page ad in the *Mohawk Republican*, free balloons for the kids, a door prize. For a few months the owner would mind the store and speak of business picking up with the warm weather. Then, in July, he'd hold a clearance sale of some sort and the curious would wander in off the street to rearrange the merchandise in the bins before wandering back out again. That it was an unlucky spot wasn't news to anybody, least of all Harry Saunders, who had commiserated with each of the legion of failed merchants over coffee they ended up unable to afford.

Given all this, Harry is a little unnerved to consider that he's agreed to buy the place and expand the grill. Seduced. He has been seduced. The word has a nasty sound. He says it out loud—"Seduced!"—and echoing off the walls of the empty diner, it sounds even worse. He says it several times more and is still saying it when his first customer, a truck driver named Herb with long red sideburns, comes in off the street. "Say what, Harry?"

"Nothing."

"Talking to yourself already?"

Herb takes his black. Still agitated, Harry slops some coffee over the side of the cup and onto the saucer. Herb is a good customer and not overly particular. He'll gladly slurp the saucer.

"Most married guys end up talking to theirselves sooner or later," Herb observes, engrossed in the menu. He knows it by heart, but studies it intently every morning before ordering.

"How would you know?" Harry says. He breaks two eggs onto the grill where they sputter happily. They'll be ready by the time Herb decides it's eggs he wants for breakfast. Harry takes a platter down from the tall stack and warms it on the edge of the grill. Herb almost always ends up ordering bacon or sausage since ham is a dime extra. Harry spatulas some home fries onto the platter along with toast.

"Couple eggs, sunny side," Herb says from behind the menu. "Sausage, I guess"

When Harry sets the platter in front of him, Herb

digs in. "Women are okay," the truck driver concedes. "Some of them."

Two more customers wander in and Harry takes their orders. Pretty soon, the counter is full. Since Harry's competition over at the Fulmont Diner had a stroke, business has been brisk. Rumor has it that the Fulmont will be reopening soon, but the cook/owner hasn't fully recovered the use of his right side, and the sight of his lopsided smile is certain to disconcert customers who expect balance in a short-order cook.

"I might even get married again someday," Herb speculates, scratching one long sideburn dreamily with an eggy forefinger. "Who knows?"

"I didn't know you ever were married."

"Just twice. Not lately."

"What happened?"

"Don't know. Something."

Herb pays and leaves. Harry's morning waitress arrives and they stay busy straight through the lunch hour. The wash-up boy sets to work at ten-thirty but can't keep up with the dirty dishes. The sight of people waiting for tables and counter space doesn't cheer Harry, who envisions a vast expanse of empty seats and stools once the wall gets knocked down and all the bad luck next door begins to seep in.

Around two-thirty Dallas Younger comes in looking red-faced. "That old lady of yours sure is touchy," he observes.

"You walk in on her again?"

In addition to buying the place next door, Harry has renovated the upstairs, which he and Mrs. Saunders now use for living quarters. That was months ago, and everybody has got the hang of it except out-of-towners and Dallas Younger, who still expects to find a poker game in progress instead of looking three doors down the street, where it has moved.

Dallas studies the picture calendar hanging from a magnet on the milk machine. "It's April, Harry. Are you gonna get this year's calender, or just let it be 1971 again?"

"I like 1971."

Dallas nods. "She's all right, I gotta admit."

30

Randall Younger had to wait a long time before anyone would give him a lift. It was the hair. He was lucky at first, getting picked up on the outskirts of Buffalo by a driver heading east on the Thruway to New York. The man dropped Randall off at Fultonville, and from there it was basically no go. He thumbed for a while, strolling slowly along the highway and across the bridge at the Mohawk River, but by the time he got to Fonda it was getting dark, so he skipped dinner and climbed the fairground fence. Beneath the grandstand he would keep dry if it decided to rain. The ground was littered with refuse let fall by last Friday night's stock-car enthusiasts, and the smell was bad, but after a while Randall got used to it. The wind made a lonely sound high up in the bleachers that jailed the night sky.

By morning the wind had died, but it was gray and cold. Randall rose stiffly and rolled up his makeshift bedding, slinging the bundle over the chain link fence, then climbing over after it. There was a greasy spoon open in Fonda, and the muttering proprietor agreed to serve Randall coffee once the young man proved he could pay. The man didn't offer to refill it, though, so Randall had to content himself with slender retaliation in the form of a nickel tip. His last nickel.

Outside, the wind had sprung up again, lifting Randall's shoulder-length hair, alerting passing motorists to the sort of person to whom they had briefly contemplated giving a lift. Always on the smallish side as a boy, he had grown during his senior year in high school and freshman year in college. He was now taller than his father, though as lanky as undertakers in the movies. With his three-day beard, he looked a good deal older than eighteen. A few motorists slowed until they got a good look at him, then found the gas pedal again. The idea that he might frighten someone amused Randall, who'd always been the least dangerous person he knew.

Midmorning and half way to Mohawk, a decrepit VW bug pulled off onto the shoulder a hundred yards up the highway and sat there hiccoughing uncertainly. Randall didn't hurry. An hour earlier some teenagers had stopped, waved to him, then peeled out when he jogged toward them. As far as he could see, there was only one person in the VW, a girl who at first glance looked a year or two younger than Randall. "Take your sweet time," she said when Randall bent down to peer in the passenger-side window.

"All right if I put my things in back?"

"Why not?"

Randall saw the answer to that when he pulled the front seat forward to squeeze his bedroll in. The floor was rusted through in several places, and the battery, strangely positioned where the backseat once was, tipped precariously, only a few inches above the blacktop.

"Let me guess, " the girl said. "Mohawk, right?"

When Randall got in next to her, she pulled back onto the highway. The car had what sounded to Randall like a death rattle. "Right."

Closer examination suggested that the girl was sixteen, tops, but she maneuvered the car as if she'd been driving for years. Something about the way she handled the wheel with the palm of her right hand, as if she'd get fewer points if she employed her fingers, convinced him that she was showing off. He smiled. He hadn't showed off for anybody in a long time, and it was even longer since anybody had thought it worth their while to show off for him. Everything on the dashboard rattled happily. "Don't worry," the girl said. "We'll make it." When she stepped on the gas and tailgated, people in front of her got out of the way, perhaps fearing that anyone crazy enough to drive this wreck might also haze them right through town. "Want to know how I guessed Mohawk?"

"There isn't a whole lot up this way," Randall said, not in the mood to do much talking. The closer he got to Mohawk, the more he wanted to just take it all in. The familiar landmarks: the Ford dealership, the Dairy Queen, the power company offices, all on the outskirts. Everything seemed oddly out of proportion, as if each building had inched closer to its neighbor since he'd been away.

Unfortunately, his companion felt like talking. That so many people exacted a conversational toll was only one of the many disadvantages of hitching. At least in this case the driver was pretty, in a dingy sort of way. Her white sweater had the bluish tint that came from washing it in the same load as a pair of jeans. The girl's complexion was smooth, but it also had this suggestion of unhealthy gray, though her features were full and soft, her hair not quite so blonde as it had first appeared. She was barefoot.

At Rose Avenue she turned left off the highway

toward downtown. "We'll take the scenic route," the girl said, "so you can see how much things've changed. They got a Kentucky Fried Chicken in next to the bank."

"Really?" Randall said, not sure he believed her. A Kentucky Fried Chicken in Mohawk. Imagine.

On lower Main were several vacant stores, including what once was a small grocery owned by the father of one of Randall's classmates. One of his sort-of friends. He had neither seen nor corresponded with anyone from high school since leaving Mohawk. Still, he was sorry to see the small grocery closed. "So, how's college?" the girl said.

"What makes you think I'm at one?"

"The hair," his companion said matter-of-factly.

"It just grows," he told her. "Whether you pay tuition or not."

"I don't see what the point is. Of college, I mean." She said it as if she really wanted to know what he thought the point might be.

Randall didn't have a handy explanation, though he liked studying. It was nice to sit around and read books without people thinking you were peculiar. You could even call it work, if you wanted to, and nobody there bothered to disagree. Randall himself had done real work and knew the difference, and he suspected that a lot of other people did too. But as complicities went, this one was harmless enough. Certainly more harmless than the one that sent people halfway around the world to kill or be killed in the name of national defense. He wondered what his grandfather would've thought of having a draft dodger for a grandson. Very soon, that's what Randall would officially become. For all he knew, he was one already. Since dropping out at the beginning of the spring semester, he hadn't made himself all that easy to locate. No doubt his mother had been collecting plenty of official documents bearing his name. That was partly the reason for his return. He had to try and explain to his mother. If Mather Grouse were still alive, Randall would've tried to explain to him, too. He doubted his grandfather would've understood, any more than he would have understood the hair and the stubble. Randall smiled at the thought of his grandfather, picturing Mather Grouse as he always did, shoveling the sidewalk or cutting the grass or weeding the small strip of garden in back of the house or stirring paint with a stick, patiently, the oil swirling gently toward the vortex in the center of the can until the mixture was smooth as velvet.

"Go to war," his grandfather would have advised him. "You will not have to kill. They will know what to do with you and the killing you object to will fall to someone else who probably will not object. You will learn about them and about yourself. You will not like what you learn, but better to learn it anyway."

"Spring break, or what?" the girl said.

They were stopped beneath the traffic light at the Four Corners. The girl had told the truth. Halfway up the block a large red-and-white bucket rotated next to the dome of the Mohawk Bank and Trust.

"I guess I'm pretty nosy, huh?"

"Just medium nosy."

"I know who you are, even."

Randall doubted that. The last time he looked at himself in a mirror, it was all he could do to recognize himself. And he'd never seen this girl before.

"You're Randall Younger," she said when the light changed. "When I was a sophomore and you were a senior, I had the biggest crush in the world on you."

Randall was surprised. "You should've said something."

"You got any money?" she said, pulling into Kentucky Fried Chicken.

"You should have caught me earlier this morning. I was loaded. I gave it all to a needy man in Fonda."

"My treat, then."

Randall was hungry, but he didn't like the idea of letting a strange girl pay for his food. There was a remote possibility that his grandfather would've learned to accept the draft evasion, but sponging a meal off a teenage girl whose car had a see-through floor was harder to justify. "It's only ten-thirty," Randall objected.

"The best time. The chicken hasn't had a chance to sit around and get soggy."

She was already ordering into a speaker mounted on the column. Nine pieces of the Colonel's Original Recipe, slaw, rolls, Cokes. "You can take me out some time if you want," she said, and soon enough was handing him the cartons, one at a time, until they formed a warm pyramid on his lap. She swung the VW into a parking space beside the dumpster. "I've still got a little crush on you. Or I would have, if you shaved and dressed up nice."

"I don't think I'm going to be in town all that long," he said. "Not that it wouldn't be nice to go out with you."

They both ate hungrily, and the chicken tasted very good, midmorning or not. There was only one spoon, so Randall made the girl eat the coleslaw.

"Probably just as well," she said. "I gotta stop with

these crushes anyhow. It's not so good when you're married."

"I'm not married," Randall said, glad that she was finally mistaken about something.

"I know," she said. "I am."

Randall stopped eating and looked at her. "You aren't old enough," he said, aware that this observation wasn't particularly intelligent.

"You're right," the girl conceded cheerfully. "Old enough to get knocked up, though. You should see my kid sometime.'

She had picked her piece of chicken clean and now deposited it in the bag. "You care if I take the other wing too?"

"Sure," Randall said. "Live."

"They're the best part. I don't care what people say."

"You're easily pleased."

"True," she admitted. "I bet you're just the opposite. I bet you aren't happy very much."

"What makes you say that?"

"I remember you from before. You always looked kind of sad in high school."

"I didn't mean to."

She shrugged.

"Did you like Mohawk High," he asked.

"Sure. Wish I didn't have to quit."

"Go back."

She thought about it, chicken wing suspended a few inches from her lips. "Nah. I like different stuff now."

Randall suddenly realized that talking to this girl had cheered him. Chatter was usually annoying, but hers was so good-natured he found himself grinning. "What stuff's that?"

"Different things. You got any grass?"

"Good Lord."

"What's the matter?"

"This is Mohawk."

"So?"

"Nothing." What the hell, now that there's a Kentucky Fried Chicken. "Sorry to disappoint you."

"Not very generous, after I paid for lunch. You probably think I'd tell where I got it."

"Tell me about your husband."

"Mostly he just rides his motorcycle. He wouldn't like the looks of you."

"That's a shame. We might become the best of friends."

The girl missed his sarcasm. "I don't think so. You're completely different."

"I bet he wouldn't be thrilled about the idea of your picking up hitchhikers either."

"He wouldn't care. He's got some girl over in Ephrata."

"You aren't living together?"

She lip-farted. "God, no! What would I want to live with him for?"

Randall hadn't any idea. They ate until the boxes were empty and the paper bag they came in was full of bones. Randall took the trash to the dumpster and breathed in air that smelled a little like Kentucky Fried Chicken, a little like Mohawk and a little like the dumpster. A few doors up the street was the Mohawk Grill, behind it the alley where he had been beaten, and further up the hill a vacant parking lot where Nathan Littler Hospital once stood. The scene of his greatest moment. The hero, Randall thought with a smile, turned draft dodger. There were people who probably didn't even remember the old hospital. For almost six years now the sirens wailed right up the highway, bypassing the town just like everything else did.

The girl wiped her hands with one of the Colonel's special lemony cloths after deeply inhaling its fragrance. "I love these things," she said. "Don't you?"

"You can have mine."

"Really?" she said, dropping the packet in her open purse. "I'll use it on the baby. You want to go to Mountain Avenue?"

Randall blinked.

"Like I said. I know all about you."

"It must've been some crush."

They drove north up Main.

"Let me out at the fire station. I'd kind of like to walk the last few blocks."

"Sure." She pulled over and he got out. To his surprise, his bedroll was still wedged behind the front seat. "I didn't even catch your name."

"Call me B.G."

"All right, B.G. Be good. Watch out for those crushes."

"Can't help it with you," she said. When she flushed, the color dispelled the faint dinginess of her complexion and she was genuinely pretty. "Actually, it goes back to when you were thirteen and I was eleven."

"Come on."

"Really. I'd never even seen you."

He wouldn't have believed the girl if she hadn't sounded so serious.

"I probably shouldn't tell you what the "G" is for, but what the hell. It's the first letter of my maiden name."

Suddenly Randall knew, though he could think of no reason for the sudden intuition. "Gaffney," he said, even as he heard her say it.

"That was my uncle you saved," she said. "I fell for you sight unseen. What's the matter?"

In fact, Randall felt suddenly awash, as if he'd unexpectedly come upon the answer to a riddle he was asked long ago and had since forgotten.

"Don't be embarrassed. You were great."

He couldn't agree. Earlier, on the outskirts of town, he had felt that everything was slightly askew, too close together. As if the disappearance of the old hospital had created a void that was drawing everything in Mohawk a little closer to the vortex, like the oil in his grandfather's paint can. He himself had been drawn all the way from Buffalo. Maybe he hadn't come to explain the present to his mother. Maybe she was the one who had something to tell him. She was Mather Grouse's daughter, and she must know.

"They're releasing him the first of the month," he heard the girl saying, and for some reason he concluded that she was talking about his grandfather.

"Releasing—"

"Yup," she said. "Wild Bill rides again. He's coming home."

31

From the back porch Anne Grouse watched her mother
through the kitchen window. Mrs. Grouse had changed
very little. At first Anne feared that Mather Grouse's
death might precipitate a rapid decline, since from the
diagnosis of his illness Mrs. Grouse had focused all her
energies on her husband and seemed ill-equipped to
continue without him. But Anne had underestimated
her mother, and now wondered if perhaps it wasn't
their unfortunate destiny always to underestimate each
other.

Mrs. Grouse was unaware of her daughter's presence
on the back porch, where Anne was getting the garbage
ready for the Thursday collection. The older woman,
having thoroughly dried the breakfast dishes with her
thin dish towel—she refused to use the plastic, drain-
board contraption her daughter had bought for her at
Woolworth's, preferring to dry each teacup by hand—
was engaged in setting the table for her noon meal,
still several hours away. She had set two places, because
Anne came home from work at noon to make sure the
morning garbage collection had gone off without a hitch.
Her mother's fretting about the trash had intensified
over the years and now occupied her thoughts out of
all proportion. When the dogs got to it before the

garbage men, she'd regale her daughter with vivid descriptions of the mess while they ate their grilled-cheese sandwiches.

Mrs. Grouse was usually talkative during these Thursday lunches, because they were "like strangers, after all," though they lived under the same roof. Anne had categorically refused to move downstairs when Randall went off to the university. Her daughter's reasons for wanting to maintain a separate household were entirely unclear to Mrs. Grouse, who discussed this strange arrangement with her sister every time the old woman visited. "Queer" was the term Milly used. Anne was officially to blame, but she knew that her mother wouldn't have things any other way and would not have allowed the introduction of her daughter's things into the downstairs flat.

Mrs. Grouse carefully arranged the cups and plates as if the plastic placemats were printed with exact geometric designs that matched the dishes and silver. She lined up the plates first, adjusting and readjusting, an inch this way, then the opposite, until it felt exactly right. Anne watched from the porch, fighting the hardening she felt in her heart. Her mother's face exhibited that faraway expression that always meant she was working out some thorny point of consequence only to herself, and possibly her sister.

Mather Grouse's death had been the final link in the sisters' symbiotic chain. Mrs. Grouse had been shaky and fearful, but began to rally once her daughter canceled her contract with the movers and found another job in Mohawk, this one paying far less. Of the two, Mrs. Grouse had adjusted far better. But then, the old woman had a blueprint to follow. Milly had suffered a similar loss, and accepted it with a stoic forebearance only slightly diminished by the fact that in the decade before his death, she and her husband had not spoken a dozen words to each other. To hear her talk, as Dan Wood often remarked, anyone would've concluded that she'd lost her soul's mate. In fact, burying her husband had given Milly something of an unfair advantage over Mrs. Grouse since both women derived great satisfaction from loading onto their slender shoulders every hardship life could impose. If anything, Mrs. Grouse now had the upper hand, having both a deceased husband and a divorced daughter to her credit. But she was too kind to press an unfair advantage, and the two agreed that each had leaden crosses to bear.

Mrs. Grouse did not stray from the kitchen table. She would stop inching the silver once she'd resolved whatever problem absorbed her. Only then would the table be set correctly, the knives and forks resting in their proper slots. Anne came inside just as her mother reached her conclusion. "Goobies," Mrs. Grouse said.

"What?"

Mrs. Grouse started, not expecting to see her daughter in the doorway. "Some goobies," she elaborated. "You know. Chocolate-covered cherries. Peanut brittle. Will you ever forget how he loved peanut brittle?"

"Dad refused to eat peanut brittle. You're confusing him with yourself."

Mrs. Grouse, suddenly perceiving another flaw in the arrangement of the cutlery, began maneuvering a fork. "I should think I'd know whether he liked peanut brittle or not. After all, I lived with him for over forty years . . . I sat up with him all night long when he couldn't catch a breath . . . I—"

"You're right, Mother. I'm sorry. I'll pick up some peanut brittle on the way home from work if you like."

"Whatever for? I'm not able to walk a few short blocks?"

"Fine, Mother. Walk, by all means."

Anne went upstairs to finish getting ready for work. She particularly hated Thursdays. She didn't go in until late morning, but didn't get home until well after the nine o'clock closing. Then she had to open the store the next morning. Sixty hours a week at roughly minimum wage. And that wasn't the hard part. The hard part was remembering that staying in Mohawk was her choice.

She was pulling on her coat when Mrs. Grouse's voice floated up hallway. "There's someone at the door, dear."

The bell hadn't rung and Anne had heard no knock. "Mine?"

"Come down," Mrs. Grouse said. Her voice was edgy, and when Anne came in she was standing next to her place setting wringing her hands nervously. "He has long hair," Mrs. Grouse explained. "He doesn't look right."

She followed her daughter into the living room. The blinds were drawn, the room dark. When Anne opened them, the flat was flooded with light, and her mother shrunk back involuntarily, either from the light or the expression on her daughter's face. "Who is it?" she said.

32

Out by the highway a cold rain was falling on the Mohawk Medical Services Center. The dampness found its way into the building, and the nurses scurrying among the corridors threw sweaters over their shoulders. Diana Wood, seated bare-armed outside Room 247, shivered and wished vaguely that she hadn't made this particular visit, especially since there was no need to. This was the way it always turned out. Her mother had brightened up as soon as they pulled into the hospital drive and told the first doctor she saw that she hadn't any idea what all the fuss was about. She'd never heard of such a thing. All this after her frantic ringing of the hand bell on the nightstand next to her bed, and the panic-stricken eyes. "I can't breathe!" she had breathed, a mere whisper, frightening Diana terribly. Only Dan had taken it in stride. "Neither can I," he remarked to his mummylike mother-in-law lost in a queen-size bed.

In a few minutes he wheeled around the corner and joined his wife in the bright corridor.

"That didn't take long," Diana said, trying to sound cheerful.

"They always have our file handy. I fill in 'complaint' and 'date.' They copy the rest."

"I'm sorry," she said.

"You always are. That's part of the ritual."

"I always mean it," Diana said. "Doesn't *that* count?"

"Of course it counts. It's the only thing that does. Just don't try to talk me out of being angry. In fact, you ought to try getting bent out of shape yourself."

"I'm bent enough, apparently."

"Forget it. That kid was a jerk."

On the way into the hospital, one of the young interns had asked if Milly and Diana were sisters. An honest mistake.

"I'm going home," Dan said.

The lights in the corridor dimmed briefly, then came back again.

"Yes," Diana said, blinking, "Go."

"Come with me. We could both use a night without the bell."

Diana hesitated, considering, but the struggle was brief. "No. I'll try to get back in an hour or so."

"Come now."

"No."

"All right, stay. Call if there's any bad news." He wheeled around and started for the exit.

"Don't make me dislike you, Dan," his wife said. They were the only two people in the corridor. "I don't think I could stand disliking you."

He stopped, turning the chair sideways. "It was a rotten crack. I apologize."

"Get Fred to help you in. The lights were on in their living room when we left. They'll still be up."

"Sure," Dan agreed.

"I mean it. You're too tired."

He wheeled out to the lobby. He was tired, but he had no intention of tooting outside his neighbor's house. Not that Fred would mind. But for some reason, he felt like risking something. Early in the day, he felt strong and had no problem pushing the chair out the passenger door, setting it up, then sliding himself into it. But when he was tired, things sometimes went wrong. Once he hadn't secured the brake, and the chair had rolled down the sloping driveway and into Kings Road, riderless, leaving him clinging to the door handle with one hand and the roof of the Lincoln with the other until he was rescued an interminable five minutes later, the last strength ebbing out of his white fingers.

In the lobby near the door was a pay phone, and Dan slipped in a dime. "I could use a hand," he said into the receiver. "I'll be the one in the souped up Lincoln with the wheelchair on the license plate. Accept no substitutes."

In the parking lot he chinned himself into the driver's seat, surprised at how strong he suddenly felt. A passerby stopped to offer assistance with the chair. "Don't bother," he said. "Do I look helpless to you?"

33

Anne pulled in behind Dan's Lincoln. It was late, and along Kings Road the Woods' house was the only one with lights on. The rain had stopped but it was cold, and the shallow puddles Anne stepped around rippled in light cast by the streetlamp.

The chair, still collapsed, sat on the driveway. "Make sure the brake is on," Dan said, and did the rest on his own. "Come in."

"I shouldn't."

"I don't see why not."

They went in through the garage, Dan flipping the switch for the kitchen overhead.

"Guess who showed up today?" she said.

"Lyndon Johnson. How the hell should I know?"

"You could go along and guess wrong a few times so I could properly astonish you."

"It *was* Lyndon Johnson?"

"No. Randall."

Dan frowned. "That doesn't sound good."

Anne considered. "It's hard to say. He's always been such a strange boy."

"Genetics."

"Go to hell."

"Actually, I was thinking of Mather and how the Grouse blood skipped a generation."

"I'm very much like him."

"You aren't like anybody. And you're even less like him than all the other people you don't resemble."

"I'll have to think about that."

"Let's try the living room. You can build a fire if you want. We haven't had one all winter. Her majesty doesn't like the smell of burning wood."

"Another false alarm?"

"Third one this month. They seem to coincide, more or less, with not getting her own way."

"Tell me about it."

"No. Let's not talk about old women. Let's drink. The liquor cabinet ought to have something in it."

Fourteen or fifteen bottles was all. Bourbon, scotch, brandy. Backups for each. "What do you want?"

"Whatever," he said. "You choose."

"Brandy."

"Only if you'll build a fire."

"I don't know how, if you can believe it."

"I'll show you. People start them all the time and they don't even mean to. Did he flunk out, or what?"

Anne opened the mesh with a poker, as if it might be hot already. "Dropped out, he says."

"A euphemism, maybe. Put some kindling in first. Those skinny sticks. Jesus, you really haven't built a fire, have you?"

"Where would I've built a fire in my father's house?"

"Enough. Now some of the small logs. Separate'em a little so they can breathe."

"I think he's telling the truth. He's always been a

pretty good kid that way. I've known him to lie, but never to make himself look good."

"So why'd he drop out?"

"He wasn't real clear about that. Something about the war."

"Wad up some newspaper and push it under the grate."

Anne did as she was told. The cool ashes from the last, long-forgotten fire felt soft as baby powder. Dan pitched a book of matches to her. "Now open the flue."

"Speak English."

"That brass handle right there by your skull. Turn it."

The newspaper shriveled quickly and orange flames snaked up into the kindling, which began to glow. "He says he doesn't think he'll go if he's drafted."

"If he'd stay in school, he wouldn't have to."

"He doesn't think that's right, either. It's so like him to force an issue."

"He'll go," Dan said. "When push comes to shove, he'll go."

"You're wrong."

Dan lifted himself out of the chair, onto the sofa. Anne joined him and they touched, rang, their snifters. "I think my father enjoyed the war," she said. "I don't think he saw any actual killing, and he hated the violence. But the interruption was good for him. It made him see possibilities. It's funny, but I think that's what Randall came home for. Not to explain to me, but because he thought maybe I could tell him what his grandfather would've thought." She paused. "I thought I knew my father pretty well, but I didn't know what to say."

"I'll tell you, if you like."

Anne frowned. "I don't like. I get Mother's version all day long. You give me yours and I'll begin to doubt he ever existed."

"Then you'll be free."

"Don't want to be."

"You'd be better off."

"Why are you always compelled to play devil's advocate?"

"Because you always benefit from reality therapy."

Suddenly Anne was furious, as if a spark had leapt from the grate at his command and landed right above her heart. But she didn't raise her voice. "I'm forty years old. I've got a nowhere job. I've missed all my chances and I'm not sure I'll get any more. I've got a mother who's pleased to remind me of all this, in case I ever forget. I've got no husband and I'm in love with a cripple who grows fonder of his wife every day and less fond of me. . . . Is there anything I've left out?"

"No," he said. "You touched all the major bases."

"Enjoy your fucking fire."

Dan caught her by the wrist when she bolted up from the couch. His eyes were full. "Don't," he said. "Don't go."

"I really should," she said. "Besides, Di's likely to be home soon."

Dan drained the remainder of his brandy and poured himself another. "Morning's my guess. The nurses will bring a chair from the lounge and she'll sleep by the foot of the bed."

Anne suddenly felt weak and sat down again. "God," she said.

"Try and change her mind."

"Randall's probably wondering where I am."

"Wondering in his sleep, is he?"

"All right. But only because the fire's nice and the brandy's good."

"That it is."

"I certainly wish *I* had money."

"Me, too."

Anne would've assumed he was joking, but for something in his tone. "You *are* joking?"

"Just between thee and me, no. Di's been thinking about going back to work. The only problem with that scheme is that the nurse we'd have to hire would cost more than she could make."

"You're broke?"

"Are we ever."

"Can't you put a mortgage on the house?"

"No, thanks. Already got one."

He smiled and drank off half his brandy. Anne could see he was getting potty. When he was younger, Dan could drink all night, but it didn't seem to take much any more.

"Do you mind my asking where it's gone?"

"Private hospital rooms."

"Medicare—"

"—pays part. I wouldn't waste much time worrying about it. Not having money won't bother me. It would be worth losing my vast empire if only I could see that old crow in a room full of eight or ten other black cormorants. You know I'm never *willingly* unkind."

"I wish you hadn't told me. I've always felt good knowing you and Diana had some money."

"Have some more brandy. And put another log on the fire, will you? I can't get warm."

Though the room was plenty warm enough, Anne laid on another log and it caught immediately, the whole pyramid ablaze. When she returned to the sofa, her eyes were red.

"Oh, don't, for God's sake."

"I'm sorry," she said. "I just feel awful, that's all."

"Well, don't. Don't cry and don't feel awful."

"I'll feel any way I want to feel," she said, choosing to sit at the opposite end of the sofa. "Why don't we run away? We could be happy, don't you think?"

"Probably not."

"When you say things like that I hate you more than anyone in the world."

"Then I won't say them any more. Come here."

She wiped her eyes and slid toward him. "Do you suppose we could do anything, or would it kill you?"

"No, it wouldn't kill me."

To shuck her clothes took no time, and then the fire's warmth kicked in. They kissed, tentatively at first, then forcefully. "You're letting yourself in for some disappointment," he said.

"No," she breathed. "No."

Outside, Kings Road was quiet until the rain slowly began again.

34

Around three in the morning the fire began to burn down and dampness again crept back into the living room, though Dan's upper body was still warm. He was sleeping soundly. Anne had dozed pleasantly, but hadn't really slept. The quilt pulled over them didn't reach her shoulders. She snuggled into the small of his back, enjoying the warmth of his skin. She did not worry much about the possibility of Diana coming home, partly because Dan wasn't worried, partly because the story of her love for her cousin's husband was more the story of abstinence than adultery, and she felt certain that neither God nor Fate would be so cruel. Still, staying on seemed an unwarranted risk. Prideful even, so she slipped off the couch and quickly dressed. Once ready to go, she decided she'd better wake him. Otherwise, if Diana returned early in the morning she might find him there, his clothes in a cold, suspicious heap beside the dying embers.

"I have to go," she whispered.

"No," he said. "Stay."

"I can't. Though I *am* willing to listen to you plead for a few minutes."

"I feel like pleading, if you want to know the truth."

"Do you need help?"

He pushed himself into a sitting position, careful to keep himself covered, and looked around. "No," he said. "You've already helped. Thanks."

She knelt beside him and touched his cheek. "Don't you dare thank me. Ever."

"All right. Nice talking to you."

"Shall we get together on a regular basis?"

"Absolutely. Once every twenty years?"

When she turned onto Mountain it seemed like a bad idea. If she went home, fatigue was likely to set in and she'd fall dead asleep, and she didn't want to. Not yet. She felt too completely good to surrender the moment to sleep's neutrality. Besides, it had been a long time since she'd just driven aimlessly, and once the car warmed up she was comfortable.

Downtown Mohawk was black and deserted, so she headed up the long hill past Myrtle Park and out onto the highway. There she had to choose between heading north into the Adirondacks or south and east toward Albany and New York. There was nothing north but blackness all the way to Canada, so she headed south toward the buzzing yellow neon, never mind that everyone in its glow was in bed. The Ford seemed to have more pep than usual and, when she stepped on the accelerator, seemed eager to strain itself forward against the cold, cleansing April rain.

At Fultonville she turned onto the Thruway, alone except for the occasional semi. As a rule Anne didn't like to drive, but tonight it felt good and she suddenly wanted to drive all the way to New York. If she stepped on it, she could make the city by eight or nine, just in time for breakfast. The midtown Hilton would be nice, and maybe Price was still living in the city. Possibly he'd meet her for melon and mimosas on some terrace or other. She was always able to count on him for breakfast, anyway.

After her separation from Dallas, Anne and Randall had moved to New York. She thought her father would approve, but he showed little enthusiasm. She began to realize that he had wanted her to get away *before* she'd made a mess of things. Afterward made little sense to him, and he didn't believe that people could simply walk away from serious errors in judgment. But she was a grown woman, not the little girl in whom he had dared to invest his dreams. Anne decided to move to New York and make herself forget to care about what her father thought—and, if she succeeded in doing that, maybe even forget Dan Wood. It was worth as many tries as it took.

She was still young and pretty, and in New York there were plenty of men. Unfortunately, most were majoring in insecurity, just starting up the corporate ladder. To her surprise, many reminded her of Dallas, despite cleaner fingernails and a decent wardrobe. She didn't meet anybody that reminded her of Dan. Or her father, for that matter. What recommended Price was that he was the first quiet man she met in the city, that and the fact that he wanted to take her out to breakfast. They had three six-thirty A.M. dates before he explained he was a professional ballplayer. Night games ruled out dinner, the theater, the movies and espresso in the Village. Anne didn't mind. She had never got the hang of letting men she didn't like spend money on her.

Before being traded to the expansion Mets, Price was the property of eight other major league teams, though he'd spent the majority of his career in the minors. She met him when things were going well. The regular Met third baseman had been sidelined with an injury, and Price was installed for what he imagined would be the rest of the season. For every home game, Price left tickets for Anne and Randall at the will-call window. The boy was cautious, but given the avalanche of baseballs and autographs found it difficult to object to the new man in his mother's life. He would've preferred the Yankee third baseman, but Price was some kind of ballplayer and the Mets were some kind of team and Randall was some kind of impressed. And Price wasn't nearly as hapless as most of his teammates. He was enjoying his best season, hitting a solid 240 and getting his body in front of the screamers that invariably whistled down the third-base line off Met pitching. He knew how to play within himself and seldom tried to do anything his chunky body wasn't capable of. Not a bad body, Anne thought, though it usually sported at least one technicolor bruise, now in the center of his chest, now the left shoulder, now the top of the thigh. Price claimed they didn't hurt, but the center of the bruised area was always leprous white at the point of impact, radiating outward in concentric circles—dark purple, blue, green, yellow.

By the middle of August the Mets had been out of contention for months and Price, in the middle of what was for him a hitting streak, was unaccountably benched. To Price the move defied all logic. No one on the team was playing better ball, and his replacement, a young kid from the Dominican Republic yanked all the way up from double-A ball, seemed always on the verge of fainting. He made the sign of the cross before every pitch, clearly praying the ball would be hit to someone else. It was age, of course. Price was thirty-four, and a middle-aged journeyman infielder had no part in the

team's future. If the Mets were going to continue losing, it was better to lose with nineteen-year-olds. Price
worked all of this out on the bench in September, and
once the season was over, he concluded sensibly that
there was no point in worrying all winter. He was seeing
a girl he liked and who liked being shown around the
city and introduced to the people he knew. He liked
the boy, too. Price would stay in shape during the off-
season and with luck get himself traded to a contending
team in need of a solid veteran.

They had a nice winter. A native Californian, Price
had never liked New York, but for sightseeing it was
a good city. Anne and Randall were enthusiastic and
grateful. He thought little about baseball and didn't
fulfill his resolution to keep in shape. The bruises gradually disappeared, along with a dozen or so aches, and
he easily convinced himself that he was mending, not
loafing. When it came time to go to Florida for spring
training, he knew he'd have to work hard. But he'd
always had to work hard.

He called Anne in March with the bad news. "This
doesn't mean much," he said of his release. "It's probably good. I'll be better off with another team." He'd
stay in Florida for a few days, maybe a week, since
people had to know where to find him. "Cheer up.
Come May, I'll probably be a Yankee," he told Randall.
"Boyer looks shaky this year." He was back in New
York a week later, though, and on opening day he took
Randall to the ballpark. He paid for the tickets. "Later
on, when the double headers start to stack up——" he
told the boy, letting the thought trail off.

Anne took her two-weeks' vacation in July. They
decided on Maine and, en route, Mohawk, for the sake
of Randall and his grandparents. Anne prepared Price

for a cool reception. During the past year she'd written to her parents several times about Price, but when her mother wrote back, she never mentioned him. And when Anne dropped his name on the telephone, Mrs. Grouse said, "Who, dear?" Nevertheless, he fully expected to win the affections of Anne's parents. He was frequently told he was a charming man, and had good reason to believe it; he could think of no one he'd ever wanted to like him who didn't. In roughly half an hour after they arrived in Mohawk, he had Mrs. Grouse eating out of his hand. It was the *idea* that she had objected to—this person who was "with" her "married" daughter. Price himself, Mrs. Grouse discovered, was not objectionable in the least. He was neither haughty nor aloof, nor superior nor any of the things she had assumed he must be, given the fact that her daughter had selected and spoken highly of him. A five-pound box of candy, a light kiss on the cheek and she suddenly had a new son-in-law, if that's where things were going.

Mather Grouse was another story. Traveling to a different city or two every week, Price had developed a casual forthrightness with strangers, and to make fast friends with a bartender took him all of two minutes and by the end of the evening he was drinking on the house. Unfortunately, Mather Grouse was not a bartender and for every ounce of Price's easy charm, Mather Grouse had two ounces of New England reserve. Only time—in goodly amount—could change their fundamental relationship as strangers, and the fact that Price came with a warm introduction and recommendation from Mather Grouse's own daughter did not alter a thing.

Fortunately, Price had known better than to push, especially since they were visiting for only one afternoon. Anne hadn't wanted to raise the issue of sleeping arrangements by spending the night in her parents' house. They would find a hotel in Saratoga that night and drive into New England the next day after a nice breakfast, perhaps on the same white porch where she and Dallas had stopped, in what now seemed a different life. Price was agreeable. He was perhaps the most agreeable man she knew, so agreeable that even Mather Grouse was having a tough time remaining stolid. Her mother squeezed fresh lemonade and they all sat outside on the porch, Mrs. Grouse and Price chatting like long-separated cousins at a family reunion, the others content to listen to their banter. After a while Price and Randall, who'd begun to talk about playing Little League next summer, went down to the front lawn so Price could show him how to put the tag on a sliding runner. Throughout the summer Price had taught him something different each day, and Anne suspected that during the two upcoming weeks the boy would probably miss these lessons more than anything.

"Here's the base," Price said. "You're the runner."

Randall slid several times, and Price demonstrated the footwork around the bag and showed him how to keep from getting hurt. "If he comes in spikes down, like he's supposed to, fine. If he comes in spikes up, step out of the way and step on him with yours."

Anne, watching her father, saw Mather Grouse's face cloud over, and when Price and Randall returned, leaving behind them a small brown patch on the manicured lawn, her father spoke. "Do you think it's wise to teach a young man to break the rules?"

"No, sir, I don't," Price replied. "Every player should know how to protect himself, that's all."

"Isn't it up to the umpire to enforce the rules?"

"That's true enough. But sometimes they miss what's going on. Sometimes they like the guy who's breaking the rules. The game goes a lot smoother when everybody knows better than to take liberties."

"So the end justifies the means."

Price shrugged. He was comfortable enough with that philosophy, but clever enough to know it wouldn't win him any points with Mather Grouse. "How would you handle it?"

"I would report the infraction to the umpire."

Price smiled. "And that would stop your leg bleeding?"

"Perhaps not," Mather Grouse said. "But you would have the satisfaction of knowing that you played honorably."

Price's grin broadened a little. "I never thought of it that way."

Anne smiled too. She suddenly realized she was very fond of Price. In fact, she might even be in love.

35

As usual, Dallas stopped at the OTB on his way to work, just long enough to pick up the sheets and see what was going on. The hard core were already there, milling around, scratching their three-day beards, looking for a sign. Several said hello and asked Dallas what was happening. He had no idea, and believing him, they asked who the hell did. The track, Dallas told them. The track had a pretty good idea what was going on. Untemeyer, the bookie, came in, caught the end of the conversation and smiled.

"Meyer here knows how to beat the track," Dallas said.

"Go soak your head," Untemeyer said. "Younger the Outlaw. I'm going to have you raided one of these days. I got connections."

"You also got thirty million dollars in quarters buried someplace. How about letting somebody else make a buck or two. You gotta have it all?"

"I don't get shit anymore, now that it's all taxed and legal," the old bookie said. "Younger the Outlaw."

He tried to duck away, but Dallas was too quick. Catching him by the elbow, Dallas held up the man's hand so that the ring on Untemeyer's stubby finger caught the light. "When you die, I'll be waiting right around the corner with a hacksaw," said Dallas, making a ripping sound in the back of his throat. Untemeyer was tired of the old joke, but the other men, who'd seen the routine just as many times, still enjoyed it.

"I'll swallow the goddam thing," Untemeyer growled, "before I let you get your hands on it."

"I'd get it anyway," Dallas smiled. "You ever gut a trout?"

"You probably would, you bastard." He gestured toward the door.

Dallas and the bookie stepped outside, where Untemeyer had to puff harder on his cigar to effectively foul the air. Even in the hottest weather, Dallas had never seen him when he wasn't wearing a baggy suit, usually black alpaca, with a slightly yellowed white shirt and black tie.

"You were married to that Grouse girl for a while, right?

Dallas nodded. "So?"

"So nothing," said Untemeyer. "See her much?"

"I bet I haven't run into her three times in the last five years. Last year, at my kid's high school graduation, was the last time."

"The old lady still alive?"

"Her mother? You couldn't kill her with a hammer. What is this—you thinking about getting hitched again?"

"Take off."

"Not a bad idea, Meyer."

"Get moving."

"You're never too old."

"Like hell. I'm too old. You too, prob'ly."

"Too smart, you mean."

"In a hundred years, maybe."

"Take care, Meyer."

"Sure thing."

"And take care of that ring."

When Dallas closed the door behind him, the telephone was ringing. It was Benny D., his former boss, wanting to put a yard and a half down on a horse running at Santa Anita. Dallas found the horse and whistled. "I'll have to check."

"What?" said Benny D.

"What, your ass. You know what."

"What?"

"The son-of-bitch'll go off twenty to one. That's a lot of action."

"You booking horses or not?"

"I'll get back to you."

Dallas tossed his coat in the corner and turned on the television. The room was big, once the offices of a closed-down department store, and it looked bare with just the sofa and television, and a black phone sitting on the stray kitchen chair. There was a good view from the curtainless window—the length of Main Street from the Four Corners all the way up to Fourth, and from the third floor Dallas could even see Myrtle Park. This was pretty much the same view he had from his high-school apartment, which was only three doors down before the wrecker got it.

Benny D. must be on to something. He was a regular, popping for four or five bets a day. The double always. A race here and there, the triple. He was pretty sharp, too, but he usually bet five or ten, usually at Belmont. Only twice before had he popped for a hundred. Both times at the California track. Both times winners.

"Hello, sweetheart," Dallas said to John's secretary. "Put him on, will you?"

"He isn't free—"

"Put him on anyway."

In a minute the lawyer's voice crackled on the line. "What?"

"Good morning to you, too."

"It's not a particularly good morning."

"Have it your way. Benny D. again."

"How much?"

"Hundred and a half."

"Take it."

"Twenty to one. Guess where."

"Take it," John barked.

"I could lay off part."

"What the hell for?"

"Suit yourself."

He dialed Benny D. "You're in the book, pal."

"I'm not your pal. You walked out on me."

"I said I was going to. Why don't you pay attention?"

"I'm the boss in that garage."

"Good. So tell me: What's with you and Santa Anita?"

"It's my lucky track. When are you coming back?"

"When you learn to stay out of it."

"It's my goddamn garage!"

"Not for long, if you keep betting twenty-to-one shots."

"I know what I'm doing. Why do you want to work for that asshole?"

"Bye."

Around one, Dallas called the Mohawk Grill's unlisted number. "We don't deliver," Harry growled. "Drag your lazy ass across the street."

"The phone won't stop ringing long enough."

"I can't spare anybody."

"When you can."

"Forget it."

But around one-thirty Harry sent one of the girls over with coffee and a sandwich. She was Dallas's favorite because she was built and had a nice way about her. On the whole he didn't have much use for Gaffneys, but he liked this one. "When are you and I going to step out?" he teased.

"I'm a married lady."

"He's a stiff, honey."

"Tell me."

"I got a weak heart anyhow," Dallas said, leering at her good-naturedly.

"Guess who I saw yesterday?"

"How should I know?"

"Randall Younger."

Dallas frowned. "He's in Buffalo."

"That's what you know. He's got real long hair."

"No."

"Him I'd go out with."

He listened to the receding sound of her footsteps and watched her dodge traffic in the street below. Feeling suddenly nervous, he took the phone off the hook and walked over to the OTB, laying off a hundred of Benny D.'s bet. If John didn't like it, too goddamn bad. He'd like getting nailed for three grand even less. Not that it wouldn't serve him right.

The phone rang the rest of the afternoon and Dallas didn't have a chance to think about anything. Benny D.'s horse ran like the wind. At six-thirty he closed up and went over to the Mohawk Grill for a hamburg steak and onions. He had just started eating when John came in looking sick, his shirttail hanging out from under his vest. He took the stool next to Dallas, who resumed his meal. "That fucking California horse *ran*, can you believe it?"

"What'd you expect?"

"I expected it to lose. Everybody expected it to lose. That's how come it was *twenty* to *one*."

"Everybody except Benny D.," Dallas paused to swallow, "who's done the same thing to you twice already."

"How could he know anything about Santa Anita, of all places?"

Dallas pushed his plate away. "Harry," he said. "A man comes in and wants to bet you a hundred bucks he can cut the ace of spades from a deck of cards. What do you do?"

Harry didn't bother to turn around. "Tell him to take a hike."

Dallas turned to John, "There you go. You don't need law school to figure that out."

John looked even sicker, "All right. Piss on me. I should've listened."

"Fortunately, I didn't. I laid off a hundred."

"No."

"I ought to keep it, too."

The lawyer looked like he'd just given birth. "Let me buy you dinner."

"I can buy my own dinner."

"I owe you."

"You'll end up owing everybody before you're through."

"You're all right," John said.

Dallas felt all right, too, and ordered a piece of pie.

John was no sooner gone than Benny D. came in and clapped Dallas on the back. "Come back and work for me," he said. "Your present employer isn't likely to stay in business much longer."

"He does all right," Dallas said, explaining what he'd done.

Benny D. was disgusted. "Why help him out? Fuck guys like him."

"You're probably right." Dallas didn't like John on principle. His old man gave the kid everything and bailed him out of every jam so he could act like a big wheel. Dallas couldn't figure it, either. The old man had worked for everything he got. How much fun was there in watching sonny boy piss it all away? "Next time I'll leave him alone."

"How'd *you* do today?" Benny D. said.

"A winner at Santa Anita."

"Prick."

They drank a cup of coffee and left together. "There's a game tonight."

Dallas shrugged. "Somebody said my kid's in town. I thought I might go see him."

"That reminds me. You ever see your sister-in-law?"

"Loraine?"

Benny D. nodded. "I hear she's out to The Velvet Pussycat all the while. Somebody said John was putting it to her."

"You're kidding."

"Gaff had to take her home in the cruiser last weekend."

Dallas shook his head. The world had a way of surprising him, though most of the time he could figure things. Like today. He'd figured everything right all day long. But even on the best of days there were things nobody could count on. His kid was in town and had long hair, his sister-in-law was hanging out in the biggest dive in town. "Why was that?"

"Too drunk to navigate, is what I heard. Let's play some poker."

"Nah."

"Come on. It's good for you when you're low."

"I don't know."

"We'll split a bottle of bourbon, have a hell of a time. And next week you'll come back to work for me. That John's no good."

"He's all right."

"But not like brothers. You and him never busted your balls together."

That much was true. Before Benny D. inherited the dealership, he and Dallas had knocked themselves out together on the road crew. They'd also chased women together, even caught a few who weren't in the mood to run away. Both had been fresh from recent divorces, and neither one all that fastidious. After Anne, Dallas enjoyed women who called their pussies pussies. Benny D. had never known any other kind. He was all right, too, and they went way back. Dallas had damn near killed him once and Benny D. never even held a grudge.

They took a good belt out of the bourbon bottle and climbed the dark stairs all the way to the third floor, toward the sound of gruff male laughter. "I thought your kid was in college someplace," Benny D. said.

"He is—or was, anyway."

"You gotta pay for that?"

Dallas shook his head. "Scholarship."

"Good deal. He'll turn out real smooth, like your friend John."

"John'll be here," Dallas warned.

Benny D. laughed. "I hope to Christ he is."

36

Their vacation in Maine was blessed by fresh warm weather, gentle ocean breezes and the leisure to enjoy them. Price made good his promise to forget baseball. He bought the paper every day and checked the box scores, which told him who was playing and how well. But he didn't introduce the subject into conversation, and seemed content to massage suntan oil into Anne's shoulderblades. By the time they got back to the city it would be August, when each team was allowed to expand its roster for the stretch drive; if anything happened, it would happen then. He rose early each morning and ran on the beach, showered, went out for pastries and returned in time to watch Anne wake up. To tan deeply took her no time at all, and her dark skin contrasted beautifully on the white sheets. Most mornings they didn't get to the pastries right away.

"Let's get married and have kids," Price said the afternoon of their last day. The proposal didn't surprise Anne as much as Price's tone. He might just as well've been suggesting they stroll down the beach for a bag of clams.

"Sure," Anne said. "Why not. Maybe."

"I always know where I stand with you. I like that."

Anne picked up a handful of white sand and rubbed

it into Price's oiled chest, making a paste-hair mixture. "I hated being pregnant."

"Don't be silly."

"Besides, if we married you'd already have a son."

At first Price didn't know what to say to that, and Anne could sense his reservations. "Men want sons of their own. I can't explain why."

"Right."

"No, really," he insisted. "Besides. I got gypped out of Randy's early years. And he's already got bad habits."

Price was so serious that Anne couldn't help but smile. "What a crummy thing to say."

He rolled over on his side and used the corner of the towel to daub the mud from his chest. "Why do you call him Randall instead of Randy?"

"Is that his bad habit?"

"He throws sidearm. I can't break him of it."

"And that prevents him from being a true son of yours."

"I guess not," Price admitted, grinning suddenly at his own seriousness. "But sidearm is a tough way to go through life. I'd spare him if I could."

"Did it ever occur to you that he might end up a lawyer?"

"There are sidearmed lawyers, too. The majority, come to think of it."

"You have the soul of a satirist."

"Bullshit," he said. "I have the soul of a third baseman."

August came and went. In the middle of September Price took a job as a bartender in a Manhattan hotel where he'd worked several off-seasons. But as the World

Series approached, he became increasingly morose, and in the end he refused to watch. They spoke no more about marriage, and each seemed to fear that the other would bring the subject up, if only to clear the air. Their work schedules didn't mesh and they spent fewer evenings together. At times Price seemed more interested in the boy.

In February he got a call from the Met organization. They wanted to know if he'd thought about the possibility of becoming an advance scout. He said he'd get back to them.

"Why not?" Anne said.

"Because I've got another year in me, maybe two. I wasn't in shape last spring, thanks to all the screwing around. I'll be ready this time. I feel good."

He was running and was up to two hundred situps a day. There was blood on his shorts from the floor's friction on his tailbone. He'd made some calls and two teams had promised him a look. "Jesus Christ," somebody said. "I thought you'd hung it up."

Then something happened. The morning before he was supposed to go to Florida, he came by early to take Anne out to breakfast. The "Today Show" was on, and Price stopped to watch a segment on spring training. A nice-looking young black boy, all of seventeen, was interviewed at length. Price watched it all, then suggested to hell with breakfast. They made love and right from the bed Price called the front office and accepted the scouting job.

Then he was gone. Perhaps because she didn't see him for weeks at a time, Anne noticed the change each time he came home. He put on weight, especially in the face, and his hard, battlescarred body began to look soft. When he was in New York, he worked with Randall every day. The boy was determined to try out for Little League. He seemed not to have extraordinary talent, but Price said talent wasn't the issue, was never the issue. One afternoon he brought Randall back to Anne's apartment with a broken nose that had swollen so badly that his eyes were mere slits. Price himself was white-faced, but he pushed the boy roughly toward the sink. "Stop crying," he said. "It was just a bad hop. Life is full of 'em."

Anne wet a washcloth and gently bathed Randall's bloddy chin and lips. Both eyes would blacken, that much she could tell. In a few minutes the boy was quiet, the pain reduced to throbbing numbness. Price poured himself a cup of coffee and sat down as if he would have gone right to the floor if the chair hadn't been there. "What happened?" Anne said finally.

Price needed only to look at her to know that the question was an accusation. "Like I said, a bad hop." He looked down at the linoleum.

"You hit it too hard," Randall said dully.

"Is that what you're going to tell the batter," Price asked. "Don't be a baby."

The baseball lay on the table between them. Randall picked it up and hurled it as hard as he could. Though he was only ten years old, they were within six feet of each other and the ball caught Price below the cheekbone. The surprise sent him over backwards in the chair and onto the kitchen floor. He started to rub the throbbing spot on his cheek, then caught himself. Before Anne could get between them, Price, his face distorted, dragged the boy from where he sat and pounced, his knees pinning Randall to the kitchen tile. For an instant Anne thought he was actually going to hit the boy with his raised fist. But then the fist went to his cheek and he rolled off Randall as if someone had snatched him from behind. He crawled all the way to the corner on his hands and knees and began to sob. Randall stood up his hands clenched as if he expected another attack. Anne went to him, but he pushed her away. This was between him and Price, and the expression of hopeless defiance on the boy's face terrified her—so black, so unconscious of pain, so unwilling to be consoled.

He never entirely lost that expression, it occurred to her. There was traffic now as she neared Albany, and the idea of driving all the way to New York for a fancy breakfast had lost most of its appeal. She turned off at the Northway Exit, then missed a turn that would have put her back on the Thruway heading home. To hell with it, she thought. The road she was on had to lead somewhere. They all went somewhere.

She had seen Price only once after the day he broke Randall's nose. He'd gone back on the road the next day and never called. Someone told her a few months later that he wasn't living in New York any more. In a way she had lost both of them at once. Randall had not wanted her to protect him, and even when the boy was healed, he never again encouraged her to hug or kiss him. She sometimes thought that perhaps he had seen her as a woman for the first time that day. Or as just a woman. Or maybe as the cause of it all, because she was a woman. He looked at her strangely, almost as if he had walked in and caught her and Price in the act of love. She didn't think he stopped caring for her. He just seemed embarrassed to.

Two years later, she saw Price again. In the meantime Dan's accident had occurred, and she used her father's illness as an excuse to return to Mohawk. One Saturday afternoon shortly after her visit, she came home from work to find the television on and Randall slipping into his room. And there was Price. The show was "Speaking of Sports." He looked trimmer than the last time she had seen him, and he acquitted himself well, far better than the other men, most of whom were clearly afraid of the camera. Price said some funny things, and when he laughed it was in response to the funny thing, not to himself for having said it. Anne was happy to see him again, so well, but was surprised to discover how little she'd missed him.

Now the rain was hard. The windshield wipers could hardly keep up, and Anne had no idea where she was. She was on two-lane black-top, and the occasional neon signs along either side advertised businesses that were dark and deserted. She could only guess that she was heading in the general direction of Mohawk. Finally the rain was so severe that she didn't dare to stay on the road, so she pulled off into the half-deserted parking lot of a shabby motel. She sat there for nearly ten minutes, feeling odd and hopeless until she recognized this as the motel where she and Dan had come some twenty years before. There was a new sign out front, but she was certain. The road was busier then, and the buildings that lined it more prosperous. One needed no crystal ball to see into their future now. There were only twelve units, and when Anne could not remember which one she and Dan had taken she began to cry and couldn't stop. When she awoke, though the light was gray in the east and she was very cold, Anne felt better. For some time she couldn't shake the conviction that if she just sat there long enough, Dan would drive up, get out of the car—the same one he'd been driving twenty years ago—and take her by the hand. He would know which room was theirs, or perhaps it wouldn't matter.

37

Officer Gaffney's brother Rory lives in the last house on Division Street, a dead end on the other side of the highway. Technically he's outside city limits, and Officer Gaffney isn't supposed to take the cruiser into the county unless he's in pursuit. Still, it's only a matter of a few hundred yards and no one around to report him. So he drives on up the hill, switching the headlights and ignition off and coasting to a stop. A light's on in the rear of the trailer.

The policeman closes the door quietly and puffs up the drive. Never trim, he has lately put on considerable weight, confident that no one will give him grief in his last year before retirement. He stops at the house to peer into the living room. His brother is stretched out on the Lazy Boy, watching television and wriggling his fat toes in the glow from the screen, the only light in the house. After catching his breath, the policeman takes the path through the trees to the trailer, making more noise than he'd like and cursing under his breath. The bedroom window curtain doesn't quite reach the sill. Inside, the girl is fully clothed. The air tonight is chill, especially for late April. Officer Gaffney watches for a few minutes, hoping, then retraces his steps through

the trees, fearful his brother will see the car and wonder.

Rory Gaffney looks up when his brother comes in
but stays in the Lazy Boy, apparently indifferent to
company. The policeman, at fifty-nine, is nearly ten
years his brother's junior, but if anything looks older.
"Thought I heard a car."

Officer Gaffney flips on the black police band radio
before sitting down. Nothing but static, and with luck
he'll get to relax an hour or so.

"Turn that down," his brother says.

"I don't want to miss anything," the policeman says.

"Sit in the car and you won't."

Officer Gaffney gets up and turns the radio down,
a little, then returns to his seat. They watch television
for a while, neither man reacting to anything on the
screen. "I like that show," the policeman says when it's
over.

Rory Gaffney says, "Well?"

"He's back,"

"That's what I heard."

"Harry give him a job at the grill washing dishes."

Rory Gaffney's eyes grow small, but he says nothing.

"Got this big new machine, Harry does. Showed me
today."

"Then what's he need with my boy?"

"Takes somebody to stack the dishes and push the
buttons. Harry figures Billy can handle that much. I
bet he can, too."

"It ever occur to Harry maybe I could use some help
around here?"

Officer Gaffney finds himself stumped. "That girl's
husband ever come home?"

Rory Gaffney looks at his brother until he gets up and turns off the police band. It's time the policeman returned to work anyway. It occurs to him that the girl's husband must be a crazy son-of-a-bitch to run off, but something stops him from saying so. He himself has never married, and lately he has begun to wish he had. Maybe he'd have been a better husband and father than the ones he ends up chauffeuring home after the bars close. He'd have treated a wife right, and the kids too. He didn't blame his brother's wife for taking off. There was a time when he'd also felt like it, and Rory was only his brother. Sometimes, he still felt like running away, but there was nowhere to go. "Harry'll be good to him," he ventures. "Harry likes him."

His brother switches off the set with the remote control, leaving them in the dark. "You got something on your mind, Walt?"

"Me?" His voice in the dark sounds strange. A couple seconds of silence and he can't stand it any more. "I just figure you should leave the boy alone, that's all."

"That's all?"

"Yeah, that's about it."

Officer Gaffney backs out and closes the door. He's been afraid of his brother all his life. He wishes he weren't, but after so many years, there doesn't seem to be anything he can do about it. Inside the trailer, the girl is now wearing a robe and has a towel wrapped around her head like a turban. Though the cold has grown even sharper, Officer Gaffney, crouching outside the trailer, begins to sweat. From the direction of the house comes a sound and he backs deeper into the shadows. Heavy footsteps approach through last fall's brittle leaves. The policeman is about to stand and face his brother, admit his transgression and beg forgiveness, when Rory Gaffney knocks on the door. Inside the girl gathers her loose terrycloth robe tight to her chest. She leaves the bedroom, but he can still see her down the hallway and her voice is audible through the thin trailer walls. His brother's low voice is lost in the outside air. "I'm fine," she's saying. "You go on home."

His brother says something.

"It's locked," the girl says. "And that's the way it's staying."

The trailer jiggles.

"You're gonna wake the baby."

Officer Gaffney feels weak and sits down on the cold ground. For a long time he stares at nothing, and comes out of it only when the door up at the house slams shut. Again the woods are still. He gets to his feet with exaggerated caution, as quietly as he can. The girl has taken off the terricloth robe. She is the most beautiful thing he has ever seen and he is crying quietly, wanting to tell her so. He watches the girl brush her long straight hair in front of the small dresser mirror. He would like to believe in reincarnation, would like to live all over again.

The wind changes direction, and the policeman hears the car radio crackling angrily way down the road. Friday night in Mohawk.

38

Summer had never been Mrs. Grouse's favorite season. Though she never complained, the heat made her flushed and irritable. Even as a child she couldn't understand summer's appeal. In mid-July, tar shimmering on the roads, her mother would add to the pulsing heat with oven-cooked dinners. The kitchen would throb and glow red while Mrs. Grouse wondered if it might not be the center of all the world's heat. The kitchen could not contain it all, and the upstairs bedroom where she and two of her sisters slept would remain stifling, undisturbed by any cooling breeze, until well after midnight. Mrs. Grouse's mother was not the kind of woman to surrender to weather; in fact, she taught her daughters that the righteous surrendered to God alone. And so, in the middle of August when the mercury climbed into the nineties and dogs fought viciously in the dust—and did worse than fighting, the hair standing straight up on the backs of their necks—her mother's oven would give birth to steaming casseroles.

Mrs. Grouse always remembered her mother fondly, especially since that good woman's final righteous surrender, and constantly wished she had been able to impress her mother's virtues on her own daughter Anne, whose habits of premature surrender were, to a woman like Mrs. Grouse, alarming. During the summer, Anne simply refused to cook a real meal, subsisting on salads and fruit. Mrs. Grouse failed to see how a person could give so much ground and still have the necessary strength to wage life's urgent battles.

Summer was full of horrors. Mrs. Grouse hated everything that crawled or flew. For a woman in her seventies, she was lethal with a flyswatter and her vigilance, where summer's insects were concerned, unsurpassed. Every spring, when the markets ran specials on Raid, Mrs. Grouse bought a brace of large cans, and soaked the baseboards daily. Consequently Anne refused to enter the downstairs flat unless all the windows were thrown open, an inference Mrs. Grouse resented deeply.

One afternoon in late June, Mrs. Grouse was sweeping the front porch when she noticed something that greatly attracted her interest. For two days it had rained, and the narrow strip of lawn between the house and the sidewalk was moist and green. When Mrs. Grouse examined it closely, however, she noticed thousands of small holes, as if some demented child with a pointed stick had spent the entire night systematically poking the ground until it was uniformly perforated. That's what they were, all right. Holes. She was on her hands and knees studying them when Mr. Murphy, who lived two doors down, discovered her. "Nightcrawlers," he said, peering over his spectacles.

Mrs. Grouse frowned up at him.

"Rain brings them up," he explained. "Worms."

39

There is a new sign above the Mohawk Grill. It is much larger than the old one and this, the new, sports fancy calligraphy. *The Grotto*, it reads. Beneath, in smaller script, *Beverly and Harold Saunders, Your Hosts.* The lunch counter hasn't changed, except that the cash register has been moved near the front door, where it is guarded by Harry's wife, who has the reddest hair Officer Gaffney has ever seen. She reminds him of a bulldog that suspects you have a bone—its bone. A redheaded bulldog.

The policeman has never been in the new restaurant, which is separate from the old room and dimly lit. He prefers the lunch counter, where the lighting is good and men can talk to one another over the tops of their racing forms, should they feel the need. Next door is mostly for women who like to eat salads in what the redhead calls "an intimate setting." The girl is a waitress in the next room, but she's in and out of the grill to pick up orders. When she leans in front of him, Officer Gaffney can smell her and see the outline of her brassiere through the fabric of her uniform. Some days she doesn't even wear a brassiere, and he then feels a hollow longing that makes him reconsider his life and wonder about many things. Sometimes he even envies Harry, who at least has The Bulldog.

"Hi, sweetheart," he says when the girl comes over to collect a burger and side order of fries. He tries to make the "sweetheart" sound casual; after all, they're related. But somehow he always sounds a little like a beggar. "How's the little one?"—though he knows the baby is fine, remembers it tugging at her breast. "Hear from that no-'count of yours?"

But she's gone again. If the girl was aware of him, she didn't think him important enough to answer. Or perhaps she's just too busy. Officer Gaffney orders a hamburger deluxe, and tells Harry to hold the onions. "Two more weeks, Harry," he observes. "Don't seem possible."

John, the lawyer, seated two stools down, looks up from his soup. "Somebody'll steal the traffic light for sure."

"You figure you'll write your memoirs, Gaff?" somebody says. "Like the Blue Knight?"

"The Blue Whale," someone suggests.

The lawyer's smiling. "You figure you'll get out of shape with nothing to do?"

"I'll have plenty to do," the policeman says. "Don't you worry about me."

"*I* won't, Gaff," the lawyer says.

"Like what?" somebody calls from the end of the counter.

"Like plenty."

"You could drive the getaway car for your brother," John says.

"Or for you," Harry observes.

"No tip today," John says, "*Harold.*"

"Today, my ass," snaps Harry, alias Harold Your Host.

"*Har*-ry!" scolds The Bulldog from the cash register.

"Yeah, Harold," John says. "I'm shocked."

"Kiss my—"

"*Har*-ry?"

The door to the kitchen swings open and the Younger boy emerges. He draws two cokes and disappears with them. Officer Gaffney catches a glimpse of Wild Bill stacking glasses in a green plastic tray on the stainless steel Hobart runway. To keep from thinking, he says, "You ought to have that kid wear a hair net or something."

Harry ignores him, once again regretting having taken on his wife as cashier.

Officer Gaffney is suspicious of this Younger and has been for years, ever since the day the old hospital came down and he was found there in the wreck of a lobby, looking as if God himself had set him down where no human boy could've possibly arrived on his own, what with all the bricks and plaster coming down. Two of the men who'd gone into the building, first for the boy and then for Wild Bill, were hurt by the falling debris, but there he had stood, all of fourteen years old, and not a scratch on him. The policeman was alone in thinking the boy's story dubious. The town had insisted on making a hero out of him, running his picture in the paper, getting him on the Albany TV news. But there was plently that didn't add up, and Gaffney was too good a policeman not to wonder. The boy had to have a reason for going into the hospital, just like he had to have a reason for turning up to take a kitchen job for two bucks an hour. This young man bore watching, even if Officer Gaffney could do the watching only for another two weeks.

The door swung open and the girl came back in. She tossed a plastic tray on top of the stack and was gone again into the kitchen on the door's backswing. Wild Bill was still standing at the Hobart, surrounded by tubs of dirty dishes. Instead of stacking them in the waiting trays, he had stooped to peer up into an inverted water glass at a single ice cube sticking to its bottom, defying gravity. To the policeman he had always seemed doglike, even as a boy. That look of expectant loyalty.

His brother had hit the boy the way you hit a dog that day. First striking him, then growling "Get over here!" when he tried to slink away, the boy returning to take another slap in the head. "You can't make me!" he said over and over again, while his father repeated "What did I tell you!"—as if those were the only two sentences they knew between them. This time Officer Gaffney himself had brought the boy home from Mountain Avenue. Standing there was all he'd been doing, not that he had any business doing even that. "You stay the hell out of this, Walt. So help me. You stay out." And so he had gone outside to wait, but out there it was even worse and he went back inside again. By then the boy's one eye was swollen shut and his brother was red-faced from hitting, but still the boy kept saying it. And still Rory Gaffney kept growling "Come here!" and instead of disobeying this order the way he did the other, he did as he was told, stupid boy, kept coming back, his eye shut and ugly, his lips swollen up thick and purple, now screaming "You can't make me!" At this pass Rory Gaffney, who'd beaten his son into this condition open-handed, closed his fist. The boy saw it, but was too sluggish to do more than turn his head. When the blow caught him on the temple, the boy dropped to his knees. For support he lunged forward and hugged his father's knees. Then both father and son were quiet, and Officer Gaffney left them like that and wandered out onto the porch. A while later, Rory Gaffney came out, blood on his hands and pants, and collapsed into the chair next to his brother. His eyes were dull. "I think I hurt my boy, Walt. That's what I think."

Officer Gaffney went inside to look. The boy lay asleep on the sofa where his father had put him. At first the policeman thought he was dead. But finally he got the boy to sit and open the eye that would open, but he couldn't keep the boy awake and finally he gave up. Rory Gaffney watched from the doorway. "You better take him to the hospital," he said. "He's hurt, Walt."

"Wait," the policeman said, unable to imagine himself carrying the boy in, having to explain, having to point the finger at his own brother. "Wait. We don't know. He may come around if we leave him be."

"I think I hurt my boy, that's what I think." Rory Gaffney said.

"You don't know. . . ."

Officer Gaffney has not wanted to remember all this again, but there it is in the bottom of his coffee cup. He hates himself once again, along with the Younger boy who had stepped in when God himself had seemed to decree that Wild Bill should die and leave off tormenting. For some time now, the policeman has understood that when he said "Wait!" he'd made the choice of his life, though he hadn't suspected it at the time, or even for years afterward. "No. Let's wait," he had said, and later, when it was clear there was no way to hide what had happened, it wasn't Rory Gaffney who'd figured out how to, but himself. He had instructed his brother where to take the boy, what to do, how long to stay away, what to tell people when he came back—all the while thinking that what he ought to do was use the gun he'd worn strapped to his hip for so long he'd forgotten it was there. Shoot him, he'd thought. Then the boy. Then yourself.

The trouble was, he could only hate himself.

The kitchen door swings open and Wild Bill emerges with his empty coke glass. He is returning it to Harry, whence it came. He cannot figure that the thing to do is to put it in the rack with the other dirty glasses. Instead he puts it in the tub under the counter. "You stay in the kitchen," Harry says. Through the swinging door Officer Gaffney is watching the kitchen. The Younger boy is slicing a head of lettuce with a gleaming knife. When the girl glides by, she kisses him on the back of the neck. He catches her before she can get away and kisses her on the lips, the knife resting along her flank. The policeman sees all this before the door settles shut, and he keeps on seeing it.

40

"I never *heard* of such a thing," said Milly, glower-ing at the patch of ground as she leaned on Mrs. Grouse's arm. "It's enough to make you go live in the highrise."

Dan had just dropped the old woman off for a visit. She'd been released from the hospital that morning, and Diana, who usually accompanied her mother on such visits, had collapsed into bed around mid-morning, and Dan had refused to let Milly wake her up. "How will I get up those steps?" she wanted to know.

"Then stay home," Dan advised. "But you aren't waking her up."

"I guess I can manage," the old woman said. "I always do."

"Right," Dan had muttered.

The two old women now supported each other, two sloping sides to the narrow based isosceles triangle. "How big are they," asked Milly.

Mrs. Grouse admitted she'd never actually seen one.

"They're turning the grass all yellow," Milly ob-served, pointing to several leprous patches of dying grass where her sister had sprayed concentrated doses of Raid.

"They come at night," Mrs. Grouse said. "Out of the ground."

"You poor dear," her sister said as they teetered their way up the porch steps.

41

When Randall rolled over to look at the girl, the trailer rocked. She was frowning at him again, the way she did whenever they made love. Pretty often, lately. "Quit that," he said.

"What?" She did a pushup, and looked down at him. She was the most charmingly immodest girl he'd ever known.

"Quit that too," he said when she attacked his neck.

"Why are all you men scared of hickies?"

Randall didn't know. "Don't change the subject."

She made her serious face. "What was the subject?"

"The subject is why you always look at me like that."

"I'm trying to figure out what you want with me."

"Some people would say I just had it."

She put her head on his chest and traced her index finger along his abdomen. "Not you," she said.

"You tell me, then. What?"

The girl sighed. "I don't know. Something weird, probably, knowing you."

Why did people say things like that about him, Randall wondered. It was as if someone had started a rumor when he was a baby and by now everybody had heard it. He never seemed strange to himself, despite the conventional wisdom. They lay quietly, and the girl was nearly asleep, her head on his chest, when the baby cried and she got up. This was Randall's first time in a trailer, and this particular one seemed so precariously balanced that whenever anybody moved, his first instinct was to grab for a support.

"I know what I like about you," she said when she returned, yawning, from the baby's bedroom. "You never fall asleep after we screw."

"You do."

"Somebody has to be first."

"I never thought of that."

"Night." She closed her eyes and went right to sleep.

What *did* he want with her? "Did you read the paper tonight?" he asked.

She grunted awake. "What?"

"Did you?"

"No."

"You should—it's full of interesting stuff. Did you know that another kid from Mohawk got killed in Vietnam?"

She didn't say anything.

"That's not even the interesting part," he said. "Would you like to know the interesting part?"

"No."

"The interesting part is that the guy who got killed beat me up once when I was a kid. Right out back of Harry's. Then your uncle showed up, saved my goose and cooked his own."

"So. What's the point?"

"No point at all. Go to sleep."

"Okay," she said, and closed her eyes. Then she opened them. "You mad?"

"Of course not."

"And there really wasn't a point?"

"Not a point in the world."

"Good," she said. "I'm always missing the point, and I hate it."

Thirty seconds later her breathing was rhythmic, her eyelids fluttering. Randall was free to watch her. The girl wasn't nearly as pretty asleep as she was awake—as if consciousness were the main focus on her beauty. Asleep, she looked seventeen-going-on-thirty-five. It had never occurred to Randall that people assumed postures in their sleep, but B.G. did. Asleep, her body lost its confidence, and he wondered what she'd look like when she really was thirty-five.

It would've been nice if she'd stayed awake long enough to talk. Not that he blamed her for conking out. Nobody at Harry's worked harder than she did, running back and forth between rooms, between the racing-formers at the counter and the argumentative old bags eating chicken salad platters. The latter required her to be handy without intruding. She was too pretty not to be an annoyance among such women, some of whom once were pretty in the same way she now was. When she was at the table, they wanted her to go away; but if she stayed away too long, they felt slighted and would scrimp on the tip. At the lunch counter the men wanted her to linger and listen to slightly off-color jokes calculated to make her blush. The men seldom came on strong, being as shy as they'd always been, but didn't like to be ignored. She found that if she joked with them and indulged their fantasies, they treated her well enough. She didn't mind the remarks they made when her back was turned, the hastily exchanged glances, the ooooh-shaped lips. At the end of the work day she wanted to play with the baby, get laid and go to sleep. She told Randall she didn't think about her husband any more, and as far as he could tell she literally meant what she said. She didn't mean that she'd stopped worrying about him, or being angry with him for abandoning her and the baby, or guilty about being unfaithful to his tainted memory. As far as she was concerned, he just didn't exist any more.

She wasn't much of a talker anyway, or even a listener. Maybe that was why Randall enjoyed talking to her. She seldom responded to anything he said; and if she had any reaction at all, it was frequently puzzlement, as if she hadn't any idea where such odd notions came from. After college professors, Randall found her refreshing, and the more she frowned at him, the more critical he became of what he heard himself saying. He had attempted, just once, to explain to her the nature of ethical dilemmas, but gave up once he realized her own daily life had little to do with choice and probably never would. Had he been able to offer her as evidence in his recent honors seminar in free will, the course would've been struck from the curriculum. Or his father, for that matter, who had spent his whole life trying to figure the odds, never perceiving the random nature of things that made horse races horse races and his own life an endless series of completely novel experiences. New teeth every other month, post time every thirty-five minutes. Place your bets.

Randall sat up in bed and swung his feet onto the floor. The trailer shifted but the girl didn't stir. He pulled on his Levis and buttoned them from the bottom up. It was a warm night and there was no need to put on a shirt. In the next room, the baby was asleep in her crib, the tiny room smelling of baby and baby powder. Small children always overwhelmed Randall with the sense of life's possibilities. Amazing, how quickly those possibilities vanished. Five-year-olds often had personalities as fixed and rigid as their parents, and if you couldn't tell who'd get killed in the street by a drunk driver, you'd be pretty safe in predicting who wouldn't grow up to be a surgeon. And anyone clever enough to predict Vietnam surely could've foreseen that the boy who'd sat cheerfully on Randall Younger's chest and punched him in the face would end up in a reddening paddy. Randall's ending up at the university was part of the same prediction, but what about his dropping out and returning to Mohawk? Maybe that too. Were there clues somewhere in his past, or his mother's, or grandfather's, if he looked hard enough? Maybe he'd quit because of something that had happened in the alley behind Harry's, or in the old Littler Hospital, or in the infield where Price hit grounders at him, or in the park where he discovered his grandfather slumped over on the park bench, staring up at the black, high branches of the lifeless trees as the other man, this girl's grandfather, retreated. And what did he want with this girl? Not love, surely, though he cared for her. Not lust, though he enjoyed her. Not admiration, though he found her grasp of reality appealing.

Outside, the night was black, a gentle breeze that hadn't found its way into the trailer. Randall sat down on the cinder block that served as a step. He carefully rolled a joint and smoked it, the orange inching toward his lips. For some reason he wasn't startled by the voice, though it was very near; as if he'd been expecting it for a long time.

"Mather Grouse," it said.

42

"Has it occurred to you," Anne Grouse asked her mother, "how much of our daily conversation is on the subject of worms?"

"If you're having a mood, dear, we needn't talk about anything."

"It's just that we've been through it all. You can't kill the worms without killing the grass. You have to poison the soil."

"What I don't understand is why they came here in the first place," Mrs. Grouse said. "They've come for something."

"God."

"Well?"

"We're still talking about worms, aren't we. They're just here, Mother. Can't we leave it at that? They aren't causing any harm—in fact they're *good* for the lawn—and they've probably been here all along. You just never noticed. Besides, it's been a rainy summer. There *are* more serious problems, if you care to talk about them."

"Randall said he'd paint the house," Mrs. Grouse offered. She was dipping her tea bag in and out of the steaming water like a yo-yo. Finally, when the liquid was perfectly brown, she deposited the bag on the saucer. After adding two heaping teaspoons of sugar, she pushed the bowl toward her daughter, who was drinking coffee, black. "For your disposition," she said.

This was as close to humor as her mother ever got. The old woman's wit always surfaced when Anne was most serious. "I'm not talking about painting, Mother. Painting is the least of our worries."

Unfortunately, the subject of house repairs was proscribed. Mrs. Grouse, having completed the canonization of her husband, was seldom in the mood to entertain the blasphemous suggestion that anything at all was wrong with his house. "He left it in *ideal* condition," she was fond of telling her sister.

It was typical of their relationship that Anne and her Mother never worried about the same things. With the roof beginning to leak, wetting the attic insulation and discoloring the wallpaper in the corners of Anne's ceiling, Mrs. Grouse could think only of the worms. Each morning she went into the cellar, as far as the landing, half expecting to find a rupture in the concrete floor, a sea of night-crawlers spilling out of the walls. Water, on the other hand, was pure—it came from heaven— and she didn't for an instant believe that anything was wrong with the roof.

"Not our worries," Mrs. Grouse said. "Mine. If repairs are ever needed, they will be my responsibility as the homeowner. I am *not* in the habit of shirking responsibilities."

Anne massaged her temples. "It isn't a question of shirking, Mother. A new roof costs thousands of dollars. I don't have it, and I don't think you do either. But unless we do something soon, the house will be worthless. You won't be able to give it away."

"I have no intention of giving it away. What makes you think I did?"

"Fine," Anne concluded, as always. Arguing with her mother was like trying to put a cat into a bag; there was always one limb left over. "Do what you want."

"Your father put on the best new roof money could buy," Mrs. Grouse said. "The very best."

"Yes. Over ten years ago, he did. Before the ice storm this winter. Before the tree fell on it."

"Well, then."

"I'm going for a drive, Mother."

Dan was sitting in front of the Lincoln, its hood up, when she pulled in. He had a wrench in one hand and a sweating cocktail in the other. "They make these goddamn things so cripples can drive them, but not work on them."

"Don't change the subject," she said.

He looked guilty, but didn't give in easily. "Don't even start. I've very nearly brained two women in the last twenty-four hours, and the regret for lost opportunities is almost more than I can bear."

"You might've called."

"I thought about it. Did Di?"

"This morning. She said Milly was, what? *out of danger.*"

"Second time this week. They'll release her tomorrow, same as always."

"I wish you'd called."

"So do I, but you can't count on me. You should know that."

Anne smiled. "I can, though. In ways you don't know." She nodded at the car. "Anything I can do?"

He studied her, frowning. "Not dressed like that.

Don't you own anything ratty?" He motioned toward a TV tray on which sat an ice bucket, a bottle of whiskey, two-thirds full, a capped bottle of club soda. "Help yourself."

"You're always so well prepared."

"Good scotch draws a crowd. Or it used to, anyhow. I guess marijuana's the party-saver these days."

"Feeling out of things?"

"Not particularly," he said. But his attempt to be cheerful cost him too much to be convincing. "My next wife is going to be a mechanic," he said, flipping the wrench over his shoulder. It richocheted off the motor and disappeared, rattling loudly until it fell free onto the concrete beneath the Lincoln. "How's your mother?"

"Still worrying about worms."

"Kill the soil and they'll go away."

"I hate to give in."

"I wouldn't."

"I always enjoy your advice."

He raised his scotch and they clinked glasses. "Thank you very much."

Anne unfolded a lawn chair and they sat together without saying anything. Suddenly Dan was crying. Noiselessly, the tears streamed down his face, though his expression had not changed. When she started to speak, he held up a hand and, in a few minutes, managed to stop. He didn't bother to wipe the tracks.

"You want to hear something good," he said. "I've started dreaming again. First time in years. I'm always twenty-three or so, a real specimen. I live on the beach and all the neighbor girls have big chests and sunbathe in the nude. I'm married to Diana. Not Diana at twenty-three, but Diana at forty-four. In the dream everybody's always asking how come I married the old lady.

I never know what to tell them. I play with the neighbor girls for a while, and then, just when things are getting interesting, I feel the paralysis coming, and suddenly I can't move. I wake up sweating, trying like a bastard."

When Anne said nothing, he drained the rest of his scotch and looked at her. "Now don't you start."

"I won't," she promised.

"Anyhow," he said. "My next wife is going to be my own age. Twenty-three. With big tits."

"And here I'd hoped—"

"Not on your life. You're too old for me."

Before she left, Anne fished the wrench out from under the car with a broom handle, and he began to curse the car again with his customary good humor. He was drunk, and when Diana came home from the hospital she'd have to pour him into bed, where he could dream of youth and beauty.

43

The game broke up when Dallas and Benny D. were good and cleaned. "Jesus, I can't stand that fuckin' John," Benny D. said when they were out in the fresh air on Main Street. It was still pretty early, only a little after one A.M. Both men were loaded, but not over the top. "Let's go someplace."

"Nah."

"Come on," Benny D. insisted.

"Nah," Dallas said, and the two men ambled up Main Street together toward Harry's. The grill was closed, like every other place downtown. The afternoon had been hot, but the night air was cool.

"I can't stand that fucker," Benny D. said. "I don't see how you can work—"

"I don't see him any more than you do. We settle up once a week. That's it."

"I don't see how you can work for him, that's all."

"He'll have a bad day tomorrow," Dallas said. Whenever he got in trouble, Dallas left a space or two in the book and filled them in later. The only way he had much luck with horses was to wait until after the race was over and then make the entry, usually in Benny D.'s name, or somebody who'd cover for him if push came to shove. But even this system wasn't foolproof. A couple weeks before, Dallas had no sooner entered the unofficial winner on the books than an inquiry was posted and they ended up taking the bastard down. Anyhow, he didn't do it very often. He'd saved John's ass plenty in the last few months, and besides, John was loaded like a Greek.

"I hope he has a rotten fuckin' day," Benny D. said. "What say you come back and work for me?"

"Because you can't keep your nose out of things. Like I've told you a thousand times."

"It's my place, you knothead. I'm not supposed to come around my own place?"

"No. You just screw things up."

"My mechanics answer to me," Benny D. said testily.

"And that's how come I'm not your mechanic."

"You'd rather work for a prick like John—"

"John's all right."

"—than a buddy like me."

"I'm going home."

"Come have a drink," Benny D. said.

"I'm tapped."

"Me too. So what?"

"All right, one drink. Let's hit The Velvet Pussycat."

Benny D. frowned. "That fuckin' place. I don't know anybody there."

"We better get some money then," Dallas said. They turned down the alley behind Harry's. The Saunderses' bedroom was on the second floor toward the back, and Harry's sleepy face appeared at the curtained window a few seconds after Dallas began to bounce pebbles off the glass. "Harry," Dallas shouted softly.

"What?" Harry spit down at them.

"Let me take fifty 'til tomorrow."

"Go to hell." His face disappeared and the curtain fell back in place.

"He's pissed," Benny D. said. "He went back to bed."

"Nah," Dallas said, leaning against the dumpster. "He's gone to get the fifty."

"Bullshit. He went back to bed."

"I'll bet you the fifty."

Benny D. frowned and looked up at the black window. The alley was quiet. "You're on. He's dead asleep."

The window creaked open and, when the men looked up, bills were fluttering down out of the darkness—five tens, three of which they caught in the air. Benny D. climbed into the dumpster for a stray. He handed Dallas three tens. "I'll give you the other twenty tomorrow. You buy the drinks. I hate that Velvet Pussycat anyhow."

Just then Wild Bill turned into the alley, walking toward them, and watching his own feet fall in front of him as if the surprise of seeing them perform so effortlessly was enough to absorb all his attention. At forty, he was a year younger than Dallas, though he looked like a man in his mid-fifties. He was bald, except for a ring of longish hair that began only a few inches above his ears, covering them and hanging over his shirt collar as well. His cheeks were sunken, as were his eyes. Wild Bill loped right by without looking up and inserted the key Harry had chained to his belt into the lock. The door opened and Dallas and Benny D. were alone again in the alley.

"I wonder what the hell he's doing out this time of night," Dallas said.

"If I was a farmer, I'd keep my calves indoors. I hear he don't talk no more at all."

"Hasn't said a word in three months, according to Harry."

"Better than that shit he used to come up with. That *'oughta'* shit. Remember that?"

By the time they got to The Velvet Pussycat, the place was hopping pretty good. At closing time the bartender stopped serving alcohol to those who didn't want any more and kept on pouring for those who did. The owner had been to court half-a-dozen times for serving after-hours, and even paid several two-hundred-dollar fines. But for the fact he took in an easy five hundred between two and five, he probably would've stopped. A local band was rattling the windows. The lead singer had shoulder-length hair, and Benny D. glowered at him. "Some fuckin' place this is."

Dallas had never been there either. And though he thought he knew everybody in Mohawk, the place was mobbed with strangers. John had beat them out there and, dancing with some woman who wasn't his wife, waved at Dallas and Benny D.

"How much you want to bet he never even buys us a drink," asked Benny D.

"He's tight," Dallas said, "as a rabbit's ass."

"How much you figure he took us for tonight?"

"He's going to pay tomorrow. His luck's already changed and he doesn't know it."

"That doesn't help me," Benny D. said sadly. He ordered scotches for himself and Dallas and sent a round over to John and his bimbo.

"I hope you won't try to shame him," Dallas said. "He's a lawyer and we only got fifty bucks."

"What good is he?"

Dallas explained how John had helped him beat a DWI a few months ago, but Benny D. wasn't listening. A young waitress had come up to the cocktail station and was emptying lime sections and maraschino cherry stems and soaked cocktail napkins into the small trash bucket on the floor. She was working without a brassiere, and every time she bent over, Benny D. did too. Not that he really needed to. Dallas could see everything perfectly from two stools down. He let his story trail off. When the girl walked away, Benny D. turned to him. "Who's she?"

"Somebody's daughter."

"Mmmm. And all growed up. Save my seat. I got to pee."

When the band stopped, John came over and bought a drink. "Remind me to take you shopping sometime," he said, running his index finger under Dallas's shirt collar. "What's with you and Benny D.?"

"What do you mean?"

"Nothing," John said.

"No *what*?"

John shrugged. "He comes up with a lot of winners is all."

"He knows horses."

"Nobody knows horses," John said.

"You don't," Dallas admitted. "I save your ass three or four times a week. I'm getting sick and tired, now that I think about it."

John held up his hand. "Don't get sore. It's funny how your pal wins all the time is all."

"I don't want to hear it."

"If he stays lucky, I'm going to have to cut you loose."

"I'm gone."

"Don't get sore, we're just talking here."

"Fuck you."

Benny D. came back from the men's room and eyed the bar. "Don't tell me this stiff actually bought a drink," he said.

"I don't like you, Benny," the lawyer said.

"Well, break my fuckin' heart," Benny D. said. "That sure is a nice shirt. Won't it stay buttoned?"

"Unload the guy," John said to Dallas. "Don't hang around with him."

"Thanks for the drink," Dallas said. "You seen my sister-in-law around?"

"Not lately," John said. "Her kid's sick or something."

"I'll have another drink," Benny D. told the bartender. "On this gentleman, the one with the hairy chest and the fish hooks in his pockets."

"I don't like you, Benny," John said.

"What's wrong with the kid?"

"I don't know. Leukemia or something."

When the lawyer raised his glass, Dallas hit him, and suddenly John looked like somebody had swabbed him with a brush full of red paint. One large piece of glass lodged in his upper lip just beneath his nose. He wobbled, but instead of falling down brushed Dallas aside so he could look at his face in the mirror above the bar. Only a few people had seen what happened.

"Jesus," John said reverently, touching the piece of glass in his lip, lifting his chin to better see the blood running down his neck and into his open necked shirt.

"Allow me," Benny D. said, pulling the glass fragment out of the upper lip.

"Ahhh!" John gasped.

"All better?" Benny handed him a swatch of cocktail napkins.

The bartender was now looking in horror at John.

"You're a witness," John said. Several other people nearby had already turned their backs.

"Sure," the man said. "What happened?"

"We better git," Benny D. said when John disappeared into the men's room. "There's a phone in there."

"I got to go see somebody anyway," Dallas said. He wished he'd waited until John put the glass down before hitting him, not that he could do anything about it now.

"You can't go over there at three in the morning," Benny D. said once they were out in the parking lot.

"Drive by," Dallas said.

They did, but the house was dark and Loraine's car wasn't in the drive.

"You better stay with me tonight," Benny D. suggested. "You're liable to have visitors."

"Who cares?"

"You will. In the morning."

"He had it coming."

"We'll call my lawyer in the morning."

"Nah."

"Nah, your ass. You're in trouble."

"Who cares?"

At Benny D.'s place, Dallas took the couch. Benny D. strayed in, wearing his boxers and scratching himself. "How 'bout you come back and work for me? I'll stay out of the garage."

"Sure," Dallas said. "Why not."

44

"Mather Grouse," the voice in the dark had said, and for a moment, Randall Younger was breathless. There was only a quarter moon, no real light, and the voice was so near, so tangible, that Randall at first thought he himself had spoken, not the man sitting on the tire a few feet away. But then a cigarette tip glowed red and faded like a light from a faraway locomotive.

"No," Randall said.

"I know," the big man said. "I know your name, Randall Younger. And I also know who you *are*. A young Mather Grouse, that's who."

"You told me that once before," Randall said. He dropped the roach and screwed it into the moist earth with his shoe. Rory Gaffney waved his cigarette, leaving a trail, a red-white smear in the air.

"A young Mather Grouse."

"He was afraid of you," Randall said suddenly, surprising himself.

"He didn't have no need," Rory Gaffney said. "No need for friends to fear one another."

That sounded too much like a question to be true. And yet, Randall knew, it couldn't be entirely false either. He got to his feet. "My grandfather wasn't your friend."

"No," Rory Gaffney admitted, as if there were no contradiction. "Mather Grouses can't have no friends. Can't fight, can't talk, can't fuck. Not really."

No, Randall thought, but not because we don't want to. It's because our minds keep drifting from the fighting and the fucking, always back to the me—what about me, is this a me I can live with, that I can suffer people to see, that I can suffer myself to see. His grandfather had felt all of this, surely. All Mather Grouses felt it; the same perverse self-consciousness that had driven Randall into the old hospital that day. Concern for Wild Bill Gaffney had come later, after everyone had told him why he had done it and he had believed them. He had been fearless, selfless, they said, never suspecting that what had pushed him forward through the falling debris was in fact fear. Fear that someone would witness him standing there and know he had done nothing.

He smiled at his self-consciousness now, but at the time it had seemed as if the whole scene had been staged as a test for one Randall Younger. The rest of humanity amounted to little more than a realistic backdrop. No one else had any obligation to enter the crumbling building, the hundreds of people girding it were not on trial. Randall scarcely cared about these props, but would conceal from them at any cost that he was part of their cowardly brotherhood. Of all the people in the world, he had thought, his grandfather would've suspected the truth, and when he didn't, Randall had doubted his own conclusions. Maybe it hadn't been fear. Maybe what the people said was true. He entertained this possibility for years, until the voice said "Mather Grouse" and the cigarette glowed red in the dark.

He could see clearly now, his eyes had adjusted. There was a fifth of whiskey nestled in the other man's groin. "He didn't have no reason to be afraid, though."

"Then why was he?"

The cigarette inscribed a long arc into the trees, and Rory Gaffney took a swig from the bottle.

"You and my granddaughter hitting it off pretty good?"

"That's a change of subject."

"Young girls today don't never say no," Rory Gaffney mused. "Your granddad, he'd of worried about it. He was that sort. The same with the leather we took. He figured it was stealing. We never could get him over the worrying."

Randall took in what the other man was saying, but slowly. This is what I have come back to learn, he thought mechanically, outside himself, watching himself learn. His stomach churned suddenly, and he tasted something vile on the back of his tongue. Remember this taste, he told himself, learn it. "No," he heard himself say. "My grandfather was no thief. He'd have starved first."

Rory Gaffney nodded. "Starved is *just* what he would of done. It's what we all would of done if a skin hadn't got itself misplaced now and then. And not just us, either. Wives and kids along with us. What the hell were we but family men? What was your granddad?"

Randall swallowed hard as an alternative to spitting into the dirt at their feet, but the taste didn't go away.

"No man was more a family man than Mather Grouse. Nobody in Mohawk was good enough for that mother of yours. My poor boy was sweet on her, like all the rest."

There was an edge to the man's voice, and Randall guessed that Rory Gaffney, too, was tasting something nasty when he dredged up the yellow past. "Ask your mother about my poor boy some day."

Inside the trailer, the baby cried just once, then both men listened to the crickets.

"I understood your granddad. A man gets a little crazy over his own, especially when she's a girl and prettier than anybody ever saw. Who wouldn't a wanted her for hisself?"

Randall started to speak, but couldn't.

"Anyways, I went along. I always tried to be Mather Grouses's friend, even though he never wanted none. They were tough times, but we all made out somehow."

Randall continued to hear the fundamental insincerity of the man, but also knew that the most effective lies were those liberally laced with truth. The lie could be ninety-nine parts truth to one part falsehood, the one tarnished part mingling with the pure until it was all tainted, more false than pure fabrication.

"You're the same," the man concluded. "A young Mather Grouse." With effort Rory Gaffney lifted himself from the truck tire he had been sitting on. He was half a head taller than Randall and seemed aware of the fact, though the boy had to admit that maybe it was he himself who was.

"No," Randall said, unsure of exactly what he was denying.

Gaffney raised the bottle. "To your granddad," he said, "and youth."

When the man offered him the bottle, Randall took it and drank without wiping the lip. The whiskey tasted only slightly better than what it washed down. Then, as the rancid liquid tracked downward toward his bowels, a strange notion occurred to Randall. *I could go to war*, he thought to himself. *I could kill a man.*

45

On Saturday night after the bars close, the only spot hotter than The Velvet Pussycat is the new Mohawk Medical Services Center, though most generally concede that the new hospital lacks the ambience of the old, whose crowded vestibule encouraged a desperate camaraderie of the bleeding. If you'd tiptoed home six hours late and your wife hit you in the face with a chair, chances were pretty good you'd be standing in line next to someone with a remarkably similar set of circumstances or, at least, an equally interesting story. That was the cozy kind of place the old hospital had been. You could compare wounds and feel either fortunate or proud.

The new hospital has a reception area like a large modern hotel, and the carpet sucked sound. You overheard no intimate revelations as the staff scurried about stuffing patients into the sterile, private cubicles that ringed the lobby, as if the institution was ashamed of its patients. In the hospital's planning stages, someone had come to the entirely erroneous conclusion that people preferred to hurt in private. From the beginning no one liked the new facility. They didn't mind particularly that the building came in over budget, nor that the lights dimmed and flickered during thunderstorms.

In fact, the place was altogether too bright. The walls were bright, the furniture bright, the paintings vivid. People were yanked out of sight before you could figure out what was wrong with them, what folly they had succumbed to. Several of the denizens of the beloved old ivy-encircled Nathan Littler Hospital let it be known that they preferred to bleed to death than be stitched up in a place like the new hospital. One citizen was good to his word, dying in the arms of his wife of thirty years, off and on, and whose agency in the matter was later examined in public proceedings.

Nor is there any challenge in the new hospital. The old, perched at the top of Hospital Hill, had required mettle. In bad weather, negotiating the incline was a test of commitment and, sometimes, manhood. People still talked about the year Homer Wells tried several runs at the incline and nearly made it, too. People watched him, fascinated, from their living room windows. He bent forward as if into a headwind and churned upward methodically, undeterred by treacherous patches of ice. The hill that day was impossible to ascend by automobile. It may have been Homer's sense of accomplishment at reaching the summit that caused him momentarily to lose his concentration and his balance on an icy patch. By the time he reached the bottom of the hill, he had built up such a head of steam that he flew cleanly over the snowbank into the street. Here he encountered the Bronson Dairy truck, whose driver later remarked that seeing old Homer on his hood was the surprise of his life, for he owed Homer money and the first thought that crossed his mind when he saw his friend's nose pressed urgently against the windshield was that Homer had come to collect. Ironically, it was this very event that had provided the impetus for the new hospital drive. It was the last thing Homer would've wanted.

Tonight, business at the Mohawk Medical Services Center is brisk, though it lacks the appearance of being so. An enormous man looms over the registration desk, flanked by two equally formidable women. He admits to having contracted a dose of the clap, and he wants to know where it came from, his wife or his girl friend. "It better be one of us, dumb fuck," the larger of the two women warns.

On the fourth floor, Diana Wood is preparing to go home. Her mother is sleeping peacefully and there's no reason to stay the rest of the night, though she often does, sleeping upright in one of the straight-backed chairs. Only one other person sits in the hospital corridor, a woman in her mid-thirties, facing the wall, resting her forehead against its cool surface, her arms hanging limply at her sides. Diana cannot see the woman's face, but the grief in her posture is so profound that Di is embarrassed to come upon her unexpected. Since on the carpeted floor there's no way to announce her presence, Diana concludes it would be best to just pass quietly by. Still, the implications of doing so are too grave to ignore, and Diana glances up when she comes parallel with the other woman, who hasn't moved. The three-by-five card on the nearest door reads YOUNGER.

Diana stops. Eventually the woman straightens, staring at the blank white wall before turning. She doesn't seem terribly surprised to see someone standing there. Rather, her eyes suggest that for her there are no more surprises. "I don't mean to intrude—" Diana says. "That's silly, though. Of course I'm intruding—"

"No," the woman says vaguely.

"It's just that my husband and I were once friends with a Dallas Younger, and I couldn't help noticing the name. . . ."

"Dallas is my brother-in-law."

"I thought perhaps he'd married," Diana explains, "and we hadn't heard."

"No. Not that I know of. I haven't seen him in a long time."

"I'm very sorry—"

"He's nothing to me," the woman says.

"I meant. . . . " Diana nods toward the door.

"Oh," she looks flustered, embarrassed. "My daughter. Who means everything. That's the way things work out, isn't it."

"She *will* get better," Diana says.

Something like hope registers in the woman's eyes, as if in her fatigue she believed momentarily that this stranger had second sight. But the hope vanishes quickly. "You're very kind," she says dully.

I know what it means to lose, Diana feels like telling her. But it wouldn't do either one of them any good. Downstairs in the lobby she has to wait for three enormous people to get through the double doors. "You happy now, dumb fuck?" one of the women says. Diana suddenly feels a blind, irrational rage. In all her life she has never once spoken out of turn, but she can't restrain herself. "Watch your language," she says. "You don't own the world. You—you're a blight on it!"

The three stand transfixed as she brushes by, stymied by her smallness and insignificance.

"Little troll," the larger woman says when Diana is out of earshot, and all three laugh.

46

With less than two weeks until retirement, Officer Gaffney wondered for the first time if he'd be able to make it. Lately he'd been troubled by dreams. In the most recent, he was caught up in a shoot-out at the Mohawk Bank and Trust. He was standing in the middle of the Four Corners intersection directing traffic when the robbers rushed out of the bank. The traffic light was showing green in all directions and, when he drew his revolver, cars began speeding by, narrowly missing him and each other. The robbers took cover behind the bank's marble lions and opened up. They had no trouble hitting Officer Gaffney, but each time he discharged his revolver, one of the passing cars intercepted the bullet, which would then ping around inside the vehicle like a penny in a tin can. The best he could do was blast the snout off one of the marble lions, which sported a shaggy mane a little like his brother's. Being shot didn't hurt much, but he was afraid to die and ashamed when the robbers got away. He woke up crying and was afraid to go to work, but did. The fear remained with him all day, even during his coffee break at Harry's. He bought the bottle of whiskey on his way home.

The policeman lived in a small upstairs flat with a view across the street of the Presbyterian church, whose belfry was always illuminated at night, the light streaming through Officer Gaffney's window like a searching beam, keeping him awake. He could've drawn the shade, but he never did.

Once the rye was half gone, sometime after midnight, Officer Gaffney went to the closet where he hung his holster on a hook and returned to the living room with his revolver. Though it was the evening of the third of July, firecrackers had been going off in the neighborhood for the last couple of evenings. A cherry bomb exploded somewhere down the street, and he heard some kids laughing. At him, probably. They all seemed to know where he lived. He went to the window and stared out into the dark night and the lighted belfry across the street, remembering his dream of the night before. The revolver was heavy and warm in his hand. He hadn't cleaned the weapon in a while, so he let the bullets clatter onto the coffee table. Then he cleaned, oiled and reloaded, pleased with the sound each bullet made when it slid home in the chamber. Bullet fit gun. Gun fit hand. Hand? What did hand fit? Man? And what did man fit? Man had to fit something. Family? It wasn't like he *had* to live all by himself across from the yellow light. His brother's house was too big for one man, and when the policeman retired he might suggest to his brother. . . .

Out in the street there was another loud bang. The rye slid down Officer Gaffney's throat painlessly. He switched off the light before going to the window and raising the screen. He fired four rounds in all, four sharp explosions, the fourth followed by shattering glass and darkness. "Good," he said. It was late, and the houses up and down the street remained dark. His own landlady below was old and deaf. He drained all but a swallow from the bottle of rye. I have just committed a crime, he thought to himself. Assaulted a belfry. He wasn't ashamed, and what's more he felt safe from the law. His brother had the right idea, doing as he pleased. Simple. Never got confused. Never found himself in the middle of the intersection beneath a jammed traffic light with cars whizzing by.

Right now his brother was probably in the girl's trailer, unless the Younger boy had beat him to it. Officer Gaffney realized that he loved his brother and was proud of his exploits. Except for the once, he couldn't remember Rory ever doing anything he himself didn't approve of. He didn't exactly like the idea of Rory and the girl, but she hardly looked at the policeman anyway. He wasn't the type girls went for, though he'd never known exactly why. Other men like himself had succeeded, at least enough in marrying homely girls. When he was younger, he figured that being a cop would itself guarantee him some sort of girl, but the uniform hadn't done the trick, and now he was too old to worry about it. He was content to watch the girl at Harry's and, now and then, in the trailer.

He liked it when she was alone, but now Younger had moved in. He'd cause trouble yet, always had been trouble. Just the other night Officer Gaffney had warned his brother again, but as usual Rory paid no attention. "Younger!" he almost spit the name. "Do you think I'd trouble myself over a Younger? The boy's a Grouse. The last of 'em. I can feel his grandfather in the ground."

"If he's a Grouse, the more reason to leave him alone," Officer Gaffney said. "Besides, I can take care of him for you. Let me run him in."

His brother reacted to the suggestion as he might to foul air. "You," he sneered.

The fact that his own brother despised him seemed to Officer Gaffney the most insupportable thing of all. He lay in bed and thought about this for a long time, and then about the girl, and before long he began to sob. He didn't know what time it was when he fell asleep.

When he awoke, it was light. He didn't have to open his eyes to know that someone had been in the room just a moment before. Everything looked as it had the previous night, which was one of the things that made him certain. Everything was too exactly the same, as if someone had moved and then replaced each item carefully. Even the whiskey bottle had been positioned precisely on its own moist brown ring. Two flies perched on the bottle rim until he waved them away and drained the last swallow. In the living room he saw the open window, and then he was sure.

On the way to Harry's, he stopped at the liquor store and bought another bottle. He cracked the seal before going into the diner. The regulars were all there, and everybody looked at him when he walked in. That was all right with him. He said nothing to them, nothing to Harry or The Bulldog, or even to the girl. When Harry set the eggs in front of him, Officer Gaffney stared at them for a long time before pushing the plate away. When the door swung open, he could see Wild Bill intently stacking dishes in the Hobart and Randall Younger, wearing one of The Bulldog's bright hair nets, cutting parsley snips and lemon wedges. When he approached the register to pay for his uneaten breakfast, everyone was still staring. "Gaff?" somebody said.

Outside, the sun was already blazing. Officer Gaffney drove up toward Myrtle Park, but failed to negotiate the sharp turn at the entrance. A young policeman found the abandoned car in the ditch later that afternoon. Off and on all day, there were reports of loud explosions in the park. But it was Independence Day, and there were loud explosions everywhere.

47

In mid-July, two days after Anne Grouse was replaced by a new personnel director at the store, there was a terrible electrical storm. She had reason to anticipate both events.

No Mohawk summer she could remember had ever passed without at least one dilly of the sort that had terrorized her childhood—beginning in the west, the thunder low and rolling on the perimeter of her sleep, altering her dreams to accommodate what her mind was marginally conscious of. Such storms were always windy and dry at first, rattling the screens fiercely, blowing tree branches up against them like scratching fingers. She always woke up and waited for her father to come close the windows, for when the storm broke, driving rain would soak the curtains and sills. She wanted him to stay with her until the thunder and lightning subsided, but he was always busy making his rounds of the house. After a light kiss on the forehead he was gone, leaving the room black and then, when the lightning flashed, bright. There was always one thunderclap that rocked the house to its foundations. In the dark, her hands covering her eyes, she awaited the storm's direct hit, always preceded by the lightning's hiss overhead, then the terrible crack that she imagined must have originated at the center of her brain. No one had ever known, because she had never told, just how terrified she was of electrical storms.

Dallas, who never understood anything, hadn't understood that either, and had clownishly imitated what was going on outside their bedroom window, hissing and poking her in the ribs with his index finger. At least he did until the night she hit him in the face with her open hand, hard enough to knock him out of bed, erection and all. These same storms made Dallas horny.

Anne wasn't particularly surprised that she had been let go at the store. Like the storm, it had been approaching in its own leisurely fashion all summer. Again, she'd been given the opportunity to transfer, and had turned it down almost without thinking. The store was doing well enough by regional standards, but the district office wasn't interested in regional standards. Eventually, she knew, the store would close, as so many others had. The ones on the highway died slower deaths than the downtown retailers, but they died just the same. She told no one but Randall, who frowned and asked what she'd do.

"I don't know," she said. "The only reason I mention it is that if you decide to go back to school, I won't be able to help much."

"I doubt I'll be going back right away," Randall said.

"I can understand that," Anne said. "With a blossoming career as a dishwasher at the Mohawk Grill, what would be the point?"

Since his return to Mohawk in the spring, Anne discovered that they had even less to say to one another than before. She began to understand her father's attitude when she had returned years ago. She didn't doubt Randall had his reasons, but doubted they were sufficient or would ever turn out to be. But then, she was an expert on good reasons that turned out not to be. Maybe her father was as well. He certainly understood how perversely loyal human beings could be to mistakes. Anyway, if there was any detectable pattern of motion in the universe, it was clearly cyclical, and for that reason she refused to be upset. Attempts to make life do what it had resisted doing in the past were mostly futile. She had run into Dallas on the street a week earlier and he had told her about Randall—that he was living with some girl. "What am *I* supposed to do about it?" she said.

"You could talk to him."

"So could his father, assuming he wanted to."

"She's married."

"I can't help that either."

But it had sickened her a little, just the same. She couldn't look at him without seeing the boy instead of the man. Talking might not be a bad idea, but the fact was she didn't really want to know about the girl, the husband or the sordid details that had a way of rendering everything understandable. She wasn't sure she wanted to understand. Probably her father had felt the same way, and it occurred to Anne that, viewed objectively, there had been an insidious moral slippage through the generations, each succeeding one surrendering a small patch of ethical territory.

It was after midnight when the branches outside her bedroom window began to scratch their urgent message on the screen. "So," she thought, "it's to be tonight." Below, a yellow patch of light reflected off the house next door, which meant that her mother was awake too, prepared to ride out the storm with a grim determination that came from having ridden out a lifetime of them, firmly believing in the efficacy of passive resistance. Storms went away, like pain and disappointment, like tough times. Not such a bad philosophy. It would've been nice to subscribe to it.

Closing her eyes, she tracked the storm's approach. The lightning registered no matter how tightly she clamped them shut. As the rumbling neared, the tree branch tapped more insistently. With any luck the storm would skirt town, but Anne had no faith it would. Once the rain started, everything would be fine. The dry electricity would wash deep into the earth. But first it had to rain, after all the howling wind and thunder. All right, the gods must've decided, cleanse them again. The hair along their forearms has been standing on end too long. Cleanse them one more time. Allow them to touch one another without fear.

Even with her eyes closed, Anne sensed a subtle change in the house, and when she opened them, the patch of yellow light on the house next door was gone. So was the luminous dial on the clock beside her bed. The room was still. Anne got out of bed and went to the living room window, hoping to see nothing, the entire street cloaked in the storm's blackness, but a light shined in the Millers' front room across the street and another upstairs in the house two doors down.

Anne cursed the house and pulled on her robe. Downstairs she found her mother sitting on the end of the sofa, staring out the front window at the deserted street. A flash of lightning froze the old woman in her seat, and she didn't react when her daughter walked in with the flashlight. Out in the street the wind was swirling everything that wasn't rooted; a lawn chair danced crazily up the hill, end over end. "I'm going up to the attic to change the fuse, Mother."

"Of course, dear," her mother responded vaguely.
"Did you hear me?"

The old woman turned and stared at her blankly.
"Where am I going?"

Mrs. Grouse blinked.

"To the attic. To change the fuse."

Mrs. Grouse smiled and went back to watching the
street.

At the attic stairway, Anne flipped the switch and,
when the light didn't come on, cursed her stupidity out
loud. She followed the flashlight beam up the narrow
stairs. Lightning illuminated the fusebox under the eave
at the far end of the attic, next to the only window,
which was banging madly. "Never touch this box," her
father had warned her when she was eight. He had
discovered her one day going through the trunks in
the attic that contained old clothes. "*Never* touch it."

She had waited for him to explain, of course.

She was much older before he told her that merely
touching the black box wouldn't kill anyone, but insisted how important it was to be careful when changing
the fuse.

"But why'd you tell me that?" she wanted to know.
Why let her think that death was close at hand, just up
the stairs?

"There are some things it's wise to be scared of."

"Why?"

"Because they hold the power to destroy us."

"But I hate being afraid," she said. "I've had nightmares about the box."

"Nightmares never killed anybody," he said flatly.
"If you hadn't had bad dreams about the box, you'd
have had them about something else."

Below the box was a small, wrinkled paper bag that

contained the fuses. Anne took one out—it felt cool, almost moist, between her thumb and forefinger. She opened the door to the fusebox and shined the flashlight on the double row of copper-pronged switches, each with its little plastic handle. The main fuse was splotched black across the paper.

Anne disconnected the switch and tapped the fuse with her forefinger before unscrewing it. She knew that once the copper switch was open, the box was safe; but her fear was far too ingrained for knowledge to count against it. Outside, the storm was suddenly quiet. Anne fitted the new fuse into the vacant slot. The fuse turned almost too easily, and she double-checked to make sure that it was screwed tight. All that was left to do was to throw the switch. Again she shined the light into the box so she could see to be sure that she had the switch by its plastic handle. When she pushed it forward, there was a sizzling sound and the attic was suddenly broad daylight. The clap of thunder that followed instantly drowned Anne's scream of rage and fear, and at the precise moment when what was inside her became part of the ambivalent night, she realized for the first time how very much she hated her father.

48

"Please," B.G. pleaded. From the next room issued the baby's cry, as if she knew the storm was coming. In the wind, the trailer crunched and popped like an empty aluminum can.

"I won't be long. I promise." Randall drew the curtain back to look out into the dark. When the old man was home, the lights up at the house were visible through the trees, but now Randall Younger saw nothing but blackness and the reflection of his own drawn face.

"Tell me what you talked about," she said, fixing him when he turned around, her eyes small and frightened.

"What?"

"I woke up. I heard the two of you out there."

"We discussed my grandfather, if you've got to know."

"I don't believe you."

They faced each other angrily.

Randall looked away first. "I'll be back in a few hours."

"Don't lie."

"Why should I leave you?"

"Tell me what you talked about with him." She fairly spit the last word.

"My grandfather."

She looked away. The baby wailed louder in the next room. Randall consulted his watch. It was time, and he had made up his mind. "Look," he said, "if I were splitting, would I ask to borrow your car?"

In this there was an ironic truth, and it calmed her down a little. The husband who had abandoned her was just the sort to steal the car. Randall would be more likely to leave one by way of apology. "Stay," she begged one last time.

"You have to give me tonight," he said. "It's a matter of business."

"With him."

"Yes. All right. Yes."

"I won't tell you why, but I want you to know I hate him."

"Good," he said. "So do I."

He backed the VW down the drive and onto the macadam. The police car was parked down the block, and when Randall passed it the headlights came on and the car lurched forward. At the intersection Randall stopped at the sign, and the police car pulled up so close that its headlights disappeared from the rearview. Randall waited for a blip and the revolving lights, but nothing happened. When he pulled away, the cruiser surged steadily behind, as if in tow. Even when Randall sped up, it kept exact pace, no more than a few feet behind.

When they came to the highway, Randall pulled over. So did the police car. Turning off the ignition, he rolled down the window and waited. The radio in the car behind barked and coughed. Finally, the door opened and Officer Gaffney, with some difficulty, got out. Even in the rearview Randall could see that he wasn't in uniform, but rather in street clothes, except for the black revolver holstered to his hip. And even in the rearview he could tell he was drunk.

Officer Gaffney leaned with both hands on the roof of the VW, almost as if someone had told him to spread 'em. For a long time he said nothing, just breathed heavily.

"What," Randall said finally.

"Give him a message."

"Your brother?"

"No. Him. You know who."

"No I don't."

"Just do it," the policeman said. "Tell him to stay away from my place. I'll shoot him down like a dog."

Officer Gaffney's eyes were red and wild.

"All right. Sure."

"I don't want him in my rooms. There's nothing there for him. I won't have him going through my things."

"I'll tell him that."

"And tell him," the policeman stopped, his chin dropping momentarily. "Just tell him to keep away. I know how he does it. I can follow his voice along the wall. Tell him I got it figured."

Randall promised he would.

"All night," Officer Gaffney said. "All night and no sleep. Listening to that *oughta* shit." He took his revolver out and showed it to Randall. "Shoot right *through* a wall. Next time . . . right where the voice is . . . bang. No more *oughta*."

"I'll make sure he understands."

Officer Gaffney put the gun away and straightened up. Randall couldn't see his face. "He was dead. The walls were coming down. How come you couldn't a just left him alone?"

Rory Gaffney was waiting in the van at the end of the street. "You're late," he said when Randall pulled alongside.

"I ran into a little problem."

"Since when is pussy a problem," the old man said. "Stay close. We gotta get loaded before the storm breaks."

They turned down a one-way street, and when the van came to the end of the pavement it slowed but kept going along a dirt road that wound through the trees. This was a part of town Randall was wholly unfamiliar with. They crossed the Cayuga Creek on a narrow bridge and stopped by a hut just short of the railroad tracks. On the far side, the Tucker Tannery was silhouetted against the night sky. The wind was blowing so hard now that several small trees dusted the ground with their topmost branches. When he got out of the van, Rory Gaffney's hair stood straight up like an angry gray flame. "Many a night your granddad and I crossed these tracks together, loaded down. The bastards never suspected us, either. Not their best men."

"You keep forgetting," Randall said. "I don't believe any of it, so why keep it up?"

"I do lie something awful, don't I? Not lie, really. It's just the way things could of been. We should of been friends, him and me. I wanted it. We weren't so different. It was just some little thing in him that couldn't let go. Otherwise he'd of been one of the world's great sinners."

Inside the shack were a press and several long tables piled high with leather. The windows were blackened and curtained so that light from the bare bulb hanging from the ceiling couldn't be seen from outside.

"You know how to get to White Plains without using the Thruway?"

Randall said he did, and the two men began loading the van. The newly tanned skins had the same rich, almost overpowering scent he'd always associated with his grandfather. It was strongest when Mather Grouse came in at the end of the day, but he was never wholly without it. Though the two men worked quickly, methodically, Rory Gaffney showing no signs of fatigue despite his age, it took nearly half an hour to load the van. Some of the skins had been cut into gloves and stacked in boxes. There were jackets and coats too, complete except for linings and buttons. Still other skins bore only pattern markings.

Once they were finished, Rory Gaffney gave him the keys to the van. "Careful," he said. "The vehicle ain't exactly mine. I'll drop off the bug," he said, holding out his hand for the keys.

Randall held them out to him. "Your brother pulled me over tonight."

That brought the old man up short. "What?"

"On the way over here. Which is why I was late."

"What the hell for?"

"Just to tell me he's hearing voices coming out of the walls. You want to know whose?"

"I'll handle him. You just drive. Carefully. You get pulled over now and you won't have to worry about the draft."

"I'm not."

"Ahhh," he said. "You just naturally like to hide out."

49

When the lightning strikes the top of what had once been the Montgomery Ward building two blocks from the diner, the thunderclap cracks several windows along Main Street, and Harry Saunders, at his wife's insistence, gets up to check things out. Harry's awake anyway. The Grotto was expensive to start up and isn't close to paying for itself.

"Is he back yet," Harry's wife asks when he returns.

"No."

"Did you look in his room?"

"I didn't have to. He isn't back yet."

"You shouldn't let him go."

"How would I stop him? Lock him in his room?"

"He wouldn't do anything you forbid."

"I don't have the heart. I won't make this a jail. He's been in jails."

"He could be getting in trouble."

"No."

"How can you be sure?"

"Because I know where he goes."

His wife's hair is aflame, bright red. "Where, then? Where does he go?"

50

Near the outskirts of town on Kings Road, the thunderclap was less severe, though it shook the windows of the Wood home. Only old Milly was able to sleep out the storm. Dan and Diana didn't even bother to turn on the bedroom light.

"I can't get her face out of my mind," Diana said. "If a painter had been able to capture it. . . . I've never seen anything like it. For once I was happy to be childless."

Dan said nothing.

"I'm sorry," she said after a moment. "I didn't mean that the way it sounded."

"I know what you meant."

"It's just that the poor girl made me feel so strange . . . about us."

Dan looked over at her, so small inside the bedclothes, so physically like her mother. "How?"

"I'm not sure I can explain. We regret the little things that don't work out, but not the big things. Seeing that woman made me realize I never told you how sorry I was—I am . . . about everything."

"You make it sound like you were driving the car."

"I wasn't thinking of that so much. I guess I'm sorry about Mother and the way things are now. Maybe about not turning out to be the kind of woman you needed me to be."

"You've been a perfect wife."

Their bedroom lit up and Diana waited for the thunder before continuing. "You needed someone to make you run like the wind."

"For that," he said, "I have your Mother."

51

The trip from Mohawk to White Plains would've taken nearly four hours if Randall Younger had had any intention of completing it. He knew he didn't even before he recrossed the one-lane bridge and brought the van out of the trees at the dark end of the one-way street. Off to the side of the cul-de-sac, the police cruiser was almost completely hidden in the trees. No one who wasn't looking for it would've noticed. But Randall Younger *was*, and he wasn't surprised when his headlights reflected something blue. There was no telling if Rory Gaffney had seen it when he emerged from the trees in the VW. Randall guessed he didn't, since the bug's headlights hadn't come on until it was fifty yards up the street. Of course there was always the possibility that Rory Gaffney didn't need to see, that the brothers were setting him up, though he doubted it. To have Randall arrested when he would immediately implicate the man who hired him made no kind of sense. Still, he didn't understand something that was going on. He kept his eye on the sideview mirror, waiting for the cruiser to come to life. Only after three blocks did a single set of headlights switch on somewhere down the dark street, and from that distance

Randall couldn't be sure it was the police car's. When he turned at the intersection, Randall tried to make out the car, but it was still too far back. He did, however, get a glimpse of Rory Gaffney's pale face up against the window of the VW. He filled the small car so full that a white, fleshy arm spilled out the open driver's side window.

The VW stayed tight behind the van as far as the highway, where both vehicles stopped for the light. It was here, an hour earlier, that the policeman had pulled up behind the VW. Randall watched the sideview, but there were no lights behind him. On green the van turned right, the VW left toward town. Randall drove well below the limit and, when the bug's tail-lights were red diamond points, pulled off onto the shoulder to wait. Back at the intersection, the police car slowed for the red light, then shot onto the highway in the same direction as the VW. Randall counted ten, then made a U-turn. He let several cars pass him for fear that a red light at the next intersection might stack up the VW, police car and van. When he got there, however, neither the bug nor the cruiser was in sight.

At the entrance to Myrtle Park, Randall turned the van up the steep grade. The high beams shot off into woods at each bend in the road, and twice they lit up bright animal eyes that seemed suspended in the air. At the summit of the park, Randall left the blacktop and steered carefully down a dirt path toward a clearing that overlooked Mohawk. The low ceiling of clouds seemed very close overhead and the air was thick with electricity.

Turning off the ignition, Randall rolled down the passenger window for some air. He took off the work gloves he'd used to load the van, but was careful not to touch anything. The only prints on the van would be Rory Gaffney's. From where he sat, it was possible to see the lightning gather around the town from all directions. Branches raked frantically at the sides of the van and the gusting wind stirred debris underneath. The concentration of lights below meant Main Street, and with that as a fulcrum Randall could gauge pretty accurately where his grandfather's house was. One of the thousands of lights below would be his mother's bedroom window. She had never told him she was terrified of electrical storms, it was just one of the things he knew—just like he'd known for many years that she was in love with a man in a wheelchair, her cousin's husband. Things like that they'd never speak of. Not long ago he had entertained the possibility of asking her about Mather Grouse. Working as one, they might fit together all the pieces: what power Rory Gaffney had wielded over his grandfather, how they'd become such enemies, how Wild Bill figured in the scheme of things. Rory Gaffney had suggested he ask her about "his poor boy," and perhaps for that reason he hadn't, certain that Gaffney wouldn't have offered if she knew anything. He couldn't imagine how he would broach the whole subject with her. Your father, my grandfather . . . is what I remember true? Did he really stand more erect than other men? Did he mean what he said, or just say it?

"I would report him to the umpire," he remembered Mather Grouse telling Price, who had smiled indulgently. Even as a boy, Randall knew his grandfather's solution was naive, that for such a philosophy to work you'd need an umpire for every player, and the umpires would have to be different in kind than the men they stood in judgment of. But he admired his grandfather's way, the purity, order and generosity of it. But in the end, he reckoned that Mather Grouse had no more faith in umpires than Price. While Randall believed little of what Rory Gaffney told him, there was no doubt that Mather Grouse had known perhaps all there was to know about his tormentor, yet had done nothing. Randall hated to think the explanation was simple fear. More likely, Mather Grouse had realized the necessity of living in the world as you found it. He remembered his grandfather's advice about Billy Gaffney, how as a boy he had been disappointed in his grandfather's too-easy conclusion that nothing could be done for the unfortunate. How strange that had sounded, coming from a man who claimed to rely on umpires.

Suddenly it was daylight and thunder rocked the van before darkness could settle in again. Randall consulted his watch. He shouldn't have to wait long. The old man wouldn't expect him back until morning and was probably in bed already. Randall would, however, wait for the storm to pass. If it awakened the old man and he looked outside to see the van in the drive, it was all over. The other sticky point was the phone tip; Randall would have to drop a dime somewhere. If the girl was asleep when he got back, he'd call from the trailer. Otherwise, a public phone. But she probably would be asleep, and her phone was in the front room. This wasn't a great plan, maybe, but it was simple.

When the rain broke, it hit the truck like a shower of stones, streaming down the windshield in a thick sheet. Randall tried the wipers, but they were useless.

The town had disappeared below, swallowed whole by the storm.

He couldn't tell just how long he'd slept, though it couldn't have been much more than half an hour. The rain was still coming down, but not so angrily, and the windshield wipers were suddenly adequate to the task. But Mohawk still was nowhere in sight.

52

The rain had been falling for quite some time before Anne heard it. As far as she was concerned, it could rain for forty days and forty nights. The streets could become rivers, and the rivers could rise and rise. The creaking of her father's house in the gusting rain gave the impression that it might already be floating away, arklike. To hell with two-by-two this time, Anne thought. This time He means business.

The flashlight lay where she dropped it, and eventually she picked it up. To remain aloft in the raging storm was foolish and self-indulgent. She got to her feet and ran her fingers through her hair, which since she had rested her head against the sloping roof was wet. Shining the flashlight along the beams, she discovered that a large portion of the ceiling was glistening. The water ran in tiny rivulets, a pool was forming beneath the metal fusebox.

Once downstairs, Anne dried her hair with a towel and watched the wallpaper grow dark high up in the corners near the already-wrinkled ceiling. This, then, was how the quarrel with her mother would end. Even Mrs. Grouse, so adept at sidestepping reality, would be forced to come to terms. Before long her own wallpaper would darken and wrinkle, and in time she'd understand. In time. That was the key. To rationalize reality took time.

In the end, Mrs. Grouse would construct a myth. In the dead of winter, during the Great Ice Storm, a limb from the Grand Oak had fallen, damaging the perfect roof. An act of God even Mather Grouse could not have provided against. The best thing for Anne to do would be to sow the seeds of this myth tonight, then stand aside and watch for signs of growth from a safe distance. So far as she knew, her mother had the money. She always had saved nickels and dimes, and now, living on her husband's slender pension, she still was probably saving them. Well, the rainy day had come.

Back in bed, Anne reset her clock. The yellow patch of light had reappeared on the house next door, which meant that her mother had not yet fallen back asleep. Morning would be soon enough to broach the subject of the roof, bring her mother upstairs and quietly summarize the evidence, the facts of the matter. It was still raining, but the thunder rumbled a good way off.

She didn't hate him, of course. But neither could she adore him any longer. She realized now that in her own way she too had canonized Mather Grouse. She and her mother simply worshiped different images. To Mrs. Grouse he had been provider, man of duty, man of honor, man of quiet reverence. To Anne he was the explorer, man of letters, inventor and more, all in the disguise of the humble leather-cutter. In his gentle ridicule of the clergyman's Sunday sermons she had seen a real blasphemer, undaunted by the traditional Christian bribes for obeisance. When times were tough and he was without work, she had always imagined that her father was being punished for something courageous—trying to organize his fellow workers, perhaps, or refusing to compromise the standards of his craft. In the end, Mather Grouse had been neither her mother's meek, dutiful conformist nor her own Prometheus. He was just a man who had put on the best roof he could afford, and now it needed replacing. He had been afraid, and she had seen the fear in his eyes the afternoon she breathed life back into him. Probably she had always been aware of his fear, rage, anguish and disappointment, though she hadn't allowed him these because she had counted on him to rescue her from her own.

She wondered if her mother was thinking about him in the bedroom below. That she hadn't turned out the light was odd.

Anne got up again and pulled on her robe. The flat downstairs was dark, except for the light in the bedroom. "Mother?" Anne said. The living room door was not completely closed, and a cool breeze riffled the curtains. It was still raining, but a sliver of moon had appeared between the clouds, enough to illuminate the street. Mrs. Grouse, dressed in her thin housecoat and slippers, was at the foot of the porch steps, slashing the ground with a long-handled ice-chopper. Clumps of earth had been cut from the lawn and now lay askew on the sidewalk. The old woman's slashing seemed only to have stirred the worms into a frenzy, and though she halved and quartered some, the only visible effect was to increase the number of glistening, writhing coils underfoot. "I don't *want* them here," Mrs. Grouse cried as her daughter gently guided her back up the porch steps. "I don't *want*—"

"I know, Mother," Anne said. "I know."

53

The rain had the curious and unanticipated effect of altering Randall Younger's purpose. He had devised the plan the very night that Rory Gaffney had offered him two hundred dollars to take the van down the line. The symmetry was appealing, and Randall felt this was exactly the sort of thing his grandfather might've done had there been only him and no wife or daughter to worry about. But now, as Mather Grouse's grandson sat high up in Myrtle Park, Mohawk invisible below, it suddenly seemed to Randall that his attempt to pay Rory Gaffney back for tormenting his grandfather was childish. He even doubted it would've received his grandfather's blessing, this dishonest act perpetrated against a dishonest man. It amounted to doing what Price had recommended, using his spikes with deadly efficiency in order to keep the game honest—except that the game was over, lost long ago, one of the contestants dead.

When the rain let up and the streetlamps of town began to sparkle, Randall backed the van onto the macadam and headed out of the park. Though it was late, he felt certain his mother was awake. He hadn't even been over to see her since moving in with the girl. Now he knew that he was going to leave Mohawk, probably for good, almost certainly in the morning, after telling Rory Gaffney that he was right about Mather Grouse's grandson. And if Randall stayed much longer, the draft board would tire of writing letters, and if they came looking, as eventually they surely would, they'd find him.

To tell his mother what he was doing with his life seemed imperative, but he couldn't and he knew she didn't expect it of him. Going to jail was hardly productive; he wasn't, it now seemed, quite that idealistic. Of course, he could go down to the draft board and make a deal. Given his race, intelligence and skills, there was a good chance he'd end up holding a typewriter-ribbon instead of an M-16. It was the Boyer Burnhoffers whose destiny it was to wake up dead one morning five thousand miles away from the friendly base of Nathan Littler's statue. The Randall Youngers were molested with haircuts, but did all right otherwise.

But he wasn't all that pragmatic, either. Which left Canada or the open road, and the latter was more appealing. Randall liked the fact that his was a sizable country, large enough to stay lost in without exactly running away. There was enough Mather Grouse in him not to like the idea of flight. On the other hand, no law obliged you had to have a permanent address, or even a forwarding one. In Mohawk he no longer had any obligations that he could think of.

There was the girl, but he had never misled her. B.G. was no worse off for having known him. Nor any better off, he had to admit. She knew, now that he thought about it, what he was going to do before he did. Leaving town, he would disappoint people—Harry and The Bulldog, even the ladies he made salads for— but they wouldn't be hurt. He had already hurt his mother by dropping out of the university, but he doubted that dropping out of Mohawk would strike her as tragic or even regrettable. It would be months before his father noticed. Who else was there to consider?

He pulled up at the intersection of Mountain and Fifth just as his mother's bedroom window went dark. The storm was spent, though the gutters were still running fast and deep. With the window down, the air smelled sweet and cool as fresh earth. Perhaps a sound caught Randall's attention, but just as he thought *there's no one else* a solitary figure belied him on the curb across the street, almost invisible against the dark line of trees. Randall pulled the van alongside, and said "Get in."

Wild Bill did as he was told. His scraggly hair was matted, his clothes heavy with water. The expression on his face implied he had just seen wild and miraculous things, and he shook all over. "Roll up the window if you're cold," Randall suggested, but he didn't respond. Shivering violently, he craned his neck far out the window to catch a last glimpse of Mather Grouse's home before it disappeared.

54

After swinging his heavy legs out of bed, Rory Gaffney sat still until the trailer settled. He was wearing nothing but a grayish T-shirt. The girl had drawn the covers up over her own nakedness and turned away from him. He had used Randall's key, then pulled the chain lock off the wall. The baby was asleep, and putting up a struggle wouldn't have changed the outcome. Rory Gaffney studied her back for a minute, till his attention was distracted by a glow outside the curtains. He listened, but heard no motor. "Don't be like that, young 'un," he said. "This is old news."

She didn't say anything at first, and when she did speak it was to the wall. "Things are different now. I told you."

Rory Gaffney stepped into his shorts and arranged himself in them carefully, as if placing a bird in a nest. "Things aren't different. They're always the same." Then he added, "Thank God."

"Don't talk about that. If there was one, he'd of settled with you a long time ago."

"That's where you're wrong. I'm made in His image, so I don't blame myself." He zipped his fly by way of punctuation and pulled his shirt from the tangle of bedding. "Who gave you this trailer to live in when you was swelled up like a balloon and no husband and no place to go?"

Tucking in his shirttail, the old man went to the window and pulled back the curtain. The rain had slowed to a drizzle.

"He'll take me away from here if I ask him."

Now she had rolled over and was looking at him. Without bending over he pushed his feet into leather moccasins.

"Sure he will," the old man said. "Admires the hell out of you, he does. Plans to marry you. Which is how come he give me the keys to the trailer and told me I could keep you company."

He took the keys out of his trouser pocket and tossed them to her.

"You don't really think I'd believe anything *you* said."

"Don't believe me. Tell *him* all about it."

"I won't have to. He'll smell you on the sheets."

"Then change 'em."

"We could put you in jail," she said, as if unsure.

"Nah," he said. "I didn't force my way in here, and you didn't put up no fuss. At least no more'n usual. Besides, who'd believe you and professor longhair?"

"I know somebody they'd believe. Your own brother. He's in love with me, in case you don't know. Everybody down to the diner says so."

"Wrong again," he said. "He loves *me*, the dumb fuck. Always has. Besides, people don't tell. Too embarrassed. They look at guys like me and see theirselves. They'll squeal on some guy that robs a bank, maybe, because they can't imagine doing it. But what we just done is what all of them are thinking about doing every time they look at a girl like you. I'm just them, and nobody rats on theirself."

"The whole world isn't like you," said the girl.

"Enough of it." He ran his fingers through his hair and stooped to examine himself in the mirror. On the way out, he peered into the darkness of the child's room.

The girl sat up in bed. "Get," she said. "I may not be able to keep you out of here, but that's one room you don't go in 'less you want to wake up with a slit throat some morning."

"The way you talk," he said, grinning over his shoulder. "Cover yourself. I'm too old for thinking about double headers."

He shut the door behind him. The rain had stopped, but the breeze blew heavy drops from the trees overhead, hitting the ground at the old man's feet like tiny grenades. The air was fresh after the storm, and Rory Gaffney felt freshened as well. On nights like this, it was good to be alive. Of course, it always *was* good to be alive, but these nights he could see himself living to a hundred.

It was roughly fifty yards through the trees to the house. He'd left a light on in the kitchen to see by, but when he started up the path, something passed between him and the yellow window. "Who is it?" Rory Gaffney said, feeling a flicker of fear. Then, "Oh, it's you."

The first bullet caught him in the shoulder and spun him around as if he'd been grabbed from behind. He regained his balance and looked at his ruined shirt. "What—" he began, but his voice was stopped by two sharp explosions and he staggered back toward the trailer. The impetus flung him off the path, but he kept running through the thick underbrush anyway. By the time he got to the trailer, everything was going black.

Even before he hit the door face first and slumped into it, his knees resting on the cinder block, he suspected that he wouldn't live to a hundred. And by the time the girl inside could get to the door that his solid body had buckled, he was dead.

55

Randall drove past the diner, but there were no lights upstairs or down and he didn't want to drop Wild Bill off in his present state. Randall hadn't expected him to speak. For years now he hadn't. But huddled in the corner of the van, shivering like a dog that's misbehaved, Bill looked even more pitiful than usual. "We'll get some coffee," Randall said. "Then I'll take you home." Wild Bill showed no sign of having heard. He was staring straight ahead, but whatever he saw was coming from inside.

Main Street glistened beneath the street lamps. Though the rain had ceased, Randall kept the wipers on, reassured by their gentle rhythm. "You're cold," he said, though the air after the storm was clear and still warm.

The closer they got to the outskirts and the Gaffney house and trailer, the more Wild Bill shook, his shoulders hunched up beneath his ears, his hands clenched prayer-fashion over his groin. "Almost home," Randall reassured him. "We'll get you taken care of."

His companion seemed far from comforted, and if they hadn't been so close, Randall would've pulled over. When they turned into the drive and something flashed in front of the van's headlights, Wild Bill howled in panic. Randall hit the brake just as Rory Gaffney rammed the side of the trailer so hard that it rocked. Bill lunged forward, his head striking the windshield, then sat back dazed, fingering the knot that immediately started forming on his brow.

Randall got out of the van. Rory Gaffney had hurtled in front of the van so suddenly that he hadn't been able to make out who it was. Now the body lay crumpled and still near the cinder block step, its back to the van's headlights. There was a large dent in the trailer door, which had sprung inward from its hinges, then jammed on the carpet. Inside, the baby was crying, the only sound besides the water dripping from the trees. Randall waited for the man to get up off the ground. Utterly still, he looked like a big pile of someone's dirty wash left outside a laundromat. Randall approached cautiously. Only when he saw the blood smear on the caved-in door did he begin to guess, and he wasn't sure the dead man was his grandfather's tormentor until he rolled him onto his back.

"Dead," said a voice a few inches away. The trailer's sprung door left a gap about three inches wide between the door and the frame. Behind it, on her knees, was B.G., and Randall could see she was naked.

Rory Gaffney was blood from shoulders to groin. "Yes," Randall said, stepping back. The headlights illuminated the old man's face, a mask of horror and perplexity.

"Good," the girl said. "You love me, then. I didn't know."

"What?"

The baby had stopped crying, and a sudden gust of air shook a shower from the trees arching overhead.

Randall could see he had blood on him from touching the dead man. "Call the police," he said.

"Don't worry," she said. "I'll tell 'em it was me. He had it coming. I'll say it was self-defense." He could see that in the split second it took to invent the lie, she had adopted it as the only reality.

"No," he said, but she was gone. Then he heard her dialing the phone in the living room. At the same moment he became aware of the policeman standing a few feet away, just outside the focused headlights. The gun in his hand was pointed at the ground. "Step away," Officer Gaffney said. "Don't touch my brother. *My* brother."

Randall was quick about it.

"This is wrong," said Officer Gaffney. "All of it. I know wrong when I see it, and this was all wrong from the beginning. I tried to tell him. All those years and all of it wrong. Not just him. The two of us. We never did nothing our whole lives that wasn't wrong." He raised the revolver and aimed it at Randall. "This here will be wrong, too."

As the policeman spoke, Randall became aware, somewhere on the periphery of his conscious thought, that a door on the van had opened and closed again. Gaffney had sighted Randall's middle along the gun barrel, then looked up, as if assailed by a sudden doubt. His sad expression was suddenly transformed into something more like fear, and the gun wavered. If he pulls the trigger now, Randall thought, astonished at his own objectivity, he'll miss me.

"I warned you. Keep him away from me. Tell him to shut up!"

Wild Bill had stepped in front of the headlights and become an approaching silhouette.

"Make him!" Officer Gaffney screamed.

"Stop," Randall shouted, but Wild Bill didn't appear to hear or notice either of them. In the glare of head-lights he stalked toward them on fire. It occurred to Randall that he could step between the gun and the man it was now fixed on, but in the time he took to decide not to the gun roared twice, then clicked several more times. As Randall drove forward, the revolver sighted him again, and he distinctly heard a click before burying his shoulder in the policeman's soft belly. Both of them went down. As Randall got to one knee, he caught a glimpse of Wild Bill, still in silhouette, bend-ing over his father. Then the shots had missed, Randall thought, before Officer Gaffney's revolver, swung like a club, found his right temple.

56

Cool. The sensation was enough to fix on. Lovely, like diving into a flooded quarry on a hot day. Maybe, Randall thought, I am underwater. If so, he made a mental note not to stay down too long or he'd . . . what? Something was bound to happen if he stayed down too long, but he couldn't think. . . . The cool moved to the back of his neck. Drown, that was it. If he stayed down too long he'd drown. He kicked toward the surface.

"Sit still," the girl's voice spoke to him from somewhere.

"Save me," he tried to say, but only gurgled.

"Don't," she said, closer now.

He opened his eyes, then shut them against the bright lights. "Off," he croaked, and the girl went away. Suddenly it was dark and he opened his eyes again. He wasn't underwater. The trailer was there and, far away among the trees, the yellow window of the Gaffney house. Something was missing, he reminded himself, something important. Rory Gaffney. Rory Gaffney was missing. No body in front of the door. One was slumped and twisted up against a tree, though. Randall couldn't see the face, which was turned away. He didn't have to. Somewhere, a siren whined.

When Randall struggled onto all fours, the girl at

first tried to prevent him from standing, then helped. To get him on his feet took a long time, and he couldn't have remained upright without her. "You shouldn't," she said. "Your head . . . they'll be here in a minute." It now seemed to Randall that there were several sirens, some close, some miles away, from all different directions. He saw that the damp rag she'd been using to bathe his head was bloody. So was the policeman slumped against the tree. So was the door of the trailer and the cinder block. Randall checked again to make sure that Rory Gaffney had not reappeared. "Bill . . . " he started.

The revolver lay on the ground a few feet from the policeman. So, Randall thought, he hadn't dreamed the dead man. "Help me," he said, not knowing what he meant, and wanting to cry because he didn't.

One of the many sirens had now drawn close, and bouncing headlight beams reflected halfway up the trees from the street below. When the cruiser pulled up next to the van, Randall and the girl were again blinded, and he briefly lost consciousness. He came to, still on his feet, a moment later. One young policeman was pointing a gun at Randall, and the other, who couldn't have been more than a year or two older than Randall, stood over the dead man, his arms hanging limply at his sides. "His face," he said to his partner. "Look at the look on his face."

"Call it in," said the other. "Step away, miss."

"He'll fall. He's hurt."

"Drunk, you mean."

"No. Come look at his head."

"I'm staying right here, and you're staying right there."

His partner hadn't budged. "Look at his goddamn face," he said.

The radio in the police car barked off and on. Randall

still heard sirens, but they were fading. "Call!" said the man with the gun. His partner finally got into the car and rolled up the window as if he were embarrassed about what he had to say and didn't want anyone to hear, not even his partner.

Randall felt himself slip in and out of awareness. The policeman with the gun was now looking at the trailer door. The streaks of blood had dried brown, but there was no doubting what they were. The policeman looked first at the door, then at the dead officer twenty yards away at the treeline. "Jesus," he said.

His partner was a long time in the car, and looked disgusted and scared when he finally returned. "We won't be getting no help."

The policeman lowered the gun and turned. "Why the hell not?"

"Everybody's up to the hospital. The son-of-a-bitch is burnin' down. I can't raise nobody."

"So what the hell are *we* supposed to do?"

"We could toss 'em in the car and head over there ourself. Captain's there. Everybody's there."

"What about Gaff?"

"Gaff's dead."

"But I mean, Jesus Christ—"

"We should go to the hospital," the girl said. "My boyfriend needs a doctor."

The two young policemen looked at each other. Clearly they were thankful for advice. Anybody's. "Go look at his head," said the policeman with the gun, again waving it at Randall. "And stay off to the side."

The young man approached Randall as he would a snake. Randall managed to stay on his feet until the young cop had a good look. Then his legs went. Next thing he knew, they were all in the back seat of the moving vehicle. Himself. The girl. The baby. The two policemen were up front, the steel grill in between providing their security. The driver braked suddenly to avoid something in the road. "What the hell?" he said.

"Drunks," said his partner.

"Didn't look it."

"Keep going," the younger cop said. "We already got trouble enough."

57

All in all, the fire at the new hospital is disappointing. From the outset it's obvious that despite the rather impressive columns of flame, the firemen will soon contain the blaze in a single wing. The drive has been barricaded too far up for spectators to enjoy the full effect. Inevitably they draw comparisons between this blaze and the razing of the Nathan Littler, which everyone agrees was high drama. There is little danger here, since the fire broke out in the maintainance wing.

The crowd can only encourage the flames to leap into the night sky. Their Saturday night has been prolonged, and they're thankful for the diversion. Some have brought bottles. "Don't let it go out 'til I get back," people say, hurrying home to call friends and neighbors or to stock up. Within half an hour, their number has quadrupled and grown festive. The Velvet Pussycat has emptied out, and the other bars are closed. Some of those gathered had come with injuries, hoping to be sewn up and gauzed, but what they find is even better. Bottles of cheap whiskey circulate and their complaints are forgotten.

When the two policemen on the barricades are called away, a phalanx of drunks picks up the sawhorses and moves forward with them, ropes and all, stopping only when the breeze shifts and brings them a blast of heat from the fire. Women hike their skirts and climb onto the shoulders of their men for a better view, which also gives some boys a better view.

A police car pokes slowly through the crowd, and the restraining ropes are lifted by two self-proclaimed valets who direct the driver with exaggerated, sweeping gestures. In the back seat sit a young woman with a child and a young man slumped over her lap. People peer in, hoping to identify them, but it's dark and the riders too huddled.

"What's with them," somebody asks.

"None of your business," says the driver. Then, to his partner, "Better lock up." Once inside the ropes, the younger cop gets out and heads up the hill to find an officer who can tell him what to do.

At this point a drum of something flammable ignites in the maintainance wing, and broken glass showers out into the night, all the way to the onlookers at the rear, who cheer enthusiastically. Somebody says it's a shame the whole place doesn't burn down; it was a piece of shit from the beginning, and the wiring contractor in particular belongs in jail. "Bullshit," another man shouts. "Somebody set it. They got the bastards over there in the cop car." This makes sense even to those who haven't even seen the car, and the arson rumor itself lights up the crowd. "People coulda been killed," calls an angry man with an open cut on his forehead. "They'll get off," says the woman riding his shoulders. "Some lawyer-sharpie will get 'em off."

Since there's no one present to stop them, the barricades are again moved forward. The police car, which had been parked well inside, is now outside the ropes and swarmed. The young policeman, returning down the drive, mistakenly concludes that the cruiser has vanished, and hurries back to report its theft. When he fails to locate his partner, he realizes his error. The car wasn't stolen. His partner's just moved it, and perhaps has taken the prisoners downtown, which is what he had wanted to do in the beginning.

"Send her down, David!" yells the fire chief, looking up at the sky. Rain clouds have rolled in, and the sliver of moon is gone.

Several boys clamber atop the police car for a better view, and the still swelling crowd packs tightly around it. The car begins to rock, much to the delight of the boys on top. "Who is it?" yells the man with the bleeding forehead, his nose flattened against the rear passenger-side window. "Tell . . . us . . . your . . . names!" Somebody pulls up a brick and hands it to him, but he balks. Luckily, the man standing next to him, already the veteran of one fight tonight, has a heavily bandaged hand. "Here," says the man with the bleeding forehead, handing him the brick. As it turns out, the bandaged hand that qualifies this one to break the glass disqualifies him from doing a good job of it. His grip on the brick is weak, and when it strikes the car window, the brick flips into the air, skitters across the roof of the car and disappears over the other side. No one over there can be made to understand the problem. A jovial group, they're thoroughly content to rock the cruiser. And within five minutes, David sends her down. Everyone knows this signals the end of the party, and only the firefighters are happy about it. In a matter of minutes the streets adjacent to the hospital are jammed with horn-blaring cars.

When there is excitement somewhere in a small town, much can happen elsewhere without attracting notice: Such is the immutable law of diversion. Only when the diversion is recognized for what it is are the more significant details—entirely overlooked at the time—recalled, and then only reluctantly, out of embarrassment. The morning after the fire at the Mohawk Medical Services Center, many remember seeing a dark figure struggling with what they had concluded was a drunken companion in his arms. But everyone had been hurrying toward the bright horizon in the southwest.

The following morning, when that same horizon began to brighten truly, a milk truck labors up Steele Avenue hill, known a few years before as Hospital Lane. The nickname didn't long outlive the old Nathan Littler. Now the hilltop is a seldom used parking lot, well paved but inconvenient to the Main Street businesses whose rooftops it overlooks. The driver of the milk truck is a man of local distinction. Nearly twenty years earlier, he was the driver whose truck killed Homer Wells, once his slide down the entire icy length of Hospital Hill was complete. Since that morning, the driver of the milk truck has given considerable thought to the notion of fate, and this morning, like most others, finds him with much on his mind. In fact, this morning's run is to be his last. The Bronson Dairy is calling it quits, the victim of supermarkets, convenience stores and cardboard cartons.

At the top of Steele Avenue, the truck shakes to a stop. In the center of the parking lot is a mound. The more the driver of the truck stares at it in the gray half-light of early morning, the more puzzled he becomes.

For some things, it's too small, and for others too large. Finally, the driver gets out and walks over to where Wild Bill Gaffney kneels, dead and cold, his arms locked in rigor mortis around his father, whose expression of mortification is later explained by many as the result of being dragged up Steele Avenue hill by a half-wit to a hospital that was demolished almost a decade before, as Wild Bill himself had good cause to remember.

Harry Saunders, up early to open the diner, hears the sirens wail up Steele Avenue and feels ill. "You better get up there," his first customer tells him, and so he goes, slower now than on the day the Nathan Littler came down. In the middle of the parking lot Harry sees a small circle of men in work clothes, who step aside when they see him. The grotesque mystery on the macadam holds no fascination for Harry, who goes white and immediately starts back down the hill. While the other men whisper in wonder of how a man with two holes in his chest had managed to carry a two-hundred-fifty-pound man up Steele Avenue hill, and why on earth he would've wanted to, Harry Saunders, as he stands before his grill, bacon spitting angrily, can only imagine the wonder and confusion of his good friend when he discovered himself mistaken and alone under the night sky in Mohawk.

58

At the bar in Greenie's were five men, along with another small group clustered around the shuffleboard machine. They all mumbled hellos to Dallas when he came in, but they weren't the usual hellos and Dallas knew it. People had been acting peculiar all day, and whenever he entered a room he felt he was already the subject of conversation. Nothing malicious, of course, and he didn't blame anybody. People just didn't know how to behave in times like this, and he wouldn't have either. Instead of joining the men at one end of the bar, he instinctively took the stool next to the one reserved for Untemeyer. It was a little after three-thirty, and the bookie showed up at four o'clock sharp.

Woody brought Dallas a draft. "Anything I can do?" he said.

"You can let me take four or five grand."

"Sure enough. I'll just take it out of petty cash." He paused. "Rudy hit the number yesterday."

Dallas shook his head. "Five hundred wouldn't help, even if he still had the five hundred, and he wouldn't be Rudy if he did."

"I'd give it to you, if I had it."

"I know that, Woody."

The bartender hovered, wondering how to start. Finally he said, "I never met your kid, but I don't believe he done that. Where they got him?"

"Up in the hospital, still. They haven't even let his mother see him yet."

Benny D. came in and pulled out the stool next to Dallas, waving Woody away. "You're something," he said to Dallas.

"What."

"Anybody else would be chasing me, but not Dallas Younger. I gotta chase him. He not only doesn't bother to show up for work, he can't even call to let people know where he'll be."

"I'm right here."

"Asshole," Benny D. took out a wad of bills and stuffed them in Dallas's pocket. "It's two grand, in case you're wondering. Say thanks."

"Thanks."

"You're tough."

"I mean it. Thanks."

"I want it back someday. They set bail?"

Dallas shook his head. "Ten grand is John's guess."

"Jesus."

"I got a thousand from a guy I know pretty good. Your two makes three. My ex-wife says she's got seven hundred or so in a savings account."

"Rudy hit the number last night."

"So I heard."

"Probably back in the local economy by now. The kid got a lawyer?"

"John said he'll go see him, but I don't know. He's still pretty sore about his face."

"He's an asshole. Let me have Dominic do it."

"I can't pay him."

"You can work it out later. Dominic's all right."

"Yeah, let's do that."

When they finished their beer Benny D. left, passing the bookie on his way in. Untemeyer assumed his usual perch. "You picked a bad time," he grumbled, brushing cigar ash off his sleeve.

"When's a good one?"

"I've been taking a beating."

"You've been taking a beating for fifty years. I don't need to hear about it."

"What do you need."

"A bundle. John says bail'll be around ten grand."

"I hear he's out of bookmaking."

"He had some tough luck."

Untemeyer nodded. "I figured he would. A man shouldn't have more than one racket. I can spot you a couple grand if it'll help."

"It would."

Untemeyer wrote out a check and, from habit, a small slip.

Dallas's pocket was getting thick, its bulge reassuring. "How the hell old are you anyway," he asked.

"Never mind. I'm not going to die before you pay up, so you can forget about that."

"Really. I'd just like to know."

"I'll piss on your grave anyhow, so what's the difference?" Greenie's was filling up. "Go away. You're bad for business, and I need a good day for once."

Dallas threw a dollar bill on the bar. "I can take up a collection if you want," the bartender offered.

"He already did," Untemeyer growled. "Your ex-wife still live around here?"

"She's almost as broke as me," Dallas said.
"The old lady still alive?"
"Her mother? As far as I know."
Untemeyer shivered.

59

The corridors of the Mohawk Medical Services Center smelled smoky, though all the windows were open and fans had been set up to circulate the air. Like many summer storms, the one that had struck the night before had granted only temporary respite. Again it was muggy and wet, and when the sun broke through everything steamed. Anne Grouse had the waiting room all to herself. There were magazines to read, but instead she watched the sun drop out of sight behind Myrtle Park. Then the street lamps came on, barely discernible in the gloaming.

No one—doctor, nurse, staff—had said anything to her for hours. She had spoken to Dan on the telephone, and of course he offered to come out, but she told him not to, then regretted it immediately. She almost wished Dallas was here to share the responsibility of waiting. He'd been by the house earlier and she'd foolishly given him her savings account for Randall's bail. She didn't mind the money, obviously, but in a weak moment had violated one of the few rules she lived by, which was never to give money to Dallas. In a way, that Dallas was off someplace trying to be useful was just as well. His company was never soothing, though it wasn't all his fault. He wanted to be taken seriously, the one thing she'd never been able to do. Briefly she felt sorry for the people he was borrowing from. If he didn't get the full amount, he'd probably drop the whole bundle on a sure thing at Saratoga. In the end she'd have to ask her mother to put a second mortgage on the house, and of course Mrs. Grouse would do it. The old woman could inspire random violence moment to moment, but for the big things could be counted on, provided that sacrifice and not intervention was called for. Anne smiled to herself. There was, after all, something to be said for sacrifice.

Mrs. Grouse had been shaky after her assault on the worms, and Anne had sat with her until she finally slept, but when she came down early in the morning, before the call about Randall, her mother had already eaten breakfast and was housecleaning. She'd even been outside to clean up the lawn. She never allowed the ship of state to list for long. Now it was back on an even keel, and Anne knew that any references to the previous night would be greeted with blank stares. That night no longer existed. When Dallas called with the news, Anne said nothing to her mother.

When the evening shift came on at the hospital, one doctor made the mistake of venturing into the waiting room. "I want you to tell me about my son," Anne told him. The doctor was young and clearly intimidated by so attractive a woman fifteen years his senior. "Let me find out what I can," he said. "They'll talk to me. I think."

Fifteen minutes later he was back, but in the interim had gathered himself and applied the mask of his profession. "He's resting well. You'd better go home and get some rest yourself."

"I'd like to sit with him a while."

"I'm sorry."

"It's the police, isn't it."

"I'm sorry."

"Yes, you are."

At nine, she gave up. In the lobby she saw Diana Wood at the admissions desk. Anne almost didn't recognize her, she was so stooped, so gnarled. There was no girl left in her, and her expression was even more vacant than Anne felt. When she looked up and saw Anne at her elbow, she flushed.

"You didn't have to come," Anne said.

"I'm ashamed," she said. "I'm not here about Randall."

"Not again."

"She's curious about the fire, I think. Has to know what's going on."

"I'm really sorry."

"Don't waste the feeling," her friend advised. "Most people assume they have an unlimited supply of emotions. They don't."

"Do you have time for coffee?"

"I better not. I always end up paying double for tardiness."

"Please, have a cup with me. You can blame the desk."

Diana shook her head. "Go see Dan. He'd love the company, and he's better at it." Before Anne could object, her cousin added, "Dallas stopped by around noon."

Anne took a sharp breath. "Oh, no."

"We didn't mind, really. I wish it could've been more."

"But you don't have it."

"If we didn't have it, we couldn't have given it. Besides, we hadn't seen him in years. Why don't you and he grow old?"

Anne reluctantly watched her cousin walk down the corridor and wait patiently for the elevator that wouldn't come.

Dan was watching television when she came in. "Don't worry," she said. "I haven't come to seduce you."

"Hmmm," he said. "Tonight I could be had, maybe."

"Not me. I feel like I've been had. And had."

"Things don't look good," he said. "I've been hearing some stuff. Turn that down, if you want."

Anne turned it off. "Tell me."

"They found a van full of stolen leather out there. Speculation is that one Gaffney brother has been stealing for years, probably with his brother's knowledge. Randall was involved somehow, probably driving the stuff downstate."

"I don't believe it."

"That's their thinking, is all. There must've been some kind of blowup. When the cops got there, they found Randall all bloody, the dead cop a few feet away. Apparently the kid was wearing gloves, too. That makes it look worse. They figure he shot the cop, then tried to make it look like suicide."

"The son was killed too? Billy?"

Dan nodded. "They found him and his old man someplace downtown. Nobody knows how they got there. The good part is that there are some things that don't add up, at least according to my sources. All of which is private, by the way. Bail is going to be out of sight, in any case."

"You shouldn't have given Dallas the money."

"I didn't mind."

"You can't make up for things that way. You can't make up for them at all."

"That's not why I did it. I'd just rather him have it than Milly. Next time she goes in, it's the ward."

"God, Dan."

"Don't look at me like that. You've got your own worries, kiddo. Besides, when the bank officers arrive, I'm going to be the happiest man in Mohawk County."

Anne sat next to him on the sofa and took his hand. "Let's run away," she said. "Like I wanted to twenty years ago."

"It hasn't been me stopping us."

"Nonsense. It's been your ethics, not mine."

"And you've been counting on them."

"Meaning what?"

"Meaning you aren't as wild as you think. You're Mather Grouse's daughter, after all. And a good deal more, thank God."

"But not an abject sinner?"

"No. Just a sinner. Garden variety. Garden of Eden variety."

When Anne got home, the living room light was on downstairs. Anne went in, never suspecting her mother might have a visitor at this hour. She did, though. Mrs. Grouse sat very straight, smoothing her thin housecoat over her slender knees. Across the room, looking even more uncomfortable, sat the man in the alpaca suit.

60

Dallas Younger arrived to meet his ex-wife at the hospital hours after the prearranged time. The place was quiet, idling between the end of visiting hours and the closing time at the bars. The wing that had burned the night before looked charred and desolate. Two rent-a-cops were protecting the ruins from adventuresome boys. In the lobby, a pretty young girl was alone at the reception desk, and Dallas smiled at her when she looked up. "Younger," he said.

The girl told him Room 237. Since he was late anyway, he decided to call Benny D., locating him eight dimes later at the Oak Lounge. "Where you been?"

"Looking for you," Dallas said.

"I'm right here. Dominic went out to the hospital."

"That's where I'm at now. I haven't been up yet."

"Don't be surprised if they don't let you in. According to Dom, he has a bad concussion and the cops haven't had a real go at him yet. They won't let anybody in until they do. Rumor has it they fucked up and let him sit in the car while the hospital was burning and then took him down to the station for questioning before admitting him. A couple of the doctors are all bent out of shape, and they'll probably testify if you decide to sue. That's the good news."

"The bad?"

"Twenty grand, Dominic figures. Minimum."

Dallas slumped into the seat in the booth. He had raised a little over eight thousand. One or two people might be able to pony up a little more, but not that much more.

"I can't make it."

"Of course you can't. How do you think they pick those figures?"

Dallas knew that, had known it all day and ignored it, glad for something to do. But there was a cop dead, and bail as high as it had to be. "It stinks," he said.

"They figure he'll skip. Turns out he was drafted and failed to report, so that doesn't help. The DA's acting pretty cocky about the whole fuckin' thing, but Dominic says he's encouraged. Over what I don't know. You can bet they'll try to protect Gaff's reputation." Benny D. paused, and Dallas heard his cigarette lighter click. "What do you figure happened out there?"

Dallas had no idea. He couldn't picture Randall shooting anybody, but then he couldn't picture Randall at all. Their paths never crossed, except at the diner, and then the boy was always in the kitchen. He never asked for anything, never seemed to want anything. Including the companionship of his father. Not that Dallas had been such a hot father, but you'd have thought the kid would have to be mad or something. Instead, it was like he hadn't even noticed.

After he hung up, Dallas just sat for a while. By now Anne would be hopping mad. She wouldn't say anything, but he'd look at her and feel unworthy, the way he always felt around her. Then it occurred to him that with any luck she'd given up by now and gone home, a possibility that cheered him considerably as he rode the elevator to the second floor. The waiting room was empty, so he ambled down the corridor glancing at the three-by-five name cards in the metal slots outside each room until he came to 237, "Younger." There were no policemen in sight, and he ducked in.

Inside were two beds, one empty and the other occupied by a young girl, asleep, her light brown hair radiating outward on the white pillowcase. Her face, neck and arms were covered with purple bruises so bright they looked painted on, since there was no swelling. Dallas' first thought was that Randall had been moved, probably to some high-security wing where the cops could grill him in peace.

A woman was seated on the edge of the girl's bed and, when she turned to see who'd come in, Dallas saw it was his brother's wife. Her eyes registered nothing when she looked straight into his face. "Younger," he'd said at the desk, not thinking.

Someone had told him a week or so ago that his niece was sick, but despite repeated efforts to make himself remember he'd succeeded in forgetting. Since the night they'd slept together, Dallas thought about her pretty often, and there were times when he would've liked to go back. But he feared it would happen all over again. And though he was angry when he heard that John, married with three kids, was hanging out with her, there wasn't a thing he could do about it. She'd lost a good deal of weight and was prettier than she'd been since before David married her.

It wasn't Loraine he looked at now, but the girl. He couldn't look away, and without wanting to he moved closer, up to the foot of the bed. His throat tightened and he couldn't breathe right. Trying to fight it off, the way he had delayed throwing up when he was a child, he tried to imagine his niece in the form before him. But there was little resemblance, and when he remembered the closet still half-full of his brother's presents, he thought it would be good to die, if only to escape what he was feeling. If there was an open window, he thought, I'd jump.

Then, to make matters worse, he realized Loraine was looking up at him and had actually taken his hand. Somehow she had found something to feel for him who couldn't have deserved it less. Suddenly he realized he was crying. He hadn't done that in twenty years, even at David's funeral, and was embarrassed for doing it now. "Don't," his brother's wife was saying. "It's not your fault. You came. You're a good man. A good man." When she said that, he let some terrible sound escape, and before he knew exactly what he was doing, he had emptied his pockets into Loraine's lap. Some of the bills fell to the floor, fifties and hundreds, all mixed together, neither counted nor organized. Then he ran out of the room and into a stairwell, at the bottom of which he made a wrong turn and found himself not in the lobby but in a dark corridor. Then he took another turn and was outside, the stars overhead sectioned into grids by the steel rafters above. He tripped, got to his feet, fell again. The ground was wet and dirty. When he emerged, the rent-a-cop grabbed him roughly. "You got no business in there," he said dutifully. "No business at all."

"I got lost," Dallas choked, the smell of the dead fire deep in his lungs, black char all over his hands and clothing.

The cop shoved him in the general direction of the parking lot. "Well, get unlost, for Chrissake." Lost? Crazy was more like it. In his long and varied career in enforcement, he'd studied people carefully and concluded that most of them were full of shit.

61

People in Mohawk still talk about the events leading up to the Randall Younger trial. Headlines in the *Mohawk Republican*, television coverage on all the tri-city TV stations and, in general, a circus atmosphere. Cameras everywhere and the issues all but lost as revelation followed closely upon revelation. It was alleged by the tanneries that Rory Gaffney, his son William and Randall Younger had been engaged in transporting stolen leather. The man who owned the van reported it stolen as soon as he heard about the trouble, but the police were suspicious and after an hour or two of interrogation he withered and directed them to the shack across the tracks from the tannery. The police chief suggested he state unequivocally that Officer Gaffney had no part in the thefts, and he complied.

Coincidentally, just as the pre-trial publicity was nearing its height, a long awaited, federally funded study was published, officially linking the abnormally high incidence of cancer, leukemia and Lou Gehrig's disease in Mohawk County to the tanneries and mills. Numerous charges of illegal chemical dumping in the Cayuga Creek as well as citations for unsafe working conditions in the shops were specified and substantiated. One mill was closed down by the state and two others closed voluntarily under the onslaught of the *Republican*'s editor, for many years the sole enemy of the tannery owners. The old arguments—that a coalition of shopowners had deviously and systematically prevented clean industries from entering the county, preferring decline to competition—were raised and examined, this time in the big city papers. As outrage and animosity toward the tanneries mounted, Rory Gaffney, who'd apparently been stealing from them for years, was elevated to folk-hero status, and the men who for decades had drunk draft beer with him at Greenie's began to recall fondly the many times Old Gaff had taken on the owners and shop stewards, very nearly unionizing the men. None of this boded particularly well for Randall Younger, who stood accused of snuffing out this simple and noble flame. Those prone to moralizing saw parallels between the fate of Rory Gaffney and that of the Kennedys, struck down by outcasts unworthy to shine their shoes.

Once the Gaffney myth was gaining decent momentum, however, there was a third revelation, this one made by none other than The Bulldog, "Your Hostess" at The Grotto, beloved wife of Harry Saunders. Indeed, Harry was probably the motivating force behind his wife's revelation. She had first met Rory Gaffney when she was just a girl, living with her mother and older sister in Cresson, a tiny community in central Pennsylvania. The sister had been married but left her husband—a godless man, she said—to live with those who cared something for her. It was this sister's husband who appeared on their doorstep one afternoon, and with him a seventeen-year-old boy who said nothing at all and stared at nothing at all out of swollen eyes that were little more than slits. The boy frightened her more than the man, she said, because she couldn't think why he was the way he was, and if anyone else knew, they wouldn't tell her. She concluded that he must've been visited by God, and guessed that it must be God he was looking at through the slits, which was why he was so puffy all over. But as the days passed, the swelling lessened and his eyes opened a little and he began to resemble a boy. At night she heard the arguments between the man and her older sister, him saying that he had a good mind to take her back and show everybody what her running off had done. That if she couldn't help heal her own flesh and blood, he'd make sure the whole world knew the kind of unnatural mother she was. One day her sister broke down completely and told her she must in God's judgment be corrupt for such a terrible thing to have happened, and to be pursued so far. And the younger girl thought her sister must've been right, because she was never the same afterwards, not even when the man and the boy were gone. "I am unholy in God's sight," her older sister told her again and again during that last year.

For months after he left, the swollen boy who made crazy sounds when he talked haunted her imagination, and she frequently expected him to reappear on the porch. Then came her sister's death, which meant that he wouldn't be coming back, thank God, but still she couldn't forget him. Then, for a long time, things didn't work out, first one thing and then another. Her mother was placed in a nursing home in Johnstown, Pennsylvania, and waiting for her to die took years. And one day a letter came for her sister, who'd been dead for well over a decade, from the man who had brought the boy, and it said the boy had gotten into a mess and to come back if she wanted to. She tore the letter up and didn't bother answering, but it got her thinking about the swollen boy again, and wondering if he was still looking at God. She didn't believe in God herself any more. Not since her mother and sister died, and she discovered that not believing didn't make such a hell of a difference. So, a month after the letter came, she went to Mohawk to find out about the boy, who by then had been taken to Utica. People said a man named Harry Saunders had been his only friend, and since Harry was a decent enough man she got him to marry her. She saw the man Gaffney once or twice—he'd changed surprisingly little, and she would've recognized him anywhere—but she never let on who she was, or that she remembered him, or that over the years she had pieced it all together. Every Christmas she sent him a card with a message inside. "Unholy in the sight of God," she scribbled every year, signing her dead sister's name—the only retribution she allowed herself.

Her story so confused people that some began to credit the protestations the girl who lived in the trailer had been making from the start, an awesomely ugly tale that no one save Randall's lawyer had wanted to believe.

From a reporter's standpoint, the best ticket in town was Dallas Younger, father of the accused, who, it turned out, had a disarming presence on television. Without coaching, he would look right into the camera and talk as if to another human being. Before long a string of reporters were following him around as best they could, this despite the fact that he clearly knew nothing. He not only knew nothing about what had happened the night the Gaffneys died, but also knew next to nothing about his son. Either he never knew or had forgotten, among other things, the boy's middle name, his birthday, his favorite subjects in school, how long he and Anne had been married when Randall came along. But if Dallas wasn't a rich source of information, his ignorance on key points was thoroughly engaging, and one reporter, famous for his human-angle method, pronounced that what Dallas knew was the story. And what Dallas knew all about was Mohawk. He *was* Mohawk, "a backcountry prophet too unself-conscious to guess that his words and attitudes were a ringing indictment of his world." In time this last assessment became received truth, but only after Dallas was interviewed on all the local stations, quoted in the major regional newspapers and offered a lucrative contract with an Albany advertising firm to promote a new line of hunting-wear. He hadn't hunted once in his life, but according to the agency his carriage and rugged face "reeked" of the woods they'd never been in either.

That Dallas could be counted on for copy was good, because during the month preceding the scheduled commencement of the trial, no reporter got a word out of the boy's mother, an attractive woman who unfortunately didn't photograph at all well. On camera her face looked harshly angular, and she made the photogs doubt their skill, briefly, before writing her off. And since she gave the reporters nothing to write, they had to make up what they didn't know, and most of them suggested vaguely that she was a piece of the tragic puzzle of her son's ruined life. One columnist suggested that "ice water ran through her veins," a line picked up again and again.

"Shall I set these swine straight?" said Dan Wood one Sunday afternoon in October, a gray day very much like the one six years earlier when they had skimmed leaves from the pool. This year the pool was drained in September and a sheet of plastic stretched across to catch leaves. The golf course was crowded, and each time Anne heard the crack of a driver on the nearby seventh tee, she flinched, half expecting the ball to come slicing over the wall.

"I don't care what they say," she told him.

"Of course you do. Anybody would."

"You're wrong. Saying is just saying. It's only the doing that scares me."

"They'll never get a conviction," Dan said. "Any place but Mohawk, they wouldn't even try."

"The men from selective service called again yesterday, frightening Mother half to death. I'm beginning to worry about her, and I never thought I would."

"The afternoon with Milly will buck her up."

"I'm not so sure. She's never been this scared before. She's just stayed inside and closed the door. Now she's talking about selling the house."

"Why's that such a bad idea?"

"I don't know. It's Dad's house."

Dan frowned at her.

"I know what you think," she said, "so there's no reason to say it. I just can't help wondering what he'd have made of all this. He never was particularly optimistic, but I doubt even he suspected things could come unglued so goddamned fast. . . . I feel like I should keep the house, even if I can't keep it in order."

"And in this fashion are the sins of the fathers bequeathed to generations yet un-bow-ern," Dan drawled.

His evangelical prattle usually made Anne laugh. "Actually, I'm just jealous, since it turns out I'm not going to be able to keep my own house."

"Can I help? At least to forestall things?" There was still a sizable chunk of money left from what she called the Untemeyer Bequest. The old man had put Mather Grouse's winnings in an interest-earning account and let it sit there for six years. Mrs. Grouse wouldn't take it, naturally, but she had no objection to her daughter doing so, especially since Anne had replaced the roof. She had also repaid the money Dallas had borrowed from the Woods. Dan wouldn't have accepted it, and was angry with his wife when he learned that she had, but in truth they needed the money badly. Randall's bail had been set at eighty thousand, far beyond Dallas and Anne's reach, though they tried. Anne had even located Price on the off chance that he'd suddenly struck it rich. He hadn't, but was glad to hear from her just the same and very sorry about Randall, whom he "would've liked to square-up with." He offered money, which Anne refused when he confessed that he was married and had two small boys. "I'll bet they throw overhand," she said.

"Not yet." Price had laughed. "We'll wait and see."

"You better hang onto it," Dan said. "When was the last time you ever had a lawyer do anything for you."

"I'm not involved," she said, which was true so far. "Dallas says he's taking care of it."

"And when do his French lessons start?"

62

Randall didn't mind jail that much, or so he told his mother. Anne almost believed him. She made sure he had what he needed and paid him awkward visits whenever she could. They didn't talk about what had happened. He simply told her he hadn't killed anybody, and she knew this was true. Neither said another word on the subject. They did, however, discuss Billy Gaffney. "For a while, every time I looked up, there he'd be," she said after explaining the afternoon outside the tannery. "I had started seeing your father then."

"He loved you," Randall said.

"Billy? I know. But we were young and he got over it. Before long he stopped standing on the corner. Then we heard about the accident—"

"He was standing in the rain outside the house that night," Randall said. "He always looked at me like he was seeing somebody else."

"Your grandfather . . . I never knew what he had against Billy, besides the obvious, I mean. He was a Mohawk boy, and to your grandfather that was enough. I don't believe Billy could have stayed in love all those years. People don't. At least not most."

She was thinking of exceptions, Randall could tell. "Your grandfather was a good man. Under different circumstances, he could've been a great one. But like most people he had blind spots, things he just couldn't see even when they were pointed out. At times I wonder. If he ever really loved—the kind of love that hurts, I mean. I think in the end he was just afraid."

All things considered, Randall was treated well enough, partly because of the misconduct lawsuit his lawyer had filed, partly because the case was showing signs of strain with every passing day. Randall had been afraid the girl would lie for him, but she didn't. In the back seat of the police car on the way to the hospital, he'd insisted that she tell the truth, and apparently she had. It was the only thing to do, of course. She might convince people that she'd shot Rory Gaffney, but she had no conceivable reason to shoot the policeman and Wild Bill. Both she and Randall stuck to their stories and offered to take lie detector tests. Neither could be budged, even on details, and that worried the district attorney, who had motive, method and opportunity, but would've preferred to have a real case. Still, there was a dead cop and the clamoring public.

Other than his mother, Randall's only visitor was B.G. A week before the trial was scheduled to begin, she brought the baby with her. "They aren't going to let us in," she said, drawing a chair up outside the cell. "They're afraid you'll take Sue hostage or something. Crazy, huh?"

She looked lovely, and as he often did, Randall thought that if somebody taught her a little about makeup and how to dress and carry herself, she might really be something. Maybe she was anyway. He hadn't given much thought to being a family man, but she and the baby looked good to him, and it might be nice to sit someplace under a shade tree and bounce the child on his knee while she played the guitar and sang. Trouble was, there weren't any shade trees so late in October, the girl didn't play the guitar and he was in jail.

"I think it's ridick. You're the nicest person I ever knew, and that's counting everybody."

This wasn't the first compliment she'd ever paid him, but it sounded unnatural. "Something wrong?" he said when she wouldn't meet his eye.

"I guess I better tell you," she said. "Andy's back in town. Saw me on the TV, I guess. He says inasmuch as we're still married and everything—"

Randall forced a smile. "Great. That's great." He stuck his thumb through the bar, and the baby caught it and hung on.

"It's good for her—to have a father and all. Not that you weren't like a father—"

"I wasn't like a father."

She shrugged. "You think he'll just run off again?"

"Not if he's smart."

"I'd rather with you, you know."

"It looks like I might be tied up for a while, one place or another."

"I hope it's the war."

"Thanks."

"You wouldn't get killed."

He didn't consider this a point worth arguing.

"I just wish Andy was a little more stable, you know? 'Cause if he takes off again, I won't have either one of you."

"Maybe he'll run off about the time I get out."

She hadn't thought of that, and the possibility of such fortuitous timing made her grin. Randall couldn't help smiling himself.

.   .   .

Dallas visited only once. "So," he said. "Son." It was the longest twenty minutes of their lives.

About the only thing Randall regretted was missing Diana Wood's funeral. Milly had an attack, a real one, in the evening and was rushed to the hospital. Instead of returning home, Diana slept in a chair in her mother's room. At five forty-five in the morning, the nurse found her there stone-cold when she came in to prepare Milly for her tests. The old woman was snoring soundly. Mrs. Grouse was summoned to break the news to her sister, who took it all in in swift stages of disbelief, disorientation and dysfunction. "Who ever *heard* of such a thing?" she said over and over again.

63

If Diana Wood's death accomplished anything, it was to prove Anne's father wrong when he suggested that if she continued to love Dan Wood, she'd be hoping for her cousin's death. Loving him was something she couldn't help, nor wanting him, and needing she couldn't help either. But she had never wanted to take him away. She knew that now. Dan had always belonged to her cousin, and always would. When they all were younger, Anne had fantasized what their lives would've been like had she and Dan married. There were any number of believable scenarios—some happy, others tragic—and the sheer variety probably meant they didn't amount to much. The only unthinkable scenario was Diana gone.

By the funeral, Anne had begun to regain marginal control of pain and rage, but at the cemetery things began to come apart again. It was another gray day, with winter heavy in the air, and nothing made much sense. The leaves gusted to life in half a dozen different directions at once. For a while they danced furiously, tiny little cyclones, then came to rest, quivering, rippling.

A great many mourners had followed to the grave, but to Anne it seemed that about a hundred people were inexplicably absent, though she couldn't think who they might be. A lot of Dan's people came in from out of town, and there were others who looked like they might be family. Dallas was there, a harlequin of mismatched clothing. He'd been the one who broke the news, Dallas-style, over the telephone. "You hear about Diana? She's dead." Somehow he had found out even before Dan. Anne hadn't believed him, assuming that as usual he was confused, that it must be Milly. In fact she almost convinced Dallas, who knew better, since he was almost never right where Anne was concerned and easily bullied. He admitted he could be wrong, or the guy who told him might be, even though he was a good guy and you could usually take what he said to the bank. "Goodbye, Dallas," she had told him.

But he was right after all, and he felt so bad about it, even after so many years of being wrong, that he called back later to apologize. "You figure Dan needs some help," he asked. "All kinds," she told him, so Dallas told Benny D. he wouldn't be working for a while and went over to the house on Kings Road and helped Dan drink. He stood now, alert behind the wheelchair as if he suspected it might have a life of its own and, if he weren't vigilant, would race off with its occupant. He'd spent too much of his life screwing up without knowing why not to have a healthy respect for the unexpected. Dan on the other hand knew all about the chair, and the way he sat in it showed more clearly than ever before how he had become an extension of it. The vague sense of his not belonging in it, so powerful sometimes, had vanished. He seemed to have shrunken inside the black armrests.

Next to Dallas and Dan, the two old sisters leaned

into each other, looking as precarious as ever to anybody who didn't know better. Mrs. Grouse said nothing, but Milly's voice could occasionally be heard above the minister's. On the fringes of the crowd, Anne recognized Dallas's sister-in-law Loraine. She was at the church, too, though Anne couldn't imagine why, since as far as she knew the two women had never met.

After the service, since no one seemed particularly solicitous of her, Anne slipped away among the gray trees. Only from a safe distance did she look back and see the procession of black cars curling out the main gate. She found her father's grave, which she hadn't visited in the nearly six years since his death, but quickly hurried away again, sure that to open a conversation there would be a mistake. At Diana's grave several men were working beneath the canopy that covered the open hole.

"She was very kind," said a voice at her elbow, causing her to start. It was Dallas's sister-in-law, and apparently she had been standing there for some time, waiting for the opportunity to speak.

"Yes," Anne said. "I wasn't aware that you knew each other."

"Only recently," she said. "She introduced herself one night. It was at the hospital. She told me things were going to work out for my little girl. I remember she said it almost like she had some inside knowledge or something. I even started to hope again."

I wish she were here, Anne thought. Maybe she'd say something to me.

"All the doctors said leukemia."

"I'm sorry," Anne said.

"That's just it," the other woman said. "They were

wrong. It turned out to be something else. The same symptoms and really rare. It was like she knew. I don't suppose she could've though."

"No. She was just an optimist."

"I wish I could be like that. Maybe I can, now. Lately, the whole world has seemed so . . . right."

"Really?"

"I know it's selfish, but I can't help it. So many wonderful things have happened. Like Dallas showing up with all that money. I don't know how it would have gotten paid for otherwise."

Anne smiled for the first time that day.

"Did he tell you what he did?"

"No. We hardly ever see each other."

The other woman was studying her carefully. "I guess I've been wondering about it. You know Dallas. He almost never has more than he needs, and he doesn't need much."

"I wouldn't worry about it," Anne said. "Anybody lucky enough to get something out of Dallas shouldn't ask too many questions. He probably had ten dollars on a number or something."

"I guess he gave you a rough time when you were married."

"No, I gave him a rough time."

Loraine looked away, embarrassed. "I should mind my own business."

"It was a long time ago. We've both forgotten. I'm almost fond of him."

"Me, too. I mean I *am* fond of him. David worshiped him, of course."

"I remember," Anne said. She liked Loraine, whose purpose was clearer than she supposed. "Dallas can be very sweet. Also very inconsiderate. Kind. Oblivious.

Savvy. Obtuse. He doesn't know how to behave, and nobody will ever teach him, but he'll turn up when you least expect it, the nicest man you know. If we'd stayed married, there'd have been no survivors, but another woman might do better."

"I don't know if I'd be up to it."

"You could try, if you felt like it. If you end up telling him to go away, he will, and he won't hold a grudge either. He'll just forget to be mad."

They were walking along the path now and stopped where the men were finishing up beneath the canopy. "Well," said one of the men, unaware that they were not alone, "that's about it. Say hello to eternity."

64

Two days before Randall Younger's trial was due to convene, the prosecutor collapsed. He had played his hand boldly, some said recklessly, but things just hadn't worked out. The young man could not be shaken from his story. In the beginning it had looked like a child could get a conviction, but the mounting testimony and evidence weakened the prosecution's case like a wasting disease. Randall's lawyer was combing the town looking for people who had witnessed peculiarities in Officer Gaffney's last days, and he didn't have much trouble. The Presbyterian minister had discovered two thirty-eight caliber shells in the wall when he went up to investigate the darkened belfry, and these the attorney was extremely interested in. Several of the regulars at Harry's were willing to testify to the policeman's condition on the Fourth, and the abandoned car in the ditch was a matter of public record. It turned out Officer Gaffney had also accosted his landlady with explicit directions never to let anyone into his flat in so wild-eyed and accusatory a manner that the old woman had been terrified.

The way the defense would tell it, Officer Gaffney, unhinged by his impending retirement, had gone loony and started shooting and stopped when there was no one left to shoot. Then he had shot himself. Ballistics would do little to discourage such a theory. The boy's lawyer was rumored to have enlisted a big shot from down the line to testify that the bullet's angle of entry was consistent with a self-inflicted wound. The prosecution's own experts would be forced to admit to possibility if not probability. To make matters worse, the prosecution would be asked to explain why Randall's gloves were covered with Rory Gaffney's blood, while the gun used to kill Rory's brother was clean. Thus reasonable doubt would be established.

The district attorney himself would tell a very different story, admirable in its consistency. If he worked hard and told it well, he would not seem a fool. He might even convince a few jurors. But the outcome? A reasonable doubt. The boy's story, most of it, would sound true. Secretly the prosecutor had to admit that it sounded true even to him, which left him with a dead cop, a dead citizen, a dead retard, an angry public, lots of media attention, the chance of a political lifetime and nothing to do but drop the charges. In desperation he called on the boy's lawyer and offered, "in the interest of all involved," to reduce the charges to first-degree manslaughter. But the son-of-a-bitch just smiled, and the game was up. "Zilch," he told his staff. "That's what we got here." His staff had offered this much off the record for weeks. And so, late Friday afternoon, three days before the biggest trial in the history of the tri-city region, the Mohawk County district attorney called a press conference to announce that all charges against Randall Younger were being dropped because the prosecution had zilch. Then, after telephoning the

Selective Service, the district attorney went south on vacation. He had three weeks coming and intended to use every minute of it.

The media were still gathered outside the courthouse when Randall Younger was taken from his cell to the second floor for final processing of his release and the restoration of his valuables, a wallet with forty-two dollars cash. From the window above the street, Randall looked down at the mob scene in the street. Directly below near the front of the crowd were two men in sedate three-piece suits and sunglasses. They seemed far more patient than the rest, and for some reason they reminded Randall of the Cobras, who had lounged idly at the base of Nathan Littler's statue outside the junior high. He slipped his wallet in his pocket.

"Well," said Dominic. "That's it. Say what you want when we get outside. Don't be afraid to rub it in."

"I have to go to the bathroom," Randall said.

"Go ahead," said his lawyer. "Piss away. You're a free man."

The men's room was two doors down and nobody followed Randall in. A single window high on the wall opened on the alley in back of the courthouse. There was also a vertical drain pipe.

The reporters and the two men in the conservative suits had to settle for zilch.

65

Benny D. had a rough night, and as usual it was all Dallas Younger's fault. He'd started looking for Dallas eight o'clock the night before, and when the sun peeked through the trees around seven the next morning, Benny was still looking. Somewhere in the course of the long, dark night he'd forgotten precisely why he was looking for his friend and sometime mechanic, but it would come back to him eventually, and in any event the quest itself had proved sufficiently absorbing.

Dallas hadn't been to work in the three days since his kid's release and disappearance, but word of his exploits had filtered back to the Pontiac dealership. The first night Dallas had closed down a bar on the Albany road and was so drunk that he backed his car into the Mohawk River, barely escaping with his life. Somebody had called Benny D. the next day and he'd taken the wrecker to haul it out. Dallas himself wasn't there, but for some reason the car was, its rear wheels and trunk underwater, its front wheels and hood on the dry bank. To Benny D. the car looked like it was trying to climb out of the river on its own. It took him an hour to haul it onto the highway and back to the lot at the Pontiac dealership, where he locked it up safe behind the chainlink fence. He would've asked the cops to drag the river for Dallas, but somebody claimed to have seen a man clawing his way up the muddy bank, and the police were inclined to go with the hypothesis that Dallas had made it.

Indeed he had, for no sooner did Benny D. sit down at his desk than simultaneous reports of Dallas's activities began to come in from such far-flung corners of the county that Benny D. began to suspect that his friend had died and spawned nine new alcoholic lives. At the Fall Inn he bought drinks for everyone in the house and disappeared before the bartender could collect. At Greenie's he was said to have cornered Untemeyer in the sour men's room, pinned him against the wall and forcibly removed a valuable diamond ring over the man's chubby knuckle.

Since Benny D. figured Dallas was having a hell of a good time, his first instinct was to join up. No one was more fun than Dallas on a binge. Unfortunately Benny D.'s wife, who three years before had walked out on him for the second time, had suddenly reappeared. He was so surprised and, at the moment, delighted to see her that he unthinkingly promised to mend his ways and act right. He promised other things, too, things he knew he would regret deeply, but which could not be undone. In Mrs. Benny's three-year absence she had taken an associate degree in business, and as one of the provisions of her resumption of wedded bliss obliged her husband to turn over to her day-to-day management of the garage and dealership, along with the checkbook. "I don't even get to write no checks," he asked. "We'll see," she answered.

Still, all around, he was pleased. She looked better than when they had married, and she'd taken to going braless like the young college girls who were her classmates. When he looked at her, he felt lucky and grateful for her return, swollen with admiration for her breasts and herself. They had drawn the office blinds and done it right there on the desktop, their cries of delight muffled by the banging and wheezing in the shop on the other side of the wall.

Indeed, the only Mohawk resident who seemed to be having a better time was Dallas Younger, whose rampage continued. The fourth night of his binge, Dallas apparently learned of Benny D.'s salvage work, because the car was gone the next morning. Somehow, Dallas had scaled the fence, subdued the vicious mutt that Benny D., who fed him, always kept at arm's length, and somehow spirited away the car that Benny D. had purposely hidden among other autos to prevent just such an event until he could be reimbursed for his considerable trouble. And still the saga continued. Dallas at the Outside Inn, Dallas at the OTB, Dallas at Greenie's to return Untemeyer's ring and apologize about the bruised knuckle. Dallas. Dallas. More Dallas. Benny D. was cruelly ashamed of himself for being such a malcontent, but he couldn't help but wish that his beloved, jiggly wife had returned a week later. He began to droop, partly out of wistfulness, partly the result of feverish activity with Mrs. Benny, who had learned somewhere that getting laid was fun. He began to philosophize about life and nearly came to the conclusion that total happiness was not in the cards for mortal men. But he was wrong, it turned out, because Mrs. Benny told him he'd better go find Dallas and bring him back to work, since the service department was backed up with troublesome Pontiacs that would listen only to him.

So, on the night of the sixth day of Dallas's rampage,

Benny D. sallied forth in search of his chief wrench, hoping desperately that he wouldn't find his friend spent. Mrs. Benny had counted him out fifty dollars with which to conduct his search, just enough to ensure success without creating a serious risk factor. He had searched for Dallas before, of course, and knew how to go about it. Following the time-honored theory of concentric circles, he started at the geographical center of town, say Greenie's, and widened his loops until he hit the county line, the enchanted boundary that Dallas, as Benny D. knew from long experience, would never penetrate. By midnight Benny D. had canvased the likely Mohawk bars and pieced together a decent picture of his friend's travels, but the trail was still cool and he began to sense that Dallas was maintaining a twenty-four-hour lead. In terms of alcohol consumed, the lead was even more impressive, though Benny did what he could to narrow the gap. He heard about a poker game at the Knights of Columbus and dropped by. Dallas wasn't there but others were, all of them happy to see Benny D., who sat down with what remained of the fifty dollars after being assured that his paper was good. What these men didn't know was that he had legally transferred the dealership to his wife, and he saw no reason to tell them. Anyway, he felt lucky and knew that sitting still wasn't a bad strategy for finding somebody in Mohawk. Running in circles within a limited space could theoretically be endless. But if you stayed put, what you were chasing sometimes found you.

This time it didn't, though, because Benny D. had the most incredible run of luck he could remember. At one stretch he won seven hands in a row and by three-thirty had cleaned everyone at the table, whereupon the game broke up and he was on the road again. He had nearly six hundred dollars in his pocket and couldn't even brag to Mrs. Benny about it, the proscription of gambling having been one of the conditions of his parole. At seven, when the sun came up, he knew he'd have to return home defeated. He felt small and puny and doubted that even the sight of Mrs. Benny's pendulous breasts would cheer him up.

What did, in fact, was the sight of Dallas Younger's water-marked car parked in the dealership lot. Dallas was alone in the garage, standing beneath Mrs. Schwartz's ailing Bonneville. He had showered and shaved and was wearing a pressed shirt which, amazingly, said *Dallas* in flowing script. "I've been looking all over hell for you," Benny D. said.

"I'm right here. Somebody's got to look after your business. You look like shit, by the way."

"How'd you get in?" Benny D. had a lot of questions, but this, strangely, was foremost in his mind.

"With a key. How'd you think?"

"I gave you a key?"

"You must've. I got one, don't I?"

It made sense, Benny D. had to admit.

"Somebody told me your old lady was back." Dallas pressed the button that lowered the Schwartz Bonneville until the tires met the cold floor and the lift whooshed in relief.

Benny D. wondered what else Dallas had heard, and decided he'd better assert his manhood. "Took the boys for a bundle last night. Your buddy John had it the worst."

"Good," Dallas said. "I could use a hundred, since you got it."

Benny D. peeled off some bills and passed them to him.

"You ever paint a house?" Dallas said.

"Not recently."

"You got brushes and stuff? A ladder?"

Benny D. shrugged. "I guess. You can come over and check in the cellar."

"All right."

A car pulled up outside and Mrs. Benny got out. When her husband saw her through the bay doors, he shoved the rest of the money he won into Dallas's back pocket. "Put it someplace for me. Someplace safe."

Mrs. Benny walked directly into the office, then noticed the two men in the garage. "See you found him," she said, approaching carefully.

"Of course I found him," Benny D. said.

"Look at you," Dallas leered appreciatively.

"Nevermind, Dallas Younger."

"Tell her to go away and come back again. Leaving does her good."

"I'm the one doing the telling," she said before closing the office door.

"So I heard," Dallas said.

Benny D. reddened. "So where the hell were you last night?"

"Home."

"Bullshit. I was by there half a dozen times."

Dallas got into Mrs. Schwartz's Bonneville and gunned the engine. No knocks or pings. Perfect timing.

Benny D. looked at him slyly. "Wouldn't be your brother's house that needs painting?"

"You should see the place."

Benny D. shook his head. "No time of year to start painting."

"I was thinking about spring."

Dallas turned off the engine and handed Benny D. the key.

"You don't suppose we're going to end up pussy-whipped, do you?" Benny D. said.

"Nah," Dallas grinned. "Not me, anyway."

66

A car was backing out of the Woods' driveway when Anne Grouse turned onto Kings Road. She recognized the driver as Dan's nephew, who'd been a bearer at her father's funeral six years before. Though they hadn't seen each other since, he smiled and rolled down his window. "Hi. Going in to see Uncle Dan?"

Anne nodded. "How is he feeling?"

"All right," he said. "A little down. I think he wanted to say his goodbyes to the place alone."

"Maybe I shouldn't bother him. Tell me, is he drinking?"

"A little." The boy reddened. "He's okay though. I never saw anybody that can drink like him." At this his voice sounded happier. "I'd be in a coma."

For some reason Anne was irritated and in no mood for small talk. "I'll just go in and say hi."

"Sure, that'd be great. You want me to hang around?"

"No need, I don't think."

"We could go out for coffee later."

"What for?" But his hurt was immediately obvious, and she apologized. She also noted that she was forty.

"Oh," he said seriously. "I didn't think."

Dan was padlocking the pool shed when she swung the gate shut with a clang. The back door of the house was open and all its rooms empty and hollow, most of the furniture sold at auction the week before, the rest put in storage. She'd seen little of him since the funeral, and they hadn't been alone at all. Nor was Anne sure how seeing him now would work out. The length of the swimming pool was between them, a distance that seemed greater than it was. "You just missed Michael," he said.

"Actually, we passed the baton in the drive," she said. "He asked me out. Pretty funny, I thought."

"So what did you say?"

"You can be a very nasty person."

"I don't mean to be," he said. "How's tricks at Forest Lawn?"

"It's not Forest Lawn, as you well know. It's Forest Towers."

She had dropped in on her mother and aunt that morning. They had moved into the small, fourth-floor apartment the previous week. There was an elevator, cable TV, a supermarket and drugstore next door. The OTB was across the street, and Milly, to her sister's horror, had actually hobbled in, elbowing her way to the counter where she extracted two musty dollar bills from her fat coin pouch, asked for and ignored advice from a man with a tattoo, then played her own daily double. She lost her money, but not her enthusiasm. "I like that gambling," she told Anne. "All those years I lived with that son-in-law of mine, I never had a minute's fun."

"How are things," Anne asked her mother once Milly was out of earshot.

"Fine," Mrs. Grouse said. "Just fine."

"It's not going to be easy."

"I know," her mother allowed. "But it's welcome to

be needed. No one's needed me since your father."

"I'm sorry," Anne said, not that Mrs. Grouse meant anything particular by her remark. The present arrangement was perfect. Her sister was probably the only soul Milly wouldn't torment with bogus complaints and needs. When the sale of Mather Grouse's house became final, the two old women would have enough to live more than comfortably. Anne planned to be out before Christmas. The new owner had bought the Grouse home for an investment and was chagrined to hear that Anne didn't intend to stay on. But he quickly rented both flats.

"I'd offer you a chair," Dan said, "if I had one to offer."

"How'd you make out?"

"Not bad, actually. The house fetched more than we thought. Than I thought. Break-even territory."

Anne looked away.

"Of course Di didn't break even, but she always knew she wouldn't."

The swimming pool seemed to stretch even longer. Neither had moved. "If we're going to part friends, you're going to have to stop trying to hurt me, Dan."

At first he didn't say anything, just looked off past the redwood fence at the sky above the golf course. "I'm not trying to hurt you. Myself, maybe. But not you."

"But we feel the same things. That's the really terrible part. We always have. You can't punish yourself without punishing me. So please stop. I've always been the one to push for us, even when I knew there couldn't really be any us. But I won't any more. I promise. We've lost practically everything there is to lose, haven't we?"

"I'm not hurting. That's the strange part. I don't mind losing the house, or anything in it. I know I should, and I'll probably feel better when I do, but right now I just feel bored. I'd even feel better if I thought there was some tragic flaw, some error in judgment I could trace everything to. If I could look back and say I'd missed a sign, and that if I hadn't, things would've been different."

"I've taken a job in Phoenix," she said, suddenly impatient with his abstractions. "When I told them yes, I fully intended to ask you to come with me. I had this idea that we might even make each other happy in the end. I should've known better. You'd rather I went out with your dippy nephew."

"I'd kill you first."

"Good," she said. "Then we're still friends."

"Let's get out of here," Dan suggested, suddenly wheeling toward her. She closed the patio gate behind them. "I'm glad I still have the car," he admitted. "Don't help now."

He swung himself inside behind the wheel, then closed the door and rolled down the window. "Where the hell is Phoenix, Arizona?"

She collapsed the chair and bundled it around to the passenger side. "Consult a map."

"I bet they don't even have ramps. It's just like you to invite me to a place that doesn't have any goddamn ramps."

"These days they're building them everywhere."

"More trouble than they're worth, believe me."

"But they *can* be built."

"I suppose," he admitted. "In time."

67

At the Mohawk Grill there are many systems for picking winners at the track, and each of the regulars who slips in off the street when Harry opens promptly at six has his own, though as they readily admit no system's perfect or the players would all live in Florida. So they compose elaborate mathematical formulas, not to determine who the winner *will* be but who the winner *would* be if the track weren't crooked. These scientific men are not chagrined by their cynical belief that the science of handicapping is seriously compromised by dishonesty and greed. Poring over the charts of workout times and track conditions, analyzing the level of competition—these are pleasurable activities in themselves, especially in the gray morning light that slants through the diner's front windows and across their racing forms. Even more cynical are those who think the horses more or less irrelevant, and that smart money's on the trainer with the best pharmacist. This view is not widely held, since there's no way of telling who has the best pharmacist on any given day; and hence the theory isn't conducive to wagering.

Harry himself bets only infrequently, though he too has a theory. He has never felt compelled to share it with the seasoned veterans who drink his coffee, losers all, with impeccable credentials and expertise, and who would mock the naive simplicity of his system. Still, it has worked well enough for Harry, and the afficionados were the first to admit you can't beat the horses. Or the dogs. Or the dice. Or the cards. All you can do is try.

When Harry bets at all he bets jockeys, and while they're harder to handicap than the horses beneath them, they're not entirely immune to scientific observation. Harry's cardinal rule is to never bet an untested jockey; they sometimes win, but mostly find ways to lose on their few good mounts. Some seem born to lose. The top jocks are more or less equally talented, and so the issue, it seems to Harry, is the human spirit: pride and concentration. Desire. These qualities are by no means constant in the human breast, as Harry well knows, and so he watches their ebb and flow until some subtle tuning fork of his own begins to throb and vibrate in sympathy, suggesting for example that Shoemaker will take five winners home in a row. Consequently, Harry will bet the Shoe every time he's up, never mind the nag, and keep betting until he senses the pride, the desire, the need ascending in another man. It's a silly theory, Harry knows, but it gives him pleasure and occasionally even works.

This morning, however, Harry has no strong feelings about any given jockey, and feels little in the way of desire himself. Today it wouldn't surprise him to learn that there were no winners anywhere in America. He says as much and this remark stirs one of the coffee drinkers sufficiently to make him look up from his form. "*Some*body's got to win, Harry. They can't *all* lose."

"All mine can," another remarks.

The door opens to admit a group of five men, among them John. As if by design, five stools remain at the counter to accommodate them. "Who's the big loser," somebody asks.

"You wouldn't believe it," says one of the gamblers, "but we played all night and broke even."

Harry flips sausage patties and smiles, his back to the lot of them. They'll tell what they want to tell whenever they're ready, so there's no need to face them.

The lawyer snorts as he picks up Harry's copy of the *Republican*. The front page proclaims that two local tannery owners have been fined over a hundred-thousand dollars for polluting Cayuga Creek. According to investigators, carcinogens were routinely dumped into this tributary of the Mohawk for over forty years. The EPA was debating whether evacuations of high-risk neighborhoods were advisable. Industry spokesmen denied all charges and detailed the number of jobs that would be lost if the tanneries were closed. Further penalties and indictments were expected.

"They'll never shut 'em down," somebody said.

"Like hell," John laughed. "They were closing anyway. Why do you think old man Tucker sold out last year? They made all the money that was here to be made thirty years ago."

"Never happen," the first man said. "Mohawk *is* leather."

"Mohawk's horseshit," the lawyer said. "Always was."

"How come you're still here?"

John didn't bother answering, but his expression suggested there was an answer just the same.

"You figure the government wants to buy my house,"

another player asked. "It's only a block from the crick."

"Might," John said. "I know some people who'll testify you're wacky, and you can claim it's from drinking the water. Just like Wild Bill."

Had John looked up from his paper, he would've had time to duck. Harry's shoulders quivered almost imperceptibly before he whirled, his spatula slicing through the newspaper like a knife. Fortunately, the *Republican* offered enough resistance to spin the utensil in Harry's grasp. With a slap it met John's cheek flat, leaving a triangle of sausage grease below the right eye. Everyone, including Harry, was speechless with surprise. The grease formed a rivulet that disappeared into the lawyer's collar. The spatula itself was so flexible that the blow didn't even leave a tingle.

To everyone but the principals it was obvious that what they'd witnessed was about the funniest thing ever. They laughed so hard that several coffee cups were overturned, and John himself soon joined in. "People sure are touchy around here lately," he remarked. His mouth still bore the scar of Dallas Younger's assault, a livid crease in his otherwise pretty mouth. He wiped off his face with one of Harry's napkins. "Was that your best shot, Harry?" The men howled and spun on their stools, one falling onto the floor, the stool twirling without him.

Suddenly Harry, too, was laughing, or crying. The tears ran down his face and he went down on his knees behind the counter. The men had to lean over to see him on the floor, and The Bulldog soon came downstairs to see what the ruckus was about.

Once the breakfasts were paid for and the men were gone, Untemeyer came in. Harry was restored to himself by now, though his eyes remained red and puffy.

"What the hell you been up to?" said the old bookie. "Cryin'?"

"Hell," Harry said. "Laughing."

"What about?"

"You had to be here."

"I wish like hell I was. I never once saw you laugh."

Harry rang *No Sale* on the register and removed some bills. "How many mounts does the Shoe have today?" he said.

Untemeyer checked his wrinkled sheet. "Eight."

Harry handed him sixteen dollars. "I got a powerful feeling about him."

Untemeyer nodded, added Harry's money to the thick roll and wrote out a slip. "He's due, all right, that son-of-a-bitch."

ABOUT THE AUTHOR

RICHARD RUSSO did his graduate studies at the University of Arizona and now teaches fiction writing at Southern Illinois University in Carbondale, where he lives with his wife, Barbara, and their two daughters. His second novel, *The Risk Pool,* is also available from Vintage. His newest novel is *Nobody's Fool.*

Bright Lights, Big City
by Jay McInerney

Living in Manhattan as if he owned it, a young man tries to outstrip the approach of dawn with nothing but his wit, good will and controlled substances in this celebrated novel.

"A dazzling debut, smart, hearfelt, and very, very funny."   —Tobias Wolff

0-394-72641-3/$9.00

Mama Day
by Gloria Naylor

This magical tale of a Georgia sea island centers around a powerful and loving matriarch who can call up lightning storms and see secrets in her dreams.

"This is a wonderful novel, full of spirit and sass and wisdom."   —*Washington Post*

0-679-72181-9/$10.00

Anywhere But Here
by Mona Simpson

An extraordinary novel that is at once a portrait of a mother and daughter and a brilliant exploration of the perennial urge to keep moving.

"Mona Simpson takes on—and reinvents—many of America's essential myths ... stunning."   —*The New York Times*

0-679-73738-3/$11.00

The Joy Luck Club
by Amy Tan

"Vivid ... wondrous ... what it is to be American, and a woman, mother, daughter, lover, wife, sister and friend—these are the troubling, loving alliances and affiliations that Tan molds into this remarkable novel."   —*San Francisco Chronicle*

"A jewel of a book."   —*The New York Times Book Review*

0-679-72768-X/$10.00

Philadelphia Fire
by John Edgar Wideman

"Reminiscent of Ralph Ellison's *Invisible Man*" (*Time*), this powerful novel is based on the 1985 bombing by police of a West Philadelphia row house owned by the Afro-centric cult, Move.

"A book brimming over with brutal, emotional honesty and moments of beautiful prose lyricism."   —Charles Johnson, *Washington Post Book World*

0-679-73650-6/$10.00

• •

Available at your local bookstore,
or call toll-free to order: 1-800-733-3000
(credit cards only). Prices subject to change.

VINTAGE
CONTEMPORARIES